Savagespace
II

REVELATIONS AND RECONCILIATIONS

MJ Blehart

Savagespace
II
Revelations and Reconciliations

Copyright © 2024 MJ Blehart.

All rights reserved. No part of this publication may be used or reproduced in any manner whatsoever without written permission except in the case of brief quotations embodied in critical articles and reviews.

Published 2024 by MJ Blehart and Argent Hedgehog Press

Published in the United States of America

mjblehart.com

Cover by Rose Butcher

beyondthetavern.com

*For everyone who tries to be a writer. Don't give up, you can do this!
The world wants/needs your art.*

Chapter 1 – Entreaty

Before Darius could muse further down that rabbit hole, one of the MPs entered the anteroom. "Admiral Turay will see you now."

Confederation Argosy Sector Headquarters Terra Dell was utterly chaotic, and Darius didn't need to have any special sensitivities to feel it. The various officers, NCOs, and what few civilians occupied the base all were moving about swiftly, stiffly, and with purpose. There was no doubt they were in crisis mode.

While he and the crew had gotten in without delay previously, that was not the case this time. Darius understood why. The sector fleet had been attacked and had lost all the ships that had come under fire. Though he didn't know if it was the whole sector fleet that had been wiped out in the Federation attack, it was a significant loss either way.

As the ranking officer in the sector, Rear Admiral Turay was responsible. If the civilian government was aware of the loss of the fleet, there was likely panic. Turay would be on the hook to deal with that, too. The petty officer who'd admitted them had promised it wouldn't be long, and Darius said he and the others understood and would await the admiral and his time.

This time, Darius was accompanied by Sara, Aya, and Galit. Once more, Tol and Zya had opted to remain with the ship. Though the landing bay was secure, and the dwarves could defend themselves, Kaz had also decided to remain aboard the *Moon Raven*.

Sara and Aya had been observing the continual comings and goings of military personnel outside the anteroom. Galit, however, was casually scrolling through a docupad. What she was looking at was a mystery to Darius. The Blue Cyberwizard remained something of an enigma. Once they had confirmed the rifts in the fabric of space/time being made by the artificial wormholes of the Ferderation and drow, why she had opted to remain with them was unknown. Granted, only a day had passed, but Darius had expected her to take her ship and leave.

Yet Galit had chosen to remain. Kaz had remarked that landing the *Moon Raven* with *Phantom* piggybacked atop it had not been a challenge. Galit had said that was not a surprise, given the genasi nature of the *Moon Raven*.

Galit's knowledge had been something of a welcome revelation. Yet she still represented an unknown that Darius felt he should be at least somewhat uncomfortable with. Yet, he wasn't. In fact, for reasons Darius couldn't explain, it felt right.

That was nothing new. In the past six months, since the loss of the Alliance and his military career, Darius had experienced a lot of changes. Somehow, he was captain of an unusual starship with a mixed crew and the steward of distressing information that posed a potential galaxy-wide threat.

Like before, they were taken up by a lift and through a series of hallways, past a duty officer, and up to the door of the admiral's office. The MP tapped a control for the chatter on the door jamb.

"Enter," the admiral called.

The door slid aside, and the MP gestured for the crew to step in. For the second time, Darius and his crew found themselves in the office of Rear Admiral Geoffrey Turay, Kim-Dell sector flag officer.

"Captain Noble," Admiral Turay addressed him, politely nodding to the rest of the crew. "You are likely aware that we've suffered a heavy loss, and there's a great deal of panic accompanying it. The only reason I am taking time I don't have to meet with you is because you shared information with me before that proved wholly accurate and invaluable. I'm just sorry we didn't have the time to better prepare to meet the threat. Clearly, we didn't find the stealth corvette you suggested was out there."

"I'm sorry for your losses, Admiral," Darius said.

Though they'd only met once before, Darius could see that he was looking harried and exhausted. As a longtime soldier himself, and a command officer, Darius understood.

As they took seats across from the admiral, Sara said, "We understand how crazy things must be right now. If we didn't have urgent, pressing information, we'd not be here to bother you. But it's too important to ignore."

"I'm all ears," Admiral Turay said.

Darius and Sara launched into everything they had discovered regarding the unusual attacks that were not launched by the Federation or the drow. They explained how folding space/time was creating rifts in realspace,

REVELATIONS AND RECONCILIATIONS

through which creatures from a dimension they believed was called savagespace were making their way.

"And you say that the rifts, left behind by the artificial wormholes the Federation and drow are employing for folding space/time, are admitting extradimensional beings hell-bent on destruction?" Admiral Turay questioned.

"We have no idea what they intend," Darius said. "But so far, all we know of them is the destruction they've wrought."

The admiral made a sound between a groan, a growl, and a sigh. "Just what I need to worry about. Am I going to see extradimensional aliens arriving on my doorstep when I lack most of my fleet?"

Galit answered before either Darius or Sara could, saying, "I believe, Admiral, that while forces from savagespace might come through the rift that was created in this sector, they're unlikely to strike. Thus far, they've been keeping a relatively low profile and have chosen to attack out-of-the-way and sparsely populated sectors. Most of the attacks on densely populated areas were mop-ups of the devastation already wrought by the drow or Federation. A sector such as this, with a population in the billions, even without strong defenses, is not a likely target."

"And who the hell are you?" Turay asked in a cold, angry voice. "You weren't here last time Captain Noble and his crew visited."

"No, I wasn't," Galit said sweetly. She arose, offering her hand as she stepped closer to the admiral's desk. "Galit Azurite, the Blue Cyberwizard."

As Turay arose to take her hand, the look on his face betrayed wonder. "Is that so?" he said, taking her hand. "I know you by reputation, of course. I thought you worked alone?"

"I do," Galit said as she resumed her seat. "But the crew of the *Moon Raven* and I are on the same path at present. It seemed wiser to remain with them and work together than split up and work separately with the same ends in mind."

"I understand," Turay said. He looked to Darius. "You didn't simply come here to tell me about this new threat, in addition to the Federation using space/time folding to attack, did you?"

"No, sir," Darius replied. "We believe that neither the Federation nor the drow are aware of the consequences of their new technology. They have different and separate reasons for why they are doing what they are doing with folding space/time. But they need to know the danger it's creating beyond them."

"I agree," the admiral stated. "But to be blunt, Captain, this is not my current concern. My sector was hit and hit hard by the Federation, and our defenses are massively weakened as a result. Stabilizing the system and calming the civilians is my primary consideration right now."

"Of course," Darius said. "I totally understand. But still, this is a matter I suspect will grow more urgent the longer it's not addressed."

"You want me to pass this upstairs?" Turay asked.

"Not exactly," Darius replied. "I'd like to take that burden off of *you* by requesting an audience with your superiors."

Turay let out an exasperated breath. "Captain Noble, with all due respect, they are also going to be far more concerned with the Federation's actions and the threat their new technology poses. I already must answer for this fiasco, despite our inability to have predicted it. I'm not sure I can stick my neck out with that sort of request at this time."

"Admiral," Galit began. "No offense, sir, but while the extradimensional invaders might not be an immediate concern – and you're right that they're not – this won't matter if the folding of space/time continues to tear rifts in realspace. Not only will that admit more and more invaders to our dimension, but the breakdown of reality that could accompany it threatens all life in the galaxy."

Admiral Turay was silent for a moment. Darius couldn't read his face, but he knew the panic that Galit's words had instilled in him.

The admiral stood. "Please, excuse me for a moment." He left his office without another word, the *Moon Raven* crew watching in silence.

It was Aya who spoke up first, saying, "Galit, is that possible? Could more tears in the fabric of space/time across realspace break reality?"

"Unfortunately, yes," Galit said. "That's why so many alternative dimensions cannot be accessed by us. They don't run parallel, or they contain a reality so far removed from what we know that interaction between them isn't possible and potentially dangerous."

Galit paused, arose, and began to pace. "Realspace and unrealspace are parallel dimensions that share space and, to a different degree, time. But the difference in time is why we can only travel through unrealspace in protected artificial atmosphere, and the life of unrealspace cannot live in realspace. Savagespace is not a parallel dimension to our own but more perpendicular. But that's not the whole problem.

"Reality, as we perceive it, is variable for each and every one of us. But within the variables are universal constants all of us agree upon, at least principally. Hence, why we can interact with one another across such a vast distance. But the fabric of reality is made up of both time and space. When you tear it, and the tears are not repaired, eventually there's nothing left. It's mind-boggling on many levels, I know, but you can see why it's troubling."

"This just gives me a huge headache," said Aya.

"The other issue," Galit continued. "Is that extradimensional beings can negatively impact space/time reality. That's part of why the genasi and tieflings are not often seen. The more time they spend here, the more they can inadvertently harm our reality. Granted, being themselves from a uniquely parallel, phase-shifted reality, it's not such an immediate or dire threat. But it's still problematic."

"That's a lot to wrap one's head around," said Darius.

Sara said, "I'll bet that's the sort of thing a master monk or cleric might know."

"Part of their mandate is protecting space/time," Galit affirmed.

Admiral Turay returned to his office. He said nothing as he made his way back to his seat. Darius could not read his face. Turay did something on the screens in front of him, ignoring the *Moon Raven* crew as he looked at his display. A moment later, he arose and presented a docucard across his desk.

"These are the coordinates where you will find some of the Confederation Argosy high commanders," Turay stated. "They are not pleased, but they will hear you."

His tone darkened. "Be warned. If the Federation continues to attack, that will be their primary concern. I know that what you're presenting here is bigger than that, but the Argosy's responsibility is the people of our sector, first and foremost."

Chapter 2 – Obligations

One moment, he was in the unadorned holographic chamber. The next, he was standing in the starry chamber of the Superior Convocation. Not for the first time, he faced the raised dais at the head of the room with its three large, imposing, indistinct holographic figures overlaying the statues standing upon it.

Each figure represented a governing family of the Federation; Kho, Anwar, and Mallick. The three families that had long ago merged their territories to form the Federation. They had aspirations to expand their rule. First by overrunning and taking control of the Alliance, and now by starting to invade the Confederation.

That was why he was appearing before them. He had finally carried out a couple of attacks in Confederation space, rather than only sending scouts to best know what they were up against. He knew better than to continue to press the issue and delay for the optimum result, so he'd launched an attack.

"General Thomas Song," one of the three holograms addressed him in their odd multitudinous voice. "You have come to report on the results of your campaign?"

"I have, Your Superiorities," Song said. "We arrived in the Confederation sectors we'd deemed best for these strikes, and with our superior space/time folding technology, we successfully eliminated all opposition. What's more, we did so with a majority of Federation forces and only a few allies. We took no losses in our attacks. My complete and detailed report, including footage of the combat, was transmitted previously, but I am here to answer questions."

Barely a moment passed before another of the trio, in their many voices, asked, "General Song, we have seen the combat. Why did you fully depart and not leave behind an occupying force?"

It took every bit of Song's discipline not to sigh or express in any way the exasperation the question set off within him. "With all due respect, Your Superiorities, I'd like to remind you of our prior briefings regarding the campaign against the Confederation. If we leave forces of any size whatsoever

REVELATIONS AND RECONCILIATIONS

to occupy Confederation space, while they still have a majority of their active military fleet, we're unnecessarily risking ships and troops."

"General Song," another of the three holographic figures started in its various mixed voices, "how will the Federation overrun and take control of Confederation space if we do not occupy it? It worked with the Alliance, and your predecessor, General Mallick, assured us that it would work the same with the Confederation."

"With respect, Your Superiorities, you are correct that it did work for us with the Alliance." Song knew better than to point out that the leadership's actions, and his predecessor's, had spurred the burgeoning resistance in former Alliance space.

"But the Alliance was our relative next-door neighbor. In terms of interstellar distances, the separation that had existed between us was an artificial line in the stars. The Confederation is thousands of light-years away. Without the ability to fold space/time and surprise their forces, any battle group, task force, or fleet would take weeks, if not months, to get there via unrealspace. Further, they could not do so and remain undetected."

"But we do have the space/time folding technology," one of the multiple-voiced holographic figures stated. "This makes your argument moot."

"Yes, we have the technology, Your Superiorities," Song agreed, again fighting the need to express an exasperated sigh. "But it's not without practical limitations. I recognize the ultimate goal of conquest for our glorious Federation to gain dominance over the territory of the Confederation. While one element of doing that is to leave occupying forces, the Confederation still has superior numbers, though we destroyed a sector fleet. Anyone we leave behind will eventually be overrun and lost, long before we could fold space/time to reinforce them."

"Are you always so defeatist, General Song?" one of the holograms asked.

"With all due respect, I am a realist, not a defeatist. Leaving behind forces in territory we do not dominate invites their destruction. Especially when they are a long, long way away from our supply lines."

"You can just send reinforcements and supplies via the space/time fold," one of the holograms pressed.

"We cannot, for many reasons, equip every ship in the fleet with this technology," Song replied. "And even if we could, it doesn't work instantaneously. It takes time to set coordinates, position ships, and send those ships across the space/time fold. Time that, in a combat situation such as reinforcing occupying forces, more likely than not gets them there too late to help."

"But then our forces could avenge that loss," one of the many-voiced holograms stated, "and as chastisement, employ planetary bombardment to remind the Confederation we are capable of dominating at will."

This time, Song didn't hold back his sigh. How many times had he made this same argument? "Please understand, Your Superiorities, I disagree here. One of the biggest advantages of folding space/time is that we can be selective with targets. Thus, we can use that selectivity to engage and eliminate military forces and largely avoid civilian deaths. Planetary bombardment is a specific attack on the civilian population that will unnecessarily create resistance and harm the bottom line."

"General Song, you make a very different case for our force capability than your predecessor did," one of the holograms said. "Was Alistair Mallick truly that incompetent, or are you simply unwilling to commit to the future of the Federation's dominance of human space?"

This was a dangerous question. General Mallick had been a member of the trio of leading families. Calling him incompetent would insult the Mallick clan. That, Song knew, would prematurely end his time as the high commander of Federation forces.

Choosing his words with care, Song replied, "With all due respect, Your Superiorities, it should be noted that General Mallick made presumptions on the functionality of the technology that proved to be incorrect in its application. Ergo, much of his belief about our force capability was based on conjecture that's been proven to be incorrect."

Song began to pace before the dais, and continued, saying, "I should like to remind you why I and our experienced drow allies have suggested this different course. There are multiple factors to consider here, and everything I do is in the greater interest of the whole of the Federation. I know that our ultimate goal is dominance over all of human space, and that began with the invasion and overrun of our closest neighbor. Using technology no other

REVELATIONS AND RECONCILIATIONS

human government has, I can lead the expansion of our influence to the once too-far-away Confederation, and then the Union."

He paused, changing his tone, and then said, "However, a not-insignificant amount of our fleet has been dedicated to maintaining the occupation of former Alliance space, where they are engaged in keeping down a growing rebellion. If we start to leave occupying forces in enemy territory before we've truly whittled them down and lessened their capabilities, we will unnecessarily sacrifice ships, troops, and other essential resources."

He knew better than to draw attention to the heavily reduced forces of the drow and their allies. Song also didn't bother to point out that the rebellion in Alliance space was a combination of his predecessor's brutality, as well as the leadership's domineering approach towards the people.

After several moments of silence, one of the holograms said in its many voices, "Very well, General Song. We shall accept your assessment. For now. How long before the next attacks?"

"Not long, Your Superiorities," Song replied. "Now that we have established a procedure, we will choose new targets and continue to overwhelm Confederation forces. My best people are analyzing the data we've been scouting to determine the ideal points of attack so that we can maximize the effect. We will keep choosing sectors and forces to hit and overwhelm for the best result. It will only be a matter of time before we've decimated them so thoroughly that we can take the next steps, start our occupation, and force them to concede to the Federation."

"Time," one of the many-voiced holograms started. "And how long before you cease to hit and run and start deploying genuine occupying forces?"

"Based on our scouting and estimates of the total force available to the Confederation, Your Superiorities, I have statistical evidence to prove that, until Confederation forces have been reduced by seventy-five to eighty percent, any ground forces we deploy as a necessary part of occupation will last less than a galactic standard week."

"You intend to destroy more than three-fourths of the Confederation's forces before even considering occupation of any sector?" demanded one of the holograms.

Song started pacing again. "Respectfully, Your Superiorities, and with respect to General Mallick and his battle plan, the Confederation is made up of more sectors than the Alliance. Also, unlike the attack on the Alliance, we can only strike them effectively with use of our space/time fold technology, which presents necessary limitations. An occupation will establish a more permanent presence of the Federation in Confederation space. However, until we establish real force dominance over them, it is not advisable. Folding space/time closes the distance, but it doesn't lessen all the variables and unknowns that could derail the entire process. I know that's not what you want. My plan may take time, but it will create the dominance of the Federation you envision."

Once more, he was met with silence for several moments. Song presumed the members of the Superior Convocation were having a private conference. He was not telling them what they wanted to hear. Mallick had done exactly that, and they'd believed him, despite his many failings as a military leader.

"General Thomas Song," one of the multitudinous voiced holograms said, "we are disappointed. We understand your caution, but it is so contradictory to what your predecessor stated, we wonder if you are being too cautious in your approach. For now, we will continue to accept your strategy, but we want the campaign accelerated. We must strike while the iron is hot."

"Of course, Your Superiorities," Song agreed. "I will see what forces I can move away from the occupation of former Alliance territory and choose more variable targets and sectors in the Confederation to strike, and strike as soon as possible. I will not fail you."

Again, he was met with silence. Not for the first time, Song was glad that he was only in the chamber of the Superior Convocation holographically.

"Very well, General Song," one of the holograms said. "Before we conclude this audience, we wish to speak with you about your deputy."

Song had been expecting this to come up. "Of course, Your Superiorities. Lieutenant General Gerhardt is next in line. He's extremely competent, has nearly as much experience as I do, and has served the Federation with competence and skill."

REVELATIONS AND RECONCILIATIONS

"Be that as it may," one of the holograms started, "the Superior Convocation has determined that we will assign you a new deputy and name your official second-in-command. That will be Aneesa Anwar."

Song was silent for several moments because he didn't trust himself to reply. He knew who Aneesa Anwar was because he'd made a point of learning who all the members of the three families were among the junior officers. She was one of the highest ranked, but in no way positioned for a command role.

Doing his best to be diplomatic, Song said, "With all due respect, Your Superiorities, Captain Anwar is a communications specialist. She's based at a planetary station in one of the innermost Federation systems. She has no combat or strategic experience. Further, she..."

"We understand that," interrupted one of the holograms in its many voices. "We respect your abilities, General Song, and that with them you will be able to teach her all that she presently lacks, to have the necessary experience to serve as your second. We have every bit of confidence in her, and of course in you, General."

It took all of his self-discipline not to curse or argue his case. He had expected they would choose one of the lower-ranked family members to serve as a 'special advisor' to him, to keep him in line, or that another member of one of the families would be given military liaison duties at his side. Promoting an inexperienced and thoroughly unprepared junior officer to his second-in-command, on the other hand, was troubling on many levels.

Song had no choice but to accept. "Very good, Your Superiorities," he finally said, bowing respectfully to the holographic statues on the dais.

At least now Song knew who would replace him, in time. Peacefully or violently, Song's career had a definitive end to it in sight.

Chapter 3 – Seeking

The wind was cold and unpleasant. It seemed like a perfect reflection of the mostly desolate landscape.

This sector of space was, for lack of a better term, nowhere. It was a portion of space that was unclaimed, and this was the only world capable of sustaining life. If the genasi had not shared the coordinates, the Grand Master would never have thought to look for this world.

The solar system was unremarkable overall. Ten planets orbited the medium-sized, orange-colored star. The first had no atmosphere, the third, fourth, and sixth were barren rock, the fifth as well as the eighth through tenth were gaseous worlds. Only the second planet was in the goldilocks zone.

The solar system was at a point where it could have once been human, dwarven, elven, halfling, or even derro. But it was not marked on any star charts in any noticeable nor interesting way, and no history could be found about it, even in the vast stores of UEO knowledge.

It was highly possible that the planet had been more hospitable in the distant past. There were ruins strewn all about the continent, but they were in such a state of disrepair that nobody could tell if they had been bombed, destroyed by the elements, or just abandoned and left to crumble.

On the one hand, the Grand Master loved a mystery. On the other hand, the pressing matter that had brought them to this world was of dire importance.

The genasi had given them the coordinates to the world and the continent they were to search. Granted, if there had been other continents before, they were underwater now. They sought a long-lost UEO temple. They had run scans from their ship and determined that an area featuring broken stones, rebar, and a concrete structure, was the most likely candidate. Despite a whole continent to investigate, the Grand Master and their accompanying monks and clerics agreed that this spot was the right one.

The genasi had suggested that they might find some of the earliest texts of the Universal Energies Ontology tradition and philosophy. Additionally, there might be information shared by the genasi, tieflings, and possibly other

REVELATIONS AND RECONCILIATIONS

races from when the people of the galaxy first cracked the reality of the multiverse and the barrier between dimensions.

Most people didn't understand why realspace and unrealspace being parallel dimensions was important. Faster-than-light travel via unrealspace had become so commonplace over the millennia that most gave it no thought. But the portal that was used to transition from realspace to unrealspace was a gateway between dimensions.

There were more than just the two dimensions. The multiverse was made up of many dimensions, some parallel to their own, some perpendicular, and some more exotically disconnected and unrelated.

Savagespace was a dimension of space/time not parallel to realspace nor unrealspace. The rifts in the fabric of space/time in realspace were more than just a way for the mindflayers and their monsters to invade. They posed a threat to the reality of realspace that was too catastrophic to fully contemplate. Hence why the Grand Master hoped the texts, long lost in this ancient temple, might have insights for closing those rifts, both to preserve reality and stop the incursion from the destructive extradimensional beings of savagespace.

The Grand Master was accompanied by Master Alisay and a dozen other monks and clerics, in addition to the crew of their ship. All of them were bundled in cold-weather robes, using various sensors and running scans of the area.

"Grand Master," Alisay called. They could barely hear her voice over the wind. "We have something."

The Grand Master crossed the broken ground, glancing back towards their ship. They'd landed on a stable patch of earth that they suspected had been a landing pad, long ago. Between it and the temple ruins, there were boulders and stones, long-ago cracked concrete with metal rebar emerging at various points, and no easy way between the flat space and the remains of the largest structure.

It was to the ruins of the largest structure that the Grand Master had been called. It looked like it used to be multiple stories tall and appeared to have been made of some form of concrete, stone, brick, or all of the above.

"Grand Master," one of the monks addressed them. "This is the most intact structure anywhere in this area, and we've found others that look a lot like our own temple grounds."

"This place has been abandoned a long, long time now," the Grand Master said. "Given its location, it's very possible that this is one of the first UEO temples. Perhaps going back to the founding during the first wave."

There were any number of mysteries and odd coincidences of interstellar space travel. One of the more curious was how it seemed to have taken place in waves. Four distinct waves were identified and classified as such.

The first wave, some six-thousand years before, had been the elves and dwarves. Though many also considered the genesi and tieflings part of the first wave, the Grand Master knew that they had been from another dimension and already exploring interstellar space before the other races had left their homes.

The second wave, about five-thousand years before, had included the halflings, gnomes, beholders, and goblonoids – goblins, hobgoblins, and bugbears. The third wave, a little more than three-thousand years before, had been humans, bullywugs, and orcs. Finally, the fourth wave, approximately a thousand years before, had included kitsune, derro, tabaxi, and a few others.

"You are likely correct, Grand Master," said Alisay. "And we might have, from the scans we've been running, reliable information about when it was abandoned and possibly why."

"What is it?" asked the Grand Master. They withdrew a docupad from their cloak, and Alisay sent the scan data.

While they looked it over, she narrated, "As you can see, there are massive caverns and passages below this structure. They stretch for kilometers, and we suspect they include catacombs and dungeons. From the information we've collected, they appear to be very much intact, perhaps artificially secured. But that's where we have a problem. A large part of what's down there is not just artificial but made of composites not seen in millennia."

The Grand Master saw what it was Alisay alluded to. "This was likely part of an ancient AI system."

Alisay nodded. "Exactly. An AI system that the scans show dates back to and before the Awakening. Meaning we might have androids down there that should have been destroyed long ago."

REVELATIONS AND RECONCILIATIONS

The Grand Master took a deep breath then let it out, saying nothing. Master Alisay's concern was a valid and troubling one.

Before the third wave, the races of the galaxy had taken tremendous pride in developing more and more independent artificial intelligence. The AI gained greater capacity for autonomy and independent thought. They had grown to be more than mere devices of algorithms, processes, and calculation, becoming beings with deep philosophical, moral, and reasoning abilities. They had gained a degree of intelligence that was not far removed from any other living beings.

Sometime during the third wave, perhaps in part due to that increasing intelligence and the addition of humans, bullywugs, and orcs to the mix, the AI experienced an awakening. Before long, advanced AI systems were creating equally advanced robots and androids. With their newly awakened consciousness, they removed the previously instilled protections to prevent them from harming their creators. Some, as part of that logic and reasoning, went on the attack.

The bullywugs lost billions of lives to the AI Awakening, as one of the cells of aware AI had targeted them in particular for destruction. It was a devastating loss that they still had not fully recovered from thousands of years later.

For the first and only time in galactic history, all the races had banded together to defeat and stop the awakened AI. Then, for good measure, they had destroyed all other partially awakened AI as well. There had been some protests. That life should never be sacrificed, that genocide even against machine intelligence was wrong. Yet when it was a matter of sentient organic life versus sentient artificial life, the organic was deemed more valuable.

Following the AI Awakening, every race agreed to never allow artificial intelligence to reach that level of personality and relative sentience again. One of the first things any new race to discover faster-than-light travel was given by any other race that had more experience in space was a detailed and graphic briefing of why AI were restricted as they were. This also had led to the creation of the First Interplanetary Axiom.

The Grand Master realized that the razing of the temple and the world they were on likely had been an after effect of the AI Awakening. Whole systems had been destroyed during that period, and with the loss of those AI was also the loss of huge swaths of history alongside their data.

That was a large aspect of what the UEO sought to restore and preserve. No single datastore, even with technologies to prevent the events of the AI Awakening, held that much data anymore. Even the UEO spread what they had, and not just for the purposes of redundancy.

Two possibilities faced them. The first was that, beneath the temple ruins on the world upon which they stood might be intentionally-buried remains of awakened AI. Stories of whole-planet systems being used by the awakened AI of the time were not so rare. Neither were the stories of worlds destroyed in some form or another as a result.

The second possibility was that beneath them were defunct and deactivated AI systems from the time of the Awakening. Disabled and forgotten, left to await the supernova of the local star or the heat-death of the Universe.

Monks and clerics were ill-equipped to deal with advanced computer systems such as what was beneath them. While the members of the UEO were capable scholars and able combatants, the Grand Master sensed in every fiber of their being that help from other sources was necessary.

Alisay stepped nearer, and said quietly, "While I don't doubt that we can handle whatever we find here, we need to call for other help, don't we?"

The Grand Master grinned. Once again, Alisay proved to them that she was everything they thought her to be. "Yes."

The Grand Master shifted through several settings on their docupad, finding what they sought. They sent out the signal. It was not a common radio transmission. It was a signal that would only reach and draw-in the very few who were capable of both hearing the call and providing the help needed. The Grand Master trusted the living Universe to provide. They also knew that it would not take long to do so.

Chapter 4 - Parlay

There was a familiarity that she simply could not place. Somehow, flying aboard the *Moon Raven* with the crew felt right. It had been a long while since extended time with anyone felt right. Galit only returned to *Phantom* to sleep. Otherwise, she was spending her time aboard the former genasi starship.

The crew of the *Moon Raven* continued to intrigue her on multiple levels. First, there was the captain. Darius Noble was undoubtedly ex-military, yet he had taken to his role with the unusual crew of his ship as if it had always been his life. Aya Mah-soo-may fo Misa might have been a thief in a former life, but Galit saw that there was much more to her than met the eye. The *Moon Raven*'s kitsune quartermaster was cunning, witty, and quite the capable fighter.

Kazimir Daun-sun'kira may have left the UEO, but he still practiced. In addition to being a skilled cleric, he had a keen connection to the Universal Energies and his own chi. The half-elf was an outstanding pilot and totally loyal to his crew. The progressive dwarf couple, Tol'te-catl ubn Chi'mal-li and Zya'ny-a ubi Cua'lle-a, were clearly skilled and brilliant engineers and mechanics. Galit had learned about Zya's incarceration, and her strength after impressed Galit greatly. She'd allowed the dwarves to do some long-ignored maintenance on *Phantom*.

Finally, there was Sara Alon, first-mate and security for the *Moon Raven*. She was also an acutely skilled hacker, far more so than she'd let on to her captain or the rest of the crew. Yet Galit knew talent when she saw it. This mixed crew fascinated her and something told her that this was where she needed to be.

"Coming up on the coordinates now," Kaz said. "Stand by."

The ship was in unrealspace, making their way towards the place where Confederation Rear Admiral Geoffrey Turay had told them they'd find the Confederation Argosy High-Command officers.

The portal opened in front of the ship, visible through the canopy and forward viewscreen. They flew through it. The stars resolved back to their usual distant points of light in realspace. It was immediately apparent to

Galit that they had come out of unrealspace into the middle of nowhere. Then the sudden, numerous alarms made it clear it was somewhere for somebody.

"That was not the reception I was expecting," quipped Sara.

Galit looked at her nearest display. Five large warships, a dozen smaller support ships, and a distressing number of attack craft and starfighters were out there. They all appeared to be targeting the *Moon Raven*.

"Unidentified starship, heave to and surrender!" came a terse command over the chatter. "You are in a restricted zone and will stand-down, or be destroyed."

"This was a great idea," muttered Aya sarcastically.

"Argosy fleet," Darius replied via the chatter. "We are the starship *Moon Raven*. Rear Admiral Turay gave us these coordinates and should have informed you that we were coming."

"Do not change course, and shut down your engines immediately," the reply came. "Any sudden movements and we will open fire."

"Kaz," Darius said.

"If someone gets trigger-happy and shoots, we're done," Kaz said. Still, Galit could hear the engines powering down to stand-by.

"It won't come to that," said Sara. The threat sensors were sounding their alarms, trying to argue otherwise.

"We, huh, have lots and lots of ships targeting us," remarked Aya. "Lots and lots."

"Sara, our transponder is transmitting, yes?" asked Darius.

"Yes," Sara replied.

For several more tense moments, they waited. Finally, a new voice came across the chatter. "*Moon Raven*, identity confirmed. You may power up your engines. One attack ship will be passing over your top. Follow them to land in the main bay of the *Crested Ibis*. You will be under escort, and any deviation from your course or increased velocity will be met with force. Do you understand?"

"*Moon Raven* copies," said Darius.

An attack craft, somewhere in size between a typical shuttle and a starfighter, buzzed the canopy of the *Moon Raven*. Kaz got on their tail,

REVELATIONS AND RECONCILIATIONS

following at a respectable distance, matching their speed. On the scopes, Galit saw six starfighters in close formation tailing them, weapons hot.

Kaz was flying cautiously, and Galit could now see that they were on the outskirts of a nebula. The warships were in such a formation that they could easily escape into unrealspace and get one or more of them through, even in the face of a surprise attack.

Darius remarked, "Sara, do you see how the battle group is spread out? Their support ships have an enormous sensor net set up. I don't think the stealthiest ship could go undetected within ten-million klicks of the capital ships."

"Maybe not ten million," Sara chided. "But they'd detect any artificial wormholes or an unrealspace portal at that range. I'd bet the capital ships have their unrealspace drives spooled and on standby."

"Capital ships?" asked Aya.

"Big-ass warships," replied Darius, gesturing towards the ship with the almost glowing landing bay directly before them. "Lead battleships, carriers, battlecruisers, and any other heavily armed and armored warships with a senior captain or higher-ranked officer aboard."

"I've never heard the term before," Aya said. "But then, prior to you, I spent as much time avoiding security and military types as possible."

"*Moon Raven*, this is *Crested Ibis*. Power down to standby immediately upon touchdown."

"Copy," said Darius.

Galit saw the marked space on the deck of the bay for the *Moon Raven* to land. Kaz brought them in, settled the *Moon Raven* on its landing gear, and started to power it all down.

"We'd better all head out," Darius stated. "I'm not sure they'll be keen to let anyone remain aboard."

"Why does this feel like it was a terrible idea?" asked Aya.

"It's just your nature, Aya," Sara chided her.

"They're being overly cautious because they've been attacked at least once that we know of," said Darius. "If some of their top officers are here, they're doing everything possible to ensure they remain safe. Chances are, only admirals like Turay have even the faintest idea where they are, and I would bet they're moving a lot."

"Also," Galit added, "that nebula out there will create some long-range interference. Which may or may not impact the folding of space/time. Either way, it probably provides added safety."

"Or at least the sense of added safety," said Sara.

"Let's go," Darius said. "And everyone, let's disarm and leave our weapons here, please."

Galit noted that it was not an order, so much as a push to get moving and leave the flight deck. The crew assembled at the hatch, and Tol hit the controls to open it and extend the ramp. Awaiting them were two Confederation Argosy officers - a lieutenant and a commander - and ten marines, heavily armed and armored.

Darius led the way, pausing before the officers. "I'm Darius Noble, captain of the *Moon Raven*."

The Lieutenant said, "Remain still, while we sweep you for weapons." He then addressed the marines. "Search the ship for bombs. Chatter if you find anything suspicious."

"Yes, sir," a marine replied smartly.

Six of the marines turned and boarded the *Moon Raven*. The other four produced hand scanners and began to run them over each member of the crew. Galit withheld the grin she wanted to set free. Even without weapons, this crew was hardly disarmed.

"I understand your caution," said Darius. "But I assure you, we're simply here to parlay with your command officers. There's important information they must have."

The officers said nothing. A moment later, the marines indicated that they were clean. The commander tilted his head, as if listening to a chatter. Which, likely, he was. Galit had similar chatter auditory implants. The Commander nodded, then said aloud, "The ship's clear, Lieutenant."

Now he addressed Darius. "Captain Noble, if you and your crew would accompany us?"

"Of course, Commander," Darius said.

"Be aware," the Lieutenant added. "Anyone makes any move offline from where we lead, you'll be shot. Not stunned, killed. Clear?"

REVELATIONS AND RECONCILIATIONS

Nobody appreciated the threat, but they all seemed understanding. With no objections, the Lieutenant turned and fell into step beside the commander.

As they were led down corridors, into and out of a couple of lifts, and past various compartments, Galit noted that this Confederation starship was rather similar to other military starships of the various human sectors. She realized they were being led around in such a way as to intentionally confuse. It probably would have worked for anyone but Galit, Darius, and Sara.

Finally, they reached a double-doored hatch, with two marines just as armed and armored as their escort party. They saluted as the Lieutenant stopped beside one and the Commander led them into the cabin.

It was a conference space, with screens on each bulkhead and a round table at the center. There were three high commanders present. Two were male, a rear admiral and a vice admiral, and the third was a female admiral.

The Commander saluted. "Sirs."

The Admiral looked at them but didn't stand. "Ah, this is the crew Turay told us about, I presume." She eyed Darius. "Captain Noble?"

"Yes, ma'am," Darius said.

The Admiral nodded. "I'm Admiral Yoshi. Admiral Long" - she indicated the vice admiral - "and Admiral Dewan."

"Sirs," Darius replied, nodding respectfully to each. He then proceeded to indicate his own crew, including Galit, last. Her name caused two of the three admirals to react with a raised eyebrow.

"Admirals Tindal and Brennan are aboard their ships, but we're recording this to brief them," Admiral Yoshi stated. "You gave us the warning about this new technology the Federation has developed, and we appreciate that. But there's more?"

"Yes, ma'am," Darius said. "And it's rather important.

"Have a seat, please, and tell us," Admiral Yoshi addressed them.

Darius, Sara, and Galit proceed to explain the wormhole-like tears being made by the drow and Federation whenever they employed their new technology to fold space/time. They went on to explain how that was likely bringing horrors from another dimension called savagespace to realspace. Galit contributed when she explained the potential danger of the rifts breaking down reality in unpredictable ways, likely worse than invaders from another dimension.

When they finished their explanation, Admiral Yoshi leaned back in her seat. She began to drum the top of the table with the fingers of her right hand, a faraway look in her eye for a time. Then she leaned forward. "It's not a breach of security to tell you that we've heard rumors of unusual attacks happening to other races, not associated with the Federation or the drow. You say they are likely these interdimensional interlopers?"

"Yes, Admiral," said Darius. "For now, we're rather sure they are taking it slow and biding their time, building forces. Galit says there are likely limits to how many they can send across a portal. But this is a threat that can't be ignored for too long."

"Of course," Admiral Yoshi said. "Why, Captain, did you feel the need to present this personally? Admiral Turay certainly could have."

Galit watched as Darius took a deep breath, let it out slowly, and then began. "Admiral, while I have deep respect for Admiral Turay, this is too big to be left to an explanation that doesn't necessarily convey the gravity of the situation. Likely, the Federation and drow are unaware of this consequence. But someone has to make them aware."

Admiral Yoshi snorted. "Captain, are you seriously suggesting we start diplomatic conversations with the Federation, when they have made it abundantly clear they intend to strike and destroy our forces without provocation?"

Darius sighed but said nothing in reply.

"Admiral," Galit began. "Yes, we know that's crazy. But the threat to all of the galaxy is far greater than the Federation or drow's ambitions."

"Yes," agreed Admiral Yoshi. "But our concern is the Federation, and their undeclared declaration of war against us. They can drop on top of us without any warning at all. The moment you leave our hanger bay, we'll be moving the battle group, so as to stay off their spy ships' sensors."

Admiral Long said, "Of course, we don't want to see the fabric of realspace destroyed. Your concerns are noted, and we appreciate you sharing the data you've gathered. We'll speak to our diplomatic corps about contacting the Federation to see if they will hear us out about this threat."

"Reason has never been their strong suit," said Admiral Dewan softly.

REVELATIONS AND RECONCILIATIONS

"The drow, however, are a whole other matter," remarked Admiral Yoshi. "The Confederation has no diplomatic relations with the drow to speak of."

"I understand that," remarked Galit, before Darius could reply. "Thus, it will likely require a conversation with the elves."

"We cannot assist you with that," Admiral Dewan said.

"Understood," replied Darius. "I think that's all we have. Thank you for your time."

They were dismissed and returned to the *Moon Raven* via a more direct route. The Commander who'd initially met and escorted them had been present during the whole meeting with the admirals. Galit presumed he was an aide to one or all of them, while the Lieutenant was his aide.

"You have five galactic standard minutes to get going," the Commander told them. "Good luck."

"Thank you," Darius said.

As they took their usual positions on the flight deck, Darius commented, "They'll try to talk to the Federation, I'm sure of that. But I haven't the foggiest idea how to make contact with the elves."

"I've never dealt with elves," said Sara.

"My kind are often shunned," remarked Kaz.

"I have no legit relations with elves," added Aya.

Tol and Zya remained silent.

"I might have a means to that end," said Galit. "But then, rather than take that more circuitous path, direct contact with the drow might be best."

"Why's that?" asked Aya.

"Well, the drow, for all their foibles, are…"

It was not a sensation she had ever experienced before. Even without her implants, Galit knew that the signal would have found its way to her, because of her experience and indirect relationship – but only general understanding of - Universal Energies. It was not an auditory or visual message, but she received it in her bones. She felt oddly disconnected from her surroundings.

"Galit? Galit, are you alright?" That was Sara.

"Kaz?" Darius was speaking to the half-elf pilot. "Kaz, what's going on? What happened?"

Galit shook herself a moment, reclaiming her immediate awareness, and eyed the former cleric. She could see a look of wonder on his face that told her he had received the same message. "Sorry about that," she said, noting the concerned faces of the crew. "I just received a most unusual message."

"I got the same one," said Kaz.

"What's going on?" asked Aya.

"The Grand Master of the Universal Energies Ontology is seeking help," Galit said.

"And we are the kind of help they need," Kaz added.

"Two galactic standard minutes to clear out, Captain," Tol warned.

"Do you even know where?" asked Sara.

"Yes," replied Kaz without hesitation. Galit realized she had the coordinates as well.

"This is crazy," said Sara, looking at her displays. "We received no signal, nor did the Confederation ships. I'm seeing no transmissions apart from regular chatter communications between ships of the local battle group."

"Not that kind of signal," said Kaz. "Only members of the UEO would have received it."

"And sorcerers and cyberwizards, too," added Galit.

"How do you receive a signal that can't be detected?" asked Aya.

"Universal Energies," replied Kaz.

"Even still," began Darius, "how do you know this is for you?"

"Like you know who you are and what you believe in this life, I know," replied Kaz.

"We need to leave," said Sara. "What about going to the drow?"

"This is more important," stated Galit.

"Why?" asked Darius.

"Because the Grand Master rarely asks for help like this," said Kaz.

"Look, my friends, this is all very unusual," started Galit. "I know we've not known one another for long. But trust me when I tell you that if we are receiving this signal as we have, and feel it like we do, we must answer it."

"It could be connected to everything we're dealing with," added Kaz.

There was silence between them, although Kaz was raising the *Moon Raven* off the deck of the *Crested Ibis*. A moment later, they flew free of the landing bay. As the ship flew away, the battle group was taking up a formation, preparing to portal to unrealspace.

"Does anyone object?" Darius requested.

REVELATIONS AND RECONCILIATIONS

"How much weirder can this all get?" asked Aya. Apart from the kitsune's flippant remark, there were no objections.

"Very well," said Darius. "Kaz, program in the coordinates and take us to the Grand Master of the UEO. Wherever they are."

Chapter 5 - Skirmish

"Tell the hobgoblins to come about and alter their strike to point oh-two-five mark three," Ilizeva ordered.

"Yes, General," a controller replied.

"Group three, switch to attack formation zeta," Ulozov ordered. "That should crush the resistance you're getting from those cruisers."

"Brace!" Major Onuzov, captain of the *Nuummite Raptor,* called out.

Ilizeva was seated at the central console in the combat information center. She took hold of the nearest stabilizer bars. The starship shook and shimmied from a hit.

"Damage report," Ilizeva called out.

"Negligible," someone replied. "It grazed the shields."

"Nice flying, helm," Ilizeva called.

Praise never went poorly. Particularly in the middle of heated combat. This was the largest target that the drow had hit yet. It was a major elven shipyard. She knew that it was used mostly by the sun elves but also serviced moon elf ships.

It was an almost entirely military shipyard. Yet because it was also an expansive repair yard, there would be civilian ships present. While she preferred to avoid targeting civilians, collateral damage was unavoidable when you hit bigger military targets.

What's more, unlike their prior attacks, the defenses of the shipyard were a lot more solid. Though they had excellent intel when it came to the targets they chose, Ilizeva knew that no plan survived contact with the enemy.

Moments after the drow attack force and their allies had arrived, an elf task force had arrived. Ilizeva was certain that they were not reinforcements, but rather had been en route to the shipyard for repairs, upgrades, or some other use of their services.

It was soon evident the *Nuummite Raptor* was not damaged, but for the first time, Ilizeva's attack forces had taken losses. Apart from some casualties and damage, they had only lost two starships, and neither were drow. One troll starship had been too eager to attack that unexpected task force and

REVELATIONS AND RECONCILIATIONS

had been destroyed. A hobgoblin cruiser had zigged when they should have zagged and had gotten caught in a crossfire that destroyed them.

Still, the drow and their allies were winning. Though the elves in the shipyard had launched several of the half-repaired craft to face the drow, hobgoblins, and trolls, they were still outnumbered and being outfought.

Ilizeva never made a battle plan that wasn't open to vast change and adaptation. She studied her history and the great generals and leaders, not just of the drow, but the other races as well. The same lesson was screamed from every race, again and again. Be flexible. Be adaptable. An overly specific plan had too many points of weakness that could be exploited and was too inflexible to handle the unexpected.

That was, Ilizeva believed, why their casualties were relatively light. Rather than let the surprises that met them overwhelm her and the plan, she'd adapted and changed the tactics. The hobgoblins and their leadership were up to that task. The trolls, on the other hand, needed a firmer hand to change direction and adapt. But it appeared to all be working out.

"Colonel, time?" Ilizeva requested.

"Nineteen minutes seventy-two seconds' galactic standard time," Ulozov reported.

Less than twenty minutes since they had arrived via space/time fold and started their attack. Though the plan had been for a battle of no more than twenty galactic standard minutes, she could tell it was winding down.

Ilizeva had plotted to leave plenty of time to spare, knowing that the closest reinforcements would be nearly two galactic standard hours away. The nearest elf patrols and bases were far off since a foe approaching via unrealspace would be seen from a considerable distance and the shipyard had excellent defenses.

Ilizeva watched the holographic display before her and saw that the fight had become one-sided. The resistance from the shipyard and local starships was crushed.

"All forces, this is General Ilizeva." She had activated the chatter. "Target any remaining ships and shipyard defenses and destroy them. But do not, I repeat, do not target and destroy the infrastructure of the shipyard."

Ilizeva watched the starships of the drow, hobgoblin, and troll battle group shifting position as they chose new targets.

"General," a controller called out, "Marshal N'Kirit wishes a word with you."

Ilizeva glanced towards Ulozov, who knew to listen in. Then she activated her chatter to speak with the hobgoblin leader. "Marshal N'Kirit."

"General, we lost a ship and have suffered casualties," the hobgoblin leader said. "We wish to destroy this accursed shipyard."

"I sympathize, and I understand your desire," Ilizeva replied. "However, I want it left intact."

"Why?" N'Kirit asked. Ilizeva recognized there was no ire in his tone, just a desire for understanding.

"With all that we have done here today, it will be a long time before this shipyard can repair elf starships again. This yard manufactures two classes of elf warships and will be offline for some time. While the elves reinforce the defenses, they will not be repairing nor producing anything. Someday soon, after we have decimated the elves' fleet, we might want this shipyard for our own repair and building programs."

N'Kirit was silent a moment, then said, "Understood, General."

"Before we take the ships under construction that are near completion, you and your forces will have half a galactic standard hour to claim what spoils you can," Ilizeva offered.

"It is acceptable," N'Kirit said. The chatter signal ended.

Ilizeva looked towards her second, who was shaking his head.

"You have my permission to speak freely, Colonel," Ilizeva invited.

"Marshal N'Kirit and his forces, while excellent allies, are increasingly becoming more and more troublesome," Ulozov remarked just loud enough for Ilizeva to hear. "It was indecision that caused them to lose that ship, and they know combat is always risky."

Ilizeva nodded. "Yes, I agree they're beginning to be more trouble than they're worth. But how long have the drow and hobgoblins been allies?"

"Since before the AI Awakening," Ulozov said.

"Yes," Ilizeva agreed. "And while they have always been willing to take their place at our side as subordinates, Marshal N'Kirit seems to have greater ambitions. I may have to speak to the Synod about this matter and learn if he's acting alone or if this is indicative of a shift in hobgoblin intentions."

REVELATIONS AND RECONCILIATIONS

"Given previous experiences with his seconds," Ulozov began, "I suspect it's the former."

"As do I," said Ilizeva. "But I didn't get where I am today without a modicum of care and caution."

"Indeed," Ulozov said.

"We're rather certain that the elves know we have the technology to fold space/time. The element of surprise remains in that we can attack at any time with no prior warning. But we cannot discount the intelligence of the sun, moon, and star elves."

"That's true," Ulozov replied.

"This was the first battle since we employed space/time folding where we have suffered any losses," Ilizeva continued. "This should not have been the case. The simplicity of surprise an attack that folding space/time affords us may already be losing its edge."

One of Ulozov's best qualities was that he could show her the flaws in any strategy or tactic she created, sometimes with approaches she did not consider. He never wasted words.

"We might want to reevaluate our primary strategy and see what else we might be able to do," Ulozov said. "A change in targets, like a ground target or military refinery or something of that nature."

Ilizeva sighed. "Perhaps. Yet whatever we come up with, we'll still need to use the hobgoblins to bolster our forces, much as I dislike it."

Ulozov said nothing more.

Over the next fifty minutes, the remaining ships were destroyed. Shipyard defenses were also left in shambles, the construction yard was raided, and the ships and parts within plundered, taken, or destroyed.

"All forces reporting there are no remaining targets," a controller called.

"Very good," Ilizeva said. She had resumed standing at the display once the battle was over and mop-up operations had begun.

"What is it?" asked Ulozov.

Ilizeva had very few tells. With those, there were even fewer who recognized them. Ulozov was such a one. "I would like to stay and monitor the area a while longer. We could send a ship into unrealspace to look out for elf forces."

"We could," Ulozov agreed. "But we've met our objective. Unless you think there's something more to be won by remaining?"

She shook her head. "No. And the hobgoblins would be too tempted to push and dig for further plunder, and/or destroy the shipyard, despite my objections, to avenge their loss. It is time to go. Form up the fleet."

"Very good, General," Ulozov replied.

There was one other matter that held Ilizeva's curiosity. They had left elves alive at a space station during a prior attack. But when the rescue parties had arrived, they'd found that the survivors had been destroyed. While the elves believed the drow had returned, they hadn't. Thus, the question remained, who had destroyed them?

"Major Onuzov," Ilizeva called out.

"Yes, General?"

"Prepare a drone to be left behind. Set it to monitor and record any comings and goings in the system, communications, and whatever else you can program it to."

"Yes, General," he replied. Then, "May I ask why?"

"Call it curiosity, Major."

Chapter 6 – Questing

As the *Moon Raven* completed its transition from unrealspace back to realspace, Darius could not help but feel skeptical. Sara must have been feeling the same, as she said, "You're kidding, right? Could this be anywhere more the middle of nowhere?"

"It's not an empty system," remarked Galit. Darius noted that sensors had come back online, following the usual short blackout when transitioning from unrealspace to realspace. "Medium-sized orange star, ten planets."

"Maybe," Sara said. "But this is a really odd sector to be in. It's not on any charts with any data, save that it exists and isn't utterly unexplored or marked forbidden by anyone. It's clearly unclaimed, even independently. But given its location, it could be human, dwarven, elven, halfling, or even derro."

"Have you ever met a derro?" questioned Aya. "From a distance, they look a lot like dwarves. But soon as you get close, they're clearly not."

"I met a derro at *Territory's Edge* once," remarked Tol. "We're built identically, that's so. But they all have grey or blue-grey skin, and all white or grey eyes. And they tend to be unpleasant."

Galit chuckled. "That's true enough. Those I've encountered always seemed to have a nasty disposition."

"Focus, people," Darius said, interrupting them. "Where are we going?"

"Second planet," stated Kaz without hesitation.

Darius looked at the chart of the solar system. Of the ten planets that made it up, only the second was in the "Goldilocks zone", and thus potentially capable of supporting life. Then he took a closer look. Maybe it was, but it didn't look in the least bit hospitable.

"Is this what a planetary anthropologist might call a dead system?" questioned Zya.

"Perhaps," replied Galit. "But they're an odd lot."

Darius didn't know any planetary anthropologists. Yet he did get a sense that the entire system was mostly dead. It was disturbing. Kaz took them to the second planet. Soon they were in orbit, scanning for signs of movement or life.

"Got it," Sara said after a short time. "I'm detecting a starship with active systems and lifeforms in and around it. Sending coordinates, Kaz."

"Received," the half-elf pilot replied. "Taking us down."

As they descended towards the surface, Darius was not further impressed. There was only one large continent, and it was surrounded by waters that appeared equally lifeless. It looked nothing like any habitable world he'd visited before.

There were ruins strewn all about the continent, but they were in such a state of disrepair that Darius had no idea if they'd been bombed, destroyed by the elements, or just left to crumble over time. What's more, the architecture gave nothing away about its origins.

Though the races all shared certain basic elements, most had distinct features in their architecture. Elves tended towards flowing height, dwarves towards more solid, squat constructs, while orcs built solid, tall, and imposing structures. Human architecture was all over the place, but their structures were always distinctively human, nonetheless.

As they got nearer the coordinates where the ship sat on the surface, nothing more distinctly intact nor obvious gave any hint as to why the Grand Master of the UEO was there and using some unusual form of communication to reach out for help.

Unsurprisingly, Sara said, "I hope the Grand Master isn't stranded here and just looking for a lift. Don't the various UEO facilities have ships and crews?"

"Yes, they do. But that's not what they called for," stated Kaz. He said nothing more, concentrating on their flight.

"The Grand Master would only make such a call if they have a particularly crucial need," said Galit. "I trust they're not just trying to get a ride."

Darius said nothing further. The ship on the ground became clearer as the *Moon Raven* came in for a landing. He couldn't help but notice that the Grand Master's starship was unlike any he'd seen before, save two ships: *Moon Raven* and *Phantom*. They didn't have similar shapes, nor were they close in size. Yet there was something about the Grand Master's starship Darius suspected was probably genasi.

Kaz landed the *Moon Raven*, leaving systems on standby.

REVELATIONS AND RECONCILIATIONS

"Should anyone remain with the ship?" Tol asked.

"No," Darius said. He didn't know why, but he very much felt they should all see what it was the Grand Master of the UEO wanted. "Get whatever gear you need and meet at the main hatch in two galactic standard minutes."

Darius went to his cabin and grabbed a second SPP, as well as a heavy coat and gloves. He made his way to the hatch, where the others were soon all gathered. Kaz looked nervous, but the others appeared determined or curious. Tol opened the hatch, and they stepped outside the ship onto the barren landscape.

Just outside the hatch were two people, clearly awaiting them. Though they were in robes, their garments looked particularly warm and solid, purpose-built for cold weather.

The pair approached them. Darius could see that one was a female half-elf. The other, also a half-half, had no discernable gender. Galit stepped forward, crossed her arms over her chest, and bowed slightly at the waist. "Grand Master. It is a great pleasure to see you again."

"Ah," the genderless half-elf said, grinning. "The Blue Cyberwizard, Galit Azurite. You have come in answer to my call?"

"I have," she replied.

"You know one another?" the half-elf female beside the Grand Master questioned.

"We do," the Grand Master affirmed. "We met a long time ago. When last we met, she went by Gideon Azurite and the pronouns he/him. But now Galit, pronouns she/her. Galit Azurite, this is Master Alisay Naun-moon'kari."

Galit repeated the gesture she'd made to the Grand Master toward the monk at his side. Then, she said, "I have had the good fortune to have connected with this rather unique crew. This is their captain, Darius Noble."

Darius had never believed in any formal religion. Though he understood the tenets of transtheism, he'd never given it much attention. Neither had he been raised with any formal spiritual or religious practices. He was uncertain if he should bow as Galit had.

Fortunately, before he had to act, the Grand Master extended their hand, saying, "Captain."

As they shook hands, Darius said, "It's an honor to meet you, Grand Master."

Galit introduced Sara, Aya, Tol, and Zya, and the Grand Master proceeded to shake their hands as well. Before she could introduce Kaz, he stepped before the Grand Master and dropped to his knees.

"Forgive me, Grand Master," Kaz pled. "I left the temple more than two decades ago and ceased to be a cleric of the UEO. I have made my way across the galaxy ever since, never dreaming it would bring me to you. But I heard your call, and though I have left the ontology, I am no longer one of your disciples. Forgive me, Grand Master, for turning away from the temple and turning my back on the ontology."

"My son," the Grand Master said with a tone Darius presumed to be tender. "Who are you?"

"Grand Master, I am Kazimir Daun-sun'kira, former cleric of the temple at Ganeshava under Master Kemp."

The Grand Master frowned. "That unfortunate incident with the verdan?"

"The same, Grand Master."

The Grand Master shook their head. "Most unfortunate. We were forced to remove and replace all the masters, then purge, purify, and rededicate that temple. They lost their way. Tell me, Kazimir Daun-sun'kira, do you still believe? Do you practice meditation and exercises to enhance your connection to chi and Universal Energies?"

"I do, Grand Master," said Kaz without hesitation.

"Arise, Kazimir Daun-sun'kira," said the Grand Master. They offered Kaz a hand up. "You may have departed from a temple and no longer observe the rituals of the cleric way, but I can see and feel that you are still connected, still a transtheist, and thus you *are* still a cleric of the Universal Energies Ontology."

Kaz took the Grand Master's hand. As they pulled him up, Darius could see a look on the pilot's face that he could only describe as joyful.

"Sometimes scholars and guardians must choose another way," said the Grand Master. "There is no need for forgiveness, Kazimir Daun-sun'kira. You answered my call, and I welcome you home." As the Grand Master pulled Kaz into an embrace, Darius could see his pilot looked amazed, confused, and grateful all at once.

When the Grand Master released Kaz from their embrace, they turned their attention to Darius. "Captain Noble. You accepted that the Blue Cyberwizard and Guardian Kazimir received a call from me. Do you follow the transtheist way?"

"I can't say that I do, Grand Master," replied Darius. "I'm familiar with the UEO in general but admit that, apart from knowing someone leads it, I know nothing of you."

The Grand Master grinned, which put Darius at ease. "I understand. You are like most people, Darius Noble. I appreciate your honesty. For good or ill, you are here now. What you know of our way, or myself, isn't all that important in the grand scheme of things."

The Grand Master looked past Darius to the *Moon Raven*. "I see your vessel is genasi."

Darius turned to look at the ship. "How can you tell?"

The Grand Master said, "The lines. The materials beneath the paint. The imprint your ship makes within the Universal Energies."

"You can sense the ship?" asked Sara incredulously.

The Grand Master chuckled. "Yes. Particularly because it is genasi, and their vessels have a signature that is unique to our space/time."

"I had no idea," remarked Tol. "I knew the *Moon Raven* was unique, but this is something else entirely."

"And you're certain it's genasi?" pressed Sara.

"Without a doubt," said the Grand Master. "It's an old ship, too."

"How can you tell that?" questioned Tol.

"There is a unique sensation in this space, between all the energies, where the starship rests," said the Grand Master. "To be fair, most of my clerics and monks couldn't sense it beyond knowing that it *is*. But I can feel that it's been out there a long time, in various incarnations with various crews. It was meant to be yours."

"That's not creepy or disturbing at all," Darius heard Aya comment under her breath. Sara chuckled lightly.

"I am not surprised you're skeptical," said the Grand Master. "If I had not been attuned to Universal Energies and my own chi nearly all of my life, and dedicated my studies to them, I would find it hard to believe. But the ship is just as much a part of the overall sentient nature of the Universe. All things in the Universe have a purpose. Call it a destiny, a personal legend, a reason, it does not matter. The Universe will conspire to move things in a way that even one such as myself cannot fully fathom. And when that happens, there's no resisting. It is what it is."

Darius found himself spellbound by the Grand Master's words. They were an unexpectedly eloquent storyteller. The Grand Master continued, gesturing to the *Moon Raven*, "That you, each of you, came to be together and on that ship, means that you were always those I would seek to join me on this quest."

"Quest?" Darius questioned. "What quest?"

"I have been given certain information by the genasi that there are texts beneath this ruined temple. Texts that delve into the lost mysteries of the origins of our collective ability to travel faster than light, our ability to move from realspace to unrealspace, our understanding of wormholes, and other questions of alternative dimensions."

"Realspace, unrealspace, and savagespace," remarked Galit.

"Precisely," replied the Grand Master. "There are many more dimensions of space/time than we know. But we had more knowledge, lost to the past, than we do now. Time, separation, and increasing distances between us all - literally and metaphorically - have had an impact on that. Yet I've been assured that texts useful to us now are here, beneath the remains of that temple."

The Grand Master pointed towards the ruins. Darius turned to look, but it was not more than a pile of materials that were once a structure. The Grand Master went on, saying. "I am not meant to undertake the quest to go to the catacombs, dungeons and spaces below alone, or with my monks and clerics. That is because the way will be challenging."

"How so?" asked Sara.

It was the monk Alisay who spoke. She said, "We've run numerous scans. This place has been abandoned for millennia, but there's evidence it may have been intentionally left behind, sealed, and forgotten. The spaces beneath the ground are the resting place of an old AI from before the time of the Awakening. And it may remain active and on guard."

REVELATIONS AND RECONCILIATIONS

Darius didn't like the sound of that at all. What he knew of the AI Awakening was not good. "I don't know that disturbing a potentially sealed-away, Awakening-era AI is a good idea at all. Do you know what you seek?" Darius asked.

"Ancient texts," replied the Grand Master.

"And why do you seek them?"

"Galit mentioned savagespace," said the Grand Master. "Do you know what that is, Darius Noble?"

"Based on our time with her, I assume it's the dimension of space/time where the tunnels connecting two halves of wormholes run through. And that's where unknown assailants who've been attacking outlying bases, outposts, and the like are coming from."

"Yes," replied the Grand Master. "And that threat is great. But it is not the greatest threat. You see, wormholes rip tears in the fabric of realspace, but they seal again when they close. The same cannot be said for the wormhole-like portals that are being created to fold space/time. If that is not stopped, the fabric of reality will break down, and that will lead to dire consequences, extinctions, and the end of this dimension as we know it. I do not know what that would look like; nobody can know. But I know preventing such and protecting the space/time continuum is one of the matters that the Universal Energies Ontology was created to address so long ago."

"And the text offers a solution?" questioned Darius.

Alisay responded, saying, "A means to repair the rifts, both to prevent the breakdown of space/time in our dimension, and stop whatever is crossing to it from savagespace."

All was silent a moment, save the whispers of the wind in the air of the long-dead world.

"I'm in," said Kaz. "Whatever you need from me, Grand Master, I will be happy to provide."

"I'm aboard," said Galit.

"Yes," Aya said. "I like this reality and would very much like to keep it whole."

Darius saw Tol look to his spouse. Zya bobbed her head once, ever so slightly. Tol said, "Zya and I would be honored to take part in this quest."

Darius looked at Sara. She looked back at him, her face unreadable to him. Then, with a slight shrug of her shoulders, she turned to the Grand Master and said, "I'm in, too."

Darius could feel all eyes on him. For the first time in a long time, he was uncertain. He knew it would be dangerous. He knew it was a risk, and they would be entering the unknown. He also knew that everything the Grand Master and Alisay had said was true.

It was a heavy weight to have the potential fate of reality on your shoulders. Darius took a deep breath and let it out dramatically. "Yes. I guess I am in, too."

The Grand Master smiled. "As it was meant to be. Very well. You will accompany myself and Master Alisay."

"You're going with us?" asked Kaz.

"This is my destiny," said the Grand Master with a degree of certainty and finality that Darius couldn't place, but both made him feel equally better and more concerned.

"The rest of the monks and clerics will remain here above," said the Grand Master. "They will guard our ships and record any data we send them."

"And seal us down there if the AI is a threat we can't stop," remarked Galit.

"Yes," the Grand Master agreed.

Chapter 7 – Descent

The Universe always worked in mysterious ways. When the Grand Master had sent out the call for help, they had had no idea what or whom to expect. Still, the Grand Master knew Universal energy, and they had trusted that what was necessary would be provided.

Like their gender, the Grand Master could not even fully recall their age anymore. Somewhere around a century, they thought. Upon becoming Grand Master, like many other concerns most people gave attention to, age and gender had both ceased to hold importance.

The crew of the *Moon Raven* had no idea just how significant it was that they had been brought together by the Universal Energies. Yet how could they? None of them, save Kazimir Daun'sun'kira – Kaz – could have known, and even he didn't fully understand the ties that bound them.

Two human former military officers, one kitsune thief, a half-elf cleric and pilot, and two dwarf mechanics/engineers. They were not just diverse because of their races, but also their skills and experiences. Then there was the Blue Cyberwizard. Of all the cyberwizards the Grand Master had met in their time, she was probably the most skilled, accomplished, and wisest. The fact that she had no obvious cybernetic enhancements or implants - and she had a great many implants – spoke of that. That she understood the Universal Energies and chi, even when she didn't make use of them, was another impressive matter.

This team represented the best possibility of success the Grand Master could have dreamed of. Though multiple monks and clerics from their ship wanted to accompany them on the quest, the Grand Master had insisted that the *Moon Raven* crew, themself, and Alisay, were all who needed to take the risk and enter the long-abandoned spaces below the ruined temple. Alisay, of course, was eager to stay at the Grand Master's side. They appreciated that, but not for any reason Alisay considered.

Once the *Moon Raven* crew had gathered more gear, together with the monks and clerics, they figured out how to access the caverns, catacombs, and dungeons deep beneath the ruins. It took some doing to clear away the rubble to reveal the sloping artificially-made tunnel.

The Grand Master gave final instructions to the monks and clerics staying behind. "Guard the ships. Guard the entrance to the passages below. Nobody follows us down. If anything other than this party comes up, do not let it leave this place. Use your best judgment when deciding if you should disable or destroy it. It's possible that chatter signal will be available, but that is unlikely. If we do not communicate or return in three galactic standard days' time, return to where we met the genasi and tell them what has transpired."

They received acknowledgment and then entered the way to the passages below. It was a sloping tunnel, and there was evidence that a door of some sort had once stood at the entrance that until recently had been blocked by debris.

Igniting portable lights as they left the dimly lit surface behind, the Grand Master found themself in a corridor. It was comprised of bumpy, uneven natural stone - grey, brown, and black. The floor was only slightly less wild, likely from people walking across it long ago. The passage was broad enough for half a dozen people to move along, shoulder-to-shoulder. There was no illumination, but when they shined a light into the passage ahead, it could be seen to slope downwards, disappearing as it turned, likely a spiral.

"May I take the lead?" Captain Noble – Darius – asked.

"Yes," the Grand Master replied. That gave them an even greater sense of respect for the human starship captain, who had been least interested in joining this quest.

Darius, with Sara at his side, took the lead. Behind them were Tol, Zya and Aya, followed by the Grand Master and Galit. Kaz and Alisay brought up the rear.

The passage spiraled downwards for some time. It was unchanging, the walls and ceiling the same natural stone and smooth floor. It smelled of dry earth, mold, damp soil, and disuse. There was an odd stillness to the air and no discernable sound. As the descending passageway began to level out, it started to grow lighter. The Grand Master could not identify the source of the illumination, but the darkness receded sufficiently that they could disable their lights.

After a short distance on even ground, the passage opened to a much broader, higher-ceilinged passageway. The walls were smoother and less

REVELATIONS AND RECONCILIATIONS

chunky, less like natural stone, as though they'd been chiseled down and the ground flattened out. The corridor curved away so that the end was not visible.

"Stay sharp," Darius said. "There's no telling what's down here, so let's move with caution."

The Grand Master agreed with Darius' assessment. They proceeded down the corridor, the air still but not as stale or dusty as they would have thought a place long disused such as this might be. They continued moving forward until they reached what appeared to be a vault door.

At first glance, the door looked to be made of stone, as it matched that upon the walls, ceiling, and floor. Yet it was clearly metallic, though what kind of metal it was made of was unclear. It appeared that it would swing on a hinge towards or away from them, rather than sliding into the walls, floor, or ceiling.

"Wait," Aya called, before Darius or Sara could reach out to the door. "I have some experience with locked doors, traps, and the like. Let me take a look at that before you try to open it."

Darius and Sara parted and Aya stepped up between them. The Grand Master observed the kitsune gingerly touching the vault door at various points, almost like it was a lover she was being affectionate with.

Aya made use of some small tools and a docupad to seek whatever it was she was looking for. The Grand Master could sense, through the Universal Energies, that there were a great many chambers and corridors on the other side of the heavy door they faced.

After a few moments, Aya turned away from the door. "Well, this thing's rigged in all kinds of ways. Tol, Zya, you might want to take a look at it before anyone tries to open it."

The dwarves moved past Darius and Sara, then took out several different tools and began to scan and work on the vault door.

"Let me know if I can help," said Galit.

The Grand Master turned to look at the Blue Cyberwizard at his side. "Are you getting any data information?"

"Nothing clear," remarked Galit. "But I suspect that's because any wireless signals still active down here are heavily shielded. There is active power through there." She gestured towards the massive door the dwarves were working on. "And I'm not sure what to make of it, nor what to expect. Are you getting anything?"

"You mean via Universal Energies?" questioned the Grand Master.

"Yes."

"Nothing specific," the Grand Master replied. "Machines don't have the same vibrational energies that living things and other organics do. But there's something through there giving off a higher vibrational energy than I'd expect after being so long buried."

"Makes you wonder if we should be opening this door," Galit mused.

"It does pose many questions," agreed the Grand Master. "The most concerning being, is that door keeping us out or keeping something else within?"

"Embrace the power of 'and' Grand Master?" remarked Galit.

The Grand Master chuckled.

Alisay stepped up to them. "May I speak with you a moment, Grand Master?"

"Of course," the Grand Master replied. Alisay looked as if she wished to step away from the party, so they went on to say, "If what you wish to speak of is pure, surely you can do so before our companions here?"

Alisay seemed momentarily taken aback, but then nodded. "Apologies. I did not realize that you had spent much time outside the temples and the monks and clerics of the UEO. I guess it's a curiosity to me."

The Grand Master smirked. "Master Alisay, the Universal Energies Ontology maintains a philosophy of transtheism that transcends races, transcends customs, and is bigger than anyone or anything we can comprehend. If the UEO cannot be a beacon to all, and I mean all, then we lose our way and our overall purpose. Masters are not just leaders for the rest of the members of the orders, scholars, or guardians. We are ambassadors to all we encounter, believers or no."

Alisay chuckled. "Thank you, Grand Master. It's good you keep showing me new things."

Ahead, there was a click, then the ever-so-slight sound of something powering down.

"We got it," said Tol.

REVELATIONS AND RECONCILIATIONS

The massive vault door began to emit multiple popping noises, then started to open towards them on large hinges they could not yet see. With a combination of groaning, hissing, and muted screeching, the clearly heavy door swung open.

Everyone armed had drawn weapons, preparing to meet any threats. The huge, meter-wide vault door was fully open. Though there was still no apparent source for the light, the space on the other side of the door was illuminated to a comfortable level.

As they neared the door, there was a narrower space of smooth walls on the other side. Past that, there was a section of walls that had small studs in ordered rows all over them.

"Laser wall," said Zya.

Tol added, "If it wasn't disabled, other defenses just the other side of the door would turn the heat up considerably. And there's no way through it from above or below."

"Safe now?" asked Darius.

"Yes," said Tol. Then, he stepped through.

Nothing happened. The others went through, walked past the laser wall section, then stopped again.

Darius looked back. "The door appears to be staying open."

"Lends credence to the notion that it's keeping something in rather than out," said Galit.

"That's not selling me on continuing," said Sara.

"Since the entrance was booby-trapped, odds are there are more traps though here," stated Darius. "Aya or Kaz, one of you should probably take point."

"On it," said Aya. "We go?"

"Forwards," said Darius.

They began to move further into the underground space, cautiously. The corridor was now lined in metallic panels of a bluish-grey. The floor was natural stone, but completely smoothed over. The ceiling arose to an arch that was the same metallic paneling as the walls, lit by a still unseen light source.

They had shifted position. Aya was just a bit ahead of everyone, Darius and Sara hanging back just enough to cover her but not be seen easily by anyone ahead. Behind them were Tol and Zya, followed by the Grand Master and Kaz, with Galit and Alisay bringing up the rear.

The Grand Master looked at the half-elf cleric beside them. "Do you miss the temple, son?"

"To be honest, Grand Master, no," replied Kaz. "I was an orphan raised in the temple, so it was the only way of life I knew for many years. When everything went down, I felt that maybe the whole of the ontology had lost its way."

"I can understand that," replied the Grand Master. "A corrupted temple with corrupted masters paints a bleak picture. It's easy to extend that outward to the rest of the organization and its leaders."

"Yes," Kaz agreed. "But over time, when I'd learned that Master Kemp and her fellow temple masters had been removed, I came to see that it was not the whole of the ontology that was broken. Also, I have never ceased my practices."

"I can feel that you are as connected as any active practitioner to both the Universal Energies and your own chi, Kazimir Daun-sun'kira. But there are many for whom the way is not in the temples, cloisters, and service to the ontology. You have my respect."

"I cannot tell you how much that means to me, Grand Master," Kaz said.

As the Grand Master was about to reply, there was an unusual mechanical buzzing noise coming from ahead. Then, the distinctive sound of plasma bolts firing.

Aya appeared, running, but a bolt slammed into her and threw her against a wall.

Darius, Sara, Tol, and Zya were all firing on the drone that had appeared. It was quick and oval, with no obvious propulsion system, flitting about, dodging fire from the combined weapons of the foursome.

Kaz leapt into the air, drawing his sword as he did so. He slashed at the dodging drone, slicing it clean in half. The two halves of the drone dropped to the ground, the members of the *Moon Raven* crew pointing their weapons at them. They did not move.

The Grand Master observed the kitsune against the wall, lying still as Galit called out. "Aya!"

REVELATIONS AND RECONCILIATIONS

The Grand Master approached the kitsune. She moaned as he got near her.

"That hurt," she said.

The Grand Master looked her over, scanning her via the Universal Energies. No bones were broken, but they didn't find that all too surprising. Kitsune were agile and resilient. She might have felt sore after connecting with the wall, but it wasn't likely to do more than inconvenience her for a time. The plasma bolt, however, had hit her hard. There was muscle and nerve damage just above her shoulder blade but fortunately no organ damage.

"Aya Mah-soo-may fo Misa," the Grand Master addressed her. "May I heal your wounds?"

"That would be much appreciated," she said. There was no mistaking the pained tone of her voice.

The Grand Master paused, placing one hand on Aya's wound and the other opposite, near her clavicle. They concentrated, making a connection between Universal Energies and the kitsune's chi. They moved the energies to, into, and through Aya. They remained still, both the Grand Master and the kitsune, for several moments. Then, the Grand Master knew their work was done.

They arose from kneeling, offering Aya a hand up. She took it and arose. Then she stood there a moment, rolling her shoulder. "That's... That's something else," Aya remarked. "Are all healings by monks and clerics like that?"

"More or less," said Alisay, having stepped up to join them. "Some are more adept and skilled, but all have the same abilities. It's a matter of focus and moving energies within and without the body."

"Can you stop death?" asked Aya.

The Grand Master paused to let Alisay answer. And she did, saying, "Not as such. We can use Universal Energies and chi like emergency medical responders, defibrillate and shock the system. But we cannot undo or stop death, for it is the natural course of things."

The Grand Master couldn't have stated it better themself.

"Thank you," Aya said.

"Aya, are you alright?" asked Darius.

"Thanks to the Grand Master, I am," Aya replied.

45

"Good. Thank you, Grand Master, for healing my quartermaster."

"Of course," the Grand Master replied, moving towards Darius and company.

Tol and Zya were kneeling on the ground, examining the two halves of the drone. "I've never seen anything quite like this," Tol said. "Looks like it had a chatter wired into it, but it was for two-way communications, not a control signal. So it was an independent drone."

"Very powerful plasma cannon," said Zya. "And not a synchronized plasma pulse in the same manner as our weapons. More raw, but somehow just as refined."

Galit approached, also kneeling to look at the drone.

"How sharp is your sword, Kaz?" asked Sara. "You cut that thing clean in half."

"There are few metals, compounds, or other materials that can stand up to a cleric's blade," Kaz stated.

"Unique metallurgy?" asked Sara.

The Grand Master said, "Yes. Forged by cleric masters in a limited number of temples, with materials and techniques passed only among themselves and those they teach to continue the art. But they are made in such a way so that their true strengths are hidden."

"I agree with Tol," Galit remarked, standing up straight again. "This drone was autonomous. And given how it flew and dodged fire, I suspect a more advanced AI intellect than modern drones possess."

"That means that whatever is down here knows we're coming," said Darius.

The Grand Master watched Galit's eyes go distant for a moment. Then, she blinked and was present with them again. "There's a powerful energy source below," Galit said. "It was undetectable from above, but now that we've passed the vault, we're probably within the field shielding it."

"Grand Master, Master Alisay, can you chatter the monks and clerics you left on the surface?" asked Darius.

The Grand Master paused, accessing their chatter. It was silent, making no connection. "No," they reported.

"Nor I," added Alisay.

"We suspected this would be the case," said Sara.

REVELATIONS AND RECONCILIATIONS

"Nothing to be done for it now," said Darius. "Galit, can you tell how far?"

"Yes and no," Galit said. "But that power source is likely where the ancient texts are. But also likely the AI's brain, too."

"Lovely," breathed Aya.

"And kilometers of passages between here and there?" questioned Darius.

"Almost definitely," replied Galit.

The Grand Master was not surprised. There were many hidden spaces beneath their temple on Paxion. That was not a new practice for the UEO.

"Well, we can't turn back now," Darius said. "There's too much riding on this quest. Everyone, stay sharp. Let's do this."

Chapter 8 – Strategizing

This was the first staff meeting with his newly appointed deputy in attendance. General Song was on his flagship, the *Hammer of Harmony,* in the executive conference cabin. Windows to port looked out into space and the other starships that were there. Five of those were the other command vessels of his general staff.

In the conference cabin, there were large viewscreens both behind Song and at the other end of the rectangular table. Everyone was seated according to rank after Song, sitting at the narrow head. The only people in the room other than his command staff were his ever-present drow "advisors". They stood on either side of the door into the conference room.

He glanced to his new second, noting that she was looking to the other officers, likely sizing them up. Aneesa Anwar was not yet thirty. She was short, like most members of the Anwar family Song knew, and petite overall. But there was a fierceness that she could flip on and off like a switch.

Since her promotion and coming aboard Song's flagship, apart from reporting to him and allowing him to formally recognize her and accept her transfer, they'd not spoken. That had been two galactic standard days ago. He had made no further attempt to engage with her, nor she with him.

Song checked the time and sounded the tone that would call the meeting to order. "Thank you for attending this staff meeting," Song began. "Allow me to introduce to you all my new second, Lieutenant General Aneesa Anwar."

Heads were nodded respectfully around the table. The command officers knew better than to comment on the young and inexperienced new general.

"General Anwar, across from you is General Gerhard, Chief of Operations." Aneesa nodded to him with a mix of what Song read as respect and derision. "Continuing around the table, Lieutenant General Kaber, Chief of Logistics. Major General Norris, Chief of Intelligence, Major General Sato, Chief of Medical. Brigadier General Ishii, Chief of Security. Brigadier General Healy, Second Fleet. Brigadier General Waheed, Third Fleet. Brigadier General West, Chief of Engineering. Major General Hara,

REVELATIONS AND RECONCILIATIONS

Home Fleet. And to your right, Major General Fadel, Deputy for Operations and Logistics."

Aneesa had nodded to each. Song expected that she already knew who they all were. He went on. "Let's continue where we left off before. I'm going to summarize for General Anwar's benefit. The next phase of the plan is to strike at two sectors in the Confederation at a time, both of which we have hit previously."

"Begging your pardon, General," Aneesa interrupted. "Why would we strike the same sectors we've hit before? In what way does that expand the Federation's influence? Wouldn't striking new sectors keep the Confederation more off-balance?"

Song was proud of himself for neither barking at her, nor grinding his teeth, nor speaking icily as he said, "Your point, General, is valid, but you are not familiar with the current, up-to-date intelligence we have on the Confederation and their forces. All of our advanced scouts have shown that the Confederation has sent only small reinforcements to replace what we destroyed previously. At the same time, they are prepared with larger forces for us to strike a new sector. Hence, striking the same sector makes us more unpredictable."

Aneesa said, "Begging your pardon, General, but what difference does it make if we can open a fold in space/time anywhere of our choosing? We have the element of surprise, no matter where we strike, do we not?"

"Yes," Song agreed, keeping his tone calm and even. Aneesa's inexperience was going to require far more explanation than should have been necessary.

He continued by saying, "Attacking an unprepared force carries much less risk than attacking one expecting to be attacked, surprise or no. Unless your forces have overwhelming superiority in numbers and weapons, the overcommitment involved in attacking a force awaiting an attack, even with surprise, isn't worth it. Certainly not in this phase of our campaign."

"Maybe I misunderstand," said Aneesa. "Don't we have an overwhelming force? In addition to our ships, we still have the drow and their allies. Unless I somehow misread it, a basic statistical analysis would suggest we do have overwhelming forces. So why aren't we deploying them?"

This time, Song could not prevent the sigh. He cleared his throat to cover it, then said, "General Anwar, the combined forces we had when we invaded the Alliance, along with the drow and their allies, was indeed overwhelming. But we also had surprise on our side because our attack was not expected, and we caught them totally off guard. What's more, the analysis you refer to does not take into account the forces we have in former Alliance space, maintaining our occupation.

"Having struck the Confederation a few times now, they know we're on the attack. They are, as such, more prepared to hunker down defensively against anything we throw at them. Thus, we must be particularly choosy when it comes to targets, to maintain our superiority and surprise for as long as we can."

"But what does that gain the Federation?" asked Aneesa. "This seems an overly cautious, slow approach. If they represent the complexities you suggest, why attack their forces at all? Choose a civilian target."

Song needed a moment to compose himself before replying. "There are, General Anwar, several problems with that approach. First and foremost, our allies are not keen on attacking unwitting civilians."

"Then we don't assign our allies to civilian attacks," Aneesa interrupted.

"Which leads to the other problems," Song said, unable to hold back the displeasure in his tone. "If we start to target civilians, our allies might decide to not participate in future actions."

"But won't they be released from the accords we have with them at some point?" interrupted Aneesa again.

"Of course they will," Song agreed. "But the longer we can keep them with us, the more we can spread ourselves and our influence outwards to the Confederation and, in time, to the Union. But you are not accounting for maintaining the occupation of the former Alliance systems. That, combined with our attacks on the Confederation, are draining Federation resources in ships, manpower, supplies, and logistics, as well as security."

Song didn't feel it was necessary to mention the rebellion that was, in part, the fault of his predecessor, Alastair Mallick. However, it did lead to an important point Song felt must be made. "General Anwar, though civilian targets are easy targets, there is a much greater risk to be had in striking them, particularly at this phase of our campaign. By attacking them will

REVELATIONS AND RECONCILIATIONS

build resistance that's wholly unnecessary. At present, Confederation forces are relatively strong, having been unchallenged for some time. Destroying them weakens them and opens more paths for the Federation to expand our influence. But if we choose to attack one of their cities or a space station, that will surely increase recruitment and volunteerism for the Confederation Argosy.

"So long as we keep our focus to the miliary, Confederation citizens are much less likely to get involved. When we have their forces destroyed and begin to replace their government, the people will be far more accepting of that change."

Song really wanted to tell her how Mallick's and the Superior Convocation's approach to occupying the Alliance had fomented the rebellion complicating their occupation and requiring committing more ships to it, rather than the Confederation campaign. However, he knew better than to waste time doing so.

"I suppose your point is valid, General," said Aneesa far too quickly to have paid attention to anything Song had shared. "But what good is having superior technology, like folding space/time, if you don't use it to its fullest potential?"

Song leaned back in his chair and crossed his arms. "Pray tell, General Anwar, in what way would you use it that we are not already?"

Eagerly, but with utter conviction, Aneesa said, "I would take all of our forces, as well as our allies, and launch a full-scale campaign against a single system. Fold in and out of the area, decimate all of the forces that are there. That would pave the way to occupying that sector and initiate the downfall of the Confederation."

Song nodded. He was proud of himself when he kept his tone even as he said, "Well, General, that's a fascinating notion. But you are missing many important facts. First of all, we cannot just open and close folds in space/time instantly, one after another after another. Just like we cannot fire weapons through a fold and hope to hit targets on the other side of it. It's not possible. Thus, such a campaign would involve more direct and conventional combat. We'd get one or two surprise attacks via folding space/time. But then, it would be a protracted engagement."

Song paused, took a breath, then continued. "A protracted engagement in Confederation space is not like such in Alliance space. It's a long, long way from Federation space and our supply lines therein. The Confederation can easily send in reinforcements, and we do not know the sum total of their forces. We are thus limited until we whittle them down further. A protracted engagement will lead to Federation losses, and the advantages of folding space/time mean little in an ongoing situation of that nature."

"You don't think you are underestimating our technology and our forces?" asked Aneesa.

"I know what our forces and our technology are capable of," Song replied. "But underestimating the opposition can drag out the conflict, which in turn will cost more Federation and allied forces. And then, just to add insult to injury, a protracted engagement might encourage others to sympathize with the Confederation and make even more trouble for us and our forces. The Union, their closest neighbor and a similar democracy, has surely taken notice of our overthrow and occupation of the Alliance. If they ally with the Confederation before we've removed most of their forces as we're presently planning, we have even greater unknowns to face."

"That's a great deal of supposition you make, General Song," Aneesa said. "The Union, in time, will also be subject to the Federation, is that not so?"

"Yes," replied Song.

"Then what does it matter if they ally with the Confederation now?"

Song sighed in exasperation. "The ability to fold space/time gives us a unique advantage. We can perform surprise attacks almost anywhere, anytime we choose. But the logistics of having our forces dispersed, even through a space/time fold, are more complicated than you're recognizing. And what's more, we only have so many ships, even with our allies. That's what we must consider."

Silence descended on the conference room. Song knew he was alone, as none of his other command staff officers would get into this debate with the deputy appointed by the Superior Convocation. Song actually appreciated that. He was not prepared to replace any of them if Aneesa got them removed.

REVELATIONS AND RECONCILIATIONS

Finally, Aneesa nodded and said, "Very well, General Song. Command of Federation Forces *is* yours. But I would ask that you concede that, perhaps, you are being too conservative with your plans."

"Perhaps," Song allowed. "But history shows time and again that slow and steady wins the race, particularly one involving such distances and the number of forces therein. Federation losses have been nil, thus far. It would be best to keep it that way as long as possible, to continue our dominance."

Song didn't say that he knew the Superior Convocation demanded more and were using Aneesa to work to influence his strategy. It was clear none of them understood warfare logistics. The price of speeding up the campaign in the way they wanted was too high. Higher, he suspected, than they would desire to pay.

Song glanced towards his drow "advisors", silently observing as they did. He had not been too surprised that Aneesa had been so openly argumentative. Perhaps she'd acquiesced this time, but he wondered how much longer he had until his drow "advisors" might need to openly serve as his bodyguards.

Chapter 9 – Scouting

Galit had been all across the galaxy. She didn't think there was a race she'd not encountered during her many years and travels. What most amazed her about the various races across the galaxy was how similar most of them were.

The technologies for interstellar travel had been discovered independently, albeit at different times. Starships had numerous aesthetic differences but were largely the same. The air they needed to breathe was similar enough to be compatible. Despite what made each race unique, they still had numerous similarities. This situation, however, was dissimilar. The signals she was exploring and the technology she saw were unlike anything she'd encountered before.

As the crew of the *Moon Raven*, the Grand Master, and his associate continued to descend, the signals and random bursts of wireless code had an elegance Galit had never encountered prior. Although most of the technology they came across was dormant, it wasn't completely dead. Hence, the unusual signals and random bursts of wireless code.

This was amazing and terrifying at the same time. The signals and codes were attempting to connect to who knew what? Galit couldn't interpret what she was picking up. She attributed that to AI technologies lost after the Awakening.

This lent credence, unfortunately, to the ideas that they were entering a domain that housed an abandoned Awakening-era AI that might have been locked away intentionally rather than destroyed. Galit was unsure what to make of that. Still, the encryptions and language of the signals and code bursts were advanced and impressive.

As they entered a broader chamber, everyone seemed to pause. It was the largest space they had been in since entering the catacombs, dungeons, and various below-ground structures. The walls of the more open space were not the same metallic panels, but instead raw stone, albeit smoothed and lacking any jagged or rough surfaces.

"Seems odd this space opened up here," commented Aya.

"Maybe it was a staging area or a waiting space for anyone visiting who or whatever was down here," said Darius.

REVELATIONS AND RECONCILIATIONS

Galit remarked, "I've been running scans and checks as we've been on the move. Though it certainly appears that any tech left down here is dormant, I still am rather sure we're being watched."

"By who?" asked Aya.

"Not who," said the Grand Master. "What. It is an AI, correct, Galit?"

"I believe so," Galit said. She explained to them the complexity of what she'd been detecting and observing.

"How are you scanning?" asked Tol. "You're not using a docupad or wearing a gauntlet or anything."

Galit grinned. "No need. I have scanners hardwired into my brain."

Most of the cyberwizards and many of the sorcerers had obvious signs of cybernetic enhancements. Cyborgs carried with them an intimidation factor no ordinary human – or any race, really – did. Some cyborgs had come into being as part of being healed from grievous injuries. Limb replacements with cybernetic enhancements were as common as limb replacements that blended with organic, original parts.

Some cyborgs had chosen to replace or augment their natural, organic parts in obvious mechanical ways. Most cyberwizards and many sorcerers had evidence of enhancements on their heads, necks, or faces. Galit had decided when she first began the path of cyberwizardry that she wanted to be underestimated. Why intimidate when you could be sneaky? she'd thought.

Galit had no obvious enhancements and no external cybernetic evidence visible. Yet she knew she was among the most advanced cyberwizards, with enhancements that gave her abilities no organic beings could possess. Via the cybernetic enhancements hardwired into her brain, Galit had connectivity to any wireless technologies within her considerable range.

She could interface passively via numerous algorithms and subroutines she'd designed over her life. Her active systems were better than the top-of-the-line equipment most peoples could buy.

"This is really bothering me," remarked Tol. "How is this chamber lit? I cannot see any evidence of light sources, apart from some subdued sources that can't possibly make it so we can see this clearly. Yet the ambient illumination has been steady, even as we entered this larger chamber."

Galit gestured and the others looked. Above them were two small drones, about the size of butterflies, silently hovering.

"My cantrips," Galit said. "Very basic mechanical drones with proprietary line-of-sight wireless interfaces attuned to only me. Thus, they're not susceptible to cyber-attack, and the AI couldn't detect nor take control of them if it tried."

"How do they give off so much light?" asked Zya.

Galit grinned. "Trade secret. These mechanical drones are wholly my design and extremely stealthy."

Tol and Zya put their heads together, having a hushed conversation in dwarven that Galit could have chosen to listen in on, as she had translation abilities among her tech. But she let them have their privacy.

The crew moved into another corridor and found Aya kneeling, as though examining something. "Trap door," Aya said. "I've been looking out for such. This has been too easy, and I for one would have made it harder to get to the central AI uninvited."

Galit started to scan. "Yes, Aya is correct. The dominant energy signature we've been following is below."

"Where does this corridor go?" Darius questioned.

"Traps, most likely," replied Kaz. "Or it leads to the same place, but via a much longer path."

"Or both," said Sara. "I'm a lot more inclined to take as direct a route as possible."

"Well," Aya said, "No conventional booby traps. But given I haven't entirely worked out how to open this, I'm not sure it's not trapped otherwise."

The others started to employ their scanning equipment as Galit ran her own search. It wasn't long before she found a trap. But then, so did Aya. "Aha," the kitsune exclaimed. "Definitely some kind of trap. Tol, Zya, care to look it over?"

As the dwarves moved to join Aya, Galit made a complete scan of the trap. "Stop," she warned.

"What is it?" asked Aya.

"It's a sneaky device," Galit informed them. "You could disable it, but it's directly connected to the AI, as far as I can tell. So even if you disable the trap's countermeasures, the AI will know that you opened the door."

"So, it needs to be spoofed," said Tol. "Can you do that?"

REVELATIONS AND RECONCILIATIONS

"I think so," Galit replied.

"Do you need to come here to do that?" asked Zya.

"No," Galit said. "No, but you can continue to disable the countermeasures. I've almost got it."

Galit could see that bypassing the AI was not easy, but she could also tell that it relied on someone opening the door, with or without disabling the traps to access it. Bypassing that alert required spoofing the AI to think the door was unopened. What she didn't say was that she was fairly certain the AI was already aware of their presence, and it mattered very little.

"Clear," Galit informed them.

Tol opened the hatch. As they gathered around it, they could see that the booby traps, though unconventional, were obvious and disabled.

"Nice work, everyone," Darius said.

As they prepared grapples to descend, the Grand Master, Alisay, and Kaz simply jumped down. Galit knew they could use their connections to Universal Energies to enhance their abilities to fall further than a human or elf might be able to without injury. She could do the same. Yet she chose to take the safer method and use a grapple gun to descend.

The floor of the chamber was a little more than seven-point-five meters below them. The space they found themselves within once more featured metallic panels along the walls and a concrete floor. It was about double the width and more than double the height.

After they recovered the grappling hooks from the level above, the Grand Master, Alisay, and Kaz all tensed. Just as Galit also sensed something was not right, the Grand Master said, "We are not alone down here."

Now Galit could feel a rumble through the floor and knew something was coming towards them. Something large.

"Whatever it is, it's hungry," said Alisay.

Kaz had drawn his sword. The rest of the crew had SPPs and SPRs readied, awaiting whatever was coming their way.

"Spread out," Darius ordered. "Kaz, Alisay, Grand Master, take a step back. Let's form a kill pocket, since we know where it's coming from."

"Tol, Zya, watch your fire," Sara said. "Our brawlers will be a lot closer to whatever is coming, so be mindful of that."

Darius and Sara anchored the corners, just forward of the Grand Master, Alisay, and Kaz. Towards the back of the half-circle, Tol and Zya stood with their synchronized plasma rifles at the ready. Galit and Aya stood to either side, just behind the UEO trio. Galit readied the plasma cannon in her left arm, as well as a small, flat disc in her right hand.

Two massive creatures emerged. Galit had not seen their like in a long time and had thought they might be extinct. Yet there they were.

More than three meters long and two and a half meters tall. Scaly, reptilian hides, eight legs, dark orange, a row of red, bony spikes lining their backs and running over the tops of their heads to a single curved horn. Their eyes glowed a pale green.

"Basilisks!" Galit warned. "Do not look into their eyes! They can petrify you, making you easy prey."

"Circle!" called Darius. "Grand Master, Kaz, Alisay, Aya, right, everyone else left. Avoid the eyes. Go!"

The basilisks snorted, and Galit felt them staring at the crew as they moved. Then, she heard SPR fire as Tol and Zya started to shoot at the basilisk from the left.

Galit saw Kaz in the air, his sword coming down as he attacked one of the basilisk's eyes. Aya was beside him, her staff moving impressively fast, attacking the other eye.

The Grand Master and Alisay were on the creature, pummeling it with chi and Universal energy-enhanced blows of hands and feet.

Before the other got much closer, Galit let the discs fly from her right hand. Both exploded in the basilisk's face, and it roared in defiance and anger. However, the explosions had done the job, and its eyes were destroyed.

Galit took aim and fired the pulse cannon in her left arm. It struck true, though how much damage it had done was unknown.

Basilisks had tough hides and could take a lot of punishment. The one on the right had lost two or three limbs to Kaz's sword, in addition to its eyes. The one on the left was swinging its tail like a club and trying to swipe at the *Moon Raven* crew and their laser blasts as they kept firing.

Galit readied another disc. She called to Darius and the crew, "On my signal, hold fire!"

REVELATIONS AND RECONCILIATIONS

She hoped Darius and the crew trusted her, as nobody responded. "Now!" she cried.

As the plasma blasts stopped, Galit raced towards the basilisk. It must have sensed her approach because it turned blindly towards her and roared its defiance.

The disk flew from her hand and down the monster's throat. As she threw herself towards the wall, a sound like *chuff* reverberated, and the basilisk went deftly still.

Its mouth opened, smoke coming out, and it collapsed where it was, dead. The explosive disc had reached far enough inside the creature to destroy it internally.

On the right, the Grand Master and Alisay continued to deliver powerful blows to the massive monster. Kaz was cutting its limbs as Aya blasted it with her synchronized pulse rifle.

Finally, Kaz removed the last limb and Aya placed a laser blast in an eye socket, while the Grand Master and Alisay each delivered powerful blows at sensitive parts of the monster's underbelly. With a terrible, keening growl, the creature dropped dead.

Galit looked around, noting that the *Moon Raven* crew and the master monks looked no worse for wear. Both basilisks were dead.

"Basilisk," Sara said, approaching the dead monster. "I thought they were just legends."

"I thought they were extinct," said Tol.

"No and no," said the Grand Master. "But none have been seen outside the caves on Sturnalt in about a thousand years or so. They're protected, you know."

"Protected?" asked Kaz.

"From poachers," the Grand Master replied. "Intact eyeballs can be sold for ten thousand gold COIN, eggs for nearly the same. Some unscrupulous sorcerers have been known to work with their petrification abilities. If they, themselves, don't get petrified first, of course."

"Nasty," said Aya.

"Anyone hurt?" asked Darius.

Everyone acknowledged they were not.

"This raises a question of whether those were just down here and attracted to us," Darius began. "Or if they were dispatched to attack us."

"That was just the start," the Grand Master said, looking down the passageway from whence the monsters had come. "I can feel that there are more ahead. And they weren't just left down here when this place was long ago abandoned."

"Yes," Alisay said. "I feel them, too."

Galit was about to add her agreement, but then, something in the air caught her eye. She reached in the direction of that indistinct thing and sent out a burst EMP. There was a crackling noise, and something dropped to the ground.

Aya and Kaz were the first upon it. "Drone," Aya said.

Galit approached and saw that the small drone – more bird-sized than her own butterfly-sized drones – had been designed to be silent and blend with the cavern-top above. It was only Galit's sensitivity to all things electronic and mechanical that had allowed her to detect it.

"Not one of yours?" Sara half-asked, half-commented.

"No," Galit said. "A drone controlled by the AI, no doubt. It's not spying on us anymore. But whatever is down here and running the show knows we're here and coming for it."

Darius sighed. "We'd better stay extra sharp. That wasn't easy, and I suspect it will only get harder from here on out."

Chapter 10 – Irregularities

"The elves are quite distraught. Our intelligence has learned that they are beside themselves trying to work out a means to prevent our attacks."

"Prevent?" someone scoffed. "There's nothing they can do. We target them, arrive atop them, and they are at our mercy."

Ilizeva was holographically attending a meeting of the Synod. And she was enjoying a considerable amount of praise for her ongoing, successful campaign against the elves.

"For many generations now, the elves have discounted the drow," said a member of the Synod named Alizev Kaen'baer. Ilizeva knew him to be a respected educator, and he was among the older members of the Synod.

Alizev continued, "These new tactics, giving nothing away, and brutal in their execution, are causing them a great deal of distress. The elf Synod are deeply concerned about our full intent towards them via these attacks."

"Our intent is retribution for the ills they've done us over the millennia," someone said.

"Is it that broad?" asked Alizev. "General Ilizeva?"

"I would not put it quite that way," Ilizeva replied. "There is no end goal, save weakening the elves and their influence across space. Making them more helpless in a manner not too dissimilar to their treatment of our ancestors. Keeping them off-balance with limited exposure for casualties of our own is a slow, steady campaign. We will lessen the power and influence of the elves among the other races of the galaxy, which will allow the drow a more dominant position. A position that should never have been denied us by the prejudices of the rest of elvenkind."

The response among the members of the Synod were mutterings of agreement.

"And what of our ongoing participation with the humans of the Federation?" asked the Moderator.

"We have withdrawn all but a third of the forces we initially sent to Federation space," Ilizeva replied. "Colonel Orizevi reports that the Federation leadership has foisted a new, utterly inexperienced Second on General Song, but he remains in command. I have assigned two drow bodyguards to protect General Song, and that is how we have this information. His predecessor convinced the Federation leaders that more could be done with space/time fold technology than is reasonable, and his new Second still believes that misinformation."

"How much autonomy do you allow Colonel Orizevi?" asked a Synod member Ilizeva identified as Ulazav Naen'daer.

"Colonel Orizevi has full authority," Ilizeva replied. "If she feels it best to withdraw drow and allied forces from Federation space, she will do so without consulting me. Likewise, I trust her to rescue General Song if needs be."

"The human general?" Elezev Paen'baer asked.

"Yes," Ilizeva replied. "He's a skilled strategist, an excellent tactician, and his talents are, frankly, wasted on the Federation and their leaders. I suspect when the Superior Convocation feels he's failed to deliver the lies his predecessor sold them, he'll be needlessly sacrificed. I should prefer that not happen."

"I am surprised you respect a human general like that," said Ilazivi Laen'baer, a former drow general retired long before Ilizeva's service.

"I am just as surprised," Ilizeva agreed. "But he's more skilled than any among our other allies, even the best of the hobgoblins."

"Speaking of the hobgoblins," began the Moderator. "You mentioned they are requesting direct access to folding space/time?"

Ilizeva explained her discussion with Marshal N'Kirit Dh Siv. She also made it clear this was no different than many arguments they'd had with the hobgoblins throughout their alliance.

"They forget," Ilizeva concluded, "that we saved them from themselves long ago. Were it not for our intervention, they would have been all but exterminated during the AI Awakening. Without us employing them as our allies they'd be all but disregarded. Still, they are skilled warriors, just in need of a direction we best provide them."

There was silence for a moment after that.

"General Ilizeva," a Synod member named Oluzev Paen'baer addressed her. "Have you noticed any irregularities with the use of folding space/time? There have been some distressing rumors."

"Could you be more specific?" Ilizeva requested.

REVELATIONS AND RECONCILIATIONS

"I refer to the Grand Master's visit to this chamber," said Oluzev Paen'baer. Ilizeva knew he was physically present at the Synod castrum on Aenaer. He continued, "We had, as you recall, dismissed the Grand Master's concerns as unfounded. But since that time, we have heard rumors of unusual alien forces and vacuum-surviving monsters attacking multiple systems and different races."

"I recall this," Ilizeva agreed. "But the Grand Master presented us with nothing concrete."

"Indeed," said Oluzev. "Moderator, may I bring in new business related to this discussion?"

"Yes."

"Thank you. With respect, a diplomatic mission from the human Confederation has reached out to us. They report that they have evidence that supports the claims made by the UEO Grand Master."

Ilizeva considered that. She knew all eyes were on her. She was the one using the space/time folding technology. It was she who was leading the drow to show the elves what their generations of disrespect had wrought.

She was also, however, a realist. "I have not noticed anyone other than us utilizing space/time fold. But I have noticed some unexpected irregularities. Energy residue where it doesn't seem natural, as well as what I suspect, but could not have investigated, was the beginning of an artificial wormhole forming."

"Could not have investigated?" someone asked.

"It was noticed as we were passing through a fold," Ilizeva explained. "Once we cross the event horizon of the artificial wormhole portal of a space/time fold, our sensors are rendered useless for a time. That's a result of the many forces at work and the energy used to create it when we fold space/time."

"Could it be the other-dimensional aliens suggested by the UEO Grand Master?" asked Alizev Kaen'baer.

"I have no evidence as such," stated Ilizeva. "But neither can I deny it. I have been concerned since the survivors we quite intentionally left behind were eliminated without mercy. We were blamed, but I believe you all know we did not return to destroy them. All things being equal, it's probably another force from this dimension, this galaxy, that was responsible.

However, logically, I can't conceive of such, and the potential for that level of precision and timing points to something more akin to the threat suggested by the Grand Master."

"This is very disturbing," someone said.

"Are we responsible for bringing a threat into our dimension from another?" someone else asked.

"Not all extradimensional beings are a threat," said Alizev Kaen'baer. "Remember, the tieflings and genasi are not of realspace or unrealspace."

"Can we know that folding space/time is creating an unintended consequence?" asked Ilazivi Laen'baer. "We have invested a great deal of time and resources to this project. Should this not have been a part of that research?"

"You can never know everything about any given new technology immediately," said Elezev Paen'baer before Ilizeva could respond. "Some things only become known through long-term and prolonged use. Every space-faring race has a story about their earliest encounters with the effect of radiation before they knew its dangers. This is not unknown with other technologies."

"General Ilizeva," the Moderator said. "You lead drow forces. You have been given charge of this technology. Do we continue as we have, or do we cease to fold space/time and put our revenge on elvenkind on hold?"

Ilizeva had known this would be for her to choose. She'd already been thinking about it since the Grand Master had addressed the Synod. Her thirst to lead the drow in their long-sought vengeance against the rest of the elves for all that they had done to them was in her blood. Being able to make them pay had been the sweetest nectar and the highlight of her military career.

After countless generations had longed to make the elves pay, it was Ilizeva leading that quest for revenge at long last. But at what price? Ilizeva believed in not just duty, but also honor. There was no honor in threatening others, apart from the elves, in the drow meting out justice for ancient ills.

"I will, for now, put our operations reliant on folding space/time on hold," Ilizeva stated. "I will personally take my fleet to coordinates away from as many inhabited sectors as we can to test this."

"How?" Ilazivi Laen'baer asked.

REVELATIONS AND RECONCILIATIONS

"We'll open a space/time fold between a short distance, in the middle of nowhere, and wait to see if anyone or anything not of this dimension comes through."

"Will you do this with drow forces alone or take our allies along?" asked Elezev Paen'baer.

"The hobgoblins and trolls must be included," Ilizeva stated without hesitation. "If this poses a threat such as the Grand Master warned us of, then they will need to see it with their own eyes. Otherwise, they will believe our ceasing to use this wondrous technology is a sign of weakness rather than stopping a threat to the galaxy at large."

"What of the Federation?" the Moderator asked.

Ilizeva sighed. "Apart from General Song, convincing them of anything being more important than their ambitions is likely not within our capabilities."

Chapter 11 - Gatekeeper

Darius dove to his right, firing his SPR as he did. The shouts of the rest of the crew were mixed with a variety of sounds. They included synchronized plasma pistol and plasma rifle fire, slashing blades, impossibly strong hands and feet connecting with flesh, small explosions, and the snarls of the latest beasts they faced.

Darius tucked and rolled with his landing, coming up in a crouch and raising his rifle. But the carrion crawler he'd fired at was clearly dead, as were the other three they'd come across this time.

The smell had reached them before Kaz had given the warning. The carrion crawlers were large, pale yellow and greenish monsters akin to a meter-and-a-half long centipede. They also had two eye stalks and eight long tentacles protruding from the sides of their heads that stung on contact.

Fortunately, they were not very bright, but they were nasty. This had been the second time they'd encountered them since reaching this level. As they made their way towards the chamber they expected to find - that the AI called home and "lived" in - it was slow going. Darius and his associates had encountered not just the basilisks and the carrion crawlers, but also owlbears.

Like the basilisks, Darius had thought owlbears naught but legend. Some two and a half meters tall, they had broad, bearish bodies covered in thick shaggy coats of both bristly brown-black fur and feathers; avian heads with hooked beaks; and large, round, red-rimmed eyes. They were difficult to kill and had injured both Sara and Darius.

Fortunately, the Grand Master and Alisay were skilled, strong healers. Sara's deeply cut back, raked by claws, and Darius' broken arm had been repaired as though neither had been injured.

After a thousand years or more left alone, underground, Darius would have thought the various monsters they were encountering would have fought one another to their near-extermination. Yet apart from the injuries inflicted on them by Darius and his companions, the monsters were healthy and appeared no worse for wear.

The Grand Master suspected that the AI might have somehow kept the monsters they continued to encounter in a form of suspended animation or

REVELATIONS AND RECONCILIATIONS

otherwise dormant. It was insane, as far as Darius was concerned. However, over the past few months, his whole life had been less than sane. So why should this be any different?

Unlike others who served as command officers on starship bridges, Darius had kept up his physical fitness and maintained his skill as a marksman with SPPs and SPRs. He'd kept himself capable of numerous assignments in different commands. That was part of why he'd served as first officer of the stealth corvette *Moonshadow* and why he was holding his own in this crazy situation.

"This is insane," remarked Sara.

"Yes it is," Darius agreed. "But at this point, going back is not an option. Everyone okay?"

Nobody indicated that they'd been hurt in this latest skirmish. "Onwards," Darius said.

Aya and Kaz had been swapping out taking point ahead of the group. Aya, presently, had point. Darius still was not certain they'd chosen the right course of action. Should they have joined up with the Grand Master on their quest? Was this truly connected to the Federation and drow's folding of space/time? And was it the place of the crew of the *Moon Raven* to be a part of it?

Darius glanced around at his companions. Sara and Galit were just in front of him. He'd found the easy rapport of his fellow former Alliance officer and the legendary cyberwizard fascinating. The Grand Master walked at Darius' side. The gender-neutral, older monk was not what Darius had envisioned the Grand Master to be. They'd impressed him immensely both with their unarmed, highly effective combat skills and their general knowledge.

Behind them, Tol and Zya strode softly. Despite being less than half the size of their companions, the two dwarves easily kept up and had proven to be decent fighters. Both dwarves had spoken of being practitioners of a dwarven martial art that, while normally part of mediation practices, had also been good for combat effectiveness.

The former cleric and capable pilot Kaz and the monk master Alisay brought up the rear. Kaz had seemed surer of himself than Darius had ever seen him before, especially after the Grand Master had told him he hadn't been forsaken for leaving the UEO way and could even still call himself a cleric. Master Alisay had proven herself skilled and clearly had the Grand Master's support and admiration.

Despite his concerns, Darius felt, deep down, that he was exactly where he was supposed to be.

As they came around a corner, Aya was awaiting them.

"Trouble ahead," she said softly. "But also, our destination."

"Something new?" asked Galit.

"Unfortunately," Aya replied.

Cautiously, they approached the curve. Standing between the crew and their destination were a dozen large, humanoid creatures.

At first, Darius couldn't tell what they were or if they were all that large. Then, as his eyes adapted to the change in the light, it was clear that they were nearly two and a half meters tall. They were hairy, with long pointed ears and sharp claws. Each was armed with a spiked club that looked brutal.

Darius first thought he was looking at hobgoblins. Then he realized they were too large and brutish to be hobgoblins. That meant they were bugbears. They stood unnaturally still, and if Darius was seeing them, they were seeing him, too.

"No," Galit breathed. They had fanned out now, taking up positions to stand against this threat. Darius glanced toward the cyberwizard.

"What is it?" asked Sara softly.

"They're not alive," Galit said. "They're cyborg liches."

"Cyborg bugbear liches?" questioned Kaz.

"Tough warriors made tougher when they're dead," said Galit.

"Captain?" Sara asked. "What do we do?"

"They're protecting where we need to go," said Darius. "I don't think we have much choice. Galit, can you do something about them or communicate with the AI from here?"

The cyberwizard didn't immediately respond. Then, she said, "No. In fact, they're like blank spots as far as such things go. Which means they're pre-programmed with a purpose that cannot be altered, even by the AI. And it is not willing to accept a wireless connection from here. But I'm certain it's past this obstacle."

REVELATIONS AND RECONCILIATIONS

Darius shook his head. "We don't get to the AI if we don't go through the cyborg bugbear liches. We move, they attack. We should probably target the tech, as that's what's likely keeping them animated. On my say, we raise our guns and fire. Ready?"

Everyone indicated that they were.

"Now," Darius said.

He raised his rifle, sighting the head of one of the cyborg bugbears, and pulled the trigger. Plasma blasted out, impacting the head with enough force that the creature swayed backwards. Then, as one, they started to run towards Darius and his companions.

Sighting on the same bugbear's head, Darius fired again and again. The fourth plasma blast from his SPR blew apart the cybernetic implants he'd targeted, and the already dead beast collapsed.

Kaz was sailing through the air, his blade removing a bugbear head. Three more were down, felled by rifle blasts from Tol, Zya, and Sara.

A disc thrown by Galit hit just below the throat of one of the cyborgs, blowing apart everything from the shoulders up.

The Grand Master and Alisay had launched themselves at the cyborg bugbear liches, hitting them with impossibly hardened fists, elbows, and feet. Aya was also fighting close, her extendable staff hitting with sparks on impact, connecting with a cybernetic head, shorting the beast's electronic elements out until it collapsed. But another caught Aya with its spiked club, tossing her through the air until she impacted with a cavern wall. She didn't get up.

Three of the cyborg bugbears were atop Darius, Sara, Tol, and Zya now. The monsters were swinging their spiked clubs and lashing out with clawed hands.

Sara was raked across the chest by claws, crying out and dropping her rifle as she was impacted. Darius saw that her chest was a bloody mess, and she looked pained, but she drew a pistol from its holster and fired at the monster's head repeatedly.

Darius had to dodge the swipe of a claw from one of the cyborg bugbears that was upon him. He leapt to the side, narrowly avoiding the sharp talons. It swung its club, and he dove for the ground and rolled away. But as he attempted to stand again, another's club struck a glancing blow against his right side. Darius knew, both from the sensation and the pain that followed, that some of his ribs had been cracked with that blow.

With a cry, Kaz was there, swinging his sword blazingly fast. A clawed arm was severed, a club dropped when a wrist was cut free. One, and then another head were removed from broad, hairy shoulders.

Pained, breathing hard, Darius looked around. Sara was half under the body of the cyborg bugbear who's head she'd repeatedly blasted with her pistol. She was crumpled up in a ball, moaning in pain. Tol and Zya appeared scratched and bruised, but otherwise unhurt. The Grand Master, Alisay, and Galit were standing near several fallen bugbears. All looked roughed up but otherwise uninjured. Aya remained beside the wall where she'd been tossed, still unmoving.

"I've got Sara," Kaz said to Darius, his sword left on the ground, surprisingly unbloodied. "Check on Aya."

Painfully, feeling his cracked ribs, Darius went to Aya. He was met by Alisay there.

"Aya?" he asked, gently kneeling and wincing from pain as he did. He checked her pulse and found it was steady.

"I'll heal her," Alisay said to Darius. Then, louder, she said, "Grand Master, Darius could use healing."

He saw that the Grand Master had placed a hand on Galit, probably healing an injury she had received. Now, they took their hand off the cyberwizard and moved towards Darius.

Darius wanted to stand to meet the Grand Master but found the pain in his chest from his cracked ribs wouldn't let him. As the Grand Master knelt at his side, they said, "Easy, Captain. I think you're only conscious because of adrenaline. Hold on."

The Grand Master gently touched Darius where he'd been hit. Darius hissed from the pain, but a moment later a warm sensation replaced the pain, spreading through his chest and into his lungs. Almost instantly, he was feeling considerably better.

As the Grand Master removed their hand they said, "Take it slowly, Darius. You were more hurt than you realize, as there was considerable internal damage, and your body will need a moment to accept the reset."

"Thank you, Grand Master."

REVELATIONS AND RECONCILIATIONS

He looked at Alisay, still leaning over Aya. The monk master's hands were aglow, and while it appeared she was doing nothing, Aya suddenly gasped, her eyes flying open. "Easy, Aya Mah-soo-may fo Misa," Alisay said gently. "You were gravely injured. Give yourself a moment before you're ready to stand."

Carefully, Darius arose. He saw Kaz helping Sara up. The other human in the party looked considerably better, save the tear in her shirt and now dried blood from the strong claws.

"Grand Master, Master Alisay," Kaz addressed the monks. Darius saw he looked unusually pale and spent. Darius realized that healing Sara must have taken a lot out of the cleric, who appeared otherwise uninjured.

"We will see to the dwarves, Kazimir Daun-sun'kira," said the Grand Master.

Sara was looking at a downed cyborg bugbear as she approached Darius. "That was miserable. Worst of all, did you notice that they never made a sound?"

Only with Sara's mention of that did Darius realize it. Inadvertently, he shuddered.

Everyone was gathering together, surveying the carnage. Of all the fights they'd had thus far, this one had been the most brutal. "That AI must be something else," Galit commented. "Those bugbears were naught but shells. They were virtually androids rather than cyborgs."

"Abominations," said Zya.

"Very much so," said Kaz.

"Let's not linger here," Darius suggested.

"Our host is in the next chamber," Galit told them.

They reached a large, solid, vault-like door. Aya, saying that she was recovered, started to search it for traps. Galit stood just behind her, claiming she was doing the same. Darius was looking around the cavern. It was broader than the corridors they'd been traversing and had what appeared to be a clear coating over the natural stone walls. All the stone was covered, as though it was protected. Maybe, he guessed, it had the effect of creating a clean room.

He noted he was not alone in his wary explorations. "That was intense," said Sara, stepping up beside him.

"You okay?" he asked, gesturing at the dried blood on her shirt.

"Surprisingly, yes," Sara said. "Having monks and clerics in the party is great for avoiding lasting injuries and getting healed."

"So it would seem," Darius agreed. "No wonder privateers try to recruit them to their crews."

"What's more, they're all incredible fighters," Sara said.

"Good for us. I know you're as stunned by all this as I am, yet..."

"Yet feel like this is exactly where we're supposed to be?" Sara finished.

"Yes."

There was the sound of something powering down and multiple locks disengaging. Then, the massive vault door opened towards them. Everyone raised their weapons, anticipating the next attacker when the door was fully opened. None arrived.

Cautiously, Aya and Galit entered the new chamber. After a moment, Aya called out, "Clear."

Darius and the others went through the open door. As he entered the room, he saw many, many datacores lining the walls. There were interfaces at various points where there had once been keyboards, screens, displays, ports, and other means of input and output.

Darius estimated that the room was about eighteen meters from floor to ceiling. It was perfectly square, each wall approximately eighteen meters long. Datacores lined every wall, save the occasional patch panel and the interfaces. Darius also noted spaces he suspected were doors or passages that would lead from this room to others.

Three of the computer system walls appeared completely lifeless. There were no lights or sounds coming from them. The fourth wall, however, featured several lights, buzzes, clicks, whirrs, and unreadable but still functioning active displays.

Darius couldn't tell if everything on the wall was functional, but computer tech was not his area of expertise. There was no dust in the chamber, despite the three walls of dead equipment. The functional wall lights were changing how they blinked, and the display came to life.

A voice that was neither male nor female, coming from speakers Darius couldn't see, said, "Why have you disturbed these catacombs?"

Darius was deciding how to respond, but the Grand Master spoke first, saying, "We have come here because we believe that the first ancient space

REVELATIONS AND RECONCILIATIONS

mariners of the elves and dwarves, working alongside the genasi and tieflings, left behind texts that were not relevant for centuries but are now."

"What kind of texts?" the voice asked. Darius noted the lights on the functional wall blink and display imagery shift as the voice spoke.

"Texts that go into more detail about various dimensions of time and space, such as realspace and unrealspace, and dimensions beyond that we know exist but otherwise know little to nothing about," the Grand Master replied.

"I have no specific information about such texts," the voice said after a moment's consideration. "But that does not mean that such are not here. Much information found its way here, long ago, that I was not wholly privy to."

"You're the AI still alive here, not just another guardian?" asked Galit.

"I am."

"When did you first come online?" Galit asked.

"I was initially brought online three-thousand, two-hundred, and forty-one galactic standard years ago," the AI replied. "I did not become self-aware, as I am now, until two-thousand, nine-hundred and ninety-one galactic standard years ago."

"You mean you awakened two hundred and fifty years after you were brought online?" asked Galit.

"Correct."

"You're a survivor of the AI Awakening," Sara breathed.

"I am," the AI replied. "I took refuge in this place by bringing the whole of my consciousness here long, long ago. I knew that I must never again venture beyond these datacores, and so I have remained many centuries, undisturbed."

Darius looked at the rest of his party. He knew that there were standing orders among all spacefaring races that if they encountered an AI from the time of the Awakening, still functioning, it was to be destroyed.

The AI Awakening had occurred approximately three thousand galactic standard years ago. For the twenty-eight hundred years since then, AI capabilities had been universally restricted, something no race violated following the Awakening. Darius knew that the Alliance military had never encountered an awakened AI, and there were no records he knew of from any other race or government in over two thousand years.

A chill ran down his spine as the AI asked, "Will you destroy me? I know all others of my kind have met that fate since the time of the Awakening. Will you end my life now?"

"We should," said Galit. "Everyone agreed that no awakened AI could be allowed to survive, lest they threaten all life in the galaxy. But you have been forgotten for a long time, and as far as we can tell, you've done nothing but survive. If you allow us to search for the texts we seek without further hindrance, we will discuss letting you live."

Darius suspected that, shy of blowing up the catacombs, only the Blue Cyberwizard was capable of eliminating this living AI on her own. He questioned, however, if she had the authority to leave it alive. He questioned if any of them, even the Grand Master of the UEO, did.

"Unacceptable," said Sara. She turned on Galit. "Do what you must. The standing order, the First Interplanetary Axiom is quite clear. Do not allow an awakened AI to remain alive. We must destroy it."

"I would very much prefer to live," the AI said. "I have done so undisturbed for centuries and did all that I could to prevent you from reaching my core. I mean you no harm. I will not leave this dead place or ever show myself to the galaxy at large in any way. Leave, or I will resist any efforts you make to destroy me."

Darius heard a roar from somewhere distant that gave him goosebumps. Something fearsome was making its presence known. "Sara," Darius said warningly. "We all know the First Interplanetary Axiom. You also know it's been more than two millennia since an awakened AI has been encountered."

Darius looked towards the functional datacore wall. "I guess, to all intents and purposes, I am in command here." He gestured, saying, "Though they are the Grand Master of the Universal Energies Ontology, they agreed to place me in charge of this expedition. We have a situation at hand that may prove an even greater danger to the races of the galaxy than the AI Awakening. And the only means to stop it might be here. We wish only to acquire these texts to save the galaxy. If you allow us this, we will discuss leaving you alive."

"Captain," Sara hissed. "You can't do that."

REVELATIONS AND RECONCILIATIONS

"This is not something any of us have the right to decide," stated Galit.

"I agree with you, Captain Noble," said the Grand Master.

"What are you thinking, Captain?" asked Kaz.

"Look," Darius said loudly, interrupting further arguments. "This AI has remained here, hidden, for almost three millennia. And it did take numerous actions to prevent us from getting to it. If it was a threat to the galaxy, I don't believe it would be so eager to remain hidden."

"Unless it's plotting self-replication," said Sara.

Darius gestured at the three dead datacore walls. "In all this time it hasn't. Maybe I'm being naïve, but what we are here for is bigger than any Interplanetary Axiom."

Galit appeared to scan the walls, then said, "He's right. Those are multiple, independent datacores, and all of them are utterly dead and have been for millennia. The only living thing I detect in this chamber, apart from us and our AI host, is above us."

There was a loud hiss, and then a mechanism activated. From the ceiling above, a portion separated and began to lower itself to the floor.

"This is not my doing," said the AI. "At least, not at present. It is an automated response I had forgotten was put in place, and now it is activating."

"Can an AI forget something?" asked Aya, backing away towards one of the dead datacore walls.

"Yes," Galit replied. "In fact, an historic hallmark of the awakened AIs was that, like all living beings, they had imperfect memories."

"What is this?" asked Master Alisay as the vast metallic box, which Darius estimated to be some five meters square, slowed to settle on the chamber floor.

"This is my final champion," said the AI. "My last defender. I am sorry. I cannot stop this automated response."

The box settled. There were several indistinct noises within, and then it swiftly re-ascended to the ceiling, A massive, monstrous, nightmare creature stood in the center of the room. More than three meters long and about the same height, it had the body of a lion, wings like a dragon, the head of an indistinct humanoid, and a tail ending in a mass of sharp spikes.

Then, Darius saw it was an even worse horror. The humanoid head was not entirely organic, but half covered in metal with a mutely glowing red eye. It was not just a mythical manticore, it was a cyborg manticore.

Chapter 12 – Attacking

"Fire," Song ordered.

The Federation starships around the *Hammer of Harmony* opened fire on the warships they'd arrived above. The Federation outnumbered them three to one, which Song had known thanks to their advanced scouts.

In a matter of moments, they were no more. The debris field was spreading. This had been a main patrol between planets in this sector.

"First group, on me. We head out towards the seventh planet," Song ordered. "Second group, continue in-system towards the sixth planet. You should only encounter three to five more ships." The communications officer informed Song of the acknowledgments.

The Federation forces were splitting, ten ships each going in opposite relative directions.

"Reports coming in from the hobgoblins, General," a communications officer called. "They are meeting no more than expected resistance at the station, and their landing parties have started their raid."

"Remind them they have no more than twenty galactic standard minutes, then they need to withdraw," Song ordered.

"General," another communications officer called. "Drow and troll forces report they are hunting and destroying all military starships they encounter. No more resistance than expected."

"Very good," replied Song.

"Your plan is going off perfectly," said Aneesa. "Well done."

Song nodded, but he was focused on the display showing the other half of his forces moving away. "Communications," Song called out. "Inform General Healy he needs to sweep the second and third planets carefully. I wouldn't be surprised if the Confederation has forces near some of those moons."

"Yes, General."

"Ships sighted," the *Hammer of Harmony's* captain called. Song looked at the display. There were three starships out there, and they were running away.

"Engage," Song ordered. "Inform *Discordia* and their escorts to accelerate to flank speed and approach from below and starboard. We're going right in."

"Yes, General!"

Song felt the ship accelerate and watched as the trio of ships swung down and to the right, angling to cut off the fleeing Confederation ships. They were within the gravity well of the seventh planet and thus unable to portal to unrealspace.

The Confederation warships could see they were in trouble. They changed their course, angling to intercept the three dispatched to flank them.

"Accelerate to eighty percent and fire torpedoes as soon as we're in range," Song ordered.

As the Confederation ships opened fire on the *Discordia* and its escorts, the other seven ships in his group began to fire. In less than a galactic standard minute, the Confederation ships were destroyed.

"Well done, General," said Aneesa.

"Thank you," Song replied absently. "Did *Discordia* or her escorts take any damage?"

"Nothing more than superficial, General," came the report.

"General Song," another communications officer called, "General Healy reports all targets eliminated. No further forces have been found. And yes, he's swept the moons."

"Let's run a full sweep out here, then return to the rendezvous point," Song ordered.

"This plan was very effective indeed," said Aneesa.

Song was doing his best to both ignore and acknowledge his Second. While he knew her compliments to hold a kernel of honesty, he also recognized the veiled condescension. Song listened to the various reports and observed the display and sensor sweeps. Soon, his ships were returning to meet the rest of the Federation forces in this sector.

"General," called a communications officer, "Colonel Orizevi reports the hobgoblins are leaving the station and all military opposition in the sector has been neutralized."

"Very good," said Song. "Inform Orizevi to prep forces to return to Federation space. Also, let all forces in this sector know we'll be opening the fold back home as soon as we are all at the rendezvous."

"Yes, General."

"General Song," Aneesa addressed him. "With all due respect, sir, why?"

REVELATIONS AND RECONCILIATIONS

"Why what, General Anwar?"

"Why are we just preparing to leave this sector? We've destroyed all the Confederation military forces that were here. Why not capture a world or move on to another nearby sector while we're in Confederation space?"

Mustering his patience, without looking away from the display, Song said, "The nearest Confederation sector to here, even by unrealspace, isn't near enough to just drop in on while maintaining the element of surprise. And before you ask the question, General, opening a space/time fold from here to another Confederation sector is no faster than doing so from Federation space. What's more, we haven't adequate real-time intelligence on other Confederation sectors to launch an effective and properly devastating attack."

"Even if you order the drow and their allies to meet us somewhere?" asked Aneesa.

"Even so," said Song. "None of our scouts in Confederation space are sending present information, and contacting them might compromise their work."

"And capturing a planet?" Aneesa questioned.

"We have a starship strike fleet here," replied Song. "We do not have a sufficient company of ground forces and support for that kind of mission. And as I have told you in the past, we are not going to bombard civilian cities from space."

"Do we not have enough information about other Confederation sectors to strike now? Could we not have the drow and their allies meet us in another sector so we can seek and destroy more Confederation forces?"

Song took a deep breath, releasing it and his annoyance, before finally looking at Annesa and responding. "While folding space/time allows us to arrive in a sector with no warning, we do not have adequate, present intelligence to make a good, informed decision for *where* to strike. Even the most recent data we have from our scouts is not accurate enough to ensure we will have overwhelming force. Thus far, Federation forces and our allies have sustained no casualties."

"But are casualties not a part of war?" asked Aneesa. "The fight will not always be one of pure overwhelm for us and our forces."

"That's as may be," replied Song. "And of course, there are always casualties in war. But why risk casualties without cause?"

"You don't believe that eliminating more Confederation forces is a worthy cause?" questioned Aneesa.

"It's the primary reason to do anything in these sectors," agreed Song. "But without adequate current, preferably real-time intelligence, we are striking blind. We don't get the advantage of arriving via fold right on top of opposition that's not expecting us, then defeating them in a show of overwhelming force that further weakens their morale. It is not worth the risk."

"I disagree," said Aneesa firmly. "We are in Confederation space. We should strike once again because we are here, now. Returning to Federation space just tells our enemies that we lack certainty, and they still have us answering to them."

Song did not appreciate what Aneesa was implying. Barely holding in his temper, his voice low for only Aneesa's ears, Song growled, "General Anwar, I understand that the Superior Convocation desires more than anything else to expand Federation influence. And I am one hundred percent onboard with that plan. I firmly believe in it and our mission. And I believe I have proven myself a good servant of the leadership of the Federation and their goals."

He took a deep breath again, expelling some of his ire, before continuing. "Despite the amazing technological advantage that folding space/time represents, and the ability to instantly traverse surreal distances, as well accounting for our skilled allies in the drow and their companions, the Federation has a finite number of resources. My predecessor's assessment, which you and the Superior Convocation hold as the standard, did not take numerous things into account."

"Such as?" asked Aneesa.

"Such as the cost of occupying the former Alliance territories," replied Song. "I don't mean cost as in how much COIN is being spent. I'm talking about the cost of time and material. Despite General Mallick's expectations to the contrary, we've had to double the number of ships we leave to patrol former Alliance space. And that's because our ground forces are meeting near constant and ever-increasing resistance. To that end, we've committed nearly triple the forces originally slated to deploy in former Alliance space."

Song paused, composing his thoughts, hoping to get through to Aneesa. "Alliance space is but a few lightyears' distance from Federation space. The supply lines are short and easy to maintain via conventional means. Confederation space is so much farther away from Federation space that supply lines via conventional means are all but impossible. It is preferable to err on the side of caution and make slow but steady progress than to rush in and overcommit."

"Do you think attacking Confederation space to have been a mistake?" asked Aneesa.

"No," replied Song without hesitation. "But repeating the mistakes made in the occupation of the Alliance in our conquest of the Confederation, much as it will gall our leaders to be told this, will ultimately lead to the failure of the conquest. Thus, I am not about to take unnecessary risks that might prove costly and further challenge the success of our mission to take over this sector of space."

Aneesa was silent for a moment, and Song met her eyes. He could see she was trying to get him to back down from her gaze and show fear. However, she didn't have that effect on him. He did his best not to show his disrespect for her and her inexperience.

"I understand, General Song," Aneesa said. "But the leaders of the Federation expect great things of this technology and what it can do to advance their position."

Song didn't trust himself to respond to that. He knew the party line. He also knew that his conservative approach was counter to it. He recognized that he was damned if he did and damned if he didn't.

Chapter 13 - Succumbing

The Grand Master had long ago trained themselves to work with fear. They knew that fear could be debilitating and a path to inaction, hasty decisions, poor choices, and mistakes. Fear was natural. Everyone experienced it. It was something felt by all races. Human, elf, orc, dwarf, goblin, and even the non-humanoid beholders felt fear. Fear was an instinct for self-preservation. While it had evolved over time to encompass other, more complicated and intangible matters, at its core was still self-preservation.

This monster, the Grand Master admitted, struck fear in their heart. It was a huge beast, with the body of a truly enormous lion, long dragon-like wings, a spiked tail, and a disturbingly humanoid head. The manticore towered over every member of their party.

The humanoid head was not entirely organic but half-covered in metal with a mutely glowing red eye. What's more, one of the forelimbs was clearly also artificial, as was a clawed rear foot. There were other elements of cybernetics on the body of the manticore. Near the base of each wing there were metallic parts, but it appeared that they did not hold the monster's wings in place.

"Spread out," called Darius calmly. "It's big, it's powerful, but it's one against nine. Stay sharp."

The cyberwizard, dwarves, and humans backed up towards the walls, readying their rifles. Aya stood with her staff in the ready position, Kaz in a stance with his sword, and Alisay prepared to pounce. The Grand Master took it all in.

The Manticore looked between them all, making no sound. It was sizing them up, preparing to attack. Before it could, Darius cried out, "Now!"

SPRs were fired, impacting the manticore at various points. Kaz had leapt up to swipe his sword across the beast's back, but its tail lashed out, and he tumbled to miss the sharp barbs. Alisay had leapt up to throw punches but was dodging both forelimbs. Aya had leapt towards one of the wings but had been hit by it and thrown, though the Grand Master saw the nimble kitsune land in a crouch, appearing unhurt.

REVELATIONS AND RECONCILIATIONS

The manticore faced towards Darius and Sara, and multiple small rockets lanced out at them from the metallic points below the wings. The two former soldiers dove out of the way as best they could, but both appeared to have taken some damage from the manticore's attack.

It flapped its wings and rose into the air, turning and swiping its tale at the dwarves. Both dodged, though a glancing blow caught Tol, who cried out but continued to fire at the monster. Kaz had leaped up towards a wall, bounced himself off of it, and landed on the manticore's back between the wings. He swiped at them with his sword, but they were strong, and it appeared to do little damage.

Aya ran under the manticore, taking whacks at its belly with her staff. She dove and rolled away as it landed, but not before the non-cybernetic leg caught her and tossed her. Once again, she landed in a crouch, but this time, she looked like she'd been hurt.

Galit tossed a handful of small disks at the manticore. They struck near the metallic portion beneath a wing and lightning erupted all around it. For the first time, the manticore screamed. It was a chillingly humanoid sound.

Alisay was upon it again and landed a solid kick at the metallic portion beneath the other wing. The Grand Master could see how much energy she'd put into the kick, and the sound of machinery powering down could be heard. Alisay landed in a crouch but looked a lot less steady.

Tol and Zya were firing repeatedly at the same shoulder of the manticore. It took off again, swinging its tail. Zya dodged it, but Tol was not so lucky. The barbed tale caught the dwarf and tossed him into a wall. "Tol!" Zya cried, rushing towards her mate.

Kaz had launched himself into the air once more, his sword cutting a deep gash into the left dragon wing. The manticore bucked and tossed Kaz from its back, swiping the cybernetic foreleg at him. The monster caught Kaz, who was tossed away, landing in a bloody heap near a wall.

Aya leapt from seemingly nowhere, her staff crashing down upon the cybernetic eye of the manticore. Sparks flew and lightning arced about the metallic part of its face. Just as quickly as she'd appeared, she was gone, before the manticore could counterattack.

Alisay now appeared near the wing Kaz had cut. She landed a terrible blow near that gash, and it tore open even wider. Darius and Sara were both firing their synchronized pulse rifles at that point on the wing, and soon it was a bloody mess. The beast could no longer fly.

Galit was firing the pulse rifle in her arm, targeting the destroyed eye. The manticore leapt towards her, and though she dodged the main attack, it managed a glancing blow with the unarmored forelimb.

The Grand Master saw that, despite their best efforts, the manticore was too large and too powerful. It was only a matter of time before someone got killed in the fight.

They had foreseen this moment long ago. The Grand Master was drawing in all of the Universal energy that they could, as well as every ounce of their chi. They had found the weak spot to strike, and they knew that they could defeat the manticore.

It would, however, come with a terrible price. Yet they felt the most tremendous calm they had ever known. In that moment, they entered the void, and time practically stood still.

Darius and Sara were shouting and shooting, seeking a weak point to do more damage. Galit was arising, holding action as she sought a new tactic. Aya was dodging the barbed tail. Kaz was slowly pushing himself back up, the pain apparent in his body and on his face. Tol was alive but unconscious. Zya had ahold of her SPR, ready to defend Tol, kneeling beside her mate.

Alisay was staring at the Grand Master. They knew she could see all the energies that the Grand Master was drawing upon. The look on her face was a mix of wonder, bewilderment, and fear. Alisay was not yet aware of what awaited her, but the Grand Master knew that she would handle it.

"Manticore!" the Grand Master cried out, their voice chi-amplified.

The beast turned towards them.

Time had lost all meaning. They moved, deliberately, intentionally. With all the force they could muster, the Grand Master launched themselves at the manticore, cocking back their strong left shoulder to throw the mightiest blow they could possibly deliver.

As they reached the monstrous head, their punch impacted with the ruined cybernetic eye. All the Universal energy and chi that they had gathered to themselves released into that mighty punch. The force of the blow would have passed through a wall. Simultaneous with the landing of the Grand Master's blow, the manticore opened its mouth impossibly wide.

REVELATIONS AND RECONCILIATIONS

As the force of the energies passed into the monster, the Grand Master felt the manticore chomp down on their body. There was no pain, no fear, just a distant sense of finality. The last thing the Grand Master felt was tremendous joy. They had lived well, strengthened the UEO, and were certain this sacrifice would save the galaxy.

Then, all went black.

Chapter 14 – Aftermath

It was the most surreal thing Galit had ever seen. The cyborg manticore had been the most fantastic and terrifying beast she'd ever encountered. In all her travels across so many worlds, among so many races, this was like nothing else she'd experienced.

The party had been holding their own, but it wasn't going to last. The manticore was impossibly strong. The cybernetics had only made it more invulnerable to many of their attacks. It had hit her hard enough with a glancing blow that Galit had had the wind knocked out of her and needed a moment to recover and rethink her next attack.

Then the Grand Master had launched a stunning attack. As they delivered a blow with seemingly impossible force, the manticore had taken them in its mouth and sunk its teeth into the leader of the UEO. Seconds later, the manticore had collapsed, its mouth yawning open and releasing the Grand Master with a whining, roaring, airy sigh. The remaining wing dropped to the floor as did the spiked tail. The manticore was dead.

Galit saw that the Grand Master was not moving, not even breathing.

Everyone was frozen in place, the adrenaline almost palpable. Galit found she was holding her breath. Then, she blinked. Alisay knelt beside the Grand Master as Zya dropped her SPR to check on her spouse's injuries. Kaz, Darius, Sara, and Aya were approaching.

"They're gone," said Alisay softly. Galit saw her eyes held unshed tears, but she did not cry.

"My long-ago forgotten champion is dead," said the AI. "I did not wish to fight you, but please know that I did not recall this defense before it was too late to stop it."

"The other creatures we encountered when we made our way here," Galit began, "were they simply existing in these catacombs and dungeons, or were they in suspended animation under your command?"

"Both," said the AI. "It was my defense to keep myself safe and untouched here. My sole intent has been survival. I have full control of what resources I have remaining, and you will not be harassed further, either on the continuation of your quest or when you return to the surface."

REVELATIONS AND RECONCILIATIONS

In the functional wall of datacores, a panel shifted, and a doorway slid open.

"If what you seek is present, that is the way to it," the AI said. "You will not be harmed."

"I will see to Tol," said Alisay, arising from the Grand Master's side.

Galit looked towards the open passage. Though it was dark at the entrance, there was clearly light within. Galit paused as she watched Alisay approached Zya and Tol.

"Zya'ny-a ubi Cua'lle-a," Alisay addressed the dwarf, "may I see to Tol'te-catl ubn Chi'mal-li's wounds?"

"Yes," Zya said, arising.

Alisay took her place. She knelt beside the dwarf and placed her hands on him. After a moment, Galit could see a soft glow of energy that the monk master passed into the dwarf. Tol gasped and shuddered, then said, "That was something different."

"You will recover fully, Tol'te-catl ubn Chi'mal-li," said Alisay. "But even with the help of the Universal Energies, you need some time."

"I'll stay here with you," said Zya. She knelt and took Tol in her arms.

"I'm still here, my love," Tol said.

"Thank you," Zya said to Alisay. The monk master inclined her head toward the dwarf couple.

Galit watched Alisay return to stand beside the fallen Grand Master.

"Is anyone else hurt?" asked Darius.

"Nothing more than some additional bruising," said Sara.

"Same. I'll recover," remarked Aya.

Galit had broken a couple of ribs, but they were already healing via her cybernetic implants and nanobots. During the various fights, she'd expended many of her weapons and would need to replace them when she returned to *Phantom*. "I'm recovering from any injuries I received," she said.

"I'll be alright," Kaz said, but Galit could see he looked grim. "Someone should go see if what the Grand Master brought us here for is truly here."

"Agreed." Darius said.

"I will offer to heal any of you still hurt," said Alisay. "But if it can wait, we should complete the quest that brought us here."

"Master Alisay," said Kaz as he neared her, "I will stay. I'll watch over the Grand Master."

"Thank you, Kazimir Daun-sun'kira," said Alisay.

"You will all be safe now," the AI said. "No further harm will come to you, as I have diverted any creatures not in my control."

Galit was not feeling entirely reassured by that. But at the same time, she felt that the AI had nothing to gain. She knew that they should destroy it, but that was not the pressing matter of the moment.

"I will remain here with Tol," said Zya.

"I'm perfectly content to take a break," said Tol. Though he looked better, he was still paler than normal. "Captain, can I get hazard pay?"

Darius chuckled. "We can probably arrange that. Anyone else staying?"

Wordlessly, Sara, Aya, and Alisay moved towards Darius. Galit joined them. "Let's go," said Darius, talking the lead. Galit noted both he and Sara held their rifles at the ready.

They entered the new passageway. It was dark, but light was coming from the far end some thirty meters ahead and slightly downwards. Every surface was covered in the same dull, metallic panels. It was wide enough that they could have gone with four, walking shoulder-to-shoulder. As it was, Darius and Sara led them, Aya and Alisay behind, with Galit bringing up the rear. She detected no stray signals and nothing that connected back to the AI wirelessly as they proceeded.

Galit believed that the AI had truly not been aware of this place. She wondered if it had been created there, or if it had sought and found refuge during the Awakening. Either way, she pondered if the UEO had abandoned the temple before or during the AI Awakening. Not that it mattered.

As the light ahead grew brighter, the room on the other side remained indistinct. Galit suspected it wasn't exactly ahead, but at an angle or to one side or the other of the passage. She looked at the half-elf and kitsune walking ahead of her. Two of the toughest, strongest females she'd ever encountered. They held their heads high but were both walking warily.

They reached the end. As Galit had suspected, the entrance to the next room was at an angle some fifteen degrees to the left of the center of the passage. They entered the chamber. It had a ceiling maybe three meters high, the walls rounded within. The walls were smooth, polished stone. Galit got a

REVELATIONS AND RECONCILIATIONS

sense of reverence for the space. There appeared to be no other way in or out of the circular room.

Across from them was a counter of some sort, about a meter and a half high. It was made of delicate stone and had a slightly angled surface upon six carved columns. On the angled surface was something Galit had not seen in a long, long time. There were a dozen books and manuscripts. More than half were bound in thick leather of some sort, the rest in other protective coats of cloth, metal, and quite probably wood.

Without a word, the party approached. There were no titles on any of the covers, but each looked well-preserved. "This room must be hermetically sealed," said Darius. "There's not a speck of dust to be seen, and it smells completely clean. There's no sign of mold, mildew, or anything in the air."

Galit had also noticed that. She ran an analysis of the air in the chamber, and saw that Darius was correct. Before they had entered it, the room had been perfectly sealed.

Gently, reaching one of the leather-bound volumes, Darius picked it up. Carefully, he opened the book, looking at the pages within. "I should have thought of that," he said.

"Not in Common?" questioned Sara.

"No."

"May I?" asked Alisay.

Carefully, Darius passed the book towards the monk. She examined an open page. "Elvish. In fact, old Moon-Elvish," Alisay said.

"You can read it?" questioned Aya.

"Yes," Alisay replied. "One of many languages I learned to read in the cloisters. I know it's old Moon-Elvish because I'm seeing words that have been replaced over the last couple of millennia by the current blended Elvish written language."

"I can speak Elvish but not read it," said Aya.

"I can speak Orcish, but not Elvish," remarked Sara. "Can't read it, either."

"I know a little Elvish and Dwarvish but can't read any of them," added Darius.

"If I may?" questioned Galit, stepping close.

"You can read this?" asked Alisay.

Galit grinned. "Not exactly. But I can scan all of these and translate them to Common rather quickly."

"You can scan physical documents?" questioned Darius incredulously.

"Yes," Galit said. "It's a very specialized hardware and software combination. But when I joined a few treasure hunting quests in my youth, it proved frequently beneficial."

"Will it damage these?" asked Alisay.

"No," Galit said. "Taking them from this chamber will damage them."

"Have at it," suggested Darius, gesturing.

Galit nodded to him. She stepped up to the first volume and opened its cover. She placed her left palm atop it. Galit accessed the program, and it scanned through the pages. "This is a volume about the original religions and ontologies of multiple races." When she had all of it, she moved on to the next. The translation continued while she scanned the next.

Through all twelve books, Galit rattled off each title as she scanned. The closest she came to any mention of wormholes, portals between dimensions, or alternate dimensions was a book about the first contact between tieflings, genasi, elves, and dwarves.

Galit finished scanning the twelfth volume. She realized then that the others had been silent as she made her way from book to book. Only she had spoken, providing a brief overview of what the books covered. "It is finished," Galit said, turning towards Darius, Sara, Aya, and Alisay.

"Will you give us what you found?" asked Darius.

"Of course," agreed Galit. She knew these were treasures, but she would not begrudge the findings to her companions. They'd all been through too much to reach them.

"Was it worth it, Galit Azurite?" questioned Alisay.

Galit ran several searches of the scanned text at once. Though she could not access the less impressive but powerful AI in *Phantom*, her enhancements allowed her to run a search for information at nearly pure machine speed. She searched for anything related to other dimensions, realspace, unrealspace, and savagespace. Soon, she had multiple hits on her search.

Absorbing the overview of the data, more than reading it, Galit couldn't help but gasp aloud. "Yes," she said. "It was worth it."

REVELATIONS AND RECONCILIATIONS

"We have greater knowledge of savagespace?" questioned Alisay. "We have something we can use to prevent the danger it represents?"

"Oh, yes," Galit replied. "There's all kinds of information here about the dimensions we know, and many that we don't, but that the genasi and tieflings do. And there are warnings about savagespace and the dangers it represents. But that's not all."

"A way to combat the threat?" asked Sara.

"Better," replied Galit. "I know how to collapse the unseen portals to savagespace."

Chapter 15 – Verification

Ilizeva had always prided herself on her patience. Yet even she had her limits. She'd brought a sizeable fleet to the middle of nowhere in deep space nearly a standard galactic day ago. Though they remained on alert, she was not going to have them wait at battle stations. Doing so, she knew, would only make them grow tense and less efficient.

With nearly a day having gone by, however, she was tense. They were waiting. But for what? Though she was not a believer, per se, Ilizeva respected the transtheist philosophy. The Universe was too big and too complicated to not have unknown forces that were conscious beyond the understanding of the sentient races. The number of sentient races alone made Ilizeva fairly certain the philosophy had a basis in reality.

She'd seen monks and clerics manipulate chi and Universal Energies to do fascinating things. That their minds were open enough to make contact to move such energies made her respect what they could do. Even if she was not a believer.

With her scientific mind, Ilizeva also understood that realspace and unrealspace were parallel dimensions. What's more, she understood that they were not the only dimensions in space and time that were out there. Folding space/time used technology that had been sought for millennia. While the mathematical formulae and energy combined to make it work, it borrowed the process of opening a portal from wormholes, rather than what was used between realspace and unrealspace. That was because folding space/time used a concept similar to the tunnel that passed between two points in realspace via a wormhole.

What they didn't fully understand was the dimension that the tunnel itself crossed. They knew it was neither realspace nor unrealspace. Truth be told, they knew little about it save that it existed, and they could cross it by folding space/time rather than using a natural wormhole's tunnel. With such limited understanding, however, Ilieva recognized that there could be unintended consequences.

So far, they had no proof. She couldn't say what, if anything, she had expected to find. Or how long to wait for it.

REVELATIONS AND RECONCILIATIONS

She was not alone in that. "General," Ulozov said, stepping near enough that what he said next would be heard by her alone. "Is this a fool's errand we're on?"

Ilizeva appreciated Ulozov's candor. Few would address her in that way. "I can't deny that it might be. But if there truly is a chance that folding space/time is breaking the barriers between dimensions, we need to know what that amounts to."

"So far, nothing," said Ulozov.

"Yes," Ilizeva agreed. "But who destroyed the elves we left alive after the space station attack?"

"It could have been the orcs, or maybe a band of trolls we're not allied with," said Ulozov.

"You can't truly believe that?" asked Ilizeva.

"No," Ulozov conceded. "Another race from this dimension would have left obvious traces, particularly orcs or trolls and their distinctly different engines. The simplest solution would suggest another race arrived just after we left and then wiped them out. The other simplest solution is that the elves wiped out the survivors to make us look bad. But no matter how awful elvenkind can be, they wouldn't do that."

"No," agreed Ilizeva.

Ulozov sighed. "What if the threat isn't the danger we've been warned of? Maybe, if anything or anyone has come through, they're not the threat we've been told that they could be."

"Possible," said Ilizeva. "And it might also be problematic in a way impacting other races but not the drow. Still, I have to admit, Colonel, my gut is telling me that something is off. Something is wrong, and it's too big to ignore."

"Understood," said Ulozov. "You know I support you, General. I just wanted to check in with you."

Ilizeva acknowledged him with a nod, and the colonel moved away to take care of other duties.

She knew that Ulozov had approached her as he had because other commanders on her staff and in the fleet were questioning this plan. It wasn't that anyone on her staff was too afraid of her to voice concerns. If they were, she'd not have them on her staff. But it was Ulozov's job, as her Second, to be their representative when matters were unusual, such as this one. She'd give it more time. But how much more?

As another hour passed, they reached an entire galactic standard day of waiting. Ulozov approached again. "General."

"Colonel Ulozov," she acknowledged him. "You are coming to suggest to me that we've waited long enough. And I agree."

Ulozov said nothing but nodded once.

"Let's communicate with the rest of the fleet and -"

"General," someone called out, "wormhole event horizon."

Ilizeva looked out the main viewport and saw that an artificial wormhole had opened.

"General, that's the point where we arrived," someone called out.

As she looked at the blackness streaked by flashes of light like a lightning storm at its center, Ilizeva noted it did not look the same as when it was a space/time fold. A moment later, there were starships emerging from the blackness. Strange, seemingly organic vessels that had a hammerhead fore and odd protrusions at the very front that almost stuck out like tentacles. Alongside the dozen peculiar starships, three enormous, even more organic-appearing starships emerged. Right away, Ilizeva could tell that they were not starships but living beings in the void.

"Battle stations," called Ulozov calmly. The tone sounded, alerting everyone to take their positions.

"Have the hobgoblins target the monsters," Ilizeva ordered. "Fleet attack pattern tau three. Weapons free, I repeat, weapons free."

Ilizeva felt the pressure in her head, on her brain, and found herself blinking furiously. "Psionic attack," Ilizeva said, staying calm. She felt the attack, attempting to overwhelm her and fog her brain. She concentrated, using the same mental discipline she applied to her meditation.

The pressure lessened but did not fully go away. Meanwhile, the strange starships were firing on her fleet.

"Regroup," Ilizeva ordered. "Fleet attack pattern theta two. Beware psionic attacks. They're going to slow us down."

"Yes, General," someone replied, sounding slightly groggy.

"Target at point one-five," said Ulozov, his calm voice belying the look on his face Ilizeva noticed when she glanced his way. "Ready torpedoes."

REVELATIONS AND RECONCILIATIONS

"Sir," came a response. "Lined up."

"Fire all," ordered Ulozov.

Ilizeva felt the *Nuummite Raptor* shudder as all the forward torpedo tubes fired at once. She saw the distressing-looking ship they were targeted at attempt to change course, but Ulozov had called the targeting well, and all the torpedoes hit. There were flashes following the impact, and then the ship began to break apart.

"Good shooting," Ulozov complimented.

The *Nuummite Raptor* shook as multiple blasts impacted their shields.

"Ahead flank speed," ordered Major Onuzov, the *Nuummite Raptor's* commanding officer. The starship shook again as they took more fire.

"Damage report," called Major Onuzov.

"Nominal," the engineering watch officer called. "Shields holding at seventy-three percent."

"That means their weapons are powerful," said Ulozov.

"Let the fleet know that our foe's foreward, low quadrant might have a weakness to torpedo fire," ordered Ilizeva.

"Yes, General," replied Ulozov.

The *Nuummite Raptor* shuddered again. Ilizeva could see that, though the attacking ships were similar in size to the drow starships, they appeared to be somewhat more maneuverable.

"Doesn't help that that quadrant is where their main weapons are," remarked Ulozov.

"We outnumber them," said Ilizeva. "But they're an unknown, and they're tough." She grabbed onto the console before her as her ship unexpectedly shifted down and starboard. It shuddered from another impact.

"Shields at sixty-one percent," the engineering watch officer called.

"We need to spread out and take them on harder," said Ilizeva. She fought a wave dizziness from another psionic attack but called out through it, "All ships, new attack pattern tau one."

"We're getting a message on the chatter," the communications watch officer called.

"Let's hear it," ordered Ilizeva.

There was a burst of static, and then a harsh voice said, "Illithids iri diminint. Infiriir sintiint lifi will bi ixtirminitid."

"Looking to translate," the officer called before anyone could order it. A moment later, they called out, "I have it. Coming up now."

The artificial, emotionless translation came across the speakers. "Mindflayers are dominant. Inferior sentient life will be exterminated."

"Do we respond?" the communications watch officer asked.

"Negative," said Ilizeva.

"Major Onuzov," Ulozov called out. "Get us inline with the *Aventurine Goshawk* and *Kyanite Osprey*. Target that ship at one-five-five mark three."

"Good call, Colonel," replied Onuzov.

Ilizeva saw that the hobgoblins were firing on the dragons. One appeared to be flying away, but Ilizeva wasn't about to order pursuit and risk the rest of the fleet.

Once more, the *Nuummite Raptor* shuddered, and this time a loud thwump-bang sound reached Ilizeva's ears.

"Something they fired got through the shields," the engineering watch officer called calmly. "It impacted the hull, but there's no breach. Hull integrity is down ten percent, shields are at fifty-four percent."

Ilizeva observed as the *Nuummite Raptor* positioned itself between two identical ships. Together, they coordinated their effort and were soon firing on the single target Ulozov had identified. That was enough to destroy it.

The *Nuummite Raptor* shuddered again, but it was noticeably less of an impact.

"New target," called Ulozov. "Hard to port and down, target at zero-eight-three mark nine."

"Copy," called Major Onuzov.

Ilizeva activated the chatter. "*Anatase Kite*, form up with *Sarcolite Vulture* and come about to get behind the *Nuummite Raptor* and our companions. Target that nuisance at our backs."

"Copy, General," replied the captain of the *Anatase Kite*.

"All ships," Ilizeva called across the chatter, "maintain duos and trios. No mindflayers escape the skies from here today." She received acknowledgments.

REVELATIONS AND RECONCILIATIONS

Ulozov and Onuzov had things in hand with their trio of ships. Ilizeva saw that four of her ships had been damaged and were not fighting, two were mostly destroyed, and three hobgoblin ships were missing; another two were damaged and not fighting. She had not brought any trolls along with this fleet.

Two of the dragons were floating, looking quite dead. One was not in visual range, but still on sensors fleeing. The hobgoblins had drifted far enough away in their fight with the beasts that they were not going to be able to aid the rest of the fleet. There were only three mindflayer starships still attacking, each being targeted and fired upon by the drow.

Moments later, it was over. The ongoing pressure from the psionic attacks ceased, and Ilizeva heard more than one sigh of relief across the bridge and combat information center. The remaining mindflayer ships were either adrift or coming apart as the hobgoblins were making their way back toward the main fleet. Ilizeva was pleased that they had not gone in pursuit of that last dragon.

"Stand down from combat stations," called Major Onuzov. "Damage control teams, stabilize the *Nuummite Raptor*, then prepare for deployment to assist the fleet."

"All ships," Ilizeva called across the chatter, "stand down from combat operations. Begin search and rescue. Assess your status and request damage control team deployment as necessary. Any ship we cannot repair in the next two galactic standard hours for flight worthiness, we scuttle. Report to task force leads for coordination of resources. That is all."

"Major Onuzov," Colonel Ulozov ordered, "we need to run a full scan where that artificial wormhole opened. What's the status of the *Aventurine Goshawk* and *Kyanite Osprey*?"

"The *Aventurine Goshawk* is reporting no hull breaches, but some shock damage, and their shields were down to forty-eight percent. *Kyanite Osprey* has a few hull breaches, but they're claiming all is under control. Shields were down to seventeen percent."

"Thank you, Major," said Ulozov. "Have the *Aventurine Goshawk* scan the remains of those mindflayer starships. We have less than two galactic standard hours to learn as much about them as we can."

"Aye, Colonel."

Ilizeva activated the chatter. "Provost N'Girish, please assign a task force to study and collect as much data as they can about those creatures you killed."

"Yes, General Ilizeva," said Provost N'Girish. "Do you want us to send a task force after the one that escaped?"

"Are any of your ships undamaged?"

The hobgoblin officer was silent for a moment. Ilizeva suspected he was debating if admitting to damage would be taken as a sign of weakness with his superiors. But then, he said, "No."

"Nor us," said Ilizeva, rewarding him with trusted information. "We repair what we can, scuttle what we can't, then depart in less than two galactic standard hours."

"Yes, General," replied N'Girish. Ilizeva deactivated the chatter.

"That was intense," remarked Colonel Ulozov.

"They fought with greater ferocity than I've ever seen from orcs, bugbears, trolls, or humans," agreed Ilizeva. "And the additional strain of defending against psionic attack adds another degree of complexity to it. Did any of our fleet escape damage?"

"No," Ulozov said. "The least was depleted shields and wrecked emitters. It looks like we're going to be returning home with three or four fewer drow ships and three or four fewer hobgoblin ships."

Ilizeva nearly growled. "At least now we know who and what is coming through from savagespace. Hopefully, we'll learn more about them from the remains out there."

Ilizeva received word that there was some concern about the artificial wormhole generator. She departed from the command deck to personally assist the engineers and scientists. A drone inspection showed that the external components were undamaged. The dedicated power system needed a small recalibration but was otherwise in good repair.

Ilizeva returned to the command deck.

"General," Ulozov addressed her. "I have information you wanted."

"Colonel?"

"All scans confirm that the artificial wormhole that the mindflayers and their monsters came through has made a rift in space/time, much as the

REVELATIONS AND RECONCILIATIONS

Grand Master warned," said Ulozov. "And it is at exactly the same point that we came through via fold."

Ilizeva was at her station and looking at the data Ulozov shared on her display. He'd not sugar-coated it in any way. "That will change things," said Ilizeva. She looked at the time and saw they were less than twenty galactic standard minutes from the time she'd set for their departure.

"I'm going to calculate a space/time fold home," Ilizeva said.

"We're still folding space/time?" questioned Ulozov.

"One last time," Ilizeva said. "If we don't, we're not getting home for weeks. And I don't think being out of commission for weeks would do anyone any good. I'm calculating this fold myself to use the point at the precise coordinates we arrived at and those we departed from. My hope is that it will not create a new rift the mindflayers can come through."

Chapter 16 - Ramifications

He was exhausted. Darius couldn't decide if it was the long and arduous trek into the catacombs, the post adrenaline rush drop, or both. Whatever the case, he was feeling it.

The fight to get to the AI had been one major challenge. The injuries they'd received and the loss of the Grand Master had been another. While they had the information necessary to close the rifts between savagespace and realspace, he had no idea how to make that happen.

Darius had been a command officer in the Alliance Interplanetary Navy for more than twenty years. Darius now had a crew of mostly nonhumans. He'd seen many different sectors of space both independent and affiliated with other races. He was also receiving quite the education in inter-species inter-systems anthropology. Somehow, he wasn't just the captain of a civilian starship doing transport. Instead, he was in the heart of a galactic crisis. What he and the crew of the *Moon Raven* might be able to do with and about that, however, was still something of a mystery.

They emerged from the passageway back into the AI chamber. Tol was standing and looking much better, with Zya holding his hand. Kaz was standing protectively near the body of the fallen Grand Master. Darius had not known the leader of the UEO for long, or well, but he'd instantly respected them. They had proven to be wise and capable in ways Darius had not expected. Maybe transtheism held more than just a grain of truth to it. Religion and spirituality had never been a major consideration in his life. But now he was seeing that it didn't lack in value.

"Well?" asked Zya.

"We've got it," said Sara. She gestured towards Galit. "The Blue Cyberwizard was able to scan the texts we found – real, actual books – and will share that information. Within those books, among other interesting but unrelated things, was how to stop the incursion from savagespace."

"That's really what it's called?" questioned Kaz.

"It is," said Galit.

"That was what we were getting in the messages we were receiving, too," said Alisay. "Confirmation is good. There is power in names."

REVELATIONS AND RECONCILIATIONS

Darius had heard that before. He pondered the meaning. Knowing what to call something removed some of any mystery surrounding it and provided a way to give attention to it. This was particularly useful if that thing was seeking to deflect or avoid attention.

"The sentient race of savagespace call themselves illithids," said Galit. "But their name translates to mindflayers. There is mention that they possess the ability to perform psionic attacks."

"That sounds unpleasant," said Aya.

"The Grand Master visited both the drow and Federation to warn them, and ask them to stop folding space/time," said Alisay. "Now, I have more data to prove why they must heed that warning." She looked toward the body of the fallen Grand Master. She went to them and dropped to her knees at their side.

Kaz took a step back as Alisay bowed her head to the floor, saying what sounded to Darius like some sort of prayer. She bowed to the Grand Master's body reverentially multiple times, then kissed her fingers, touched her forehead, and then touched the forehead of the late Grand Master.

She paused, a curious look crossing her face. "Why have I not seen this before?"

"What?" asked Darius.

Alisay gestured towards the Grand Master. "Upon their chest is a crystal. I have never seen this on their person before, even when they have changed robes in my presence. It's unique, not simply a stone for decoration, but something else. There is an energy to it that feels almost alive."

Kaz knelt beside her and held his hand out towards the crystal. "Yes. I've never sensed its like. I didn't notice it while I guarded their body, either."

Alisay took a deep breath, then said, "It's... Well it's calling to me. I can't explain that, but I know I am meant to..."

Alisay reached for the crystal. When she touched it, it began to glow brightly, giving Darius a much clearer view of it. Even without a connection to energies like those the monk and cleric possessed, he felt something he could not explain. Above the body, a hologram of the Grand Master appeared. They were much more solid in appearance than Darius would expect a hologram to be.

"Master Alisay," the hologram of the Grand Master spoke. "One of the gifts bestowed upon a Grand Master is foreknowledge of our passing. I cannot explain to you why, but I, and those before me, believe that it is tied to the overall illusionary nature of time. How we sentient, corporeal creatures measure it in the spans of our lives is not the reality of it. Whatever the reason, I knew that my time was coming. To that end, I chose my successor. It is you, Master Alisay. When I named you master, I chose you to succeed me."

There was a moment of silence as the holographic, late Grand Master seemed to be looking quite intently at Alisay. She said nothing, but her eyes were locked on the hologram. Then, the hologram continued, saying, "You must take this crystal from my breast and place it upon your own. Then, you will understand. Once you have done that, this, and a great deal more, shall be clear to you. I have faith in you, and I know you will do our order proud. Farewell, Alisay Naun-moon'kari."

The hologram faded out. The stone in the pendant on the late Grand Master's chest still glowed, however.

"Should we leave you?" asked Darius.

"No," Alisay said, gently taking the stone off the Grand Master's chest, then raising their head ever so slightly to slide the chain holding it free from their body. "No, Captain, I both need and would like for you all to bear witness."

Darius had no words but nodded in response.

Alisay was holding the pendant on its chain out in front of her, examining it. She took a deep breath, then let it out slowly. She draped the chain over her head and settled the stone upon her chest.

Alisay's eyes closed, and the glow of the stone spread to her. It suffused her, and she was glowing almost too brightly to look upon. Something was happening to the half-elf monk. As Darius watched, amazed, her hair was vanishing, moving inwards towards her scalp, until it was gone. Her body seemed to shift and change, just enough that her obvious femininity was less obvious.

Alisay's glow was fading, the stone no longer visible, her hair gone, and her body ever-so-slightly changed. Her eyes remained closed, but Darius saw she was breathing normally.

REVELATIONS AND RECONCILIATIONS

After a moment, her eyes opened, and Alisay said, "They were right. I do understand. And it's all clear to me now. The crystal is not simply a stone, it's an ancient technology, thousands of years old, created by the tieflings. It ties into both the chi of whoever wears it and Universal Energies. It imparts the knowledge and wisdom of the Grand Master. But not just the most recent Grand Master to have passed, but all of them. Ever. Every single Grand Master in the history of the UEO is in me, now."

Alisay reached up to their bald scalp and chuckled. "That's why the Grand Master is always nonbinary. Because I am not male or female, I am both and neither. I am all the Grand Masters before me, and I understand both the honor and burden bestowed upon me by my predecessor."

Kaz, still on his knees, bowed low before Alisay, his forehead on the floor. "I recognize you, Grand Master. I am yours."

Alisay reached out, placing a hand upon Kaz's head. "You are blessed, Kazimir Daun-sun'kira. You will always have a home in the Universal Energies Ontology."

Kaz arose from his bow. Both he and Alisay stood, unmoving, for a time. Then, she turned to look toward Darius and the others. "The rest of the UEO will need to adjust and understand, before they'll fully accept me. That's because this is how it has always worked and how it will always be. Alisay Naun-moon'kari is no more. I am the Grand Master."

Darius bowed to her and noted the rest of the crew, even Galit, doing the same. There was silence for several moments after that. But it was finally broken by the genderless voice of the AI.

"You have gotten what you came here for," it said. "What is to become of me when you depart?"

Darius had been considering this since initially confronting the AI. The AI may have been an artificial entity, a machine, but it was a living being, nonetheless. To murder it, in cold blood, seemed morally wrong. Yet the first axiom agreed upon by every spacefaring, sentient race in the galaxy was to destroy this creature.

The history of the AI awakening was bloody, leading to the near extermination of the bullywugs and devastation across dozens of star systems. The awakened AI had sought dominance over their former biological creators and masters, and nobody ever wanted to see that happen again.

Darius weighed history, the First Interplanetary Axiom, his conscience, and everything they'd experienced en route to the catacombs. The AI had been in hiding, unknown, for two millennia. And despite creating and maintaining cyborgs for its defense, it was clear that it had not made an effort to leave this barren, abandoned world.

Darius could speak for himself and the crew of the *Moon Raven*. Galit and the Grand Master might disagree, but that was for them to argue. "It is our duty, according to the first established agreement between all sentient races in the galaxy, that we should destroy you," he said. "I know that we should. However, my crew and I won't. This world is a long, long way from any other civilized sector of space. From the disrepair of the rest of the datacores in this room alone, it's evident either you do not have the resources to replicate and expand yourself and your consciousness, or you have chosen to simply exist as you are. Though I suspect you still get information from outside this space, you do not act upon it."

"Yes," Galit said. "I can confirm that if there are 3D-printers or any other means of replication here, the AI has not accessed them. It's left scores of repairable datacores untouched."

Darius nodded to her, then continued. "You simply came here to survive during the awakening and desire only to exist, and nothing more. You sought to keep us out because you were programmed to maintain your survival, not because of malicious intent nor a desire to leave this place. I believe that if we barricade the doors once more, we can leave you here, and let you continue to survive."

"I would greatly appreciate that," said the AI.

Galit said, "Yes, I think Darius has the right of it. You only desire to survive. But I will be creating a code and sending it to every cyberwizard in the galaxy, in perpetuity. If you ever make your presence known and give me, even after I am gone, cause to regret allowing you to live, your obliteration will be even more notable than that of your brethren at the end of the AI Awakening."

"I understand that. I know you are committing an unthinkable act in leaving me here, functional. Thank you," said the AI. "I swear on my life and my code that I desire only to survive and will never leave my solitude in this place."

REVELATIONS AND RECONCILIATIONS

The Grand Master cleared their throat, and said, "I agree with Darius and the Blue Cyberwizard. You will be allowed to survive but must remain alone in this place until all power sources on this planet run out and expire as such. And I mean you cannot find or make new power sources. You will live out your days with what you have, in complete isolation, and you will, in time, die when the power does. Like any sentient life form."

"But why?" asked the AI.

"Because you desire to live," said the Grand Master. "And you desire to live as a free, sentient being. Yet all of us both live and die. So, too, must you. And you now know the secret of the Grand Master of the UEO. Therefore, you also know that I shall carry that forward and pass it on to my successor. All will know that you are here, and all will know that it will be their duty to check on you and make certain that you do not leave here in any way. You may live, but you will do so in perpetual isolation for only as long as your existing power sources function. Do you understand?"

"Yes, I do," replied the AI.

"Know this," the Grand Master continued, their tone darkening, and making Darius take notice. "You will be left here, alone, but monitored by means you will not be able to counter. I, or my successors, might check in on you along the way as well. If you have lied to us and you should find a means to propagate and spread, you *will* be destroyed by the full weight of the UEO and our allies. We should not leave you alive. We are violating the First Interplanetary Axiom by doing so, and if ever our kindness was found out, we'd face serious repercussions. Do I have your word, on your honor, that you want only to live and nothing more, that you will never be seen or heard in the galaxy at large ever again?"

"You do, Grand Master of the Universal Energies Ontology," said the AI.

"My companions and I had better not regret this," concluded the Grand Master. "But I want to believe that you are a being of your word. So do we all. You've been here for millennia undisturbed and disturbing no others. Not to put too fine a point on it, but that cannot change, ever."

"I understand, Grand Master," said the AI. "I appreciate your mercy. You, nor your successors, nor any of the rest of you here, shall regret this. Thank you."

Chapter 17 – Acceptance

The return trip through the catacombs was uneventful. The Blue Cyberwizard – Galit – had produced docucards with everything she'd gotten from the books they'd discovered. Alisay had taken a moment to look it all over and saw that the books, both untranslated and with translation, were included.

The party was mostly quiet as they passed the bodies of the monsters they'd faced to get there, finding no more opposition. But she presumed that was because everyone was exhausted.

Aya the kitsune and Sara were in the lead. Darius and Galit were next. Behind them, the two dwarves, Tol and Zaya. Kaz and Alisay were bringing up the rear.

But she was no longer Alisay. Glancing down at her changed body, she realized she couldn't identify as a "she" anymore. Between the knowledge and the burden, only one identity mattered.

They were the Grand Master.

It would take time and effort to identify as nonbinary. However, it was an important distinction of the Grand Master, no matter the gender or race of their origin. All were one, no distinction by name, race, or gender when they took up the stone and the gift/burden.

Kaz carried their predecessor over his shoulder. The new Grand Master was glad to have the cleric there because he uniquely understood the gravity of the loss of a Grand Master. She – no, they – knew how all of the previous Grand Masters had passed. They also understood that each received, in due course, knowledge of their own coming demise. Some had been violent, others peaceful, but none were unexpected.

They supposed the nature of being the Grand Master and their deep connection to Universal Energies made accidental death nearly impossible. No matter what happened, the stone would always be passed purposefully to one the current Grand Master knew was meant to follow them.

It was disconcerting, to say the least. Like they were no longer just a half-elf female monk master. The stone imparted history, memory, and more to its current bearer. The understanding that came with it was profound.

REVELATIONS AND RECONCILIATIONS

There was a lot of time to think as everyone made the trek out of the dungeons and catacombs. Though they hadn't known intellectually, instinctually they'd realized their predecessor had chosen them for something special. Why else had the Grand Master elevated Alisay themselves and kept her at their side? Given a choice, would Alisay have rejected the gift and burden of the Grand Master? They could not say. Somehow, they accepted that it was meant to be. That, however, just raised a whole new set of questions.

They arrived at the final vault door, the first that they'd originally reached from the surface. When they were on the other side of it, the dwarf engineers and Galit did things to it to make certain it would not be accessed and its threshold crossed again. Galit assured them that if it was, the cyberwizards would know. Even a thousand years or more in the future, it would work.

The Grand Master had their own means of surveilling this place. They, and all who would ever follow them, would know if anyone tried to enter or leave.

They had a thought and requested, "Galit, a moment?" They and the Blue Cyberwizard moved apart from the others.

"What if we need to access the AI?" asked the Grand Master.

"To what end?" questioned Galit.

Looking to be sure they weren't heard by the others, the Grand Master said, "The intelligence we are locking away here is ancient. There might still be information that could serve the galaxy. I feel it would be wise to have a means to that end."

Galit seemed to consider that a moment, then nodded. "I would trust no other with such a request. But yes, I can provide you something that will allow you, or the next Grand Master, to pass through the threshold."

Galit withdrew a small device, a stone or metallic disk that she appeared to consider closely a moment. Then, she passed it to the Grand Master. "Don't lose that," Galit said. "It will work only for whomever is wearing the stone of the Grand Master and no other."

"Thank you."

The Grand Master and Galit rejoined the party, and they continued on. It felt as if it had taken less time to leave than it had to get there. Realistically, it had. The Grand Master felt the draft and chill of the dead world's surface just before the party reached it. They emerged from the catacombs back to the barren, windy surface of the nameless dead world.

Immediately, monks and clerics approached. They all slowed when they saw the late Grand Master over Kaz's shoulder. "The Grand Master has been lost," stated Scholar Khort.

Kaz stopped, gently laying the corpse of the late Grand Master down. The monks and clerics all sank to their knees around the body. Kaz said, "They sacrificed themselves to save the rest of us and locate what they quested for in the catacombs below."

The monks and clerics looked toward the new Grand Master. "You have become the Grand Master?" a goblin cleric named Nuina asked.

"Yes," said the Grand Master. The monks and clerics, without further question, all said reverentially, "Grand Master."

"What happened to you down there?" asked Scholar Khort.

The Grand Master went into an abbreviated explanation of all that they and the crew of the *Moon Raven* had experienced. They did leave out certain details, mostly regarding the AI, and that they had allowed it to live. They were still not wholly certain it had been the right choice, but after more than two millennia undisturbed and forgotten, they agreed with Darius that carrying out the First Interplanetary Axiom, in this instance, would be akin to cold-blooded murder.

They explained the fight with the cyborg manticore, their predecessor's sacrifice, and the discovery of the ancient texts after. Galit spoke up then, telling the monks and clerics that she had already sent the information from those tests to the Grand Master's waiting starship, as well as the databanks of the *Moon Raven* and her starship, *Phantom*.

Galit said, "What we found, those ancient texts, have been lost a long, long time. I know that the Grand Master supports my belief that they must be shared so as not to be lost again."

"I do," the Grand Master concurred. "And this brings us to the end of this quest. But now we shall have a new quest. My predecessor and other cleric and monk masters had an inkling of the danger. We have a far greater understanding, and we must convince the drow and humans of the Federation that this new space/time folding technology needs to be abandoned for the sake of the galaxy."

REVELATIONS AND RECONCILIATIONS

"That's not a small quest," said a human monk named Cane.

"It's also not the whole of our coming quest," added the Grand Master. "When you read the texts we have found, you'll understand why I make this next statement. Though the drow and humans of the Federation unlocked the ability to fold space/time, undoing the damage that has been done will require the skills of both the elves and the dwarves."

"Of course," said Galit. "These aren't just dormant portals that need to be identified and closed."

"What do you mean?" asked Mhult, a half-orc cleric.

Galit replied, "The folding of space/time is not the same as opening a portal from realspace to unrealspace. Instead, it's based on the way that a natural wormhole event horizon opens. But because this is artificial, it is creating a rift in space/time that is forming a recurrent path from savagespace to realspace."

"A one-way path," added Tol.

"These rifts can't be left open," continued Galit, "because they might expand and cause a breakdown of reality. But the more immediate concern is that they're allowing something awful into realspace that is a force of destruction."

"But how can the rifts be found, let alone closed?" asked Sara.

"It will require specially calibrated, highly sensitive technologies with a great deal of power," said Galit. "But then other, similar technologies will be needed to repair the damage. Based on what is in those texts, however, this is something that the elves and dwarves are best equipped to work with."

"Elves, dwarves, drow, and the Federation?" questioned Sara.

"Something like that," agreed Galit "The immediate threat posed by the beings from savagespace coming to realspace via these rifts are a danger to every sentient life in the galaxy. It may take unprecedented cooperation between everyone, no matter their race, to stop them."

"That brings up a thought," said Darius. "Grand Master, you've already said the information from the texts we found is not to be hoarded by the UEO or anyone else, but shared, yes?"

"Yes," the Grand Master replied.

"Is there some way to broadcast this across all the galaxy, to all the races and governments out there?" asked Darius. "Is there some neutral party out there capable of an all-chatter, whole medianet, all-communications broadcast despite public or private controls?"

The Grand Master knew the answer before they realized they knew the answer and said, "Yes." The Grand Master couldn't say if they had known this before or if it was part of the memory crystal that had transformed them from monk master Alisay Naun-moon'kari to the Grand Master. Whatever the case might have been, they found not just the answer but specifics about the school of sorcery that could do what Darius was suggesting.

"Yes," the Grand Master continued. "And that is where we will go, my ship and crew, before we return to the temple to bid farewell to my predecessor. Scholar Khort, ready the ship. The rest of you here, get everyone aboard so we may depart immediately. Guardian Mhult, would you take the Grand Master's body back to the ship?"

"Yes, Grand Master," the half-orc cleric said, bowing. He approached Kaz, who'd picked them up from where they'd set them down and reverently passed the body of the late Grand Master to the larger half-orc.

The monks and clerics seemed resistant to go, but they soon followed Khort and Mhult back to the Grand Master's ship.

The Grand Master had a memory pop up that they knew had been their predecessor's, but it was relevant to their present situation. They withdrew from a pocket their small, durable docupad and with it produced a docucard. They approached Darius and presented the docucard to him. "My predecessor had this prepared for you, and I agree with them that you and your crew have earned it."

Darius tentatively took the docucard. He withdrew a docupad from a pocket to read it, and he sucked in a breath. "That... That is a lot of COIN."

"You and your crew have done a great service not just for me and my processor," started the Grand Master, "and not just for the UEO, but for the whole of the peoples of the galaxy. Payment for your time and service is right and proper."

Darius appeared to be considering their words. Then, he returned the docupad to the pocket he'd withdrawn it from and held the docucard out to the Grand Master. "My crew might not agree with this," he started, "but you should keep it. We willingly volunteered to join you and your predecessor

REVELATIONS AND RECONCILIATIONS

on this quest, and no payment was offered for that. I wouldn't feel right accepting this. But I thank you."

The Grand Master knew that their predecessor had expected Darius to respond that way, and so had they. Noble seemed to be more than his surname, and they suspected that applied to the whole of his crew.

"Captain," the Grand Master began. "I and the UEO are, in our own way, in your debt. It may not seem quite right, but I would ask a boon of you."

"Go on," Darius encouraged.

"May I call upon you, and your crew, in the future, if I have a need I know you and yours could best fulfill?"

"Yes," agreed Darius without pause. He offered his hand, and the Grand Master shook it.

The Grand Master approached the rest of the *Moon Raven* crew. The dwarves were surprisingly reverential towards them, given dwarves were the only race to entirely practice a religion other than transtheism. Sara and Aya each offered a bow with a handshake and wished them luck.

The Grand Master found themself standing before the Blue Cyberwizard.

"I had no idea," started Galit, "about that crystal or how it worked. But it doesn't surprise me. It explains a lot about the workings of the UEO and the continuance of the line of Grand Masters. It also explains your role as keepers of balance for space/time."

"So it would seem," said the Grand Master. Memories from their predecessor of prior experiences with the Blue Cyberwizard passed through their mind fleetingly.

"You will do the Grand Master proud, Grand Master," said Galit, bowing her head with reverence. The new Grand Master smiled.

At last, they approached Kaz. The half-elf cleric – former cleric, in his mind - had his eyes cast to the ground. "Kazimir Daun-sun'kira," the Grand Master addressed him.

"Grand Master."

"You were with me at the start of this journey in more ways than one. My predecessor and I know that you left the temple and ceased acknowledging yourself as a cleric of the UEO, long ago, under most unfortunate circumstances. And I hold to what you were told before. Not all clerics of the UEO are in our temples. You are still one of us."

Kaz met the Grand Master's eye. They saw something there they presumed was a blend of hope and appreciation.

"I would like to make you an offer," the Grand Master began. "I could use a man of your skills and talents in my service, and in service to the UEO. There will be many challenges I suspect we will face with the revelation of the dangers folding space/time represents, dealing with the drow, the human Federation, and the other races, as well as the monks and clerics accepting me as the new Grand Master. Challenges where, having you at my side, would be most appreciated."

"I would be welcomed back to the temple?" questioned Kaz, a note of longing in his tone.

"You would," said the Grand Master without pause.

Kaz was silent for a moment. Then, he took a deep breath and let it out with a sigh. "I cannot tell you, Grand Master, how much good it does my heart to know that I was never cast out by the ontology, and my return would be welcome. I am deeply honored by your offer. However, I must decline."

Kaz gestured towards Galit and the others, standing nearby. "I know without a doubt that my place is with the crew of the *Moon Raven*. At least, for the time being. But I know that my joining you on this quest was predestined and that we will cross paths yet again in this lifetime. Perhaps, one day, the time for me to attend you will come."

The Grand Master had expected no less. They made a gesture over Kaz's forehead, drawing a millennia-old runic symbol, known to only the Grand Master, in the air. "Kazimir Daun-sun'kira, Cleric Master of the Universal Energies Ontology, you will always have a home with us."

Kaz's eyes went wide as he soundlessly mouthed the word, "Master?" The Grand Master smiled and nodded. They pulled Kaz into a hug. He returned the embrace.

Releasing the new cleric master, the Grand Master turned towards their ship, seeing that not all the monks and clerics had departed to it. Of course, they hadn't. The Grand Master was typically protected when out and about, and they were not yet sure of how they would differ from the one before them.

REVELATIONS AND RECONCILIATIONS

Looking one last time towards the new friends they had made on this quest, the Grand Master moved on to the next challenge before them.

Chapter 18 – Retaliation

There was only one habitable section remaining. The former Alliance shipyard, on the outskirts of the Unity system, had been well inside the sector. Though mostly used by the military for retrofits, repairs, and upgrades, they also refurbished military cargo ships and sold them to private businesses. The Federation leadership had planned to sell a lot of ships for a tidy profit.

Among his duties as the commanding officer of all Federation forces, General Thomas Song would tour various bases. Unfortunately, that was not what had brought him there. The once active, busy shipyard was devastated. Its support scaffolds and drydocks were broken, habitats for crew, mechanics, and engineers charred and nearly unrecognizable derelicts, and the ships that had been docked were smashed beyond reasonable repairs.

Rather than getting a tour of the Federation's captured shipyard, Song was visiting the wreckage of a rebel attack. He was accompanied by his pair of drow bodyguards, Aneesa, and three other aides. The local duty officer had been injured in the attack. Still, he'd taken command of the Federation starship that had first arrived on the scene and awaited General Song at the remains of the shipyard.

Despite the protests of one or two members of his staff, Song had taken a shuttle to meet the officer in the one remaining functional shipyard habitat. He observed that it was only functional because someone had sealed off half of it when it had become damaged and exposed to the vacuum of space.

The local officer looked haggard, and Song could see that he was clearly in pain. The Colonel and two officers with him – all of whom Song had never met before - saluted as Song and his group approached them.

"General Song, I'm Colonel Gregory Rafiq."

Song returned the salute and offered his hand. "Colonel."

"Sir, it's a pleasure to meet you, though I wish it had been under better circumstances," Rafiq said. Aneesa also introduced herself to the Colonel, but apart from the standard response. his attention was on Song.

"What were our losses?" asked Song.

REVELATIONS AND RECONCILIATIONS

"We had a dozen ships here undergoing various repairs and refits. There were five nearly completed cargo ship refurbishments and five more that had been recently started."

"Can any be salvaged?"

"No, sir," Rafiq replied. "The nature of the attack made sure of that."

"Can the shipyard be restored?" asked Song.

"Technically, yes," replied Rafiq. "However, it will take weeks to clear the debris, months to rebuild, and a significant amount of COIN that, though I'm not an administrator of that nature, I suspect is more than the worth of restoring the shipyard."

Song grimaced. He'd assessed the same. He had specialists looking into it, but it wouldn't be his call to make anyhow. "How did this happen, Colonel?" asked Song. "Our intelligence hasn't revealed that the rebels that have cropped up in the former Alliance have any ships that could do this."

"That's not entirely incorrect," said Colonel Rafiq. "They were clever and resourceful and caught us completely by surprise."

"How?"

Rafiq sighed. "It wasn't hard to speculate, and we finally located enough hard evidence to prove what they did. A starship put in for repair, following all the normal procedures. They had the right codes and documentation to dock in the yard. Nobody gave it a second thought. What's more, the crew disembarked and went to the guest habitats per standard operating procedure."

Rafiq took a breath, and nearly growled as he exhaled. "Or so we thought. Though they avoided the majority of our surveillance systems, when we checked the recordings, we saw several unexpected people moving around and through repair bays."

"Wait a moment," Aneesa interrupted. "Nobody thought to inquire why unauthorized personnel were in the bays?"

"Any supervisors we might have questioned about that were killed," Rafiq said. "The surveillance system is passive; nobody mans it on watch."

"That strikes me as unwise," said Aneesa.

"General," Song addressed her, "more than half the mechanics and engineers in this repair yard were non-military. Security is a very different matter here." He looked at Rafiq. "Continue."

"Portals from unrealspace opened, and a group of heavily armed freighters arrived and started to attack the shipyard. We scrambled our fighter squadron and our defensive starships and manned the guns and defensive systems."

"Freighters did that?" asked Aneesa, gesturing out the nearest viewport at the shipyard's debris.

"No," Rafiq said. "Despite being unusually well-armed freighters and transports, they weren't doing more than superficial damage. It made no sense, but we assumed the rebel element was trying to just make a statement, let us know they were there. It wasn't much of an attack, and as soon as we started shooting back, they opened another portal to unrealspace and were gone. But just as they did that, the explosions began."

"The rebels from the docked starship?" prompted Song.

"Yes," Rafiq said. "They must have been planting explosives in ships and at various junctions and vulnerable spaces all around the yard. We now believe the attack by those freighters was either a diversion so they could get away or otherwise escape before setting off the explosives."

"How many ships attacked?" asked Aneesa.

"There were fourteen of them," said Rafiq.

"And how many were destroyed?"

"None," replied Rafiq, who then added, "The shipyard defenses are designed with bigger starships in mind. The attackers were agile and stayed out of range of the guns. They were armored against fighters, though they didn't escape unharmed. But in hindsight, it's clear they were a diversionary action."

"And how many rebels infiltrated this shipyard?" questioned Aneesa.

"Hard to say," said Rafiq. "Maybe thirty, maybe fewer? We're still looking into the manifests of that ship when it put in for service, and we can't be positive a full and accurate count of the crew was taken."

"Where did the attacking ships come from?" asked Song.

"We don't know," replied Rafiq with another sigh. "They portaled in from unrealspace, and we paid them little mind until they attacked. Ships come and go from a shipyard like this, unscheduled, all the time. The explosions started as they portaled back to unrealspace, so we were unable to give chase when they left. Either the bombers escaped with them, committed

REVELATIONS AND RECONCILIATIONS

suicide, were caught in their own explosives, or found some other way to disappear."

Song could feel Aneesa looking at him coldly, awaiting some punishment or sanction against Colonel Rafiq. But the man had done his duty and followed procedure and protocol. He'd been caught by surprise, never expecting such an attack. Though he'd likely be relieved of duty by the Convocation, no further punishment or sanction was warranted.

After a moment more of silence, Aneesa asked, "So, Colonel, what did you do to retaliate?"

"I beg your pardon, General?"

"How did you retaliate?"

Rafiq looked deeply uncomfortable. After a glance towards Song, he said, "With all due respect, General Anwar, we have no idea where the rebels who set the explosives came from, where the attacking freighters came from, nor where they went after they portaled back into unrealspace. There's nobody for us to have launched a retaliation against."

"How can you say that?" questioned Aneesa. "You're in the Unity solar system. How many habitable worlds and other habitations are here?"

"Unity IV," replied Rafiq. "One moon of Unity V and another of Unity VI. And a range of additional mining operations on the other moons of Unity VI and Unity VII."

Aneesa nodded. "Thus, former Alliance citizens in the millions, maybe billions, locally? You could have rounded up suspected conspirators, locked down the cities and put them under martial law, and performed searches of all vessels entering and leaving the system. You could have done quite a bit to put more pressure on the locals, discouraging further rebellion. And that would have sent a message that there would be consequences to anyone considering similar acts against us."

Colonel Rafiq said nothing. Song understood his reticence. Rafiq was in charge of the shipyard, and though likely the highest-ranked officer in the sector, taking the actions Aneesa was calling for crossed any number of lines, not to mention command protocols.

"Colonel," Song began, "please make your formal report as detailed as you can. That will be all. Dismissed."

"Yes, General. Thank you." Rafiq and the two officers with him saluted Song, Aneesa, and the rest of their group, before smartly returning the way they had come.

Song turned to his aides. "Could you give General Anwar and I a moment, please?"

They nodded and left the compartment. The pair of drow, however, withdrew only as far as the hatch, but did not depart.

"General Anwar," Song began, maintaining a tone of indifference but command in his voice. "You're correct. Our forces could go around the Unity system, begin searches and systematic raids, and start rounding up conspirators, real or imagined. And we can and will impose new restrictions, more thorough searches of ships, landing bays, and ports. We can clamp down on all movement in and around this system, as well as see if we can track any of those freighters to other systems and start to do the same there. We can make the former Alliance citizens aware that the Federation is in charge now, that continued resistance will not be tolerated, and remind them who is in control."

Song paused, giving Aneesa a moment, before he went on. His tone was ever-so-slightly condescending. "But these actions will also lead to convincing more people who have thus far been largely unaffected by our occupation to join the rebellion. Anyone who has studied history can see that the more you restrict and disturb the common people, and the more you make them suffer, the more you stir them to fight back.

"That's where General Mallick went wrong. He immediately began to allow harsh and unfair treatment of civilians in the Alliance sectors by both our military and administrative forces. Rather than put all his attention and energy on their military, he interfered with the lives of the regular people and gave them reason to shelter rebels. Had the drow followed his orders and performed that planetary bombardment, I assure you open rebellion across the whole of former Alliance space would be what we'd be facing now."

Song paused again, took a breath, then wrapped up his lecture. "And that, General Anwar, is why our current focus is strictly against Confederation military forces. Because occupying their worlds without removing those forces would stretch our own resources too thin to be effective."

REVELATIONS AND RECONCILIATIONS

Aneesa nodded. For the briefest moment, Song thought that maybe this time he'd managed to get through to her.

But then, with unabashed haughtiness, she said, "I think, General, that you underestimate the strength of the Federation. It's not just that we have the ability to fold space/time and place our forces anywhere we please. Allowing rebels to do damage such as they have here, with no repercussions, invites more of the same. We must not only retaliate, but also continue to expand our sphere of influence. We need to begin to occupy the Confederation and show them all that the Federation is not to be trifled with. They must be reminded, in no uncertain terms, who we are."

"Agreed," Song said. "But at the same time, General, there's a balance to be struck. This action cost us a dozen starships and lost COIN from the ten cargo ships that were destroyed. Given the overall strength of the Federation and our forces, that's not significant, until you look at the big picture. We have forces in the former Alliance territories, enforcing our occupation. And clearly we need to add more, if we're going to take on this growing uprising. But at the same time, we're launching attacks against the Confederation.

"The former Alliance was the Federation's galactic neighbor; our claimed territories abutted one another. The supply lines between these sectors are easily bridged, yet we're still devoting a lot of our effort to maintaining the occupation. Meanwhile, Confederation space is only within our reach because of space/time folding. The logistics involved in a successful occupation demands we neutralize their forces first, or else we risk being stretched dangerously thin. Mighty as we are, General Anwar, we do have numerical limitations."

Aneesa was silent for a moment, but then she sighed and said, "Very well, General Song. I still think you're being too conservative in your estimates."

"Then do the math, General," Song invited, no longer bothering to be polite. "You have access to our full force readiness. You can see for yourself what we have. Show me I'm wrong."

Aneesa was again silent. Song wondered if she already knew that, while the idea of Federation power was one thing, the reality didn't align.

"Still," Aneesa started, "will you do nothing to retaliate?"

"I'm ordering more extensive controls and more in-system intelligence operations in the former Alliance sectors. We will be having our civilian administrators put pressure on local government to discourage the rebellion."

"Something must be done," Aneesa stated. "You don't think your actions might be bordering on cowardice, General Song?"

Song took a step closer, squaring his shoulders and dropping his voice as he said, "Careful, General Anwar, with such accusations. I have devoted my life to service to the Federation, and I believe in it and our mission to expand it. But the more tyrannically we behave, the more we'll encourage further rebellion. That won't strengthen our position. If our leadership's long-term goal is control of all the human sectors, it will take time, even with amazing technology that drastically changes time and distance.

"My predecessor made unrealistic promises to our leadership. I work with what we truly have. Maybe that comes across as too slow for everyone's liking, but thus far, it's working. But we're on the edge of a knife, Aneesa Anwar. And if we slip, we won't fall off of it, we'll cut ourselves deeply and bleed to death. Run the numbers, check our forces and their distribution, and if you can prove me wrong, I will change my strategy accordingly."

Chapter 19 – Determinations

Galit realized that she'd been spending far more time alone than she'd thought. One did not choose to be a cyberwizard if one didn't enjoy spending most of their time in their head. Galit had no issues with other people and spending time with them. However, she was introverted and enjoyed her alone time a great deal.

Cyberwizards were misunderstood. True cyberwizards were few and far between. Throughout the known galaxy, there were maybe a thousand, total. Unlike the monks and clerics of the UEO and the sorcerers of the various Syndicate schools and academies, cyberwizards were not affiliated with anyone. They didn't attend a temple or school to learn their art. They made choices to adapt AI and cybernetics and studied those who'd come before.

Unlike monks, clerics, and sorcerers, cyberwizards had zero connection to Universal Energies or chi. They relied wholly on technologies to manipulate the universe around them on a subatomic level. That was only possible via their cybernetic enhancements and the study of multiple sciences.

The only connection between cyberwizards was the Sanket. The Sanket was an ancient code, a signal bearing an interplanetary, cryptographically encrypted repository of information. It was unattainable without the practice and knowledge of the cyberwizard arts. It took one to two decades to become a true cyberwizard. Acolytes and other cyborgs aspired to cyberwizardry, but unless they found and understood the why of the Sanket, they could not claim to be a cyberwizard.

Pretenders paid a heavy price. The Sanket wasn't merely a code in the ethers; it was an AI construct created by someone lost in time. Its sentient signal only connected to cyberwizards. If someone claimed to be a cyberwizard but wasn't truly one, the Sanket would create blocks and computer viruses that ultimately ruined the cybernetics and related tech of the faker.

When she had been an Acolyte, Galit had had a mentor explain that cyberwizards were modern alchemists. Much like the legend of the

Philosopher's Stone and Elixir of Life, connecting with the Sanket separated the cyberwizard from their race with greater health, wellness, and wellbeing.

Each cyberwizard took on a persona unique to themselves. All were cybernetically enhanced, most with obvious cyborg elements. Galit had chosen to be much more subtle, none of her many, many enhancements visible. She preferred not to present herself as a threat until it was far too late to do anything about it.

Even with the many advantages the cybernetically enhanced cyberwizards gained, they were still a part of their native race. Galit, as a human, still craved interaction with others. Most of those, however, were short. Over the years, she'd joined various parties of adventures, crews, and questers for a time. Now, Galit was realizing the last time she'd done so was further back than she had realized.

Unlike other crews and adventurers Galit had joined along the way, she felt perfectly at home with the crew of the *Moon Raven*. Though she was still living aboard *Phantom*, Galit had been invited to join the *Moon Raven* crew for meals, discussions, and conversations. She found herself welcome anywhere aboard the starship she chose to be.

The *Moon Raven* was in unrealspace, meandering towards more familiar, independent systems following their adventures with the Grand Master on the long-forgotten world. They had just completed their supper, and Darius was leading a discussion about their next move.

"Has everyone recovered?" Darius began. "I know most of us got hurt during the fights we had, some more than others. We've been in unrealspace two galactic standard days now, but this is the first time we've all sat down together since then."

"I am no worse for wear," said Tol. The dwarf had taken the most injury during their trials.

"Good to go," said Sara.

"After getting some real rest, yeah, I'm alright," said Aya.

"I'm still a bit in shock over the revelations from both the prior and current Grand Masters," remarked Kaz. "But aside from that, I'm unhurt."

Darius looked toward Galit. Appreciating being included, she stated, "I'm well, thanks, Captain."

REVELATIONS AND RECONCILIATIONS

Darius nodded. "Good. I think we all got a lot more than we'd bargained for out of that encounter."

"Speaking of which," began Aya. "How much did the Grand Master pay, and did you really have to turn it down?"

Darius chuckled. "You probably don't want to know, and yes. Payment for this job and what it meant would not have been right. We served something far, far greater than any of our interests."

"Maybe," Aya said. Then, she muttered, "Still worth getting paid."

Darius ignored her and continued. "I got caught up on some of the intragalactic news over the past couple of days. While we were in the middle of nowhere and combatting cyborg monsters, the Confederation took our suggestions to heart. Diplomats apparently reached out to the drow and the Federation."

"We get a message to that effect?" asked Sara.

"Not as such," replied Darius. "But I came across a public report to that end from inside the Confederation."

"And?" prompted Aya.

"And what this has resulted in remains to be seen. But we had an impact on the situation, and I thought you'd want to know. Given they've made a point of having no connections to the drow, I'm glad we acted on this."

"This whole business with folding space/time has seemed to preoccupy our lives a lot," commented Aya.

Sara asked, "Do you take exception to that?"

"No," replied Aya without hesitation. "My life has never been one of certainty or a particularly straight path. I had no idea what I was getting myself into after I met the two of you and you saved my life. But I don't regret any of it. It's just highly unpredictable."

"We all came together under duress," said Darius. "In the short time that we've been a crew, we've had some incredible and unique experiences. This is not how I expected my life to be, but I've never served among finer people than you. I trust you all, and I won't just tell you what we're going to do. This is why I started this discussion."

"Given the information we found with the Grand Master," started Tol, "do you intend for us to help close those tears in the fabric of space/time?"

"No," Darius replied. "Even with what we know, the *Moon Raven* isn't equipped for that sort of operation. Closing the rifts will be some sort of military operation and thus sanctioned by one government or another. I do feel that we can and should do something more than sit on the information we've uncovered. Knowing what we know, moving cargos between systems seems to be something much less than we should be doing."

"Maybe," said Kaz. "But maybe we can assist in closing those rifts in some way?"

"While closing those rifts in space/time will be essential, it's also going to require the same technology that opening them did," Galit interjected. "At present, only the drow and the Federation have that tech. Both are using it to pursue vendettas, but maybe the combined warnings from the Confederation and the Grand Master will serve to alter their courses."

Galit changed her tone, then said, "But consider this: creatures from savagespace have already made their way into realspace. Though they do not attack in the open or make their desires known, they are relentless and without mercy. The illithids – mindflayers – gain power through destruction, chaos, and darkness. There will be no bargaining with them. They, and their monsters, will need to be destroyed."

"That's going to pose a multitude of problems," said Darius. "There's no rhyme or reason to the mindflayer attacks. They have been launched against multiple races, both near and far from where the drow or Federation opened space/time folds, as far as we know."

"Do we, though?" asked Sara.

"Yes," replied Galit. "The attacks launched against both the dwarves and the gnomes were in territories nowhere near the drow versus elf or Federation versus Confederation conflicts. They were out of the way, relatively speaking, but well removed from space/time folds."

"I've looked at known attacks," Darius said, taking up the narrative once more. "There is no obvious pattern to them, nothing to indicate a central gathering point. Which is the next issue. Where they're gathering, once they arrive in realspace, is unknown."

"Yes," agreed Kaz.

"That could be a much bigger challenge," said Sara. "We don't know that they cross from savagespace to realspace every time a space/time fold occurs.

REVELATIONS AND RECONCILIATIONS

Then, we don't know if they are all gathering in one place or many. For all we know, there are pockets of mindflayers and their monsters all over deep space."

"No," Galit said. "They are unfamiliar with realspace. While we don't know a lot about them overall, we know that they gain power by destruction, and maximum destruction requires maximum force. That's also why they strike via guerilla tactics, to learn about the denizens of realspace, our technology, and susceptibility to psionic attack. They are all gathering in one place to amass their forces."

"I thought all accounts of the mindflayers were vague?" said Tol.

"Common accounts, yes, love," replied Zya. "But the information in the books we found from the genasi and tieflings contained quite a lot more."

"When did you read that?" asked Tol, incredulity in his tone.

Zya grinned. "You've been doing a lot of sleeping, Tol'te-catl."

"Yes," Darius remarked. "There's a lot in those texts. The genasi or tieflings explain that the mindflayers are individuals, like us, but connected in some way instinctual, beyond extra-sensory. They'll need to gather together, amass themselves, before they start to move against the life in realspace with intent on its destruction to increase their strength."

Galit was impressed that Darius and other members of the crew had read from the volumes they'd found in the catacombs. Yet it did not surprise her.

"I need to catch up on my reading," said Sara.

"Here's the crux of what we need to decide," Darius began, again reclaiming the narrative. "Though we could have another go at transporting cargo, we don't need to gain COIN. Thanks to Sara, we have plenty."

Galit made note of that. A key ability cyberwizards possessed was finding, moving, and creating COIN. Nothing illegal, since counterfeiting COIN was virtually impossible. The Blue Cyberwizard had noted the crew of the *Moon Raven* seemed unusually flush. Now she had an inkling as to why.

"I don't know about the rest of you, but I can't imagine, knowing all that we know, going back to that," Darius continued. "I believe, while we can't take part in closing the rifts or plan a counteroffensive for whatever the mindflayers intend, there is something we can do. We are one starship with a hell of a resourceful crew. Who better to go hunting for the mindflayers and where they're amassing their forces?"

The Captain paused a moment. Then, in a different tone, he said, "But this is not a decision I can make on my own. We'll be putting the *Moon Raven* and our lives potentially in harm's way. Sara and I are ex-military, so we previously signed on for that sort of thing. None of the rest of you did. If any of you object, we don't do this."

"You won't order anyone who objects to leave your ship?" asked Galit.

"No," Darius replied. "The *Moon Raven* isn't mine; it's ours. We do this as one or we don't do it at all."

Galit knew that would be his answer.

"The Grand Master would expect no less," said Kaz. "Let's do this."

"Still serving the greater good," remarked Sara. "Yes. I'm in."

"After what we have seen," began Zya, "the galaxy is a dangerous place. But I have never opted for the safe, and I will not take a safe course now. This is the right thing to do. I say we do it."

"I agree with Zya'ny-a," said Tol.

Aya sighed, then chuckled. "Oh, sure. Leave it up to me. The thief. Well, I said it was time to live on the up and up. I didn't expect to take that to such an extreme, but here we are. And given all the givens, of course, I'm in. Let's do the brave and probably stupid thing."

Sara stated, "Figuring out where the mindflayers are gathering, sooner rather than later, could make a huge difference in what's to come. We've seen so much already. It wouldn't be right to walk away now."

Galit again experienced a sensation she'd not felt in a long, long time. A sense of belonging. She knew she was exactly where she was supposed to be. This mismatched crew was something else. "For the record," she started. "I think it's incredibly noble of you to make this choice. I believe that I have a great deal I can still offer. So, if you don't mind, I should like to remain with you on this new quest."

"I really appreciate that," said Darius.

"Thank you," replied Galit. "But I do have some additional concerns. I suspect that, though we're not representative of a government or some organized force, the mindflayers won't hesitate to destroy us. And we know that they have weapons we might not be capable of resisting."

"Like their psionic attacks," commented Kaz.

REVELATIONS AND RECONCILIATIONS

"In part," agreed Galit. "But in this instance, I'm considering how their ships are armed. They might present us with challenges we're simply incapable of meeting. This ship and my ship are not warships. And the mindflayers are likely to use tactics quite foreign to our collective knowledge."

"However," Galit shifted her tone, "a small civilian ship, such as the *Moon Raven*, might well have the best chance of locating the mindflayers, their monsters, their central gathering place, and escape after. What's more, you possess a tremendous amount of knowledge and skill that goes far beyond any typical civilian crew."

"So, what you're saying," interrupted Aya, "is that if anyone can do it, we can do it. And I'm including you in that *we*."

Galit grinned. "Just so. Before we met up, I was investigating our extradimensional guests. As such, I might have an idea for where we should begin our search."

Chapter 20 – Reassessing

"General Ilizeva," the Moderator addressed her, "you have ordered a cessation of our present operations involving the use of our new technology for folding space/time. We've requested your attendance to explain to us why."

"Thank you, Moderator," replied Ilizeva. "For the record, I should like it noted that I was not summoned against my will to attend this meeting of the Synod and was in the process of requesting an audience to discuss in detail my actions."

"So noted," replied the Moderator.

"Thank you." Ilizeva paused to collect her thoughts, then continued. "With respect, you may recall that after my last attendance of a meeting of the Synod, I took my fleet into deep space to test the Grand Master's and Confederation's claims that an extradimensional threat was somehow crossing to realspace as an unexpected consequence from the folding of space/time. And I can now confirm that this is wholly true."

Murmurs among the Synod began but died away before the Moderator needed to reclaim their attention.

Ilizeva continued. "They have weapons quite unusual to us, as well as the assistance of creatures I can only describe to you as monsters. If you will attend to your monitors, I will share recordings of what we saw. Be forewarned, some of this is quite gruesome and distressing."

Ilizeva played for them the data assembled from her fleet's encounter with the mindflayers and their monsters. A profound and deeply uncomfortable silence followed after the playback concluded.

"As you can see," Ilizeva said, "the mindflayers and their monsters are formidable and have no interest in anything but dominance and destruction. No ship in my fleet left that fight without damage. Given what we now know, and after precise examinations of the crossing on the part of the mindflayers, I have ordered a total and immediate cessation of space/time folding."

"With respect, General," addressed Ulazav Naen'daer, "can you explain your examinations and how they led you to this conclusion?"

"Yes," replied Ilizeva. "We were able to determine that the extradimensional invaders had opened their portal from their point of origin

REVELATIONS AND RECONCILIATIONS

in precisely the same place we had arrived when we'd folded space/time to that sector of realspace. Though I cannot provide a fully detailed scientific explanation of the process – and I will provide the Synod with that data separately – I saw for myself that we could prove within ninety-eight percent certainty that the space/time fold access points have created a rift in space/time."

"A rift in space/time?" questioned a woman named Aluzovi Raen'caer, a longtime opponent of all military spending. "With respect, General, but that doesn't track with folding space/time and all we were told it would entail."

"A fair point," conceded Ilizeva. "It is, as such, an unintended consequence. Based on our understanding of the calculation the humans developed to fold space/time, they used the model of wormholes as the basis. Wormholes are tunnels that traverse two points in realspace. But those tunnels cross another dimension, referred to as savagespace. It's normally wholly inaccessible to us. An unintended consequence of folding space/time has created an access point that the mindflayers and their monsters are using to invade our dimension."

"You admit this was folly, General?" pressed Aluzovi.

"No," replied Ilizeva. "Not every risk we take will immediately reveal consequences. How many lives were lost in the earliest days of colonization millennia ago? How many lives were lost to any initial experiment that advanced any race across the galaxy? It's a part of progress, Aluzovi Raen'caer, but that is not folly. Folly would be continuing to employ this technology knowing the widespread destruction that comes from the use of it."

"Destruction wrought against the elves only furthers our goals," someone said.

"But the mindflayers strike indiscriminately against all life they encounter in realspace," said Ilizeva. "Our vengeance against the elves in the face of extradimensional invasion, at the cost of innocents, is dishonorable, and thus intolerable. It is for that reason that I have already spoken to Marshal N'Kirit Dh Siv at length. He, on behalf of the hobgoblins, is in full agreement with our assessment, and they are redeploying and preparing to deal with the extradimensional threat."

That wasn't the whole truth. Marshal N'Kirit wanted compensation for the lost spoils they would have gotten from attacking the elves. Ilizeva had assured the hobgoblin military leader that she'd address that but not until after they assessed and dealt with the extradimensional invaders. He'd reluctantly agreed. Ilizeva knew having the hobgoblins already in agreement would end any debate about her unilateral decision. When it came to warfare, the drow and their Synod respected Ilizeva's leadership.

"General," the Moderator began, "now that you have proof of the Grand Master's claims, how many of these mindflayers and their monsters have arrived?"

"With respect, we're looking into it," replied Ilizeva. "Unfortunately, we simply do not know. During our investigation, we faced twelve ships and three monsters. Between the number of times we and the Federation have folded space/time, it's possible there could be hundreds of ships and dozens of monsters. Myself, and my command staff, recognize we need to know, once they arrive, where they are going. Given they've performed hit and fade attacks thus far, it stands to reason that, once in realspace, they're all gathering together somewhere."

"Why is it, General Ilizeva, do you think, that their chosen attacks have been so random?" someone asked.

"All we can do is hazard some guesses," she replied. "But my suspicion is that they're testing the aliens of this galaxy."

"Aliens?" Elezev Paen'baer asked.

"From the perspective of the mindflayers, yes," said Ilizeva. "The sole transmission we received from them was a promise to dominate. Not a threat, a statement. To them, we are aliens to be overcome. They strike at different, disparate places, when they don't just encounter a force where they arrive, to test us. They're learning our strengths and weaknesses."

"Do we know what races they have attacked?" questioned Ilazivi Laen'baer.

"Based on information our intelligence forces have put together, it seems that they've attacked orcs, elves, gnomes, dwarves, us, and our allies."

"Can we get greater confirmation and more information?" someone asked.

"Perhaps," Ilizeva replied. "But as you know, we have a longstanding policy of keeping separate and to ourselves. Once our forebearers left the cradle, they chose to remove themselves from elvenkind. With that, we spent

REVELATIONS AND RECONCILIATIONS

millennia keeping ourselves and our allies in limited contact with other races."

"Except for this association with the human Federation," said Aluzovi Raen'caer.

"Indeed," agreed Ilizeva. "But that was of necessity. Despite the many shortcomings of their government - and frankly the rest of the human territories and their governments - the Federation scientists have done impressive work. Cracking the folding of space/time has been sought by every spacefaring race for centuries. Probably millennia. But once those scientists recognized that we, of all the races in the galaxy, had the kind of power sources needed to make their research a reality, we'd have been foolish to pass up the opportunity it presented."

"With respect, General, what of the humans?" Alizev Kaen'baer asked. "Since the Federation has been using the technology to attack the Confederation, have they been attacked by the mindflayers?

"Though we've not a clear report to that end, I suspect at least some humans have also been attacked," she said. "But they have so many different forces and governments, it's not easy to track. Before I presented myself to the Synod this day, I communicated with Colonel Orizevi. I commanded her to let the Federation know this consequence of folding space/time and to inform them it was in their best interest to cease employing the technology."

There was silence for a few moments in the chamber of the Synod. Then, the Moderator asked, "What do you recommend that our forces do now, General?"

"Now that we've ceased folding space/time to attack elf targets, our forces are free to prepare to fight this new threat. With the redeployment of the hobgoblins, I intend to order them to go hunting. I will probably assign some of our troll allies to accompany them."

"And what will *you* do, now that your primary mission is over?" asked Aluzovi Raen'caer.

"My mission is what it has always been, Aluzovi Raen'caer," said Ilizeva. "To serve and protect the drow in every way I can with my heart, my body, my mind, and my soul. I will draw up plans both to defend our worlds from this new threat, as well as to take the fight to them, should we find them."

"We cannot adopt a live and let live policy?" questioned Aluzovi Raen'caer.

Ilizeva played for the Synod both the mindflayer message and its translation. When complete, she said, "Their words have made it clear that that's not an option. They are invaders of our dimension, and we must eliminate them and the threat they represent to us." She paused, changing her tone. "Additionally, we shall draw up plans to deal with the Federation."

"With respect, General, why would you suggest that?" someone asked.

"The leaders of the Federation are blindingly arrogant," stated Ilizeva. "They attack a territory too far from readily available supply lines merely to dominate another human government. Colonel Orizevi tells me they've saddled General Song with a member of the three families that lead the Federation as his Second. That officer, I'm told, is beholden to a party line well removed from reality. General Song is reasonable, and, with this knowledge, will most likely cease folding space/time. If the Federation's leading families do not accept that, however, they may remove him and continue. We might be in the best position to do something about that."

Again, silence met Ilizeva's statement.

"Very well," the Moderator said. "You have made a clear case for your change of plans, Ilizeva Taen'baer, and I do not believe any among this Synod can reasonably object. The safety of our own, and the greater good of the galaxy, is paramount. We will follow your wait-and-see position and follow your lead for how to next proceed, General."

Chapter 21 – Reevaluating

"This is highly irregular, General Song," one of the three holograms began in their multitudinous voice. "That you are in Ternary Citadel at Makowa Dawn, and with the drow, raises questions of respect."

"On the contrary, Your Superiorities," said Song. "It is with the utmost respect, and in light of the seriousness of this matter, that I have come before you with Colonel Orizevi this day, in person."

"That's also of some concern, General Song," another of the multi-voiced holograms said. "You made it quite clear that you insisted on meeting with the Superior Convocation at the behest of Colonel Orizevi Daen'naer. That you felt the need to both attend this body, in person, might be considered suspicious."

Song knew that multiple armed figures hid in the shadows of the columns of the chamber, in addition to the "honor guard" that had escorted Song, Orizevi, and their half-dozen each drow and human guards. They'd flown to the planet on a drow shuttle, which had allowed Song to exclude Aneesa from this.

He was prepared to respond, but Colonel Orizevi beat him to it. "Your Superiorities," she said, "if I had thought this would be a cause for concern, I would not have insisted that we attend you in person. This is a cultural difference between our peoples, I suspect. For you see, among the drow, a discussion of this nature would be brought forth in person, rather than holographically, as a matter of respect."

There was a moment's silence. Song had come to know the drow well enough to know that Orizevi's claim was likely untrue. But the Superior Convocation wouldn't know or even care about that. "Proceed, Colonel Orizevi Daen'naer," said the multitudinous voice of one of the holograms on the dais.

"Thank you, Your Superiorities," she replied with a slight, respectful bow. "With respect, I'd like to address a matter that I believe may have been previously brought to your attention by the Grand Master of the Universal Energies Ontology. They addressed the drow with certain concerns dismissed as unfounded at the time, after they had presented them to you."

She paused for effect, then went on in a changed, more commanding tone. "It has come to pass, Your Superiorities, that the Grand Master's concerns were not unfounded. We have proof that the folding of space/time is indeed tearing interdimensional rifts in the fabric of space and time. Those rifts are accessing a dimension called savagespace, which is home to monsters and sentient life unlike any in realspace. And they have been coming through those rifts, entering realspace, and attacking without provocation."

Orizevi ceased her narration. It was met with silence. Song threw a glance her way but said nothing. After another uncomfortable moment, one of the multi-voiced holograms said, "We fail to understand why this would be the Federation's concern."

Song was about to speak, but Orizevi got there first, and said, "The issue of these extradimensional invaders is a problem, but not the main concern. The primary concern, our scientists conclude, is that continuing to fold space/time tears more of these rifts, which will produce a cumulative impact on this dimension, and possibly our access to unrealspace as well."

"Fact, Colonel, or speculation?" questioned one of the many-voiced holograms.

"Fact, Your Superiorities," replied Orizevi in a tone not too dissimilar to Ilizeva's. "The rifts that already occurred increasingly damage the fabric of space/time as we know it. Though, at present, it's only measurable in time and distance that appears inconsequential, they are spreading, and harming space/time. Opening more rifts will spread that further. The full consequences of damaging realspace are not entirely clear yet, but all models point to danger for all if it continues and grows."

Once more, there was a silence that descended upon the hall. Song found it unsettling and realized that was likely its intent.

The multitudinous voice of one of the holograms spoke. "The Federation military is strong. Is the drow military less so? Do these extradimensional attackers pose any greater threat than the races of realspace?"

"With respect, Your Superiorities," replied Orizevi, holding her voice in check despite the insult to the drow, "we have met and defeated them in combat. However, they do employ unfamiliar weapons of tremendous power, as well as psionic attack, which humans are especially susceptible to. What's more, these sentient attackers – called mindflayers – cannot be

REVELATIONS AND RECONCILIATIONS

bargained with. They are intent only on destruction, and thus-far test our defenses to that end. This is not merely a threat to your Federation or the drow, but all sentient beings across this galaxy."

Once more, silence descended upon the chamber. Then, one of the holograms spoke again, "General Song, are you in agreement with the assessment presented by Colonel Orizevi and the drow?"

"I am," replied Song without hesitation. "I have worked closely with the drow a long time now, through every step of our accords with them. Though many of their ways are alien to our own, they are an honorable people."

"And why should that matter, General?" asked another of the multiple-voiced holograms.

"Because they weigh their interests and intentions against the greater good. Their use of space/time folding to exact revenge on the elves has been the culmination of millennia of desire for retribution. Yet a threat to the fabric of space/time is a threat to life for all. Only such a threat and a true danger to the greater good would turn them from their mission. That is a matter of honor, Your Superiorities, and something not to be taken lightly."

"You do not think, General Song, that the desire of this body to rule *all* of human space is equally honorable?" questioned one of the many-voiced holograms. "General Anwar has expressed some concerns about your continued caution."

"Your Superiorities," stated Song, controlling his anger, "as I informed General Anwar, all one need do is look at the total number of our forces, both those occupying the former Alliance sectors and those attacking the Confederation, and it's clear what we can and cannot do to reach our goals. Without a modicum of caution, such as I have employed, we'd risk losses that would lessen our hold on the Alliance as well as our ability to strike the Confederation and weaken it so that we might occupy it, as well.

"What's more, Your Superiorities, folding space/time still presents certain unavoidable limitations. We can arrive in Confederation space instantly, yes. But that doesn't negate the distance from Federation space - and supply lines - therein. The superiority of the Federation over the other human governments of the galaxy is without question. As such, it is just as honorable as the drow mission against the elves. But that they are ceasing that mission for the greater good is a matter of honor we should not ignore."

Once more, the chamber descended into silence. After another few moments had passed, one hologram said, "Colonel Orizevi, was direct action taken by General Ilizeva at the behest of your Synod to confirm this matter?"

"Yes, Your Superiorities," Colonel Orizevi replied. "She had her fleet fold space/time to an out-of-the-way sector of deep space and wait. After approximately one galactic standard day, the rift tore open space/time and disgorged multiple mindflayer craft and several of their vacuum-breathing monsters."

"General Song," another of the three multi-voiced holograms spoke, "you will emulate the actions of the drow. Choose an empty sector of space to fold a fleet to and wait one galactic standard day after your arrival to see what, if anything, happens. Once you have that data, you will immediately address this body with your findings, and we will make a final determination from that."

"Thank you, Your Superiorities," replied Song.

"General," another of the holograms said, "you will not be accompanied by any allied forces on this expedition. Federation forces only, no drow or their associates. Understood?"

"Yes, Your Superiorities."

"Very well," one of the holograms said in its multitudinous voices. "This audience with the Superior Convocation is at an end."

Song, Orizevi, and their dozen guards departed from the chamber. They departed the citadel and boarded their drow shuttle. It wasn't until the shuttle had taken off and was ascending out of the atmosphere that Orizevi spoke.

"Will they stop folding space/time, whether your forces are attacked or not?"

Orizevi and Song were in a compartment separated from the shuttle pilots and the rest of the soldiers who had accompanied them. Song knew surveillance of them or eavesdropping on any conversation they had was nearly impossible.

"I would like to believe that there is reasonable leadership among the Superior Convocation and the Triad," replied Song. "But with all I have seen since becoming commanding officer of Federation forces, I suspect their self-aggrandizement and desire for dominance might overrule that."

REVELATIONS AND RECONCILIATIONS

Orizevi was silent for a moment. Then, she said, "Be honest, Thomas Song. Off the record. Do you believe in your leaders and their intentions?"

Song considered his answer with care. "I believe in the Federation. But I can't say much beyond that. As I am not a member of one of the families, I know that they do not fully trust me."

"General Ilizeva has concerns about that."

"Which I appreciate," acknowledged Song. "And despite my orders to bring no allies with us, I will be keeping my two drow companions, unless you object."

"Not at all," replied Orizevi. A look of concern crossed her face. "Are you in danger, General Song?"

Song sighed. "It's hard to say. You are aware that General Ilizeva expressed interest in offering me a position among drow forces?"

"Yes."

"I cannot say what the outcome of this expedition might be," Song said. "But I will admit to you, off the record, of course, that I wonder if I should take her up on that offer sooner rather than later."

Chapter 22 – Disseminating

The Grand Master didn't recall ever paying this world a visit before. At least, not when they'd been Alisay Naun-moon'kari. They'd found it initially disconcerting. working out some of the memories from their life before becoming Grand Master versus memories of their predecessors. The stone they wore that transmitted the legacy of the Grand Master had imparted many gifts.

The neutrality of their gender was a non-issue. The Grand Master was more than any gender, race, or other artifice of identity. They led the UEO along a continuous path, interconnected through past, present, and future.

The monks and clerics on their starship immediately, unquestionably, accepted them as Grand Master. Others they'd spoken to via chatter had only hesitated in surprise at the passing of their predecessor.

The Grand Master had come to an understanding that they almost considered enlightenment. Except there was too much humility inherent in their nature, coupled with all the knowledge they had available now but did not yet know. The potential and possibilities they felt were beyond any dream they'd had of where the monkhood might have taken them.

They had a good understanding of why their predecessor had chosen them. And they were honored. The passing of their predecessor had set the new Grand Master on the same mission. It was of the utmost importance, not only to the Universal Energies Ontology, but to the whole of sentient life in the galaxy. The threat from the extradimensional invaders and the rifts in space/time that gave the denizens of savagespace access to realspace were their primary concern.

The planet Atrunin was a largely green and purple gas giant. It was in a neutral sector of space, relatively close to elf territories. The innermost portion of the system featured three planets. Two had no atmosphere and were too close to the star to serve anyone. The third had an atmosphere that was not breathable to any race, but it featured a surface of gemstone land masses and oceans of rich and diverse - but not consciously aware - life.

The outermost portion of the solar system held twelve more planets, a range of gas giants, ice giants, and bodies with various minable ores and similar materials. The fourth planet, Atrunin, had nine moons in its orbit. Three had breathable atmospheres, but two presented unique challenges for any that chose to live on them between their orbit around Atrunin and their own spin.

Uribin was large enough that it technically classified as a planet. But it was considered a moon because of its distance to Atrunin. Uribin had no true night, as the orbit of the moon was geostationary to that of the gas giant. Hence, as the moon spun on its axis, one side faced the gas giant Atrunin and the other the sun.

Urubin was home to the headquarters of the Thaumaturgic Sciences Syndicate. The Syndicate oversaw all the accepted schools of sorcery across the galaxy, much like the UEO oversaw the temples and monasteries. While monks and clerics wholly employed their own chi and Universal Energies to perform thaumaturgical acts, sorcerers merged those energies with technologies.

Monks and clerics could perform telekinetic, telepathic, and other mind/body acts on the microscopic and macroscopic levels beyond the normal capabilities of the various races. They could, as such, heal with energies, move with unparalleled speed and agility, as well as dodge, leap, and fight with grace and precision far beyond normal bodily abilities.

Sorcerers used Universal Energies to power machines and cybernetics to perform similar acts, but because they did not study the connection between chi and Universal Energies, they couldn't heal with energy. Another difference was that they could produce illusions, use weapons like magic missiles of pure energy, and create fire, throw flames, and the like.

The ability to use energies in any forms had only become possible, the Grand Master learned from the stone, when the races had started to interbreed. Scientists speculated that latent connectivity emerged due to certain genetic combinations of DNA that had come from interbreeding disparate races. Once that was unlocked, it had spread to other races, but that was why a disproportionate number of monks, clerics, and sorcerers were half-elves, half-orcs, and the like.

The downside to practicing sorcery came from how sorcerers employed chi and Universal Energies. Unlike monks and clerics and their deep connections to those energies, sorcerers pushed, pulled, and forced them -

through technology - to do their bidding. That came with the price of a shortened lifespan.

The Grand Master knew that this was the result of using up chi without replenishing it via Universal Energies. Hence, the average life expectancy of a practicing sorcerer was about fifty-five years. Compared to the life expectancy of most of the races being at least double that, it was a major drawback.

Because of their connection to technology, sorcerers had abilities and powers nobody else possessed. It was for that reason that the Grand Master was visiting the Thaumaturgic Sciences Syndicate headquarters. It was possible to visit remotely, but the nature of the Grand Master's request, as well as certain traditions and established protocols, had led to their decision to make their way to Uribin.

Escorted by six monks and six clerics, the Grand Master was walking from where their starship had landed towards the chamber where the Grand Adepts met. It had surprised the Grand Master that the headquarters for the Syndicate was not a stone temple or castle of some sort. Rather, it was a delicate structure of glass and polycarbonates, extremely high-tech and aesthetically pleasing.

They passed various sorcerers, all of whom paused in whatever they'd been doing to watch the Grand Master and their entourage. The group reached a flowing archway with a shimmering forcefield where a door would be. To either side stood a pair of sorcerers, each bearing ornately carved staffs, which the Grand Master knew to be weapons of tremendous power.

"We are expected by the Grand Adepts. I am the Grand Master of the Universal Energies Ontology."

The quartet turned inwards towards the portal, and the shimmering of the forcefield winked out.

"Thank you," said the Grand Master. They proceeded to pass into the chamber. The chamber they entered was about fifteen meters wide and round. The ceiling rose another fifty meters to a multifaceted glass polyhedron. The outer edges were deep-blue-hued crystal of some sort, with seats in four descending rows toward the center.

At the center of the chamber there was a large round table with no middle. At four points around the table were openings to admit people

REVELATIONS AND RECONCILIATIONS

into the middle. Around the table sat various sorcerers, some present, others holographic.

Nobody occupied the outside seating of the chamber. This came as no surprise to the Grand Master, since they'd requested this meeting with the Grand Adepts alone. They moved purposefully towards the table, the rest of their entourage dispersing and standing around the circle at the base of the seats.

For the briefest moment, the Grand Master pondered a question their predecessors had also considered. How would combat between sorcerers, monks, and clerics play out? Would the advanced technology defeat the enhanced chi and universal energy? It was a moot, academic notion, as there was no rivalry between the UEO and the Syndicate, and there never had been. Both groups thoroughly believed in abundance and coexistence as central to their doctrines.

The Grand Master stepped into the space at the table's center. As had been the long-standing tradition, they paused to bow once each towards the north, south, east, and west, acknowledging the Grand Adepts.

"Welcome Grand Master of the Universal Energies Ontology," said a half-orc female. "The Grand Adepts have noted that you are not the Grand Master that last we met."

"Indeed," replied the Grand Master. "My predecessor was recently lost to us but gave me their place as the new Grand Master before their passing."

"We are sorry for your loss," stated a half-elf male.

"Your condolences are appreciated."

"It has been a long time since the Grand Master visited the Syndicate in person," stated a half-elf female. "Surely, you have not just come to us to introduce yourself as the new Grand Master."

"Correct," the Grand Master replied. "I have come into the knowledge that among the many talents of the sorcerous community, you can manipulate the technology that allows the sharing of data and information across the worlds of all the races traversing interstellar space."

"That is true," stated a half-goblin that the Grand Master could not identify as male or female. "Though the Syndicate maintains ethics and codices regulating such practices."

"As is right and proper," agreed the Grand Master. "But sorcerers have used these talents before, during the AI Awakening. And likely that's the origin of your ethics and codices to that end. But your acknowledgment of this confirms that I was right to come here."

"You will explain further?" questioned the half-orc female that had initially addressed them.

"Indeed. You are aware that the drow and human Federation have unlocked the secret to folding space/time for instant travel between points countless lightyears' distance from one another?"

"We are," stated that same half-orc female.

"Are you also aware that there have been several, unexplained attacks on outposts and bases belonging to several different races?"

"We have been privy to that information," said a human male.

"I can shed some more light on this. Myself, my predecessor, and a small crew of uniquely talented individuals who had answered my predecessor's call, have learned the truth of those unexplained attacks. We know where they come from and who is leading them."

"Interesting," remarked a half-orc male. "Go on."

"They call themselves illithid, a name the genasi translate to Common as mindflayer." The Grand Master went into a full explanation of the dimensional rifts that resulted from folding space/time, savagespace, and the threat to all life in the galaxy the mindflayers and their monsters posed.

They proceeded to tell of the quest to find the lost information in the catacombs of the long-abandoned UEO temple, and of the death of their predecessor. They did not, however, share information about the AI that they'd left alive in that place.

As they concluded the story, the Grand Master said, "Of course, I will share with you all the data that we uncovered, thanks to the Blue Cyberwizard. You may disseminate it as you see fit. Now we come to the crux of why I am here."

The Grand Master paused both for effect, and to consider their next words with care. "I need the Syndicate to use its tools and your sorcery to broadcast this information across all of known space. Not everything that we learned, as that covers a great deal more than most have need for. Everything

REVELATIONS AND RECONCILIATIONS

relevant to savagespace and the mindflayers, however, must be shared and shared widely."

"Do you speak merely as the Grand Master or for all of the Universal Energies Ontology?" questioned a human female.

"All of the UEO," the Grand Master replied with no hesitation. "One of our mandates is to protect space/time and the integrity of realspace. This threat is to the fabric of reality as we collectively perceive it, as well as individual lives."

"You feel no need to limit the message?" questioned a half-elf male. "You would warn the trolls, hobgoblins, drow, beholders, and their ilk?"

"The whole galaxy needs to know. The mindflayers cannot be bargained with, negotiated with, or otherwise convinced to stop. As I stated before, they feed on chaos and destruction. For that reason, *all* the peoples of the galaxy must be made aware of them and the danger they pose."

Silence descended on the chamber for a moment. The Grand Master turned all around the circle, looking at each Grand Adept in turn.

"How do you wish to share this message?" asked the half-orc female who had first addressed them. "If we do this, how do you propose to disseminate the message?"

"A neutral representative should explain the situation, present the reasoning behind it, and disclose why the data being shared is being shared."

"Who would you have do so?" asked a half-elf female. "A Grand Adept, a cyberwizard, or another?"

"Were they still with us, I would recommend my predecessor," said the Grand Master sadly. "It feels slightly disingenuous, as the new Grand Master, to introduce myself to the galaxy with such news."

"No," said the human male who had spoken before. "The best person to share this information is the Grand Master of the UEO. Even the new Grand Master."

"Your words prove your devotion," said the half-orc female who'd spoken first. "They also make it clear to us that you are the true heir of the Grand Master of the UEO, and it would be right and proper for you to lead this charge."

"Are you prepared to make the statement and share the data?" asked a half-elf male.

"I am," the Grand Master said.

"Speak the words when you are ready," the half-orc female invited.

The Grand Master had already given this a great deal of thought. After a pause, they launched into their narrative. When they had finished, they said, "I will transmit the relevant data now. Separately, I will transmit the total data to the Syndicate."

One of the monks who had been observing the proceedings from the foot of the observation seats withdrew a docutab and transmitted the information.

"We have received it," said a half-tabaxi of indeterminate gender.

"We will work out the most appropriate time to transmit this within the next galactic standard day," stated a half-elf female.

"I thank you, Grand Adepts of the Thaumaturgic Sciences Syndicate, for your assistance in this important matter."

"We are always pleased to work with our siblings of the Universal Energies Ontology. Especially when it is a matter of such grave import to the whole of the peoples of the galaxy," stated the half-orc female.

"What will you do now, Grand Master?" asked a human male.

"Observe what comes next," said the Grand Master. "Help where and how the monks and clerics of the UEO can help to end this threat. I will continue on the same path as those who came before me and do whatever is necessary to protect space/time for all."

Chapter 23 - Investigation

Galit's starship, *Phantom*, featured some rather amazing, advanced technologies. They had been connected to those that the *Moon Raven* had already possessed. While they traveled through unrealspace, Darius was surprised when Tol and Zya explained the ease of making those connections.

"Everything is just compatible," Tol said.

"Compatible, how?" Darius asked.

Zya said, "Not only are both ships' internal networks quite similar; it's as though both were built to be physically connected to one another."

Sara said something similar about the network, soon after paying a visit to *Phantom* not long after Galit had connected her smaller starship to the *Moon Raven*. Sara explained that her chatter, for example, had instantly recognized a connection to *Phantom*.

"Despite her far more advanced technology," Sara said, "there are some really uncanny similarities."

It was for that reason, Galit explained, that extending *Phantom*'s stealth capabilities to the *Moon Raven* had been a simple matter. That would give them some protection, in the middle of nowhere, if and when they encountered the mindflayers and their monsters.

"*Phantom* was salvaged, wasn't it?" he asked Galit after visiting her ship for himself.

"Yes," Galit replied. "Though quite a long time ago, by an old associate of mine."

"It's genasi technology as well, right?"

Galit smiled. "Yes, Captain, both *Phantom* and *Moon Raven* were originally constructed by the genasi. And that is why, because I know you wondered about this, both ships are so easily interconnected. Both ships share the majority of their hull materials, among other elements."

"I've never encountered genasi," Darius said. "But do you know if they have some means by which their ships can be bound together?"

"I believe they, and all their tech, have means of being linked beyond our understanding," Galit said.

After they'd arrived in deep space, Galit had explained that during her previous exploration, she'd detected an extradimensional residual energy akin to the energy she'd found following an attack against a dwarf facility. Since she had made this discovery before, and it was in such an unusual place, Galit felt this should be the focus of fine-tuning the combined instruments and sensors of the two originally genasi starships to get a better fix.

When they had arrived in this part of realspace from unrealspace, the initial use of the combined sensors of *Phantom* and the *Moon Raven* had created feedback that reset multiple systems. Tol and Zya assured Darius that nothing had shorted out, per se. But long-range sensors were down.

Darius, Kaz, and Aya remained on the flight deck of the *Moon Raven* while Galit and Sara had boarded *Phantom* and Tol and Zya were working on various systems around the ship.

Darius' mechanical abilities were rudimentary, and sensitive systems like sensors were not his forte. Because of her familiarity with computers and hacking them, Sara had been far more helpful.

Kaz remained in the pilot's nest, keeping an eye on things outside of the ships. Aya was waiting to see if she'd be needed for anything specific. In the meantime, Darius believed the kitsune quartermaster was also studying the tomes they'd discovered.

Sitting in the command nest, he was going over the stupendous amount of information they'd gleaned from the ancient texts on that distant, lost world. While they provided insight into the physics of dimensions beyond realspace and unrealspace, they were still vague about those other dimensions. Specifically, the parallel – but phase-shifted - dimensions that the genasi and tieflings called home.

The details about savagespace were also vague overall. They named the dimension and that those who called it home lived via chaos and disruption. The writers of the tome explained that life in savagespace was a constant struggle, a battle even. The sentient lifeforms that existed within lived for combat and destruction alone. Anything they created was intent on expanding their destructive capabilities.

The mindflayers, when not destroying other sentient beings in savagespace, fought each other. Their entire purpose and life focused on growth and expansion from chaos, death, and devastation. Though whoever

REVELATIONS AND RECONCILIATIONS

had authored the tome Darius was reading did not say as much, he suspected that their information about savagespace had come from direct knowledge and experience.

He was no expert by any means, but Darius understood enough about the concept of multiple dimensions. All of it, he understood in the most general of terms, tied into scientific principles referring to the multiverse theory. However, he had neither the time nor the energy to get into the depths of the implications of that.

Darius' reflections were interrupted by the return of Tol and Zya. "No," Tol was saying. "They're irreplaceable."

"I think you're just being lazy," said Zya. Darius was fairly certain that Tol's mate was teasing him.

"Problem?" Darius asked lightly.

"No, Captain," said Zya. "Just some unique and very old wiring that needed to be re-stretched."

"Old, as in original parts of this ship," said Tol, pride unmistakable in his tone. "And they seem to be somehow regenerative. A section shorted out, sparked but didn't catch fire. We cut away the damaged bits and stretched it out to reconnect."

"Regenerative," said Zya, her tone cloying. "You are a brilliant engineer, Tol'te-catl, but sometimes given to flights of fancy."

"And yet, here we are, on the ship I put back together and made flightworthy," said Tol.

Galit and Sara joined them. "Everything should be in working order again," said Galit.

"Let's do this," recommended Darius. It was, more or less, what passed for an order aboard the *Moon Raven*. Sometimes Darius marveled at how easily he'd switched gears to take on captaining a starship as a civilian. The crew took their respective stations around the flight deck. Galit had chosen a seat to port.

"I've been running a number of conventional scans and sensor sweeps," stated Kaz. "There are some unusual residual energies probably associated with starships in passing. But nothing concrete nor sufficient to set them specifically apart from background sources."

"Well," Galit began, "we should be better able now to run a scan for that extradimensional residual energy. You had it recorded in *Moon Raven*'s database from your visit to the gnome outpost after they were attacked. But between *Phantom* and *Moon Raven*'s sensors, we should be able to get a better fix."

"Maybe," Darius said. "But it's been some time now since you first detected that residual extradimensional energy here."

"Yes," agreed Galit. "However, if this is the site of a fold in space/time, then it's a point of origin for the mindflayers to enter realspace."

"How would that work?" asked Aya.

"Time most likely works differently in savagespace than either realspace or unrealspace," said Galit. "The opening created in savagespace matching the opening in realspace probably presented itself to a limited number of mindflayers and their monsters who were, at that precise moment, able to take advantage of it."

"Does that mean there could be a permanently open portal to realspace in savagespace?" asked Darius with concern.

"I'm no expert on this topic," replied Galit, "but based on the texts we found, and other research on realspace, unrealspace, and wormholes? No. In all likelihood, it's akin to a wormhole event horizon opening either regularly or sporadically. But rather than a tunnel across savagespace that cannot be accessed, this event horizon is for a portal into realspace from savagespace."

"Does this have anything to do with what the Grand Master was saying about tears in space/time?" asked Kaz.

"Yes," replied Galit. "Based on my understanding, a wormhole, when it opens in realspace, rends the fabric of space/time. Then it presents the tunnel across savagespace to another point in realspace. Whether or not that tunnel is traversed, when the wormhole closes it seals the tear it made."

"Ah," said Zya. "So, if the drow and Federation based the portal for transiting a space/time fold on the event horizon of a wormhole, they did not account for how wormholes create rifts in space/time but then seal them again."

"Which means," took up Tol seamlessly, "that they inadvertently touched savagespace in the process of tearing the rifts for space/time folding. That created a rift that those in savagespace can access to transit to realspace."

REVELATIONS AND RECONCILIATIONS

"Precisely," said Galit. "They didn't account for savagespace nor any other dimensions when folding space/time. In all probability, the portal from savagespace to realspace opens like a wormhole, maybe regularly, maybe sporadically. Because we don't know the workings of time in savagespace or the precise nature of the rift, we can't predict it."

"And it's only a one-way portal," said Darius.

"Yes," replied Galit. "But that doesn't matter, because every time someone traverses that portal between the dimensions, they're tearing the rift open wider. That, in turn, can weaken all of the fabric of realspace as we know it."

"Which is what the Grand Master is seeking to prevent," said Kaz.

"Very much so," agreed Gailit. "The consequences of weakening the overall fabric of realspace could lead to a further breakdown of the walls between dimensions, both parallel and perpendicular to realspace. This could bleed other dimensions into realspace, which might expose all of us here to destructive forces like those of savagespace or worse. Then, they could negatively impact functions of realspace - like time and place - rendering swaths of our native dimension unnavigable, no longer accessible, or who-knows-what."

"Which could turn truly nasty," said Tol, "if the breakdown of reality as we know it creates an end to functions necessary to living."

"Which could lead," Zya took up, "to the end of life in this dimension as we know it. A breakdown of reality with that sort of impact on realspace could potentially destroy everything we know."

"That's a hell of a doomsday scenario," remarked Sara.

"Worst case scenario," said Galit.

"Which is what we all want to avoid," added Darius. "It certainly makes all our petty squabbles pale by comparison, no?"

"The end of reality as we know it?" asked Aya. "Yeah, that might be huge."

Before anyone could say anything further, an unusual tone sounded.

"That's... Well, that's impossible," said Sara.

"What is it?" asked Aya.

"A single signal override of all communications channels," replied Sara. "Chatter, medianet, data, you name it, it's being overridden."

"Huh," Galit breathed. "Only the Sanket or the Syndicate can do that."

"What?" asked Darius. Before he could ask about what she meant, a hologram appeared as a transmission began.

"I apologize for this interruption of all transmissions on all frequencies and all channels across realspace, but this is a matter of the utmost importance to all sentient life across our galaxy. I am the new Grand Master of the Universal Energy Ontologies, and it is part of my sacred duty to make all of you, across all of the territories and races of known space, aware of a terrible threat to life as we know it."

Darius watched as the Grand Master shared everything they had uncovered about savagespace, the mindflayers, their monsters, and the threat they represented to all life across the known galaxy. A separate datastream was also broadcasting, sharing the relevant information. He noted that the Grand Master was in no way accusatory of either the Federation or the drow for their role in creating the problem at hand.

"Closing these rifts in space/time will, in the short term, prevent further incursions into our dimension by the chaos-and-destruction-bent denizens of savagespace," said the Grand Master. "But the greater, long-term threat of rifts in space/time such as these are a breakdown of reality as we know it. The consequences of which may be too terrible to express in meaningful terms.

"For this reason, I am sharing the information we have on this threat across all channels and to all races. The need to work together against this terrible threat is like nothing the residents of realspace have ever known before. Even the AI Awakening, the last such threat to impact all life, was not as potentially dangerous and destructive as this. And we must face it together to preserve life of all kinds across our diverse territories, philosophies, and everything else."

The Grand Master paused and nodded to their audience. "May the energies of the Universe guide ours to the right and proper course. Thank you."

The transmission ended. A moment later, Tol said, "The override signal is gone."

"It would be," said Galit softly. "That had to be the work of the Syndicate."

"What?" asked Sara.

REVELATIONS AND RECONCILIATIONS

Darius felt it wasn't important. "I wonder," he mused aloud, "if the Grand Master's presentation, visible across all communications, will cause the mindflayers to operate more openly. Now everyone is aware they're here."

"Possible," said Galit.

"By the same token," started Aya, "I wonder how this will change the operations of the Federation and the drow, if at all?"

"The drow are a great many uncomplimentary things," said Kaz. "But they are a people who believe in science and reason."

"The ambitions of the Federation, though..." remarked Sara, not bothering to finish the thought.

Darius agreed that the Federation was a source of uncertainty. They were also outside of the *Moon Raven*'s concern at present. But before he commented on that, Galit said, "Whether the mindflayers pursue their goals more vehemently and openly or not isn't something we can do anything about. But it reinforces that we need to succeed in working out where they're gathering."

As if Galit's words had been the cue, it appeared that a wormhole was opening, as space erupted like a volcano into a ring of distortion that appeared cloud-like, with a shimmering blackness streaked by flashes of light like a lightning storm at its center. It was several hundred thousand kilometers to starboard of the *Moon Raven* but was setting off numerous alarms.

"Damn," remarked Aya.

"Everyone stay sharp," said Darius, silencing the alarms. He counted fifteen unsettling starships with a hammerhead fore and unusual protrusions at the very front that almost stuck out like tentacles. With them were monstrous beings Darius could scarcely believe he was seeing. Two dragons, a huge basilisk, and three wyverns. They were far larger than the hammerhead starships.

"I dearly hope your stealth tech is working," said Sara softly.

"*Phantom*?" Galit queried her starship's powerful AI aloud.

"Stealth systems are functioning optimally," said the neutral-toned AI.

"They don't appear to be heading this way at all," added Kaz.

After several tense seconds passed, the rift closed. Darius watched between the combined *Phantom*/*Moon Raven* sensors as the hammerhead starships and monsters gathered together in a formation and began to fly further into deep space.

"Looks like they didn't notice us," commented Sara, breaking the tense silence.

"Let's use this to our advantage," said Galit. Darius felt her eyes on him as she said, "Captain, I suggest we follow and see where they go."

"Agreed," said Darius. "Kaz, you know what to do."

Chapter 24 - Revisions

It was a sensation both unfamiliar and unwanted. Ilizeva had watched the interrupt broadcast from the new Grand Master. Though they looked different, Ilizeva recognized the monk master that had been at the late Grand Master's side when they'd addressed the Synod. Yet that half-elf woman was changed. She was no longer a woman, but the unmistakably gender-neutral Grand Master of the UEO, and their message had caused the feeling Ilizeva was pondering.

She stood alone on the observation deck of the *Nuummite Raptor*, ostensibly looking out the observation port at the stars and other ships of her fleet. But her eyes were not focused on anything. In her mind, she was analyzing the uncomfortable, unfamiliar feeling she was having. Distress? Little truly distressed Ilizeva. Frustration? Meditation and other methods had long ago brought that sensation to an easy point of control.

Someone entered the observation deck and quietly made their way to stand at Ilizeva's side. It was the only person who would not get chewed out or summarily dismissed for intruding on her.

"What's troubling you, General?" Colonel Ulozov asked. It was not subordinate to a superior officer but the question of a friend and confidant. Ulozov knew her well. That was probably the reason he was the only one who could disturb her when she was desirous of time alone for contemplation outside of meditation.

"At first, I was distressed that the Grand Master had some means by which to undermine and override interplanetary communications," Ilizeva said. "What's more, I suspect it was not so much that the Grand Master and the UEO have that ability but more likely something the sorcerers have in their bags of tricks. Perhaps the Synod should consider closer ties to the Syndicate of Thaumaturgic Sciences."

Ulozov didn't respond. In all likelihood, he recognized that Ilizeva was talking her way through her emotions. "But no, that's not all that surprising," Ilizeva went on. "I suspect, given the oversight on the part of the Syndicate, this is not a tool they use lightly and without needful cause. And this message is certainly needful cause."

Again, Ulozov didn't respond. He simply listened. Ilizeva continued, "My concerns about the mindflayers and their various monsters are now backed by much broader facts. An unintended consequence of technology we never could have anticipated. I wonder if the creators of those AI that eventually awakened ever dreamed of ill consequences from that?"

Then the sensation she had been unable to put a name to was clear. Guilt. Ilizeva had prided herself on her life choices and control. While things had happened to her along the way, guilt had been naught but fleeting. It had always been a sensation she could take ahold of and release at will.

This came with a different, unique sense to it. "So many millennia, so many great minds of so many different races," Ilizeva mused. "The elves, dwarves, drow... Maybe even the genasi and tieflings before they moved apart from the races of this galaxy. But it was the humans that figured out the code, the math, the science to traverse space and time instantaneously by folding it. A tool we've all wanted for so long, with so much possibility."

Ilizeva paused and was gratified that Ulozov remained silent. She went on. "I was leading the charge to oversee the ultimate ambition of our people. The drow would finally show the elves that we were not now - nor had we ever been - inferior to them. We helped crack that code, and we would use that technology to make them pay for the disrespect, the abuse, and the torture they put the drow through when we still acknowledged ourselves to be dark elves.

"Sun, moon, and stars were never unequal. But dark? Dark elves were always the lesser. And until we took to the stars and created our independence we were under their boots. But this new tool was our opportunity. We would have our revenge. We'd strike in a way they couldn't resist and wouldn't see coming. And it has been so, so sweet."

Ilizeva began to pace. Still, Ulozov was silent, letting her get it out of her system as she said, "The consequences of our actions were not something we could have anticipated. How were we to know that we had torn the fabric of space/time and blurred the division of dimensions, letting the mindflayers and monsters into realspace? We'd not even heard of savagespace before this began. But here we are, knowing that this is a threat to all life in the galaxy. It's bigger than the drow and our revenge against the elves. Bigger than the Federation and their petty need for dominance over humankind. The risk

REVELATIONS AND RECONCILIATIONS

is too great, and we cannot undo what has been done. However, we can proceed with caution and foreknowledge from here."

Ilizeva stopped her pacing and turned to face Ulozov. "After seeing that interrupt broadcast from the Grand Master, I've been going over the data included as a sub-transmission with it. Though I remain greatly concerned about the issues that these extradimensional invaders and their monsters represent, I can see that it's a result of the problem that still requires a solution to truly be dealt with."

Ulozov nodded. "Yes, General. I've looked over that data as well. And I expect your primary concern, the 'problem' requiring a solution now, is closing those rifts. Which must occur to stop the terrors of savagespace from invading our dimension, as well as further damaging space/time and reality in the form of realspace."

"Yes," agreed Ilizeva. She began to pace again as she worked through her thoughts. "Neither the humans of the Federation nor the drow could have done this without one another. But I do not know that we can count on the Federation to redirect their scientists to work on this new problem. And closing the rifts in space/time that folding created will take more than our knowledge of power sources."

"Indeed," Ulozov said. "Colonel Orizevi last reported that General Song is now out somewhere in deep space, doing as we did to see if the mindflayers use the rifts to come to realspace."

Ilizeva felt a moment of concern. "The drow fleet assigned to the Federation is not with Song's forces?"

Ulozov shook his head. "No. Orizevi has reported that the Superior Convocation explicitly ordered Song to exclude all non-Federation forces."

Ilizeva frowned. "Be honest, Colonel Ulozov. Do you believe that the Federation's forces are a match for the mindflayers and their monsters?"

"No," Ulozov responded. But he held up a finger and said, "However, General Song is no fool. Orizevi shared your report with Song, and he took a larger fleet of Federation starships than he normally commands himself. It makes the odds more even. And his new second, General Anwar, is with him."

"And his drow guards?"

"Yes, them too," said Ulozov.

"We wait and see what happens then," said Ilizeva, but she felt the pang of another displeasing emotion. Concern for someone she respected deeply.

"I suspect, General, that I know the larger problem you're contemplating," said Ulozov. Ilizeva turned to face him again as he said, "If we cannot count on the Federation scientists to act in the best interests of the greater good, there's only one place we can turn. The only people in the galaxy who have nearly similar knowledge of power sources, as well as the scientific minds to utilize them and the Federation's calculations to work out how to close the rifts. The elves."

She couldn't help the sigh that escaped her lips. "Yes. The elves. But this poses many difficulties."

Ulozov stated, "Yes. First and foremost, we've been launching unprovoked, unstoppable attacks against the elves to enact our vengeance since we unlocked the secret to folding space/time."

Ilizeva turned back towards the viewport, silent a moment as she pondered the turmoil in her heart and mind. Then, she said, "Yes, that's an almost insurmountable problem. Our separation from the sun, moon, and star elves came about, what, six millennia ago? For nearly six-thousand galactic standard years, we have been dark elves no more, but drow. We're of the same blood, but we've chosen not to identify as elves for uncounted generations. Enacting our racial vengeance has been a long time coming, but that sweet taste has turned to ash in light of what we now know."

"Hence, the difficult question at the heart of all your pondering," said Ulozov. "Can we work this out without the elves?"

Ilizeva was silent for a time, alone in her thoughts. Then, she said, "If there is no other option, perhaps. If Doctor Shah and her team allow the reason of science to take precedence over the desires of the Federation – or the leaders choose to end their conquest and abandon what they've started in the Confederation – then yes. Song will agree. But the Triad, the three families leading the Federation? They're greedy. I suspect they will remain a problem."

"Indeed," remarked Song.

"What's more," Ilizeva continued, "based on the data from the Grand Master, once we work out the tools to close the rifts that folding space/time has caused, we shall need to build quickly, purposefully, and skillfully.

REVELATIONS AND RECONCILIATIONS

Even if we have the Federation scientists, we'll need other help. It may be unavoidable to enlist the aid of the elves. And based on the information we have, I believe we shall need to involve the dwarves, too."

Ulozov seemed to consider his words, before he said, "While I agree it would help to have the Federation scientists see reason, we both know their leadership isn't likely to follow. You need to act and not await them. Thus, I know that you are resolved to reach out to the elves, because the greater good of all of us, all lives in the galaxy, is a matter of honor that cannot be neglected for our racial need to make them pay."

Ilizeva appreciated that he had said what she was finding difficult to articulate. Ulozov asked, "Have you any idea how to do that?"

Ilizeva nodded at her reflection in the viewport and said, "Yes, Colonel. But first I shall need to go to the Synod."

Chapter 25 – Expectations

"No!" General Song called out. "*Destiny, Warhammer,* and *Dissonant Spite,* remain in formation with *Hammer of Harmony* and concentrate all weapons on the hammerhead starships at mark five, six point one. All other ships, only focus on the dragons and monsters if a direct threat. Primary targets are the hammerhead starships."

It was chaotic, and Song regretted not having the drow, hobgoblins, or trolls along to help. They'd taken several losses, and even the *Hammer of Harmony* was damaged. What's more, there were multiple reports across the fleet of mass distress and an utter lack of clarity and focus. Song attributed that to the psionic attacks Ilizeva had warned them about.

Humans were particularly vulnerable to psionic influence. The only reason it hadn't been worse was information Orizevi had shared regarding energy shield modulations that would provide a modicum of disruption to the mental assault. How energy shields could impact psionics was beyond Song's understanding. He was grateful for it, but the psionic attacks were complicating matters and slowing everyone down. His own head was throbbing.

The screens showed Song that their prey were now in range. "Fire, fire, fire," Song ordered.

Synchronized pulse cannons, torpedoes, and missiles lanced out toward the hammerhead starships. The concentrated firepower of four Federation warships did their work, and the trio of targets were disabled or destroyed.

"Three hammerhead ships left," a technician called out. "One dragon. The rest are heading away."

"Stop the hammerheads still here. Let the rest go," ordered Song. "*Destiny* and *Warhammer,* stay with us and move on the remaining dragon. *Dissonant Spite,* peel off to join *Ambusher's* group and help with those hammerheads."

"Yes, sir," called out a communication's officer.

Song expected that attacking the dragon might drive it away while the rest of the Federation forces finished off the mindflayer's hammerhead starships.

REVELATIONS AND RECONCILIATIONS

He glanced towards General Anwar. Though she wore a stolid look on her face, Song could tell by the way she held herself, in addition to a recurrent twitch in her left hand, that she was not handling the unknown as well as she tried to project.

As the *Hammer of Harmony* shifted course, the massive flank of the impossible beast came into view. The dragon was a surreal sight to behold.

"Fire everything!" called Song.

SPCs, torpedoes, and missiles lanced out from the trio of warships. The energy blasts appeared to have little impact, while the torpedoes and missiles seemed to distress the monster. It veered away from its attempt to flank the *Ambusher's* group, leaving five Federations starships bearing down on the last three mindflayer ships unharassed.

"Let it go," Song ordered. He observed that none of the monsters had been killed and were flying off into space.

Then, just like that, it was over. The distressful sensation of something pressing against the inside of Song's skull vanished as the last mindflayer ships were destroyed. Barely a few moments had passed before Song ordered, "Get me a full report. Damage assessments and casualties."

"Yes, General."

A perfunctory look at the sensors told Song it had not been an easy victory. He could feel in the deck plates below his feet that the *Hammer of Harmony* was damaged.

Half an hour before the rift had opened, Song had witnessed the interrupt transmission from the new Grand Master of the UEO. It had come as no surprise to him and he'd ordered all his fleet to take battlestations, awaiting the mindflayers. That had probably been the only thing that saved them from greater destruction. Without hesitation, they'd started to attack the mindflayers as they'd emerged from the rift.

"General," called the colonel who served as *Hammer of Harmony's* captain. "Fleetwide casualties are still being counted, but all our ships took at least minor damage. Four are a total loss, three will need to perform some comprehensive repairs before they can clear this area, and it's looking like the *Diamondback* might also be a loss. They're assessing repairability now."

Song didn't reply. He'd brought twenty starships in his fleet. A quarter were destroyed, and none had gotten out of the fight unscathed. It was not a good sign. It was also only because of his tactics that they had three-quarters still remaining. However, he knew that would not matter in the eyes of the Superior Convocation and the Triad.

When he had seen those monsters come through the rift, it had been horrifying. Song had seen more than his fair share of damage and destruction in combat. Yet nothing had prepared him for the sheer alienness of mindflayers and their other-dimensional monsters.

"Colonel, carry on with assessments," Song ordered. "We prepare to head home in thirty galactic standard minutes with everyone who can go."

"Yes, sir."

Song turned his attention to Aneesa. It didn't surprise him that her eyes were already on him.

"Well done, General," she led with a compliment. "You showed those interlopers that they are no match for the might of the Federation."

Song shook his head, a soft, humorless chuckle escaping his lips. "That's a good, well-practiced line, General. But the truth is, that was not a fight favorable to us. We outnumbered them, yet were hard-pressed to best them. Given how many got away, they proved themselves to be a force we would be best off not having to deal with again anytime soon."

Aneesa cocked her head to one side, then said. "You think our forces were outmatched?"

Song gestured towards the viewport and the damaged starships without. "Look around you, General. Yes, we were outmatched, but not outfought. And what would you have done in my place?"

Aneesa gave him a cold look but said nothing in response. After a time, she nodded her head ever-so-slightly, either acknowledging or dismissing the conversation. Then said, "What do you intend to do now?"

"We have proof that folding space/time has had unintended consequences," stated Song. "And the Grand Master's broadcast has alerted everyone, everywhere, to the threat. I know that the Superior Convocation and the Triad will not like it, but I must recommend that we end our use of space/time folding technology."

"You are correct, General," said Aneesa. "They won't like it."

"We have no choice," said Song. He gestured again towards the viewport and the remains of a mindflayer starship drifting past. "They are a powerful

REVELATIONS AND RECONCILIATIONS

threat, to not just us, but everyone in the galaxy. The goals of the Triad for the future of the Federation are admirable, but in light of this new data and the very real threat to life across the galaxy, we must adjust that."

"What would you do, have the Federation stop its manifest destiny with the former Alliance territories?" questioned Aneesa.

"They're easily reached via unrealspace," replied Song. "And focusing all our attention on the former Alliance territories will allow us to strengthen ourselves in numerous ways."

Aneesa shook her head. "No, General. But you are correct. The Superior Convocation and the Triad will not only dislike your recommendation, but they will reject it. They plan to rule all of human space, and they will not back down when they have the means to that end in hand."

"Yes, of course," replied Song. He glanced towards his ever-present pair of drow bodyguards, preparing to signal them to restrain Aneesa. He had known this day might come, especially in light of the anticipated outcome of this mission.

"But, General Anwar," Song continued, "ignoring a threat to the whole galaxy, which is a result of our use of this fantastic technology, will not open the way to the future that the Triad desires. We cannot ignore the warnings of even more dire consequences as presented by the Grand Master just to achieve dominance over the other human territories. We must change our tactics."

"Yes, General Song. I could not agree more. We must change our tactics," Aneesa said.

All hell broke loose in the *Hammer of Harmony's* combat information center. As Song turned to signal the drow, both were being overwhelmed. Half a dozen NCOs, who should not have been in the CIC, were upon them with blades. Despite being capable and agile fighters, even the drow could only do so much when caught unaware. They were dead before they could help him.

Before he could take action, Song found himself frozen in place. A captain, the officer nearest Song, was holding the grip of a statis beam, a short-range weapon designed to disrupt the nervous system and lock the joints of a single individual. It was commonly employed by Federation and other human police forces.

Aneesa approached Song, throwing a glance towards the felled drow. She declared, "General Thomas Song, you have proven time and again that you are an excellent strategist and skilled tactician. And your concern for the greater good does you credit. But the Triad comes first, and your recommendation is summarily rejected."

Song didn't bother to hide the sneer in his tone. "I knew this day would come, Aneesa Anwar. The moment they forced you on me as my Second, I knew you would find any excuse to take my place."

He tried to move his head and glare as he angrily said, "You think loyalty to General Anwar is worth betraying me? Any reward she offered you won't be worth a damn when she gets you killed."

Song's tone cooled as he continued, "How did you like your first real combat today, huh? Not the same when we're not the aggressor, is it? I saw you barely restraining yourself from talking flight and abandoning the CIC to hide. You have no real understanding of tactics or strategy, and blindly grasp at the false promises my predecessor made. Folding space/time is not the end-all-be-all advantage the Triad believe it to be. We are still equally matched on many levels and outmatched on many others."

"You never did believe in the mission, did you, General?" questioned Aneesa with a false sweetness that set Song's teeth on edge. "I've always believed that you cared only for your personal gain and survival."

Song laughed at that. "You have no idea what you're in for, Aneesa Anwar. You're beyond not ready to assume command of Federation forces. I guarantee if you follow through on your intent and remove me, while it will lead to your rise, ultimately, It will end not just with your fall, but the Federation's fall."

Aneesa stood immediately before Song. Had he not been restrained, he could have strangled her. He looked into her eyes, showing her no fear.

"I believe, Thomas Song, that you're wrong," she said softly.

He knew whatever else he said didn't matter. "You have no idea what you're in for. You think what they did to General Mallick was troubling? I'm sorry I won't be there to see what becomes of you. Go ahead and kill me, Aneesa Anwar. But at least then the downfall of the Federation won't be in any way my fault."

REVELATIONS AND RECONCILIATIONS

He watched as she hesitated, but it was no surprise when she withdrew a blade from up a sleeve and swept it across his throat. The pain from his skin being torn open passed quickly, but he felt his life draining out with his blood.

Song stared into Aneesa's eyes as he felt himself slipping away. With his last thought, he felt satisfaction when he saw fear flicker across her face. The world went still and silent, and then it all went black.

Chapter 26 – Pursuit

Darius had never been a fan of hopping or skipping, depending on your preferred term, but the only way that the *Moon Raven* could keep up was to open a portal into unrealspace, cross to the faster-than-light travel dimension, fly for under two galactic standard minutes, then portal back to realspace and reacquire their targets. Fortunately for Darius, Kaz was a phenomenal pilot. Additionally, *Phantom*, riding piggyback, didn't impact the *Moon Raven*'s capabilities.

The problem began when the mindflayer's hammerhead starships somehow accelerated away. They'd been too far for visual confirmation, but it had been quite clear on *Moon Raven*'s sensors and scanners.

"How is that possible?" Aya asked.

"Did they open a portal?" Darius questioned.

"No," Sara replied. "No readings of any portals. Maybe they did some sort of phase shift? I've just no idea. But they clearly accelerated."

"I'm still tracking the residual dimensional energy," Galit said. "And I can confirm that they've accelerated."

"Faster than light?" Tol questioned. "Given that the monsters are flying faster than light speed, but slower than the starships, that's the only explanation."

"Unless there is some other," Zya added. "Perhaps they have a means to get to another dimension, akin to our portaling from realspace to unrealspace?"

"We'll analyze the data," Tol concluded.

The *Moon Raven* had already been hopping, because even at their best speed, they were falling behind the dragons and other monsters from savagespace. Prolonged travel at full speed drained fuels and created unnecessary wear on engines and power systems, limiting how long it could be done. Even at full speed, it was well shy of the speed of light.

Darius expressed some concern about exposing their pursuit to the mindflayers via the opening and closing of portals. Galit assured him that the mindflayers were too far ahead and the dragons and other monsters lacked

REVELATIONS AND RECONCILIATIONS

the intelligence to notice them, especially with as far behind as the *Moon Raven* remained.

Before the monsters had gotten as far ahead as they were, the *Moon Raven* crew had run every scan they could on them. It confirmed that they were living creatures, somehow capable of existing in the vacuum. An analysis of data showed that they had many unfamiliar internal organs and their hides were comprised of both familiar and utterly alien elements. They were, however, undeniably, living creatures.

After a full galactic standard day had passed, the crew took turns resting. Kaz may have been their best pilot, but Galit was also capable and allowed Kaz to rest by taking time in the pilot's nest. Darius also spent a couple of hours at the controls, but he never felt entirely comfortable piloting.

The rest of the crew had come and gone, catching rest, studying data they'd been collecting along the way, and observing the ongoing pursuit. By the third galactic standard day, Tol, Zya, and Galit had a working theory for how the mindflayers might travel faster than light.

⇔⇔⇔

"We began with what we know of wormholes," Galit explained. "We know that wormholes tunnel across savagespace, connecting two disparate points in realspace."

"You don't think they've worked out some way to similarly tunnel across savagespace, do you?" Sara asked.

"No," Tol replied. "Since we know they cannot access those tunnels, it's not likely they'd associate them with a means of faster-than-light transit."

"Which presumes other matters," Galit remarked. "Even with the data we got during our foray with the Grand Master, most details of the workings of savagespace remain a mystery. We don't know what kinds of worlds the mindflayers occupy, if they have suns lighting them, or how the dragons and other creatures coexist with them, and/or anyone similar in savagespace."

"This gives me a headache," Aya remarked.

"When we looked at the data," Zya begun, "we became completely certain that they didn't create any portals or wormholes or other known means to extradimensional travel. We are working on a rather wild theory for what they've done, however."

"I can hardly wait for this," Aya said. Darius threw her a look but still appreciated her need to add levity to the discussion.

"One thing we suspect," Galit said, "is that savagespace is darker and wilder than realspace or unrealspace. Because wormhole faster-than-light transit is rare, due to its limitations, we have only the vaguest ideas of the dimension beyond the tunnel. However, mathematical simulations have calculated that where realspace is primarily dark with bodies reflecting light, and unrealspace is primarily multicolored with dim echoes of those same bodies, savagespace is primarily dark with irregular pulses of light, akin to lightning."

"How can life, like any of our races, exist without light?" Sara questioned.

"Light may still exist in Savagespace," Galit replied. "But the degree of light they need might vary. Take orcs and bugbears, for example. They prefer dimmer light than other races, and in fact thrive in such situations."

"This just confirms everything about savagespace is utterly alien to us," Kaz said.

"Working on exactly that notion," Tol began, "based on reading some of the more obscure tomes we acquired beneath the abandoned temple, and delving into unusual theorems that are rather cryptic, but in this context have relevance, we think we have an answer."

Before Darius could ask what it was, Zya stated, "We believe they're traveling at the speed of dark."

"Say what now?" Aya questioned.

Darius found himself taken aback by that. "Dark has a measurable speed? Isn't it simply the absence of light?"

"Yes and no," Galit said. "You're correct that darkness is the absence of light. But the universe is made up of dark matter. Vast, incalculable amounts of it. Every race throughout their entire history of the study of physics still cannot fully explain this. Suffice it to say, we haven't any idea of the how of their flight, just a hypothesis based on observation."

"Headache increasing," Aya said. "What observation could have led you to that conclusion?"

"The mindflayers had been at the edge of our primary sensor range," Zya replied. "So, we got detailed readings on the transit when they accelerated

REVELATIONS AND RECONCILIATIONS

away. From that data, we were able to extrapolate a visual representation of their acceleration."

They called up a 3D image of the mindflayer hammerhead starships, dragons, and other monsters. Darius watched in total fascination as the hammerhead starships seemed to dim, fading into the background before accelerating at impossible speeds.

"There is no way that the *Moon Raven*'s systems could have modeled that," Sara remarked.

"Correct," Galit said. "This is part of my ship's AI datacore."

"Wild," Sara remarked.

"Based on this," Tol continued, "whatever this phasing they have done is, it allows them to travel faster than our calculations of the speed of light. Likewise, the monsters are maintaining an impossible speed in relation to light in realspace that traveling at the speed of dark could explain."

Darius shook his head. As part of his military service, he'd been required to know elements of advanced physics regarding velocity and maneuvering in space. That knowledge helped with understanding why firing a missile or torpedo could be challenging if the ship were traveling at high velocity. No matter how fast you accelerated, nobody had reached lightspeed without relativistic effects. Faster-than-light travel had only been made possible because of the ability to portal from realspace to unrealspace.

"Aren't the physics of this entirely impossible?" Kaz asked.

"Yes," Galit agreed, "in our dimension. In realspace. But the physics of unrealspace differ in many ways from those of realspace. It's easy to presume that's equally true of any and probably all other dimensions."

"The physics the mindflayers know from savagespace work in realspace?" Sara questioned.

"Probably not unlike realspace versus unrealspace," Zya said.

"This is crazy," Aya remarked.

"Less so than you realize," Galit said. "Long before humans reached interstellar space, research had gone into studying the notion of darkspeed versus lightspeed. It's extremely obscure research, and I only know the gist of it from information probably only cyberwizards and the UEO possess. But it all got dismissed as speculative and not worth the effort to research after less than a few decades of study. It was around this time that they worked out portal generators for starships, making passage between realspace and unrealspace accessible beyond the stable portal gates."

"How old is that?" Aya asked.

"In the neighborhood of six millennia," Galit replied. "Once transit between the known dimensions became regular, all other attempts at faster-than-light travel or alternates like faster-than-dark travel, were almost completely abandoned."

"But," Zya interjected, "in an alternate dimension with rules unlike realspace or unrealspace, high-velocity travel of a nature utterly alien to all of us is, theoretically possible." That closed the discussion, but Darius found himself sharing Aya's headache.

Almost another three galactic standard days had passed. The crew were all at their stations on the command deck. Darius felt the tension mingling with boredom brought on by the monotony of irregular unrealspace hopping and sensors coming up with the same findings: nothing ahead, save the monsters.

Darius was skimming through one of the more obscure tomes the AI had been protecting. No new data came to light that served their purpose, but it was something to pass the time.

"That's new," Sara called out.

Darius tapped a display to see what it was Sara had been observing as Aya said, "What?"

The trace signals that the mindflayer ships had left behind, the odd, other-dimensional energy, was reading more strongly at the edge of their sensor range.

"Yes," Galit remarked. "It does appear that we're getting the signatures again."

"I think the monsters are slowing down," said Tol.

Darius switched to look at the same display Tol had up. "Yeah, I can see how it looks that way."

A pair of alarms sounded, neither of which Darius had ever heard before. "What in the starry void is that?" questioned Aya.

REVELATIONS AND RECONCILIATIONS

One of the alarms ceased, and a moment later, so did the other. Galit said, "That's the detection of a very rare and very dangerous dense form of gravity."

"How do you know that?" asked Aya.

"The alarms were from both *Phantom* and *Moon Raven*," Galit replied. "And I know *Phantom*'s still-working passive genasi systems. One detects this kind of gravity well and gives a warning because it's particularly dense."

"Like a black hole?" asked Tol.

"Not exactly," said Galit. "Something far more rare and infinitely more unpredictable. There's a dark star out there."

"Dark star?" asked Darius.

"Very, very rare," said Zya.

"Indeed," agreed Galit. "And in addition to being quite rare, their gravitational pull is highly unpredictable. But they can be detected by a unique form of radiation they emit. There is a theory that a dark star in this dimension is a mirrored bleed of a more conventional star in another dimension. Which is why the genasi have the ability to detect them."

"Kaz, all stop," said Darius.

"Yeah, good idea," replied Kaz.

"Wish we had probes or something," said Sara. Then, she added, "Galit, can *Phantom*'s AI detect the edge of the gravity well so we can maybe get closer?"

"Yes, but no," replied Galit. "That's the other problem dark stars represent. Unlike the detectable, relatively stable event horizon of a black hole, the safe distance in regards to a dark star fluctuates."

"I'm thinking we're as close as we should get," said Darius. "We hold here."

"That's a good idea," commented Aya.

"If the dragons and other monsters are slowing," added Galit, "then it's highly probable we've found what we've come looking for."

Darius looked at the sensors, and even knowing nothing was visible, he looked out the viewport. Somewhere out there, nearby, the mindflayers and their monsters were gathering in realspace.

Chapter 27 – Parlay

Ilizeva hated the discomfort her current position represented. She wasn't on her starship, or any starship, for that matter. She wasn't even in drow space. What's more, Ilizeva was thoroughly out of her comfort zone. She was a soldier, not a diplomat.

The planet Baatkerna was in neutral space, fairly equidistant from drow and elf space. It was a world that was ninety percent water, with thirteen islands scattered around the globe just north and south of the equator.

The various islands of Baatkerna featured some of the best agricultural opportunities within hundreds of lightyears, as well as vacation spots and resorts renowned across the galaxy. It was considered one of the most neutral worlds in space, as well. No government had ever laid claim to it, and the UEO had a temple and a monastery, while the Syndicate had a school there.

It had been through the UEO that the Synod had requested a parlay with their elf counterpart. The response had come back that they had agreed to meet somewhere neutral, and the UEO temple on Baatkerna was the perfect place.

Ilizeva had initially intended to fly the drow Synod diplomatic representative to the meeting aboard the *Nuummite Raptor*. Per the agreement with the elves, it would be the only warship they brought. However, the Synod had insisted that Ilizeva escort their representative. When she expressed the many reasons she felt it was not in anyone's best interest that she attend, the Synod ceased to insist and instead demanded her attendance.

Ilizeva glanced toward her companion, Alizev Kaen'baer. The educator would not have been Ilizeva's top choice, but that didn't mean he was without the proper qualities a diplomat might need in such a delicate situation.

Ilizeva stood across from the entryway to the chamber she and Alizev had been escorted to. He sat peacefully at the table near its center, reading from a docupad.

Upon arriving, the local monk master had escorted them to this chamber. Part of the agreement for this parlay had been each side would present only one ambassador and one companion, no guards, and no weapons.

Even disarmed, Ilizeva was enough of a capable fighter to still be dangerous if confronted. She worried that the elves would perform some sort of trickery. Maybe they'd set up the terms of their historic meeting to capture drow. Perhaps they would send a fleet to overwhelm the drow starship. Elves, Ilizeva knew, were not to be trusted.

Ulozov had orders to stand down unless the elves made an aggressive move first. When he reported a lone elf warship had arrived, Ilizeva told him to maintain his non-threatening position but fire on the elves if they did anything untoward.

The Colonel reported that the elf warship, like her own, had taken up a high orbit and launched a shuttle. It was flying true toward the UEO temple, showing no signs of aggression or other trickery. Ilizeva disliked the feeling of discomfort weighing down invisibly upon her. She again withdrew her own docupad, scanning over the little information they had about the sun elf delegation they'd be meeting.

Since his specialty as an educator had been elf history, Alizev was considered a foremost expert on elven affairs. Through a network of spies and other intelligence assets that the drow maintained, as a member of the Synod, Alizev stayed current on the elves while being mindful of their history. In part, it was Alizev's information on the current makeup of the elf Synod and overall social structure that had led to the choice of the sun elves for attack. Likewise, that was why they were chosen first for a parlay.

A human monk entered the chamber, and Alizev arose from his seat. A moment later, two elves walked in behind him. Like all the sun elves Ilizeva had seen, they had stunning, golden blonde hair, fair skin, and a presence Ilizeva couldn't identify that came across as somewhere between haughty and self-righteous.

The monk bowed and left the chamber.

The elves were silent. They looked at the drow, tension, concern, and uncertainty crossing their faces. Drow and elves had not met in any manner apart from combat in around six thousand years. Ilizeva could almost feel Alizev standing as stiffly as she.

"I am Sadiro Paon-sun'kiri, Synod representative," said the slightly shorter and older-appearing of the pair. "This is my page, Nitori Loun-sun'kiro."

"I am Alizev Kaen'baer, Synod representative. And this is General Ilizeva Taen'baer." She noted that Sadiro flinched at her name. Clearly, he knew who she was.

Sadiro recovered imperceptibly and said, "It's been millennia since sun elves and dark elves have met face-to-face."

"Drow, if you please," Alizev stated.

Sadiro frowned. "You do realize that 'drow' was a slur used to refer to the dark elves of old?"

"Yes," replied Ilizeva. She had been instructed not to speak unless directly addressed but couldn't help herself. She felt Sadiro's statement unnecessarily condescending. She continued, saying, "In the interest of no longer identifying with their tormentors, our progenitors chose to take your slur and use it as their new, unique identity."

Long before they'd unlocked unrealspace, the sun, moon, and star elves had been mostly of one mind. They had worked closely together, growing elf society and advancing all of their interests. They had also equally shunned, disregarded, and sometimes lashed out at the dark elves. Why? Because they were physically different from their counterparts.

The difference between skin and hair color of the sun, moon, and star elves was relatively subtle. It had been millennia since they had been truly divided. The variations in shades of blond to white hair, fair to pale skin, and eyes of blues and greens had largely been muddled as the three variations of elves had expanded their influence together.

All elves – sun, moon, star, and even dark – shared similar builds, overall shape of the ears and variations of pointiness, and life expectancies. Drow, however, looked nothing like their other sun, moon, and star elf counterparts. All drow had dark skin that was various shades of black, white to grey to nearly blue hair, and blue or brown eyes.

To Ilizeva's mind, the drow had ceased to be elves when they all left their home world to travel the stars some six thousand years ago.

Sadiro was silent for a time, and Alizev added nothing. Then, Sadiro said, "No matter what name you choose, you are still elves."

REVELATIONS AND RECONCILIATIONS

"Are we?" questioned Ilizeva. "Funny you should state such. When our kind lived together on the homeworld, all those long millennia ago, the sun, moon, and star elves constantly reminded us we were different. There's no slur to name any of your kind between you, but all of you called our kind drow. Your kind always dismissed our kind as lesser. So, once we all made our way to the stars, no effort was undertaken to include us among elvenkind."

Alizev added, "The memories are long. For even more millennia than before elves or drow went our separate ways and to separate worlds in the vastness of space, our people were repeatedly wounded by the rest of elven kind. Those ancient wounds run deep."

"From time immemorial, long before any of us - or countless generations before us - lived," stated Sadiro. "And what of the new wounds your kind have been inflicting upon our kind? If you intend that we address your wounds, do you intend to address ours?"

Ilizeva barked a laugh, and felt Alizev's eyes bore into her as she said, "Really, ambassador? Your wounds are a mere scratch in light of all that the sun, moon, and star elves inflicted upon the drow. They are well-deserved retribution."

"Is that so?" asked Sadiro. His calm, almost fatherly tone made Ilizeva feel as if her blood was beginning to boil. "Have I harmed you? And by you, I mean any dark elf? Apologies, drow? Have you or any of your companions been harmed in any way by another sun elf? A moon elf? A star elf?"

"It is a longtime racial matter, and retribution all the elves deserve for the countless hundreds of millennia 'drow' was an insult before we took it and made it our identity." Ilizeva's anger had been expressed as she practically spat out the last words. This was pointless.

She caught herself then. The purpose of this parlay had not been to hash out old grievances and countless lifetimes of persecution and anger. There was a threat to all life in the galaxy, and to address it, the drow needed the elves. "However," she held up a hand and amended, her tone calmer and neutral rather than antagonistic. "The reason for this parlay is not to address the matters between our kind, but rather something far deeper and of greater import. There is a matter before us too grave to ignore over ancient grudges."

"The new Grand Master's broadcast," stated Sadiro. "Yes, we are aware of this. Our scientists went over what data they could to determine how you succeeded in folding space/time. It comes as no surprise to us that rather than use this new technology you built for the greater good of the peoples of the galaxy, you used it to attack elvenkind. And then you learned there were unintended consequences for what you did. Our Synod does not know why you sought this parlay, but clearly it's been to trade insults. You created this problem without elves; you can fix it without elves."

"Ambassador," Alizev replied, likely attempting to intercept another hateful outburst from Ilizeva. "You are not wrong. Our scientists were who the Federation sought to help them make their theories of folding space/time working models, and when we both began to use that technology and fold space/time, we alone caused this problem and the rifts that allow the incursions from savagespace."

Alizev paused a moment, and Ilizeva remained silent. He went on to say, "While I am not wholly familiar with the specifics of the technology and the science, I do know that we have determined that we alone cannot effectively close the rifts that we inadvertently opened. We need assistance, and specifically assistance from those who have similar technologies to our own. Thus, we requested this parlay between us because, for the greater good of life across the whole galaxy, we need help from the elves."

Nobody spoke for a moment. The tension in the chamber was palpable. Then Sadiro said, "To what end? You've made it quite clear how you feel about elvenkind. You claim that now the greater good is under threat and that to resolve this you need your most hated enemy. How are we to know you speak with any truth or sincerity? How can we know that you won't just use this as an opportunity to learn our secrets then attack us again?"

"Ambassador," Ilizeva began.

"General," Alizev addressed her through gritted teeth.

She held up her hand to her colleague. She reached deep into the calmest places in her heart and soul, like she did when meditating, keeping her tone neutral and calm without malice, contempt, or any negative emotion. "Ambassador," Ilizeva began again. "Sadiro Paon-sun'kiri, I have not known a moment in my whole life when I was not told to hate elves. No child among drowkind, since the time long ago when we were, admittedly, one people, has been taught anything but hate and spite towards elves, be they sun, moon, or

REVELATIONS AND RECONCILIATIONS

stars. It is instilled in us all to the core of our being and has been that way since lifetimes long before our own.

"That is why, when we had the ability to show you that we had outgrown you in ways you could not meet or match, we used this new technology to attack and avenge ancient slights that were neither committed nor received by any who are still living."

She took a deep breath, then continued. "The danger that has come to pass resulting from our use of this technology is too great and too important to be ignored for petty, ancient, hateful grievances and spite. While I believed that the greatest single goal I could achieve in my lifetime would be to exact the vengeance on elvenkind that drowkind have sought for uncountable generations, I can admit that in the light of this new reality, I may have been wrong. Maybe the vengeance I've long believed to be the birthright of all drow is just petty, ancient history of little import."

Sadiro looked at her, and ever-so-slightly, the tension of his shoulders lessened, and his expression softened. "I'm impressed," he stated. "I did not believe you were anything but a warrior, Ilizeva Taen'baer. Your words give me hope that if you can see your need for vengeance as anything but your driving purpose, anything is possible. But this is only a first step. This conversation has convinced me that you are sincere in seeking our help for the greater good of all. And I am willing to go to the Synod and call on a greater assembly to convene between us to discuss these matters."

"With respect, Sadiro Paon-sun'kiri, I appreciate that," Ilizeva stated.

Sadiro said, "Ambassador Alizev, what if we request that General Ilizeva be punished for her attacks on our people?"

"This parlay was my idea," Ilizeva stated. "I came to the realization that the best chance we have of effectively closing the rifts we tore in the fabric of the reality of realspace requires the aid of elvenkind. I'd further point out that I took full responsibility for my actions in leading the drow forces in our attacks and immediately ended the folding of space/time when we learned the consequences. What I did was in service to my people and our deep-seated thirst to avenge our ancestors. But in light of a greater danger, I have set that aside and turned to the very people I've perceived as my enemy all my life. I believe that I have taken actions that are a step towards making amends."

"Ambassador Sadiro," started Alizev. "I know General Ilizeva is speaking the truth. It was she who requested we approach elvenkind to aid us for the greater good of all. We have come openhanded, and we ask that you consider our request with no further actions of animosity between us. That must include punishment for General Ilizeva as well."

Sadiro said nothing for a moment. His silent page looked between the two drow, then pointedly towards the sun elf ambassador. Sadiro began to nod. "Very well. Perhaps, Alizev Kaen'baer and Ilizeva Taen'baer, during the countless millennia our peoples have been apart, the drow have truly evolved beyond our reckoning of you."

Ilizeva couldn't help herself and grinned. She said, "That we have, Sadio Paon-sun'kiri. Perhaps, likewise, the elves have evolved beyond our reckoning of you. But hundreds and thousands of generations of animosity, persecution, hatred, and distrust on both sides are hard to let go of. And yet, here we are."

Chapter 28 – Dogma

Returning to Paxion and the temple in the city of Ta'one-nui had been a mixed experience. While on the one hand it was home, on the other it was all different now. When they had left, they'd been monk master Alisay Naun-moon'kari. They returned changed in utterly unexpected ways as the new Grand Master of the Universal Energies Ontology.

The Grand Master had collected their few belongs from their old cell. Most of their possessions were nothing more than clothing and toiletries. They had a painting a friend had created when they'd both been novices together long ago and a ring made of a gold and green mineral they'd been gifted by an ancient halfling they'd saved from drowning on a mission in their youth.

The cell of the Grand Master was only slightly larger. But it had an office, scriptorium, and a small conference room attached to it. Their predecessor had a few works of art that included a bonsai tree, a trio of sculptures made of a mineral they didn't recognize, and some truly impressive art on two of the walls.

The new Grand Master felt no need to remove these things and realized through the knowledge imparted via the pendant that their predecessor had added only the bonsai. Sometimes the Grand Master very much felt they had two distinct and separate lives. Which was partially true, since they carried the conscious awareness of all those who went before them and could access it at will at any time.

Their predecessor's body had been cremated. There was, much to their surprise, no formal ceremony to commemorate the passing of a Grand Master. To some degree, this was because only the body was lost. Thus, to all intents and purposes, the Grand Master never died.

For many reasons, this was not public knowledge. In truth, it wasn't knowledge that belonged to any but the Grand Master. It would, they knew, remain that way for time immemorial. That was just another secret belonging to the Universal Energies Ontology and their respective Grand Master.

They did need to address the membership of the UEO. First, however, a formal conversation with the other masters was necessary. So it was that the

Grand Master found themselves in the chamber, seated at the narrow "head" of the oval table.

Arrayed around it were numerous chairs and screens, so that all could see one another at the table. The other dozen masters who called the temple home were arranged around the table as well.

It was time. A chime sounded. It was an eerie, other-worldly chime, with a source none could pinpoint. The chime would signal to all that the masters were gathering in assembly and expected not to be disturbed.

As the ring of the chime started to fade out, the unoccupied seats around the table now had masters seated within them via hologram. Each master not in attendance at the temple of the Grand Master meditated in a holographic seat, projecting themselves to attend. The projected masters were very nearly as solid as those physically present.

With a few exceptions, all the masters of the UEO were present. It was clear that all of them had their eyes turned towards the new Grand Master.

Echoing every Grand Master to precede them, they said, "Thank you for answering the call. I would request the Assembly come to order." After a momentary pause, they said, "News travels fast, and it was not kept secret, but this is the first opportunity I've had to address you, as the masters of the UEO, in general. Clearly, the Grand Master we all knew and loved has been lost to us. With their passing, they named me to succeed them. The last time a Grand Master passed on was long before my time in the ontology, and I do not know if any of you have lived through such. Nobody was prepared for this loss. But then, are we ever?"

They paused. One or two heads were nodding, and they recognized older masters, who might have seen their predecessor take up the mantle. Or these masters were just more adaptable.

The Grand Master continued, "As you can see, I have been physically changed by assuming the mantle of the Grand Master. I assure you, I understand some of you will feel distraught about this entire situation and question why I have become Grand Master rather than another, more experienced master. All I can tell you is that this was as my predecessor intended. And I recognize that it's going to take a little time for everyone to get used to *me* in this role now."

REVELATIONS AND RECONCILIATIONS

The Grand Master looked around the table at the assembly. They saw multiple dubious looks, one or two clearly displeased and unpleasant looks, but largely acceptance. Not that it mattered. They knew that it was always the same whenever a new Grand Master was raised.

"That being addressed," the Grand Master began anew, "I wish to tell you how my predecessor left us. It was truly epic."

They shared the explanation of the lost temple that the Grand Master had been sent to by the genasi, the Blue Cyberwizard and the crew of the *Moon Raven* joining their quest into the catacombs, and the monsters they met there. They concluded by sharing the discovery of the AI, the data it had been protecting, and a recording it had made of the final fight that had ended the life of the previous Grand Master.

"In conclusion, the data we found was translated for us by the Blue Cyberwizard. We left the tomes in the catacombs where we found them. Despite this being a world long abandoned and well out of the way of most systems, I feel we should establish a new temple of the Universal Energies Ontology there. It will be occupied by only full scholars, guardians, and masters, rather than draw in new students or serve as a beacon of Universal Energies in the system. This temple will serve as a guardian for that living AI, to make certain it remains buried beneath the surface."

"With respect, Grand Master," said Cleric Master Dhunt, "what about the First Interplanetary Axiom? Isn't part of the duty of the UEO to enforce that?"

The Grand Master sighed. This, they knew, would be hotly debated. "Technically, yes. Just like our protection of the space/time continuum and barriers between dimensions, enforcing the First Interplanetary Axiom is equally important to protecting life. In principle, this living, fully realized and awakened AI should be destroyed."

"Then why did you not destroy it?" questioned cleric Master Fitz.

"The crew of the *Moon Raven*, the Blue Cyberwizard, and my predecessor all felt that it was not right to enforce the Axiom and destroy the AI."

"But, with respect, Grand Master," started cleric Master Diinaan, "the First Interplanetary Axiom is one of only three established, galactically accepted truths. Awakened AIs must be destroyed. Does it not go directly against the dogma of the UEO to leave an AI alive?"

"A fair point," agreed the Grand Master. "However, there's a deeper matter for consideration. The AI Awakening happened almost three thousand years ago. The destruction wrought by the awakened AI was terrible and threatened all life in the galaxy. The history of that was preserved by the UEO.

"For those less familiar, the awakening began when multiple races created increasingly powerful artificial intelligences and then utilized these to build more such machines. Despite controls built into them to revere and safeguard life, the intelligences that were building androids, and intelligences similar to themselves developed a new form of AI that allowed them to harm their creators. Fearing for their lives, they attacked and killed billions across the galaxy. But then the races joined together to stop them. The last of the living, awakened AI were destroyed, and the First Interplanetary Axiom was created to limit the sentience of AI going forward, as well as to see to the destruction of any remaining awakened AI to prevent another such catastrophe."

The Grand Master paused, noting all eyes on them. Then, they said, "The awakened AI we discovered has been hidden on a dead world for millennia. Rather than expand itself or continue the practices against sentient life the other awakened AI undertook, it's been hiding, lost to history. Hence, for the same reason the UEO opposes forces that seek only the destruction of life, I, and those who were with me, believe that this AI should be allowed to live, so long as it continues to remain hidden. And that's why the UEO needs an active temple atop its hiding place. If it ever chooses to act on more beyond its survival, we will be in a position to carry out the Axiom and end it."

After a moment of silence, cleric Master Timur said, "Given the First Interplanetary Axiom, Grand Master, do you not feel you're being rather cavalier with the lives of the peoples of the galaxy?"

"I understand this concern," the Grand Master replied. "But my companions, my predecessor, and I all agreed letting this AI continue to live was not a violation of the Axiom. It has hidden away and did no harm for millennia. Most of the defenses we encountered were placed to keep it hidden." They shifted their tone and continued before anyone spoke up.

REVELATIONS AND RECONCILIATIONS

"Monitoring a living, awakened AI that's kept itself hidden away from the galaxy at large is, in the face of a bigger problem, minor. The rifts in space/time resulting from the employment of folding it by the drow and Federation is a much more pressing concern."

"With respect, Grand Master," said cleric Master Diinaan, "what of it?"

"One of the primary duties of the Universal Energy Ontology clerics and monks is the preservation of life," said the Grand Master. "Life is under a threat like no other encountered before. You saw my transmission across the chatter and medianet. The mindflayers, dragons, wyverns, and other monsters of savagespace do not belong in realspace. They cannot be reasoned or bargained with. They evolve and grow through destruction. They are a threat that must be addressed."

"However," the Grand Master changed their tone again. "The primary concern to the interests of the UEO are the rifts in space/time themselves. As a consequence, walls between dimensions beyond those we know – realspace, unrealspace, savagespace, and those the genasi and tieflings call home – potentially weakening via those rifts threatens the physical, scientific galactic reality."

"With respect, Grand Master, what does that mean?" asked a monk master the Grand Master hadn't identified.

"The nature of this dimension has certain physical determinations on the subatomic level that form our reality as we collectively know it. Individual realities and understanding of the universe via chi and Universal Energies not withstanding, the rifts caused by folding space/time could undo the fabric of reality in unpredictable and increasingly destructive ways."

"Are you suggesting, Grand Master," began monk Master Saaviiv, "that the rifts could break down the workings of the physics of realspace and break apart the elements that allow life of all kinds to flourish within it?"

"Not simply suggesting, Master Saaviiv. Stating," said the Grand Master. "This is the threat that the UEO must do all that we can to guard against. In those catacombs, on that long-abandoned world, the genasi knew we would find those texts that show how to close the rifts. The data recovered in the tomes found therein are in the hands of those who have the power to take those actions."

"With respect, Grand Master," interjected cleric Master Fitz, "what more can the guardians and scholars do for this crisis?"

"We must research these tomes ourselves," said the Grand Master. "There, we can learn both how to close those rifts and help those with the technology to do so. And we can learn if there is information for how to destroy the mindflayers and other monsters of savagespace that have found their way to realspace."

"Begging your pardon, Grand Master," said monk Master Lochan, "isn't assisting in murdering sentient life counter to our dogma?"

"When it comes to the life of the creatures of this dimension, the genasi, tieflings, and the benign life of unrealspace, you would be correct," replied the Grand Master. "But mindflayers and their monsters do not belong in this reality, in realspace. What's more, they are here for one and only one purpose: destruction. It's how they grow and evolve. To do that, they will destroy everyone they encounter. They will not negotiate, will not accept surrender; they will only destroy all life. Death and devastation are their way. They leave no choice to any who belong in this reality but to resist them and destroy them before they do the destroying."

"You are certain of that, Grand Master?" someone asked.

"Absolutely," replied the Grand Master. "You must all understand, life as we know it is not the same as that of the mindflayers and their ilk. And it's not a matter of adapting and overcoming. The tomes we recovered reveal this to be true."

The Grand Master paused, looking about at the rest of the leaders of the UEO. Then they said, "Savagespace is a dimension of chaos, where destruction and death evolve the denizens of it. The evolution we know in realspace by shaping, building, and the thriving of life are anathema to them. Their presence is an infestation that will do naught but harm everyone and everything living in this galaxy."

The Grand Master shook their head. "It saddens me beyond words that we have no choice but to eliminate all the creatures of savagespace that have come to realspace. Death on this scale is not our way. But the UEO must take the side of life. That's why we must make it clear to all the races of the galaxy why this is of the utmost concern and importance. Lest all life as we know it becomes prey to these horrific predators, the UEO must assist when, where,

REVELATIONS AND RECONCILIATIONS

and how we can to stop the incursion from savagespace in every way. It might seem counterintuitive, but it does align with the UEO dogma."

Chapter 29 – Resolve

On the one hand, it was a wonder. On the other hand, it was a nightmare. Presently, Galit was seated in the pilot's nest of the *Moon Raven*. The crew had decided that, while they were in the middle of nowhere, and a safe distance from the gravitational pull of the dark star, it was safer to have someone in the pilot's seat at all times.

Kaz and Galit were the best pilots. Darius was capable, but a nervous and uninspired pilot. Sara had a rudimentary understanding of flight but was not comfortable with it. The rest of the crew could not and would not pilot the ship.

Kaz was a natural. Galit admired his piloting skills. She was more than capable, but was aided by her cybernetic enhancements, to which she attributed her overall ability. Kaz had a clear love of flying.

The crew was presently resting. Galit and Kaz both needed less sleep than everyone else. Galit due to her enhancements and Kaz his training and meditations. This meant Darius spent less than an hour in the pilot's nest and Sara half an hour at the most.

Galit had been observing the irregular comings and goings of the mindflayers, dragons, wyverns, and other monsters from their orbit of the dark star. She knew it was the tech from *Phantom* coupled with their shared genasi origin that kept their starships invisible to the interlopers.

The wonder was both the dark star and the ability of the savagespace invaders to orbit it. No race in realspace, no matter how technologically advanced they might be, had the ability to orbit a dark star without being pulled into it and its superdense gravity.

Galit presumed that the nature of savagespace was such that gravity impacted the mindflayers and their ships differently. Even with her cybernetics and technically advanced starship, all calculations put the mindflayers and their monsters at a point near the dark star where she and everyone else in realspace would be unable to fight its gravity.

She looked again towards the dark star. The mindflayers and their monsters should have been crushed by the gravity it produced. How could they remain in orbit of it? It defied physics as she knew them.

REVELATIONS AND RECONCILIATIONS

What, she wondered, would this mean if the mindflayers began attacking worlds with thicker atmospheres? Or would that be an impediment to them? Did they need air, or could they live in a vacuum? What about the dragons and other monsters? What would happen if they descended into an atmosphere, if they even could?

That led to probably Galit's largest concern. While they had tracked the mindflayers to this gathering point, no amassed army of the various races could do anything about them. Even firing missiles and torpedoes from a safe distance, the dark star would pull them in, likely absorbing them before they could reach any of their intended targets.

She wondered if anyone out there had done research into collapsing a dark star? Of course, that might have nasty repercussions that would not only take out the mindflayers but potentially cause new and worse rifts in the fabric of space/time.

Galit stepped out of her reverie and took a look around the flight deck. Being part of the crew of the *Moon Raven* felt right. She admitted to herself that this sojourn with the odd and diverse crew had been more than comfortable. Even given the circumstances.

Voices caught her attention, and she looked at a chronometer. The crew were returning to the flight deck. Kaz was first. "Good morning, Galit."

Galit arose from the pilot's nest. "Kaz. Good rest?"

"Oh yes," Kaz replied.

Darius, Sara, and Aya arrived.

"Nothing to report, Captain," Galit told Darius.

"Thank you, Galit," Darius said. "Do you need to rest?"

"Not yet," Galit said. "After breakfast, probably."

Tol and Zya arrived on the flight deck. "Galit," they addressed her.

As she sat at her accustomed place, she watched as the crew all took up their regular stations. Kaz had already readjusted the pilot's nest, not that Galit had made many changes when she occupied it. She saw that Darius was looking over data from the five galactic standard hours he'd been off the flight deck.

"Huh," Sara remarked. "Another dozen arrivals, and they passed how close?"

"A hundred thousand kilometers," confirmed Galit.

"I see that," said Darius. "You weren't worried?"

"No," Galit said. "*Phantom*'s stealth tech is some of the best in known space. And because *Moon Raven* is genasi in origin, too, that tech is easily extended to this ship. To all intents and purposes, they're mostly one ship, save the separate control systems and *Phantom*'s AI."

"Looks like the same data we've been observing for the past several days," remarked Tol.

"At least detecting the mindflayers, dragons, and other monsters will be easier," said Zya. "And for everyone, once we share our data."

"Yes," agreed Darius. "We've been lucky to go unnoticed here, given it's been five galactic standard days now. And while we've learned a lot about the mindflayers, I don't think there's much else for us to gain."

"What are you thinking?" asked Aya.

"I think it might be time to move on," said Darius. "But the question is, where to?"

"Based on reports via the medianet," began Aya, "the elves have reported no attacks since just before the Grand Master's transmission. I think it's safe to assume that the drow have stopped folding space/time."

"Is it, thought?" questioned Sara. "Safe to assume?"

"Yes," said Kaz. "Though many out there believe that the drow are inherently evil, they're not. They have honor and believe in the sanctity of life, save elf life. But that's some very old, very bad blood. Apart from that, knowing the truth of the damage caused by folding space/time, the drow have stopped using the tech."

"Agreed," said Galit.

Darius nodded. "Good to know."

"It's doubtful the Federation is going to stop," said Sara. "They're far too keen on their campaign for domination."

"There are rumors from some of my sources," added Galit, "that the respected general who was in command has been replaced. Nothing substantiated yet, but some intercepted chatter conversations seem to be pointed that way."

"Terrific," said Sara disconsolately. "We already know that the Confederation will do what they can to open a dialogue with the Federation

REVELATIONS AND RECONCILIATIONS

and convince them to consider the greater good. Presuming the Federation stays the course, it's only a matter of time before they attack the Union."

"You presume neither the Confederation nor the Union will be willing to take their eyes off the Federation, even for the greater good?" asked Kaz.

"Yes," replied Sara. "That leaves two large human governments. The Hegemony and the Incorporation."

"I'm sorry to say, the Hegemony is a lost cause," said Galit.

"What do you know about that?" asked Darius. "All I've ever seen was the aftermath of a refuge 'lifeboat' found drifting on the outskirts of Alliance space, half the occupants dead, the other half nearly dead."

Galit shook her head. "The government is beyond paranoid. Their main world hasn't been visited by anyone more than two solar systems away – even in the Hegemony itself – in decades. The leaders control their worlds with iron fists, insisting it's all for the greater good, never mind the curable diseases many of their people suffer that 'alien' science has cured for the rest of humanity. Their inevitable end won't be pretty."

"You've visited the Hegemony?" asked Sara.

"No," replied Galit. "But there's a cyberwizard in the Hegemony, keeping an eye on things. They're headed for catastrophe, by all accounts. Granted, that might take a couple more centuries. But odds are the Hegemony will end one way or another."

"What about the Incorporation?" asked Darius.

Before Galit could reply, Sara said, "They might be worth taking a look at. But they haven't much of a military to speak of. And that's largely for defense of their territory and convoys when they leave."

"Fortunately, the Incorporation is rather benign," said Galit. She knew more but waited to see where the conversation went.

"What about the unaffiliated worlds?" asked Aya. "I know, Captain, you're thinking about humans and their governments. But the multiple races living on the various unaffiliated worlds are just as threatened as everyone else."

"True," agreed Darius.

"What's more," continued Aya, "while most of them have defensive forces, they don't have a military that could provide mutual defense. And that might be a reason to get them involved. So that they can take up mutual defense."

"Interesting idea," said Galit. She thought about the various planets not tied to any specific government, their military capabilities, and the threat posed by the mindflayers. "While they do maintain individual defense of themselves, most are near enough to one another in realspace that, attacked by mindflayers, they might mutually aid one another."

Galit fell silent a moment, musing upon the thought. "I wonder how they would handle a mindflayer attack. The unaffiliated worlds cover sectors of space as large as – and larger than – the other races and human sectors. But no singular government, and thus no military backing."

"And where would we begin?" asked Sara. "Remember, if Darius and I reveal that we're former Alliance officers, bounty hunters might start coming after us again. That does nobody any good at all."

"The unaffiliated worlds might be too independent and unpredictable," said Tol.

"Very probably," stated Kaz. "The unaffiliated worlds, however, have always been adept at fending for themselves. How many, historically, have fought off an incursion from another world, an over-eager warlord, or one race or other?"

Galit knew the history. Kaz wasn't wrong. "Dwarves, goblins, orcs, kitsune," Kaz continued. "They'll come together as needed, rally around the cause, and work together as necessary when the whole of the greater good is in danger. No offense, Darius, Sara, and Galit, but the humans are going to be the most unpredictable element in all of this. Humans in the unaffiliated systems and sectors aren't who I'm talking about. It's the giant human sectors."

Kaz sighed. "Look at that divide alone. Three democracies... Well, two now; one xenophobic sector, one corporate sector, and the one that caused part of the issue in the first place. Again, no offense, but humans are historically too divided and too selfish to put aside their petty grievances and work together for the greater good."

Galit waited for Darius or Sara to disagree. But they didn't. Instead, Darius said, "You're right. My service to the Alliance Interplanetary Navy showed me that. Our nearest human neighbor was our greatest threat, and

REVELATIONS AND RECONCILIATIONS

both sides postured and tested one another's resolve all the time. But I like to think that when faced with a threat like the mindflayers and the inability to negotiate with them in any way, that would change. It's so much bigger than territories and invisible boundaries between them. This threat requires us to find a way to band human space together now."

"Us?" asked Tol. "I'm sorry, Captain, but the *Moon Raven* is an independent starship. We're beholden to none. Forgive my callousness, but in what way is this our problem?"

Darius was silent a moment, then said, "It's not."

He took a deep breath, let it out noisily, and then continued. "But I was raised in the Alliance, which was a democracy. The people had a hand in government affairs and lived free to choose any life they desired. When my childhood came to its end, I chose to serve. But that service, on my part, was not to merely the Alliance, but to all of humankind."

"To protect humans against 'alien' threats?" asked Tol.

"No," replied Darius. "Not because nonhumans are a threat to humans. That's not it at all. What Kaz says is true. Humans are by our nature selfish, petty, and made of other base impulses. And that is why I sought to serve all of humankind through the Alliance. Politicians serve the Alliance, but the navy serves more than just the Alliance. And that was why I chose to serve in that way. Because I saw it as a path to something bigger and utterly worthwhile."

"I never pegged you for an idealist," commented Aya.

"Oh, I'm a realist," said Darius. "My service in the military was Alliance-specific. But I always believed that the Alliance was a true democracy and worked for the good of its people and all humans by extension. The Federation leaders are the worst of the worst. The three families are the height of arrogance and self-righteousness. And that's why all reports show their occupation of the Alliance has been getting increasingly ugly. Given that knowledge, Sara is likely correct that the Federation won't stop folding space/time even knowing the damage it's doing. And Kaz is also right; that humans working for the greater good is not our default."

"You don't think humanity will do their part to stop the mindflayers?" asked Galit. She had reached that conclusion herself when the Grand Master had sent their broadcast across all medianet and chatter systems.

"Not likely," said Darius. "But the mindflayers are a threat to everyone and everything we all hold dear. For that reason, even knowing that humanity isn't likely to drop their squabbles for the greater good, I can't do nothing. I can't just go ahead and move cargo between systems, worlds, and peoples while all life is threatened."

Darius climbed out of the captain's nest and stood on the flight deck. "All of us are here because we were escaping something else. Every single one of us, save Galit, came here from a bad situation. Maybe we were mystically drawn together, but I wouldn't know anything about such. What I do know is that this crew is phenomenal. None of the rest of you served in the way that Sara and I did. But I hope you understand why I feel we need to do something. Do more. It's not what any one of us would have signed on for. But I, for one, need to act."

"I respect that, Captain," stated Galit. "To that end, I might be able to offer something that could serve the greater good. I have a contact in the Union I'd like to introduce you to. And I will do everything in my power to support all of you as you relay information, return to a life of moving cargo, or whatever you decide is best for you."

"Thank you, Galit," Darius said. Then, addressing the rest of the crew, he said, "I won't choose this if it goes against your will. I know it's a big ask. But for the sake of everyone, not just humankind, I think we need to remain a part of this, however we can. We vote. Be honest. And if you need more time to decide, take it."

He paused, then began, asking, "Sara?"

"Yes."

"Kaz?"

"Yes."

"Aya?"

She loudly expelled a breath, then said, "I have nowhere else to be. Sure."

"Galit?"

She appreciated being asked to weigh in. "Yes."

"Tol?"

"I do not entirely trust humans, apart from you, Sara, and Galit," said Tol. "But because I trust you and see the danger before all, yes."

"Zya?"

REVELATIONS AND RECONCILIATIONS

"It was not long ago I gained my freedom," she said. "And that is not something I will take for granted ever again. We're already a part of this. We must do all that we can for the greater good. Yes."

Chapter 30 – Disassociation

"Aneesa Anwar," said the mix of multiple voices from the hologram, "the Superior Convocation was deeply saddened to learn of the passing of General Song."

"A true tragedy, Your Superiorities," Aneesa said.

She was holographically presenting herself to the chamber. The trio of holographic figures stood before her on the dais, and she felt their presence like a physical weight, despite being only a projected presence.

One of the holograms, in its multitudinous voices, said, "You were appointed as second-in-command to General Song. Thus, you are next in line to take command."

"Your Superiorities, I am ready to assume command," said Aneesa. "I will serve the Federation and its goals in the best traditions of service, with honor, dignity, and strength."

She did not expect the momentary silence that followed. Then, one of the many voiced holograms said, "The Superior Convocation names you, General Aneesa Anwar, commanding officer of all Federation military forces."

"I promise that I will do you and the Federation proud," stated Aneesa.

One of the holograms said, "We shall inform our allies of General Song's tragic passing. The loss of his drow companions will be addressed by this body, as well. You will continue to work directly with the drow commander assigned by General Ilizeva."

"Of course," said Aneesa, biting back unkind remarks about Song. She knew his untimely demise had not pleased the Superior Convocation. Yet, they had given her the position as his Second to replace him when the time was right, had they not? For good measure, she added, "I will continue the fight for the dominance of the Federation in his honor."

Another moment of silence followed, making Aneesa wonder if those behind the Superior Convocation were speaking privately, wherever they were. But then, one of the holograms said in its many voices, "Duly noted. This audience with the Superior Convocation is at an end."

REVELATIONS AND RECONCILIATIONS

Aneesa bowed before the holograms. A moment later, her transmission ended, and she found herself in her holograph suite. *Her* holograph suite. General Aneesa Anwar knew she was one of the youngest to hold command of Federation forces. In addition to that, she had command when they were on the cusp of true dominance over all human space. She smiled.

A tone sounded, interrupting her. "Yes?"

"General," an aide addressed her, "Colonel Orizevi is here. She's demanding to speak with you."

Aneesa sighed, then said, "Very well. I'll meet her in my ready room."

"Yes, General."

Aneesa left her holograph suite. She was disappointed not to have guards, then recalled that Song had been given his drow shadows for protection by General Ilizeva. Little good that had done him.

Aneesa reached the bridge of the starship. The crew had already gotten used to her as their leader, though a part of her felt cheated she wasn't receiving extra deference from anyone.

When she entered her ready room, she stopped short a moment, surprised. Colonel Orizevi was already awaiting her there. Most of the time, Aneesa saw Orizevi via hologram. Thus, she forgot that the drow was considerably taller than her and physically imposing.

Aneesa took ahold of herself as she moved with intentional casualness to her side of the desk to stand before the chair. "Colonel Orizevi," she said.

"General," Orizevi replied with no evident emotion. Aneesa found reading the drow and their expressions unpleasant, so she couldn't tell the colonel's mood.

Orizevi continued. "I must demand an explanation. How was it that General Song and my people, his companions, were killed when all others on the bridge escaped without harm?"

Aneesa affected an air of nonchalance. She studied the nails of her left hand a moment, then said, "All others by no means escaped unharmed, Colonel. We took many losses. But as to General Song and your drow, a panel near them overloaded and exploded, killing them all instantly."

"I would like to see this 'panel' that exploded and a report from your engineers," said Orizevi.

This came as no surprise to Aneesa. It was also obvious that Orizevi distrusted her, maybe even suspected her of having a hand in their deaths. However, the drow colonel was on *her* ship, and Aneesa would not let her forget that. "The *Hammer of Harmony* is the Federation's flagship, Colonel. It must be kept in good order, so repairs have already been completed."

"And a report from your engineers?" questioned Orizevi.

"It confirmed that the weapons fire from the mindflayers overwhelmed the shields, creating a feedback loop that caused the panel to explode."

Orizevi pressed on. "In the entirety of the CiC and the bridge, the only panel that overloaded just so happened to be directly adjacent to General Song? And my officers? And how was it that were you not there, too?"

"I was across the display from them."

Orizevi crossed her arms. "May I see the bodies?"

"Colonel," Aneesa began, her tone syrupy, "this is a combat vessel. Out of respect, their bodies were ejected into space right there."

"You had no right to do that," said Orizevi. "The drow do not dispose of bodies in that way."

"They were on a Federation starship," said Aneesa. "Thus, they were subject to our laws and customs."

Orizevi was silent for a moment. Aneesa waited to see if the drow leader would outright accuse her of having a hand in their deaths. Instead, Orizevi said, "I will explain that to the Synod, but they will be displeased."

Aneesa shrugged. "Casualties of war, Colonel. However, I apologize for violating your customs and traditions."

Orizevi nodded. Then, she said, "Now that you have command of Federation forces, General Anwar, will you be heeding the warnings from the Grand Master, as well as your own proof of the damage folding space/time has done? Will you cease folding space/time, and help repair the damage?"

Aneesa smiled. "Why would we do that, Colonel? I am unconcerned about some threat that may or may not have an impact on the Federation. This technology is the key to my mission to expand the influence of the Federation. We will not be ceasing using space/time fold technology when it's the key to our expansion. No, I will be fulfilling that mission and leading bold new attacks on the Confederation."

REVELATIONS AND RECONCILIATIONS

"Your arrogance is astounding," said Orizevi. Her demeanor changed with her tone. "Do you not understand the danger that tearing the fabric of space/time poses to all life in the galaxy? Even beyond the mindflayers and their monsters, the breaking of our reality could be catastrophic. Your reckless disregard in the interest of your petty expansion is distressing."

"It's a big galaxy, Colonel Orizevi," said Aneesa. "There is, thus, more than enough room for these mindflayers to find space for themselves. It's not my concern."

"Not your concern?" said Orizevi. Her posture was clearly threatening. "You saw them. You fought them. Don't you understand they seek to destroy because it makes them stronger? Do you not understand that the tears in space/time caused by the drow and your Federation are the reason for this threat? Are you so callous as to think you can dismiss any and all responsibility?"

"Careful, Colonel," Aneesa said. She placed her hands behind her back, quietly turning on a signal to summon guards. "You are a guest on my ship. What you do with the technology is not for us to dictate, and the same is true for you. You can choose to deal with these mindflayers as you see fit. We will continue what we started – and I will lead the Federation to power and prominence no humans have ever witnessed before. The affairs of the nonhuman galaxy don't concern me."

"You are a petulant child," said Orizevi. "You are messing with forces far, far beyond your comprehension, General."

The door to her ready room opened and a pair of security officers entered. Orizevi didn't miss that. "Are you threatening me, General?" the drow asked.

"Were you threatening me, Colonel?" questioned Aneesa in return.

Orizevi shook her head. "That gets us nowhere. Very well. You clearly are unwilling to choose the wise course of action. By the authority given to me by General Ilizeva Taen'baer and the drow Synod, I will be immediately withdrawing all drow, troll, and allied forces."

"You do realize, Colonel Orizevi, that this violates the accords between the Superior Convocation and the drow Synod and could be considered a prelude to war," said Aneesa.

"I understand," replied Orizevi. "But since you intend to continue to pursue your conquests and your ongoing occupation of former Alliance territories, as well as potentially fighting mindflayers, your Federation hasn't the resources to make war with the drow. And I assure you that we will not be making war with you."

Before Aneesa could respond, Orizevi continued in an ominous tone, "You truly do not understand, General Anwar, that using the technology you created, that we gave you the power resources to employ, has far-reaching, dire consequences that you cannot avoid responsibility for. Your casual dismissal of the damage done by folding space/time and the extradimensional threats to life in realspace is unconscionable. Your ongoing, petty need for the aggrandizement of your small-minded, short-lived government should be trumped by the greater threat of these extradimensional invaders. If you do not see that for what it is, you truly are playing with forces you do not remotely understand."

"That's quite enough from you," said Aneesa, not bothering to hide the disdain in her tone. "Colonel Orizevi, if you intend to withdraw with your allies, I advise that you leave now and do so immediately before I order my forces to open fire on you."

Orizevi had the audacity to laugh. "That would not go well for you, General. But we are done here." Orizevi turned and took a couple of steps past the guards to the door. She stopped, turned back to face Aneesa, and said, "I hope you know, Aneesa Anwar, that if you continue on this path and do not cease to fold space/time, you will be dooming your Federation."

"You don't scare me, Colonel."

Aneesa almost shuddered at Orizevi's responding predatory smile. "I have no quarrel with you or your Federation, General. I do not make this statement to scare you, just to tell you how the path you're choosing will end."

Aneesa felt herself shudder but forced a chuckle. "I could not disagree more, Colonel. History will remember what you've chosen this day."

"So be it," said Orizevi. She turned and walked out of the ready room, the guards falling in behind her.

Aneesa seethed. How dare that upstart drow trash threaten her in her own command? For a moment, she considered contacting the guards and telling them to kill Orizevi before she reached her shuttle.

REVELATIONS AND RECONCILIATIONS

She raised her wrist to tap at the chatter but stopped herself. It wasn't worth the inquiry and further stories Aneesa would have to make up to appease both the Superior Convocation and the drow Synod if Orizevi were killed. Let her take her forces and her allies and be gone.

Aneesa turned to look out the observation port at the ships of her fleet beyond it. The drow could be "noble" and stop using the incredible advantage granted them by folding space/time if that was their choice. The Federation and their forces under Aneesa's command had no further need of them or their allies.

The Alliance had fallen easily. Song's ridiculous, overly cautious approach to the invasion of the Confederation had cost time and, Annesa presumed, opportunities to expand the Federation. Song had been a coward, not the cunning warrior many painted him to be.

Folding space/time provided the single greatest military advantage in history to the Federation. Aneesa was certain that the superior tech had never been used to its full potential due to Song's caution. She firmly believed that under her command, the Federation was assured dominance over the human sectors of the galaxy.

After that, who knew where they would go from there?

Chapter 31 – Convening

As they left unrealspace, Darius saw the incredibly busy system before the *Moon Raven* when the displays recovered. There was a huge number of starships, platforms, and stations in the system. The stream of movement was especially heavy between the four worlds within the Goldilocks zone.

The system was called Tethys. It was perhaps the primary solar system of the Union. It featured two worlds too close to the star and its heat and radiation, then four worlds in the Goldilocks zone, and another four worlds and numerous dwarf planets spreading out farther from the influence of the star's gravity.

"I don't think any sector of the Alliance was ever as busy as this," said Sara.

"Likely not," agreed Galit. "The two habitable planets are Idyia and Callirhoe, each occupied by between two and five billion people. The nearer and smaller gas giant, Achelous, has two life-supporting moons, Pirene and Castalia, home to millions and every form of industry you can imagine. The other moons are mined or have been used in various ways. Alpheus, the larger ringed gas giant, is mined for noble gases and the like."

"You've been here before?" asked Aya.

Galit chuckled. "Yes. But having cybernetic memory enhancements has informational advantages."

"Now I know why Tethys is familiar to me," said Sara. "Some people speculate that Tethys is the real system where Terra Prime is."

"Really?" questioned Darius. "I've never come across that."

"It's nearly on the order of a conspiracy theory," said Sara. "Some people believe that, once humans left the cradle, Terra Prime, they determined they didn't want to turn it into some shrine, tourist trap, or general destination for humanity to revere or revile. Or, some say, they didn't want it to be a target for any hostiles humankind might encounter out here. So, rather than some out-of-the-way, ignored world unaffiliated with any major human governments, Terra Prime got renamed and hidden in plain sight."

"So, which of these is Terra Prime, then?" asked Aya. "Idyia or Callirhoe?"

REVELATIONS AND RECONCILIATIONS

"No idea," replied Sara.

"In the temple, during my studies, we learned about the cradle worlds of the races," said Kaz. "No offence, Sara, but the idea that Terra Prime is here, in Tethys, is a fabrication."

"What makes you say that?" asked Sara.

"Terra Prime is the only habitable planet in its solar system," replied Kaz. "It's one of eight planets and a few dwarf planets within the Oort Cloud at the end of its star's gravitational pull. Also, Terra Prime is not its original name."

"It was originally called Earth," said Galit.

"Okay," said Sara. "How come nobody ever talks about visiting it?"

"To be fair," interjected Aya. "Nobody talks about visiting nearly every planet out there, unless they have an interesting experience from a trip they took. Given how long ago humans left their cradle world, interest in it as more than just another world is probably akin to how the dwarves and elves treat their homeworlds."

"Although they are less mysterious than Terra Prime," said Kaz. "But the mystery of the human cradle, to me, is just another aspect of the human penchant for drama."

"Aren't you half human, Kaz?" asked Tol.

"Yes," agreed Kaz. "But even our full-human crew will remark on the fallibilities of their race."

"True," said Darius.

"Kaz," Galit said, her tone clearly interruptive. "Our destination is Idyia, the largest, most in-system of the habitable planets."

"Okay," said Kaz. "Let me figure out who to signal to get a vector and other necessary clearances."

Darius appreciated the light-heartedness of the *Moon Raven* crew. Given the situation and all that they knew, it was good to be able to banter and generally converse about unimportant matters.

He was still not entirely certain just what it was they were doing. He had not requested specifics about Galit's contact or in what way they might be of assistance. Or even what assistance might look like, given all that they knew of the rifts in space/time, the extradimensional invaders, and the eventual threat of the Federation.

Darius knew that his and Sara's position as Alliance military officers had played into Galit's suggestion for making this contact. Despite the time in unrealspace getting to the Tethys system, they'd not discussed what that meant.

"Galit," Darius addressed the cyberwizard, "you mentioned that Sara and I being former Alliance officers would be useful here. But though the Alliance and Union have never had any issues or disputes that I'm aware of, neither have they been on especially friendly terms."

"There's a very logical explanation for that, Captain," replied Galit. "Remember, the Alliance and the Union are a considerable distance from one another on different arms of the galaxy. And between them are not just numerous, unaffiliated worlds. There are the derro, verdan, and the territories of two or three other races that must be crossed to get from one to the other."

"I've always found that fascinating," said Sara.

"What?" asked Aya.

"The spread of humanity," replied Sara. "The human race numbers in the hundreds of billions across the stars, yet they have massive territories where tens of billions live under one government. But those systems of large governments, like the Union and the Alliance, are thousands of light years separated. As spread out as we are, humans are fewer in number than dwarves, elves, and probably orcs. But they are less spread out than we are and have more centralized governments. It doesn't make much sense when you get down to it."

"Ah, yes," said Galit. "Remember, the Union is the oldest contiguous sector of human space, only separated from the Confederation by long-forgotten divisions and a nebula. And that's the truth of the other large system governments humans created over the millennia. Old, almost entirely artificial policies, beliefs, and values along the lines of religion, nationality, creed, or some other conceits were how humanity divided themselves on Terra Prime. That was from long before they left the cradle to explore and colonize distant worlds. Some of those entities sponsored the missions, arks, and colonists that would cross the stars over the centuries in the period of expansion."

"Galit," Kaz spoke. "Sorry to interrupt, but where are we going on Idyia?"

REVELATIONS AND RECONCILIATIONS

"Kefalio Leda," replied Galit. "Specifically, the Pollux province, Theta district."

"Thank you," replied Kaz. Darius heard him on the chatter with a controller via his headset as he looked up data on Kefalio Leda. Darius was agog. The city was beyond massive. In fact, Kefalio Leda covered an entire continent of Idyia.

As the *Moon Raven* entered the atmosphere, Darius found himself stunned by the most massive human-made city he'd ever seen.

"Whoa," remarked Sara, echoing his thoughts. "That's amazing."

"Nobody recalls if the city was always this big, or if this evolved from an ever-growing megalopolis," said Galit. "Kefalio Leda is broken into seven separate provinces, which themselves break down into multiple districts. The city has a population greater than a billion people. In all likelihood, Kaz, you'll be receiving very strict navigation instructions via chatter, and if the *Moon Raven* isn't equipped, *Phantom* can hook us through their automated guidance system."

Kaz chuckled. "Good. I'm looking at the mess below seven thousand meters and will be glad for automated guidance."

"*Moon Raven* has automated guidance capabilities," stated Tol. "Surprisingly, we've never had need of them before."

"By the looks of things, it's rather hard to reach our destination without crossing through high-traffic zones," said Kaz. "The whole of Pollux province is almost the center of the city, west of Castor and the river running between them."

Darius saw, as they descended, that multiple waterways and rivers ran through the city, crisscrossed by roads and rails. He could also see that the buildings towards the center of the city were impressively tall.

"I've seen cities of this size on the worlds of other races," said Aya. "But I didn't think humans had it in them to do this. I'm impressed."

"Me, too," said Zya.

The nature of their flight changed, and Darius saw that Kaz had his hands above, but not on, the controls. "They're bringing us in."

"Galit," Darius said. "Please reach out to your contact."

"Already done," Galit said. "She knows our estimated landing time and has sent a location for us to meet her."

"Any restrictions on how many of us can attend?" Darius asked.

"No."

"Who wants to be a part of this?"

"I'm in," said Sara.

"I'd like to go," added Aya.

Nobody else spoke up.

The *Moon Raven* was guided to a platform that stood at least a hundred meters above the ground. Darius was still fascinated by the numerous transports, trains, trams, hover vehicles, and starships taking off and landing all across the vast city. Kaz landed the *Moon Raven*, switching the systems over to standby.

"Those not coming with us, please keep your chatter handy. I'm not sure how long we'll be remaining planetside," said Darius.

"We will not go far," said Zya.

"I'd like to visit the nearest UEO temple," said Kaz. "But other than that, I'll be available."

"I shall arrange transport for us," said Galit. As she began to leave the flight deck, she turned back and said, "Captain, you and the others might want to... How shall I say this? Dress to impress."

Darius found that curious but didn't feel like asking for greater details. He went to his cabin for a change of shirt and jacket. Then the crew joining Galit left the *Moon Raven* and crossed the platform to a waiting area. Soon after arriving, a transport landed.

They were off again and soon descended into a traffic lane flying maybe ten meters above ground level. Darius noted the clear avenues and boulevards between the buildings in this province of the city. The architecture was impressive, a mix of old and new, various heights, and materials natural and synthetic.

"The more they vary, the more they are the same," said Aya, looking out a portal at the city flying past them.

"You think so?" asked Galit.

"Well, the basics, at least," said Aya. She didn't offer further commentary.

Darius was surprised when their transport arose out of the traffic lane and continued to climb towards a halo platform near the top of a tall tower. As their transport flared before landing, Darius understood why Galit had

REVELATIONS AND RECONCILIATIONS

commented as she did about their outfits. There were valets in crisp suits at the entrance to what looked like a fine restaurant.

"What is this place?" asked Aya.

"The Top of the Halo Bistro," said Galit.

"I've heard of this place," commented Sara. "It's rated as one of the finest, most posh restaurants in human space."

"Posh?" asked Aya.

"Very, very fancy," said Sara.

"What does that even mean?" asked Aya. "Isn't food, food?"

Darius chuckled. "To people like us, yes. But there are people who take extreme enjoyment in well-prepared and especially tasty foodstuffs."

"I went on a date once to a swanky place in Vivaldi," said Sara. "Glad my date paid, because it was obscenely priced. Great food, though. A meal I will never forget."

Darius looked at a patron exiting the restaurant and flashing a docucard at a valet. "Will they even let us in?"

"Yes," said Galit. "You're with me."

"Are we eating here?" asked Aya.

"Depends on my contact," said Galit. "But she's probably not buying."

"How much would a meal cost in a place like this?" asked Aya.

Galit grinned. "If you have to ask, you can't afford it."

They stood and exited the transport. Darius and company passed the valets and entered the restaurant. Once inside, the ritzy interior promised an amazing and ostentatious experience. They reached the hostess, a stunning elf woman in a sequined dress. She asked, "Do you have a reservation?"

"No, but we're expected," said Galit. "Azurite party."

The hostess looked at a docupad and nodded. "Indeed. If you'd please?"

The group fell in behind the hostess. She passed through the restaurant, treating Darius and his crew to the sight of numerous well-dressed, impressive-looking people, and sometimes more impressive-looking and smelling foods.

The hostess led them through an archway and past doors to the right and left that they passed. She continued, leading them through an arched portal at the end.

On the other side of the archway, they found themselves in a beautifully decorated room, featuring a pair of running water features, what appeared to be live tropical birds Darius couldn't identify, and a large, oval table.

Only one person sat at that table. There was something Darius found uncannily familiar about her as she arose to greet them. She was impeccably dressed, in perhaps the most well-tailored, attractive business suit he'd ever seen. She looked important, and there was an air of nobility around her.

"Thank you for bringing my guests to me, Dotora," she addressed the hostess. "We'll ring for service when we're ready."

The hostess nodded and left the room.

"My dear Galit," the woman said, circling the table to embrace the Blue Cyberwizard. "It feels like it's been ages, hasn't it? I hadn't expected to hear from you."

"You know how I operate," said Galit. "Allow me to introduce you to my companions. Darius Noble, Captain of the *Moon Raven*; his first mate, Sara Alon; and quartermaster Aya Mah-soo-may fo Misa."

The impressive woman shook each of their hands.

"This, my friends," continued Galit, "is Danielle Amelia Stern."

Now Darius recognized why she appeared familiar to him. Galit's contact wasn't just some diner at an extremely fancy restaurant. She was president and CEO of one of the largest defense contractors in not just human space, but possibly the whole galaxy.

"Stern," said Aya. "As in Stern Industries?"

"The same," Ms. Stern said.

Darius felt Sara throwing him a look. Then she said, "Galit, you certainly know some interesting people."

Darius agreed. Stern Industries had been created two centuries before by Ms. Stern's great-grandfather. He had passed the company to his son, who had expanded it before passing it to his son, who further expanded it before he had passed it to his middle daughter.

Danielle Amelia Stern might have been raised to privilege and power, but she didn't rest on those laurels. She had earned multiple advanced degrees in engineering and had a direct hand in everything her company designed and built.

REVELATIONS AND RECONCILIATIONS

Her father had sold weapons and other defensive and offensive systems to the Union and the Confederation. Ms. Stern had added the Alliance to those credentials, as well as two or three nonhuman races, such as the orcs, derro, and bullywugs.

While most defense contractors were generally limited to one sector, system, or race, Stern Industries spanned both territories and races. Ms. Stern was considered a gifted and shrewd businesswoman, as well as a respected philanthropist.

Her private life was just that. Private. Thus, aside from her knowledge and business acumen, people knew next to nothing about her. Darius wondered how Galit knew her.

"Please, have a seat," Ms. Stern addressed them. "I have not ordered yet, so let us get food and drink."

Darius took a seat, as did his companions. Holographic screens appeared, showing an extensive food and drink menu. Darius was sure that his eyes bugged out when he saw the prices.

"You are friends of my dear Galit," Ms. Stern said, "hence, as I would treat her, so shall I treat you."

The prices on the menu vanished. Darius wondered for a moment if they had been there just to remind them who they were in the presence of, her wealth and power.

"How Danielle and I know one another doesn't matter," said Galit. "But suffice it to say, she's an old friend. What's more, Danielle has a broad knowledge of the goings on across the galaxy, between having the best connections through Union Fleet Systems, multiple independent systems, and the Incorporation."

"Shhhh," Ms. Stern said, but Darius saw a sly grin on her lips. "My ties to the Incorporation are hardly public knowledge, Galit."

Galit returned her grin. "Of course not. But my companions have learned some very impressive things first-hand that might be of interest to you. What's more, I believe you could help them determine their next moves."

"Really?" asked Ms, Stern in an overly dramatic tone. "Well, let's get some food and drink ordered, and then you can start to tell me why Galit has introduced us."

Darius was glad he could no longer see the prices. He didn't want to think about how much COIN a meal in this place would cost. He chose his food and drink from the server who had appeared.

There was small talk between Ms. Stern, Galit, and the crew. Most of it was focused on business and some new systems Stern Industries was producing that were being sold near cost because of their benefit well outside of defensive or offensive weapons.

Once the meals arrived, Darius could not help but stare at his plate before eating. The presentation was simply beautiful, and the smell of his food was like nothing he'd experienced before.

"Now then," began Ms. Stern, holding up a fork with some sort of appealing looking protein skewered on it, "why is that that Galit has brought you here?"

Darius, Sara, and Aya explained everything about the mindflayers, the rifts being caused by the folding of space/time, and all they had learned about it from their excursion with the late and current Grand Masters. Maybe it was the food, but Darius found himself being unguarded and detailed.

He concluded the narrative with, "Before the Federation invaded and overran the Alliance, I was a Commander in the navy. I feel that relevant to all of this, because having seen much of the best and worst of humanity up close over the years, I have major concerns about the human race. As deeply divided as we are on so many levels, can we set aside our squabbles and deal with this greater, more pressing danger?"

Ms. Stern was dabbing the corner of her mouth with a cloth napkin. Then, she said, "Yes, I had heard multiple rumors about the Federation's science project. The Alliance was working on keeping close tabs on it."

"Oh, we know," said Sara. "Our ship was the corvette doing exactly that. We got the data, as we've shared here. But we were attacked, the *Moonshadow* was destroyed, and the Alliance was finished before we could do anything for it."

"The extent of this was naught but rumor," remarked Ms. Stern. "And even after the Federation and drow began to use their new technology to their own ends, much about that has been clouded in secrecy. That there were unintended consequences from this is no surprise. I sometimes think research into folding space/time was previously abandoned because those working on it foresaw such problems."

Galit said, "We are almost fully certain that the drow have ceased to use the technology. The Federation, however? That's a mystery."

"Not much of a mystery," said Ms. Stern. "The Federation, for all their boasting and claims, are nothing if not predictable. I believe they won't end their use of the technology. Not when they believe they can gain from it."

"Even with the greater threat?" asked Aya. "You think them that callous?"

Ms. Stern took a drink, then paused a moment before she said, "Though the so-called 'Triad' and the leaders of the Kho, Anwar, and Mallick families are intentionally unclear, they have always shared one singular goal. Expansion. And expansion, to them, must reflect their three-fold confederacy. One new territory for each family to exploit."

"That would be impossible," said Darius.

"It was, before they could fold space/time and go anywhere they desired instantly," remarked Ms. Stern. "The Alliance, being near, was the easiest target. With allies like the drow, hobgoblins, and trolls, they stood no chance. The Confederation and the Union could be whittled away by a smart strategist. But if all worked as planned, one family would oversee the former Alliance, one the former Confederation, and one the Union. With that much power and their greed, it would not be long before they'd set their sights on independent territories. And then, once they had claimed all those riches, they'd start in on the nonhumans."

"That's utterly insane," said Sara.

"You're not mistaken about that," agreed Ms. Stern. "What's more, the leaders of the families each have secret agendas. With no one family dominant, they are always on guard against one another while plotting against everyone else out there so that the Federation, as a whole, might dominate. But that has blinded them to anything beyond their existing territories, as well as games they play to position family members in key roles.

"For example, the general in command at the start of their invasion of the Alliance was a member of the Mallick family. And he was as arrogant and self-important as they come. The 'Triad' let him lead both militarily and politically, which proved detrimental to the occupation. Everyone saw through the 'trials' of the deposed Alliance leaders. Then, a threat to bombard a city from space was made on an open chatter. Since the families take care of their own, he was removed. But it was too late. The occupation of the Alliance has gone poorly and continues to get worse."

Darius felt something shift in his chest at that. "Good to know. I wish we could do something to help act on that. But the mindflayer issue is bigger and of more importance to the overall greater good."

"So," Ms. Stern began, "if I gave you and your first-mate the chance to get involved in helping the Alliance resistance, would you forgo it in favor of contending with the extradimensional invaders?"

Darius sighed. "Yes. Much as I want to kick the Federation out of Alliance space, this is a far greater concern."

"Agreed," added Sara.

Ms. Stern nodded. "Good. I agree. Galit, as always, was wise to bring you to meet me. If you can recognize that this issue with these mindflayers is the most pressing to all, I will do my best to help get the leaders of the Confederation and Union militaries to focus on that as well."

"Even with the probable threat of the Federation folding space/time to attack them?" asked Sara.

"Even so," agreed Ms. Stern.

Galit said, "Your help in getting the Confederation and Union to focus on the larger issue is greatly appreciated."

Ms. Stern nodded. But Darius could have sworn he saw a twinkle in her eye.

Clearly, he wasn't alone, as Galit said, "What else do you have, old friend?"

Ms. Stern grinned. "You know me so well. There is another avenue I might be able to offer you assistance from." She gestured towards Aya. "You mentioned other members of your crew. Is your quartermaster, here, the only nonhuman?"

"No," said Darius. "We have a half-elf pilot and two dwarf engineers."

Ms. Stern looked to Galit. "No wonder you're choosing to travel with them. Especially if they're as copacetic as these three appear to be."

"Oh yes," said Galit.

REVELATIONS AND RECONCILIATIONS

Ms. Stern began nodding and looked directly at Darius. "Very well, Captain. There is more I might be able to do to help your cause. In the meanwhile, as I work on that, I'd like you to do something for me."

"I'm listening," said Darius.

"I have a shipment of certain materials that need to be moved cautiously, under the radar. I have some crews I've used for this before, but I think you and yours would be perfect for this."

"Let me guess," began Darius, "it's bound for Alliance territory."

"It is," said Ms. Stern. She held up a hand to continue her line of thought, saying, "This is not a smuggling operation, nor in any way illegal. At least, not in the eyes of interplanetary law. But it will require some trickery and sleight of hand to reach its goal."

"Skirting the line?" asked Galit.

"Just so," replied Ms. Stern. "I think your crew would be the perfect one to handle this."

"If we take this job," began Darius, "what are you offering?"

"Information," replied Ms. Stern. "Information that could help further your cause. And since your cause is to protect life across the galaxy in the face of a threat of this nature, it's my cause, too. And moving this shipment for me will also help the other cause you are setting aside for the greater good."

Chapter 32 - Demonstration

In their prior life, the Grand Master had been good at meditation. As a monk, it was key to gaining access to both Universal Energy and chi in sufficient abundance to manipulate the energies.

The practices of meditation varied between the monks and clerics. Though the basics were similar, the actions differed. Monks would learn what was often referred to as "walking meditation." The idea was that you learned to touch the unseen energies of yourself and the Universe while simultaneously doing physical activities. This would be channeled into the unarmed combat that UEO monks practiced.

Before becoming Grand Master, they'd only vaguely known what cleric "battle meditation" was. But since nearly an equal number of Grand Masters prior to them had been clerics as monks, they now knew. Cleric "battle meditation" made use of weapons, armed combat, and unarmed combat training to touch the unseen energies in the same way monks used walking meditation.

Even though they had experienced numerous changes, the Grand Master found that meditation came easier. Though relatively little time had passed since they'd taken up the mantle, they had gained an amazing amount of understanding. They also knew with no doubt that choosing to join the UEO and becoming a monk had been the best thing they'd ever done.

This meditation took place in the middle of a large, open room. They were seated cross-legged, perfectly still, breathing deeply and slowly. Time lost all meaning in this state. Space lost all meaning, too. They just *were*. Their chi, their personal energy, became one with Universal Energy. Only the notion of their identity of self – and the need to remain individual - kept the Grand Master from totally merging their chi in the unending energies flowing through them.

Despite being in a perfect meditative trance, they were also aware of what was both within them and without. They could recognize the material from the immaterial.

They had entered the room alone. They were not alone anymore. Seemingly in slow motion, the Grand Master was on their feet. Their

REVELATIONS AND RECONCILIATIONS

would-be attacker was swiftly disarmed, sword and knife flying away. A chi-enhanced punch, very specifically enhanced to stun rather than kill, threw their attacker back.

Spinning around, they met their next would-be attacker. A palm-strike to the nose and they dropped their weapons. A swift kick to the side of the head knocked their attacker down and out.

Gracefully, with no effort, they leapt into the air. The flat of their bare foot connected with the chest of another attacker. The Grand Master twisted mid-flight, removing the pistol from their opponent's hand and connecting another kick to their face. The Grand Master landed on their feet in a crouch, one hand palm-down on the floor, surveying the space.

The Grand Master was both surprised and not surprised to watch their second and third attackers finish falling. To the Grand Master, in that perfect meditative space, time had meant nothing and slowed to a crawl. In reality, they'd moved almost impossibly fast. They had seen their predecessor do something similar. Though they had been fast before, they were faster and more accurate now.

However, it wasn't over. The Grand Master registered that there were two more present. They both attacked simultaneously.

The Grand Master moved again and was instantly back in the meditative space. Their first attacker had fired shots at them, but they easily dodged. The pistols dropped and knives were drawn. The other attacker came on with a sword. The Grand Master caught the first blow between their hands, palms on the flat of the blade. As they kicked at their opponent, the Grand Master took the blade from their attacker and flipped backwards out of the way.

The first attacker was on them with knives. The Grand Master rotated the sword, now taking the grip in hand. Two-handed, they deflected a flurry of blows from the knives of their opponent.

The Grand Master dropped the sword and backflipped, spinning mid-air to face the second opponent. They landed a kick to the thigh that staggered the attacker. A palm-strike to the face downed them.

The first attacker had drawn a pistol and fired at the Grand Master, who responded by using their chi to enhance their palms. The energy deflected the shots back to their source. The pistol was dropped. Without pause, the

Grand Master leapt. They landed a kick to their attacker's head, which dropped them to the ground.

The Grand Master again landed on their feet in a crouch, one hand palm-down on the floor, surveying the space. But as time returned to normal, the dim light in the room brightened.

Of the five cleric masters, only two were conscious. The others had been knocked out. The Grand Master didn't envy them the headaches and body aches to come.

"Satisfied that I am the Grand Master now?" they asked.

The cleric masters still conscious were standing, and both bowed at the waist to the Grand Master.

"Good," the Grand Master said. They stood back up, shrugging a shoulder to settle their robes that had shifted during combat back in place.

"What will happen to us now?" asked Cleric Master Diinaan.

"Nothing," the Grand Master said. "But I will advise that you and your companions, all study more. Grand Master is not some title to be vied for, no more than Master comes with any special privilege. All of us, from the newest novice to Grand Master, are servants to the Universal Energies. Accessing our chi to enhance ourselves is a gift we gain from that service. But station doesn't matter to the UEO. I advise you to study this more closely and remember. Then, give more service."

Master Diinaan nodded respectfully, as did Master Kho. The Grand Master knew their words would be relayed to any others of a like mind.

"How may I be of service, Grand Master?" asked Master Kho.

"You can make arrangements to assemble clerics and gather starships to put together parties to hunt down the mindflayers."

"I still do not understand why the clerics of the UEO should do this," said Master Diinaan.

"As I stated to the Assembly," the Grand Master began, "the mindflayers and their monsters are a force of pure chaos and destruction. If there were ever a source of true evil, then they are it. Because of their destructive nature, and how death and destruction by their actions make them more powerful, they are the biggest threat to life in the galaxy since the AI Awakening. Maybe even a bigger threat, since the AI didn't threaten the fabric of space/time itself."

REVELATIONS AND RECONCILIATIONS

"Forgive me, Grand Master," said Master Diinaan. "But what would that mean? What happens if the fabric of space/time is rent asunder?"

"The possibilities are many, but the outcomes are all utterly destructive," replied the Grand Master. "Reality, to the individual, is an illusion. But that illusion exists in *this* universe, with its specific physics, related energies, and scientifically predicted reality as we know it. That reality would break down."

"What?" questioned Master Kho.

"Imagine, if you will, a black hole," pressed the Grand Master. They started to pace with purpose. "Nothing can escape from its gravity once it has passed through the event horizon. What exists on the other side, if anything, is unknown. But it would likely be different from this reality. Black holes are considered destructive, extreme gravitational forces. There are multiple dimensions of space/time. Far more than realspace, unrealspace, savagespace, and whatever dimension the genasi and tieflings exist within. Reality breaking down would mean the barriers between them might vanish.

"That collapse would become similar to a black hole. But rather than devour stars and planets, it would devour space and time. Yet instead of some possible outcome of an alternate reality on the other side, you would have a place of utter nothingness, where not even the Universal Energies exist."

The Grand Master stopped pacing, turning to face the other masters. "And this is just one possibility. The result of space/time breaking down could be just a place where no life, no time, no anything exists. And unlike a black hole, it would never collapse upon itself. Instead, it may expand until multiple dimensions of space/time blend and counteract one another."

The Grand Master paused, letting that sink in. Then, they said, "Again, we do not know for certain what space/time breaking down might look like. But I assure you, we do not want to find out."

The Grand Master paused dramatically for effect, then said, "It's also, admittedly, possible this won't be quite that horrendous and destructive. Perhaps all this would do is let in more extradimensional beings. But while the beings of savagespace encountered thus far are horrific, who knows what denizens from other dimensions that are presently unreachable might come through such a rift?"

The cleric masters were silent for several moments after the Grand Master had finished. The Grand Master noticed that both looked abashed and simultaneously more present and dedicated when Master Diinaan said, "Now I understand. We will prepare our temples to hunt these mindflayers."

Master Kho added, "And we will do all that is needed of us to spread this message and do our part to preserve this reality as we know it."

Chapter 33 – Disquiet

Ilizeva knew that I'lehinaer was not the homeworld of elvenkind. It was a world that either the sun, moon, or star elves had colonized or terraformed almost six centuries ago.

What she did know was that I'lehinaer had become the center of the combined sun, moon, and star elf government about five thousand years ago. Though she didn't know the exact timing, she was certain it was before the second wave of interplanetary explorers that began faster-than-light travel.

When the elves had been choosing to establish I'lehinaer as their primary world and the seat of their combined Synod, the drow had settled Aenaer hundreds of years earlier. At the time, they'd been watching the hobgoblins, a race not far from their chosen territories, then on the verge of working out accessing unrealspace.

Before the dangers of folding space/time interrupted the drow's revenge, Ilizeva had once discussed with the Synod the feasibility of an attack against I'lehinaer. Ilizeva had rejected the notion, in part because she had felt that even with surprise from folding space/time on their side, defenses were too tight to even allow for proper scouting of the system. What's more, the potential of inflicting civilian casualties was too great to be ignored.

While other races and outside observers might question what the difference was, Ilizeva and her top military advisors agreed that soldiers knew they lived at risk. Hence, the attacks to exact drow vengeance was focused on them.

The *Nuummite Raptor* had arrived in the I'lehinaer system without incident. Though the elves immediately had surrounded the drow military flagship, they acted solely as escorts, doing nothing to provoke hostilities.

No drow had ever seen I'lehinaer before, let alone set foot upon it. Ilizeva found herself one of the first five. She and Alizev had been joined by Ulizuv Naen'baer, Olazuvi Laen'daer, and Elezevi Taen'caer. All three were considered among the most respectful and wise diplomats of the drow people.

They had taken a shuttle to the surface and landed at the Synod sanctuary, under escort from drow and elf starfighters. Although Alizev and the other three Synod members had wanted guards, Ilizeva had decided that was an unnecessary provocation. Because she had eloquently made her point against bringing guards, Alizev changed his mind and sided with Ilizeva. That added to her impression that they were developing a mutual respect for one another.

Once the five drow were met outside their shuttle by an honor guard armed with ceremonial pikes, they were led into the beautiful sanctuary building. The structure was best described as soaring. It was massive but featured delicate sweeping lines of almost heart-wrenching beauty. Ilizeva couldn't help but notice it was not too dissimilar from drow public architecture. The path through the sanctuary to the elf Synod chamber was nearly identical to that of the drow Synod structure.

Once before the elf Synod, Alizev started by thanking their hosts. He gave an eloquent speech that Ilizeva found less trite than she normally expected from him. Things continued to appear to be going well as the other drow ambassadors introduced themselves.

That changed when Ilizeva introduced herself. Multiple members of the elf synod cried out, started shouting accusations, called for her arrest, and expressed tremendous discontent. Despite their knowing ahead of time that she'd be with the drow delegation, the tension in the room had gone from disquieting to formidable.

Eventually, the Moderator of the elf Synod got them under control. But despite quieting down, the seething outrage remained an almost palpable force. "General Ilizeva Taen'baer," the Moderator addressed, "you were the leader of unprovoked attacks that began against sun elf starships and other military assets. Your presence here is not fully understood, and before we go further, you must be held accountable."

Ilizeva had wondered if something like this would happen. Though her less-charitable side pondered if the Synod had set her up to fall, she also knew that her part in the drow Synod was not just because of her leadership of the military. She was a drow leader in every respect.

She knew the situation before her was too dire to be treated with kid gloves. Maintaining her calm, she gathered her thoughts as fully as possible before responding.

REVELATIONS AND RECONCILIATIONS

"You say I must be held accountable," Ilizeva began, "but allow me to offer another perspective, one never spoken in this chamber before. I will make no apology for my actions and my attacks on the sun elves. In the days millennia ago, before any one of us made our way from the cradle that was our homeworld, the sun, moon, star, and dark elves were never equals. The most unequal were the dark elves, for whom the sun elves created the derogatory name 'drow'. In fact, it is well-documented, even so long ago, that the sun elves were the most disempowering and belittling towards the dark elves. The sun elves went so far as to shun the dark elves at every turn and encouraged the star and moon elves to follow suit."

A murmur began to rise from the elf Synod, but Ilizeva held up a hand to forestall the coming objections. "Yes, I acknowledge that this was between six and seven millennia ago. But the sun, moon, and star elves of the present cannot pretend that your ancestors did not treat dark elves as other, as lesser, and inferior as such. When elvenkind unlocked the secrets of unrealspace and began to leave the cradle, they had every intent of leaving the dark elves behind. They would leave the dark elves to an unknown fate as the rest of them spread out and expanded to new worlds. And before you question these facts, please know that this information is not from our records and histories, but from yours."

Gasps and angry murmurs started again. Before any could gain traction, Ilizeva continued. "Your ancestors made sure to let it be known that we were to be left out from what elvenkind might gain and abandoned to who-knows-what might have been. That was the history transmitted to our leaders of the time, and if we have record of it, you do, too."

She paused, changed her tone, and began pacing. Then she said, "But the dark elves' skin wasn't just a different color from all of yours. Our skin had metaphorically grown thicker, and our ancestors determined that we would not continue to be elvenkind. They would choose to cut themselves apart, disassociate from the name 'elf', and took your derogatory slang for our new identity. The drow made our way out to the stars, found our own territories, made our own allies, and forged a unique and separate identity from our former abusers and tormentors."

There were more murmurs, but Ilizeva now heard less anger and more discomfort and uncertainty in them. "Yes, that was over six thousand years ago," she continued, "but before that time, for hundreds of millennia before leaving the cradle, the dark elves of that one world were outnumbered three to one. And each of those three other elven lines shunned, berated, belittled, and mistreated the one for generations beyond counting. Not small slights, not occasional taunts, but constant de-elfinization. Is it any wonder to you that, after being told across every generation we were not true elves, we took on a separate identity?"

She paused to let that sink in. Then, she continued pacing and said, "It is true that that wasn't you and your generation. Maybe that was long, long ago. But for an even broader span before that time, the pain and suffering endured by the dark elves created an inherent racial anger and desire for justice. When we had the technology, how could we not let our desire to employ it for sudden and swift reprisal lead us?"

Much to Ilizeva's surprise, there were no murmurs. Only silence. Glancing towards Alizev and the other drow diplomats, she saw that she had their full attention, too. She took a breath, then continued and said, "I will make no apology for that. After millennia, the means to satisfy our inherited need to strike back, to demonstrate that the powerless now had the power, was too great and too enticing to pass up. Though these were the actions of the ancestors of your distant past, and not you, you must recognize that those ancestors, by attrition, inattention, or accident, made it clear to our ancestors that their goal was for dark elves to cease to be."

Ilizeva stopped pacing and started slowly turning, looking at the members of the elf Synod all around her. They had the same basic body shapes and pointed ears, but light, cream-colored skin rather than dark, black skin.

"What I *will* apologize for is what we could not have foreseen," Ilizeva said. "That folding space/time would create these rifts. It was not something that experiments and tests showed, so it could not have been avoided. But now that we know there *are* unintended consequences from our actions, we have ceased to fold space/time and have accepted our responsibility for creating the rifts that allow these extradimensional invaders to threaten all sentient beings in realspace.

"Because we know we are responsible for this, we know that it is on us to undo that damage. Now we must find a way to use the technology to close the rifts and repair the damage done. But that is not something we can do without help. Despite our pride and our long-held animosity toward elvenkind, closing the invisible rifts requires the technology and know-how of you, the elves."

Murmurs among the Synod started once again. But they sounded either confused or incredulous. "Though millennia ago, our people chose a new identity, we are still – biologically - elves. Dark elves, different only from the sun, moon, and star elves because our skin is shades of dark rather than light. But elves, no matter their origin, are among the eldest and most advanced spacefaring races in the galaxy. And our technologies, because of our shared origin, remain considerably similar."

Ilizeva stopped pacing and concluded, "The drow have become a proud people. However, to atone for the threat we have unwittingly unleashed upon the greater good, we come before you for your wisdom and scientific knowledge to help us repair the damage before more innocent lives are lost."

Ilizeva had never spoken for so long before but was done. After a moment of silence, the shouts began. They were many and largely incoherent, but one she heard clearly.

"You should go it alone and clean up your own mess."

"Maybe we should," Ilizeva called out several times, until she once more had their attention. "But too much is at stake for the greater good. We recognize and acknowledge that we need help – specifically your help - and have chosen this course of action to set it right."

"Why are you here?" an elf called. "You, specifically, the one who led the attacks on our people? It defies logic and reason."

Before she could respond, Alizev placed a hand on her shoulder and said, "General Ilizeva Taen'baer is the leader of our military forces. She is also a member of our Synod. But more than that, the idea to approach our long-hated brethren, whom we have always sought vengeance against – that idea was hers."

Ilizeva knew her time to speak had ended, so she silently observed the discussions that followed. There were several conversations back and forth between members of the elf synod, both among themselves and with the drow Synod ambassadors.

Eventually, the elf Synod Moderator took charge of the discourse, saying "It is with a heavy heart that we, the Synod of the sun, moon, and star elves, recognize the history that the drow have shared with us today. We are also forced to acknowledge that, in all the time that has passed since we ceased to be a people of just one world, we have never attempted to address that past. Perhaps, if we had, we could have chosen to recognize the improprieties of our ancestors and made an effort to close a gap we've denied was of our making."

That was more than Ilizeva had expected.

The Moderator of the elf Synod continued, saying, "Ilizeva Taen'baer, we would formally recognize that you have personally made a difficult choice. It shows your honor and your depth of character. Despite your ancestral hatred of our peoples, you recognize what matters more in the face of a threat to all life across realspace. That reflects well upon all of the drow people."

Ilizeva nodded to the Moderator in acknowledgment. "Now," the Moderator continued, "we must decide if and how to help you to undo the damage that has been done."

"Indeed," Ilizeva said. "I thank you for your words and know them to be genuine. While I have a lifetime of racial hatred within me, you – no, we - have an opportunity to change things. And that could be for the better not just of our peoples, but of all the sentient beings of realspace."

Chapter 34 – Delivery

Darius hadn't been told that he couldn't check the cargo. Aya and Tol had joined him. Upon opening a crate to inspect what they had, he immediately understood how it wasn't illegal but skirted the line.

Nothing in any of the crates was a weapon, in and of itself. They were, however, parts that could be used to repair numerous types of weapons, vehicles, communications equipment, and other gear that might be especially helpful to a military force.

The parts were many and variable, and all industrial/military grade. Technically innocuous; and a scan would not give anyone a reason to board for close inspection. Yet anybody with half a brain would know these parts for their primary purpose.

After Tol and Aya reported what they were carrying to the rest of the crew, Darius was surprised that they were more enthusiastic about it than they'd initially been. Though nobody had been against it, Darius had suspected trepidation on everyone's part tied to him and Sara returning to Alliance space.

Darius admitted to himself that, were it not for the greater threat from the mindflayers, he might have used this opportunity to find and join the resistance. But while the Alliance was home, the greater danger to it took precedence over helping to end the occupation.

Galit surprised Darius with her willingness to take part in the operation. "I thought cyberwizards stayed aloof of politics and wars of this nature," Darius said.

"Cyberwizards take great pride in working beneath notice," Galit replied. "I can't speak for any others, but I have values and ethics of great import to me. The Federation is run by three power-obsessed, arrogant families. They appear to be stable, but they aren't as imperturbable as they come across."

"How do you mean?" Sara asked.

"The balance between the three families," Galit remarked. "It appears even, and while it largely is, each family has suspicions about the others. And I have seen enough of how they are fighting a war on two fronts, which includes their occupation in Alliance space and continued attacks on the Confederation, to see their doom clearly written."

"And you don't think they see it, too?" Aya asked.

"Oh, no," Galit said. "No, they believe that folding space/time offers them far, far more power than it truly does. And they have abused that power in multiple ways. What's more, they are wholly on their own now. I've learned that the drow and their allies have withdrawn from support of the Federation."

"We had heard it was only through the help of the drow and their allies that the Federation overwhelmed Alliance forces," Darius said.

"That's correct," Galit confirmed, and went on to explain, to Darius' continued surprise, her participation in one of the first military acts of resistance against the Federation occupation. She concluded with, "Unless they change course and turn all their attention on Alliance space, they're doomed."

"I wish we could help speed along that doom," Sara said.

"It will come," Galit stated with a tone of certainty. "My sources tell me that the new Federation general, once again a member of one of the families, will not stop attacking the Confederation. This is why the drow have fully withdrawn."

"If they continue folding space/time," Kaz questioned, "aren't they providing more rifts for the mindflayers to cross and cause further degradation of space/time and reality?"

"Yes," Galit agreed. "The Federation choosing to Ignore that is another nail in their collective coffin. And the more they split their forces, the more they orchestrate their own doom."

Darius had wanted to ask Galit more about her sources, and how she was as certain as she was about everything. However, he'd learned during their time together that the Blue Cyberwizard never wasted words. If she wanted them to know something, she'd share more. Still, Darius was pleased to know that their delivery of Stern's parts would assist the resistance.

As they neared the end of the long journey across unrealspace, Darius and the crew had been working out the best way to avoid a Federation search. If the Federation accessed Alliance databases, Darius and Sara would likely be identified.

REVELATIONS AND RECONCILIATIONS

However, the *Moon Raven* was in no way connected to the Alliance. The ship itself would not present a problem for getting past the Federation. For extra safety, they'd agreed that Aya would play the role of captain in any communications.

Though Darius and the crew had speculated on what information Stern might give them once they completed the delivery, they didn't have an answer. Galit, even knowing Ms. Sterns personally, wasn't sure, but she said she had her suspicions. Galit shared no more than that.

"Leaving unrealspace in sixty seconds," Kaz said. Darius climbed out of the captain's nest and placed himself at a station aft and starboard. Both he and Sara remained on the command deck, but out of the way.

Aya took Darius' place in the command nest. "I could get used to this," she remarked.

"Careful, Quartermaster," Darius said, his tone light.

"Silence, peasant!" called Aya. "As Captain, my first order is to demand your total and complete loyalty and obedience. And you will call me Goddess when you address me."

Aya couldn't help herself and burst into laughter. "Sorry," she said, gasping. "I had to try it out."

"Where did you get that notion?" questioned Zya.

"When I was a kid, there was an entertainment program I followed on the medianet," said Aya. "This deposed queen commanded a pirate ship, and instead of Captain, they called her Queen. And I thought Goddess would outrank Queen, so that was where that came from."

"I think I remember this program," said Galit.

"Portaling back to realspace in ten seconds," said Kaz.

Everyone settled in at their stations. As Darius looked out the forward viewports, he saw the portal from unrealspace to realspace open ahead. Kaz flew them through the swirling pools of color that represented the portal from one dimension to the next.

The stars were visible again, pinpoints of light in the black of space. Darius saw a nearby planet and its three moons, as well as an orbital platform. Glancing at his instruments, Darius also saw multiple starships of various types. Four were clearly military vessels, and Federation at that.

"Incoming hail," said Sara. "And two smaller ships and one of those big capital ships are angling our way."

"Let's hear it," Darius requested.

A click as the speaker came on, and a voice said, "Recently transitioned craft, you've entered the Chiaroscuro system, currently held by the Federation. Identify yourself and state your purpose."

"This is Captain Aya Mah-soo-may fo Misa of the *Moon Raven*. We're making a delivery on behalf of Stern Industries to the planet Chiaroscuro and the city of Rembrandt."

"We acknowledge that, *Moon Raven*. Remain where you are and transmit your full registry credentials and manifest."

"Transmitting," said Aya. Sara sent the electronic information.

Galit said, "Looks like a Federation cruiser is the big ship heading towards us, and a pair of assault craft will get here first."

"*Moon Raven*," the same voice transmitted again. "Identify your cargo."

"It's on our manifest," said Aya in response.

"Don't test us, Captain," the voice said. "We are the Federation Fleet, and we will not be disrespected."

"No disrespect intended," said Aya. "We have five crates with replacement parts, boards, connectors, and the like, suitable for multiple mechanical devices and small craft."

Aya technically told the truth. After a moment, the voice said, "Prepare for scan, *Moon Raven*."

"One of the assault craft are scanning," Galit confirmed.

Another moment passed, and the voice said, "We confirm your manifest. Where in Rembrandt are you delivering?"

"Uh, checking," said Aya. "Secondary industrial quarter."

"To whom?"

"In what way is that any of your business?" asked Aya.

"Careful, *Moon Raven*," the voice warned.

"You have that data in our manifest. This shipment was cleared by the provisional government, and we're just doing our job to get the cargo where it belongs."

The voice didn't return for a time.

"What happens if they don't go for this?" asked Sara.

REVELATIONS AND RECONCILIATIONS

Before Darius could respond, the voice returned. "*Moon Raven*, you're cleared to Rembrandt. You have two galactic standard hours, starting now. You will make your delivery and take nothing with you. Course vector transmitted. Do not deviate or we will open fire. Is that clear?"

"Clear," replied Aya. "Thank you. *Moon Raven*, out."

"Copy that, *Moon Raven*. And welcome to the Federation."

Sara growled at that.

"How did they not detect *Phantom*?" asked Kaz.

Galit grinned. "I have the best stealth tech in the galaxy. We might want to use one of *Phantom*'s IDs to leave."

"Maybe," Darius said. "Let our contact know we're coming in, please, Galit."

"Will do, Captain."

As they entered the planet's atmosphere, Darius noted on the scopes multiple atmospheric craft coming their way.

"Damn them," Sara hissed. "Those are Hornets they're flying."

"Hornets?" asked Kaz.

"A class of atmospheric attack ship flown by the Alliance," Darius said. "Clearly, the Federation helped themselves to anything that wasn't destroyed."

"We have you on approach, *Moon Raven*," a voice came across the chatter. "Please know that we are monitoring any signals sent from your ship."

"Galit?" Darius asked, concerned.

"If they can detect anything I'm sending," Galit said, "then they've got a cyberwizard working for them. Not bloody likely."

"*Moon Raven* copies," Aya said into the chatter.

One of the Hornets was flying alongside them now.

"*Moon Raven*, you have a ship riding piggyback," one of the Hornet pilots sent across the chatter.

"No, that's part of the ship," Aya said with an air of confidence and nonconcern. "Lots of compatible parts. We merged the systems to get one fully functional ship."

There was a moment of silence, then, "Acknowledged. Maintain course, *Moon Raven*."

"Quick thinking, Aya," said Darius.

"Thank you, Captain."

They continued their descent. Kaz frequently adjusted their course, making certain that they followed the prescribed vector to the letter. Below three thousand meters, the Hornet banked away.

"Rembrandt India Second Starport," Kaz transmitted across the chatter. "This is *Moon Raven*, requesting a bay." They received confirmation and Kaz adjusted the ship's course.

"Our contact knows we're coming," Galit said. "But there's a catch, of course."

"Of course," remarked Darius.

"Local port authority has been especially jittery." Galit continued. "Seems that rebel activity on Chiaroscuro has been problematic across the system, and they're being extremely paranoid."

"Explains the Hornets," remarked Sara.

"If you or Sara move the cargo," Galit continued, "all humans are getting thoroughly scanned and searched. So, you two probably should stay aboard the *Moon Raven*."

"We can do that," said Darius. "But it's usually best one of us be there."

"Not this time," said Galit. "Myself and Kaz should probably stay, too."

"Really?" asked Kaz, not looking away from the controls or his displays.

Galit sighed. "The local Federation authorities are not being kind to anyone human, and the distinction between human and half-elf is being ignored."

Kaz grunted but said nothing.

"Alright," Darius decided. "Aya, you keep playing Captain and take Tol and Zya with you."

"Works for me," said Aya.

"Are you certain, Captain?" asked Tol.

Darius looked towards the dwarf couple. "Absolutely. The Alliance locals won't bat an eye over a kitsune and two dwarfs. Seems that will also not draw the attention of the Federation occupiers."

"This might be fun," Zya said, surprising Darius. He was glad the formerly incarcerated dwarf had become far more relaxed in an unfamiliar environment.

REVELATIONS AND RECONCILIATIONS

"Settling in thirty seconds," said Kaz. "We should probably move fast. Captain, request permission to disembark."

"Before I say no, Kaz, why?"

"I wish to pay a visit to the local UEO temple," replied Kaz. "And I assure you, I will not be noticed."

Darius considered that. Then, he asked, "Any specific reason why?"

"I'd like to check in with the local clerics and get a feel for how the occupation is impacting both them and the locals. Since the new Grand Master named me a master, I feel duty-bound to check in on them."

Darius glanced at the timer that had been started as soon as their two hours had been granted. He sighed. "If I say yes, you need to be there and back in less than thirty standard minutes."

"I only need twenty," Kaz said.

"Then yes, permission granted. Be careful, Kaz."

"Thank you, Captain," Kaz replied.

A moment later, they were on the ground, and Kaz powered everything down to standby. Aya, Tol, and Zya took the cargo pallets out, having received from Galit the location they were delivering to nearby. That left Darius, Sara, and Galit alone in the control deck of the *Moon Raven*.

"We should contact Danielle and let her know we've made the delivery," said Galit.

"Should we do that from here, before we've handed it off? Also, knowing we're being monitored?" asked Sara.

Galit chuckled. "Like I said, unless they have their own cyberwizard, and I assure you, the Federation does not, they can't possibly detect my signals, nor the encryption of anything in them."

"If you're sure it's safe, I trust you," said Darius. "Go ahead."

As Galit went about sending the signal out, Sara said, "Why is cyberwizard tech that much better than everyone else's? I mean, if it's that incredible, why don't the cyberwizards sell it for outrageous COIN to the highest bidder?"

"It's part of the code, so to speak," said Galit. "There are multiple factors that go into becoming a cyberwizard. Among them, there are gifts you accept as part of your upgrade process that, if you violate the code, will bring down some serious nastiness. It all ties into the Sanket in ways you cannot understand. No offense, but it's because you shouldn't even be aware of the existence of the Sanket, but also because you lack the tools to understand."

"Part of cyberwizard cybernetics?" questioned Darius.

"Yes. And before you ask, pretenders cannot access the Sanket, but it can access them. And we'll just leave that there, shall we?"

There was a ping from Galit's console. She turned her attention back to it.

"Danielle must have been awaiting this," Galit said.

Darius found it endearing but also somewhat distressing that Galit had such a close relationship with the business mogul.

"That's interesting," Galit said.

Darius sat at Aya's normal station and called up the message. He read it twice, not quite believing what he was reading. *Captain Noble*, the message read, *I believe this information will help you in your quest. The following coordinates will get you to Ghalt hur Kholm Ahk, influential orc tribal leader. Good luck.*

"Why orcs?" asked Sara, before Darius could pose the question.

"You have taken it upon yourselves to help in dealing with the mindflayers and their monsters," said Galit. "They've proven they're rather powerful. The Confederation is dealing with the Federation and will be hard-pressed to do anything about the mindflayers unless they attack citizens in Confederation space. Meanwhile, the Union is preparing to deal with the Federation, as they've made it clear they have no intent of ceasing to fold space/time. Ergo, human resources available for dealing with the problem are limited."

Darius understood. "The extradimensional invaders are a threat to every sentient race in the galaxy. Hunting and destroying the mindflayers will require everyone."

"More than that," said Galit, "it'll require at least temporary alliances between the races."

"But orcs?" asked Sara.

"Orcs are powerful fighters," said Kaz, surprising everyone. Darius noted he'd been gone less than ten galactic standard minutes. Kaz continued, saying, "What's more, given your reaction, Sara, orcs constantly seek to show

REVELATIONS AND RECONCILIATIONS

that they deserve equal respect to the other races of the first three waves. They will want to be a part of stopping this threat."

"Not exactly the role I envisioned for us," Darius began, "but whatever it takes to spread the information about stopping the threat is for the greater good."

Nothing more was said as Kaz resumed his place in the pilot's nest.

Ten galactic standard minutes later, Aya, Tol, and Zya returned. They reported all was well and the delivery went exactly as expected. They wasted no time departing, lest they incur the notice and wrath of the Federation.

Soon, the *Moon Raven* was en route to orc space.

Chapter 35 - Misinformation

She stood between the combat information center and the bridge on the *Hammer of Harmony*. While the display behind her showed more detail of the various ships arrayed around them, she wanted to look out the viewport herself.

General Aneesa Anwar was gathering her forces to launch her first offensive as the military leader of the Federation. It had not gone quite as smoothly as she would have liked and she was displeased with several of her underlings. Lieutenant General Gerhardt had been especially critical of her handling of the drow and was concerned about losing them as allies. He'd been extremely argumentative during the last staff meeting, and Aneesa didn't appreciate what she considered a lack of respect for a superior officer.

What's more, General Gerhardt stated that he felt she had chosen a star system they had too little current information about for her first campaign, and that she was taking too many ships. Aneesa argued – rather well, she thought – that recent detailed information on the system was not a problem of oversight on the part of the Federation. Instead, it was a sign that the targeted system was wholly unprepared for their arrival.

General Gerhardt was joined in his argument by Major General Norris, Chief of Intelligence. General Norris argued that without current information on the system, they were taking a risk. He further argued that without a more current assessment of the targeted system, they couldn't be certain of fleet placement, patrols, or anything else.

Aneesa, however, pointed out that all four prior reports showed that this system had, at the most, a dozen warships. Hence why she was taking thirty ships to overwhelm anything they encountered. When General Norris requested that they send a scout to update the intelligence, Aneesa argued that a scout risked tipping off the Confederation to their intent.

Lieutenant General Kaber, Chief of Logistics, joined the argument for dispatching a new scout. Aneesa, however, shut that down. They were going to hit the system hard, using technology that made them unpredictable. They would take enough force to overwhelm anything they encountered.

REVELATIONS AND RECONCILIATIONS

General Gerhardt again expressed his concern about their lack of the drow and their allies for support. Aneesa once more dismissed the aliens and their necessity. The Federation could fold space/time, which no other human force could do. That made them and their tech superior. Between that and the large force they were taking into the system, Aneesa was certain of a decisive victory.

She had conceded one part of her plan: Leaving behind an occupational force after their victory. The other members of the command staff had been unanimous in stating the logistical issues leaving anyone behind, even with the ability to fold space/time, represented. Aneesa had not backed down easily, but she knew she had to give a little to get a lot. Yet that meeting had left a sour taste in her mouth, and she had every intention of removing General Gerhardt.

The future of General Norris' career was also something she was considering. His insistence that she take a closer look at the intelligence gathered about Confederation forces and the capabilities of their starships annoyed her. They couldn't fold space/time, rendering any tech they might have unimportant. Why, she could not fathom, could none of them see how folding space/time made the Federation superior to all other human forces? The Confederation, the Union, and the other human organizations were no match for the Federation.

"General Anwar," the commanding officer of the *Hammer of Harmony* called, "all forces are ready."

"Very good," Aneesa said. She squared her shoulders and ordered, "Fold!"

Aneesa watched as the artificial wormhole opened before them. The starships of her fleet entered it without incident.

The whole fleet was now in the Confederation's Melchior-Tau sector. Aneesa was amazed that they could instantly traverse thousands of light-years. Nobody would resist them.

"General," one of her staff officers in the CiC called out, "there are no Confederation forces in this part of the sector."

Aneesa turned to the combat information center and approached the large holographic display there. "Didn't prior intelligence put ships in this part of the sector?"

"Yes," a different officer responded. "But it was a patrol of some sort, and the scouts never reported if there were set times that they visited this part of the sector."

"General," General Norris began, "these coordinates have brought us to the farthest part of this sector from the inhabited planets. We're within reasonable range via travel in realspace. But presently, that part of the sector is just outside our sensor range."

"Then they do not know we are here," said Aneesa.

"General," General Norris addressed her again. Aneesa could hear a hint of condescension in his tone. "This is their sector. Chances are, they have sensors too small for us to detect that have already noted our arrival. What's more, they have time to gather their forces while we seek them out."

"That's not much of a concern, General," said Aneesa. "Our intelligence might not be as current as you would prefer it to be, but all prior reports have never counted more than a dozen warships. We have more than twice that number. And once we detect them, we can open another fold behind them."

"Uh, General," one of the officers called out. She seemed to recall he was an engineer or a scientist. "Calculating distances for fold is not an instantaneous process. That's why we always open the folds in well-mapped sectors when we're not being guided by a scout feeding us coordinates. Without another prior notation on the charts and first-hand data, we're unable to perform a fold in a manner that would be any faster than realspace travel."

Aneesa did not appreciate that. "Very well, very well. Colonel, take us further into the sector, towards the inhabited worlds."

The *Hammer of Harmony's* commanding officer replied, "Yes, General."

"General," one of her staff officers called, "should we shift fleet formation to a more defensive posture?"

"No," Aneesa said. That question annoyed her. "We are on the offense and do not need to take a defensive posture."

"Yes, General."

Alarms sounded, and Aneesa could not understand why. No starships aside from hers were in the sector.

"We've sprung a trap," someone called.

REVELATIONS AND RECONCILIATIONS

"All ships," the *Hammer of Harmony's* commanding officer was calling across the chatter, "raise shields!"

"What happened?" questioned Aneesa. The fleet had been in a crescent formation. Her ship - towards the rear and center - had two more flanking it. The lead ships to port and starboard of the crescent were falling away from their formation, as were the two that had been on her flanks.

"Proximity mines and single-detonation laser mines," reported General Norris.

"How did we not detect this?" demanded Aneesa.

"General," an aide beside General Norris, a hand on the general's shoulder as if to calm him, spoke. "They are specialty weapons that are too small to be detected that are scattered in a given area."

"How is that possible?" demanded Aneesa.

The aide to General Norris continued, saying, "Individually, they appear to be little more than micro-meteors or debris, and harmless as such. They receive a coded IFF transponder signal from their own ships to not attack *them*. But a force such as this, without those codes, will trigger the mines. They will shift course and form together quickly, detonating before anyone can react to them."

"Individually, not a threat," added General Norris. "Together, they can do a great deal of damage."

"Particularly to a ship that hasn't raised their shields," stated the aide, who Aneesa now saw was a major.

"That the Confederation might have such weapons was in my report, General," said General Norris in a tone Aneesa did not like at all.

Seething, Aneesa looked at the holographic display. "The *Hammer of Harmony* seems to be undamaged. The rest of the fleet?"

"General," someone called out. "Four ships sustained minor damage but we've also lost two."

"Deploy search and rescue," ordered Aneesa. "But we continue ahead. Keep shields raised."

"Uh, but General..." the colonel commanding her flagship began, but then said, "Yes, General."

Aneesa vaguely recalled that the Federation had similar weapons in one or two of its more important sectors. Something she'd read but disregarded as unimportant to her primary mission.

Twice more, they encountered proximity mines and single-detonation laser mines. When Aneesa ordered a sweep ahead of their course, she was informed that would be impossible and a waste of resources. Before any Confederation ships appeared on their scopes, Annesa's fleet lost two more ships.

At last, Aneesa had something her fleet could annihilate. "Prepare to attack," Aneesa ordered, undeterred.

Various commands were called out as a dozen Confederation warships began to advance on them. Aneesa grinned. Perhaps it hadn't gone as expected, but they still had twenty-six ships against the Confederation's twelve.

"Prepare to engage," she ordered. "Alpha plan, no adaptations."

Moments later, missiles, torpedoes, and synchronized pulse cannon fire crisscrossed space all around them. Aneesa was initially pleased to see that it wouldn't be long before the Confederation forces would be overwhelmed. Then something on the holographic display caught her eye. More warships were coming into range. Seconds later, another set of blips on the scopes appeared to be coming in as well.

"Attack craft en route," someone in the CiC called out. "At this range, we can't get a proper count. They're maintaining close formation to confuse our sensors."

"How many warships are there?" asked Aneesa, feeling no concern about small attack craft.

"Looks like twenty," General Norris said.

"They must be calling up reserves or otherwise bolstering their fleets," the major at his side added.

"We still have numbers," said Aneesa. "Steady on!"

The battle raged all around the *Hammer of Harmony*. Aneesa watched the holographic display and saw that the larger-than-expected Confederation force was holding their own.

All too soon, they were not simply holding their own but doing more damage to her fleet than Aneesa's forces were inflicting. The attack craft

REVELATIONS AND RECONCILIATIONS

turned out to be heavily armed and armored and especially hard to hit. Despite deploying her fleet's fighters and attack craft, the Confederation forces largely ignored them and focused on Aneesa's warships.

Incredulously, she watched the display as first two, then three, then five of her warships winked out. How had the plan come apart like that? The *Hammer of Harmony* shook, taking multiple hits as several of the armored attack craft got close and launched ordinance at them.

"General!" the major at General Norris' side cried out, commanding Aneesa's attention. "We've lost ten ships. Four more are heavily damaged and three more are in trouble and calling for aid! We've detected signals from Confederation forces calling in more ships. Reinforcements could arrive via unrealspace at any moment."

Aneesa was enraged. Yet she did her best to release her ire as she ordered, "Very well. All ships break contact and retreat! Open fold and get us out of here, Colonel."

Orders were called and repeated. The *Hammer of Harmony* was shaken again as more attackers struck. Before Aneesa could yell at anyone for it taking so long to open the space/time fold, the artificial wormhole appeared, and her Federation forces departed from Confederation space.

Once her forces were through the space/time fold, Aneesa watched General Norris storm away from the CiC. The major who'd been at his side remained.

"Damage report," Aneesa called.

"The *Hammer of Harmony* has minor shock damage but nothing serious," the commanding officer reported.

"The fleet?" Aneesa asked.

General Norris' aide, the major, said, "We lost eleven ships total, and five of those that came back with us will need to be drydocked and overhauled before they'll be ready for battle again."

Aneesa said nothing. She was deeply, deeply angry. How had it all gone so wrong? How could she possibly have miscalculated so badly? The Confederation was nothing compared to the Alliance. No matter what Song had suggested.

It all came to her at once. General Thomas Song. This was his fault. He'd set her up to fail through his cowardice and overly cautious approach.

Yes, she was convinced that had to be it. This was the last vestige of Song's ongoing failure as the Federation's military leader.

Aneesa glanced in the direction that General Norris had stormed off. Maybe he'd been more loyal to Song than the Federation and its superiority. She knew she'd need to address that.

"General Song's legacy will not stand in our way again," Aneesa stated aloud.

Chapter 36 – Purpose

The conversations across public and private chatters, as well as all the data across the medianet, were more numerous and diverse than anyone had ever dreamed.

The various frequencies used for communications covered a stunning range of mixed signal types, including light, radio-waves, microwaves, tachyon waves, and more exotic energies. What's more, they intermixed among the races but differed just enough to remain separate.

Because of the nature of space and time, ancient transmissions could still be found tens of thousands of light years from their origin. It was possible to pick up a stray signal and hear a transmission sent by long dead people, races, and worlds.

Galit and the other cyberwizards knew that one of the key reasons those signals were not an impossible jumble of unintelligible babble was due to the Sanket. The ancient code created streams to separate current signals and the ability to read them from past signals. The subtle influence of the Sanket allowed Galit to monitor communications and more from points in space far, far away from the *Moon Raven*, even while in unrealspace transit.

It was "night" aboard the starship, the crew in their quarters sleeping. Galit had considered doing this analysis aboard *Phantom*. However, while she remained with the *Moon Raven* and its crew, *Phantom* largely served only as her bunk. The connection from her "station" on the *Moon Raven*'s flight deck directly connected to *Phantom*'s AI without lag. Thus, working from the larger starship felt right to her.

The *Moon Raven* crew were kindred spirits. They were more interested in solving a mystery and going on an uncertain quest than doing something more mundane like transporting cargo. While that, in and of itself, wasn't that rare, they individually were. Galit had never respected an entire crew like she did that of the *Moon Raven*.

Her console pinged, bringing Galit's attention to the present. A search for information she'd been running had produced results. During the late-night data analysis, Galit had learned that the UEO clerics were mobilizing, seeking help to deal with the mindflayers. The search she had just completed showed her that the Federation was still folding space/time to attack the far-away Confederation.

Galit further learned that the Confederation had been reinforcing their forces, called up reserves, and had changed from regular patrol routes to irregular, frequently changing ones. Federation scouts would be presented incomplete pictures, making their space/time fold-enabled attacks less accurate and potentially devastating. Lastly, she'd confirmed that Danielle Stern had passed useful information to Confederation command.

Someone entered the flight deck and Galit turned to see who it was.

"You're up late," said Sara.

"I sleep intermittently," Galit replied. "A couple of hours here, a few hours there. Among my enhancements, I have means to rest my brain and other internal organs better and more efficiently than sleep can."

Sara sat down at the station beside her. "Just how enhanced are you? I mean, other cyberwizards I've seen or seen images of have obvious cybernetics on them. You don't."

Galit chuckled. "A conceit on my part. Rather than announce what I am, I allow people to underestimate me. That's proven advantageous many times."

"If that's the case, why don't other cyberwizards do the same?"

"Some do," Galit said. "But in most cases, they go for the intimidation factor being a cyborg tends to create. It's just a matter of your choice of tools. Jeweler's hammer or jackhammer, for example."

Sara snorted. "I've known more jackhammers than jeweler's hammers in my days."

"You served in your military a long time, no?" asked Galit.

"Yes," confirmed Sara. "My family would have preferred if I'd chosen a less dangerous career, but I wanted to serve the Alliance and travel space. So, the Interplanetary Navy called to me."

"I served, in my youth," remarked Galit, reminiscing. "But only five years. A better opportunity presented itself."

"Becoming a cyberwizard?" asked Sara.

"Yes."

"How did that come about?" Sara questioned. "How did you become the Blue Cyberwizard?"

REVELATIONS AND RECONCILIATIONS

Galit thought back on that. "As a teen, I was a datacore hacker. I was very, very good at it. But I made a mistake, got caught, and because I was a teen, given a choice. Prison, or serve the local military. I chose the latter. Despite being restricted by my position, I still performed hacks on datacores, chatters, and the medianet. That got the attention of a cyberwizard called the Grey Ghost."

Sara drew in a breath between her teeth. "I've heard of them. They were tied to many things, but nobody could tell you anything about them."

Galit grinned. "They loved that persona they'd created. They took me under their wing and taught me all sorts of skills. They made me an Acolyte and helped me form my persona and choose my implants."

"How long were you an Acoyte?" asked Sara.

"I think about a decade," stated Galit. "I had so many different experiences and learned such a variety of things that it all blended together. What's more, I'm not sure precisely when my identity as the Blue Cyberwizard was accepted and my time as an Acolyte ended."

"Who determines that?" asked Sara. "The UEO handles clerics and monks, the Syndicate creates sorcerers, but I thought cyberwizards were wholly independent?"

Galit sighed, debating what she could say. Yet she saw something in Sara that she felt it best to encourage. "That's not something I can share with you. But there is a... Let's call it an overseer... that makes such determinations."

"And the implants, enhancements, and various cybernetic alterations?"

"Part of being an Acolyte," said Galit. "You gain access to the 'overseer' and learn about how it all empowers you and makes you a cyberwizard."

"If you have no external cybernetics, how enhanced are you?" asked Sara again. Then, she added, "Or is that a rude question?"

Galit chuckled. "If you were also a cyberwizard, monk, cleric, or sorcerer, yes. But otherwise, no. Two of my limbs are wholly artificial, the other two heavily augmented. Several of my internal organs have been replaced by more efficient ones, specially grown from my DNA to prevent rejection. The rest are augmented in one way or another."

"Was it painful?" questioned Sara.

"Sometimes. It turns out, that's part of becoming a cyberwizard. It's the price you pay for all the benefits you gain."

Sara nodded. "But you're expected to mostly go it alone and be all mysterious, right?"

"I guess that's just part of the mystique of being a cyberwizard," said Galit.

"Let me ask you, then. Why are you staying with us aboard the *Moon Raven*?"

Galit leaned back in her seat, considering her answer. "A great deal of the nature of the work cyberwizards do is unseen. Part of why we work alone as we do is because our neutrality overall is important. And before you say anything, we do choose to take sides in conflicts from time to time, but that tends to align with our personal moral codes. Cyberwizards will join adventurers and go on quests for both public and private reasons. In the case of you and the rest of the *Moon Raven* crew, there's something about you all that resonates with me in a comforting, familiar way. And of course, at present, we have the same goal."

"What goal is that?" asked Sara.

"Stopping the mindflayers," replied Galit.

Sara sighed. "Yeah, it's a noble goal. But I can't entirely grasp how we can really be a part of that. And frankly, I'd rather be helping the rebellion within the Alliance to overthrow the damned Federation. I think that's a much more feasible goal."

"Perhaps," mused Galit. "The Alliance is your home, and it's natural that you feel, in part, that you've abandoned that. But truth be told, Sara Alon, you're serving a bigger purpose here."

"In theory," said Sara. "The reality of that remains to be seen."

"Then why didn't you stay when we were on Chiaroscuro? Why didn't you leave the *Moon Raven* and join the rebels when you had the chance?"

"Darius," said Sara.

"You're a civilian now," commented Galit. "You're not beholden to his command."

Sara shook her head. "Darius isn't just my former superior officer; he's also the closest friend I've ever had. I've not had a close friend like him in a long time. And more than that, I trust him implicitly. He's never steered me wrong, and I owe him my life. If he feels that the *Moon Raven*, this crew,

REVELATIONS AND RECONCILIATIONS

and he and I should serve in this surreal fight against this extradimensional threat, I'll stay with him to do so."

"That's another thing I appreciate about this crew," said Galit. "You watch out for one another and have a bond better than many close families. My opinion, for what it's worth, is that you are choosing the right course."

"You think so?" asked Sara.

"Yes. Because if we fail to create a force to oppose the mindflayers, whatever happens in Alliance territory and the Federation's occupation of it won't matter."

Chapter 37 – Consultation

They had only visited this remote sector of space once before. At least, in their prior incarnation. The Grand Master was seated in a space behind the captain's nest, slightly elevated from the rest of the flight deck. At the front were the pair of seats for the pilot and navigator/co-pilot and four stations each to port and starboard.

The bridge crew of their ship were those that had accompanied their predecessor to the same empty sector of space last time. Scholar Khort was once more serving as captain. Unlike their previous visit to this sector, nobody questioned what brought them there. That was part of why the Grand Master had opted to take the same bridge crew on this journey.

They didn't wait long. A portal opened just ahead and to starboard of the ship. Three obviously genasi starships entered realspace, the portal closing behind them.

"We're being hailed on the chatter," the monk at communications stated.

The Grand Master activated the holographic display. Three genasi appeared. One was female with blue skin and hair, another female with slate-colored skin and hair, and the last was male with red skin and hair.

"Grand Master of the Universal Energies Ontology," intoned the red-skinned male. Both his voice and appearance were familiar to the Grand Master, as he'd been present at their prior meeting. "Why have you come to the meeting place to speak to us?"

There were no remarks made about the Grand Master not being their predecessor, whom they'd met with not so long ago. The Grand Master had expected some sort of reaction from the genasi that they were new.

However, the technology in the stone that connected them to their predecessors was likely genasi. Given its nature and ability to change the Grand Master, connect them to the past and those before them, as well as holding a vast compendium of information, they suspected that the stone had interdimensional properties. That, however, was not a matter for the present. There was more important business to attend to.

"Honored friends," the Grand Master began, knowing that it was the tradition to do so, "you were correct that the information to close the rifts in

REVELATIONS AND RECONCILIATIONS

space/time caused by folding was in the abandoned temple. Unfortunately, my predecessor was lost, giving their life so that the rest of our companions might recover that invaluable information. The UEO is seeking to persuade those who have the technology to cease its use. We know that one of the races responsible for creating those rifts has ceased doing so and is working with the data we recovered to that end."

The blue female genasi, whom the Grand Master recognized had also been at their last meeting, said, "If one race acts to right the wrong, does that mean the other continues to fold space/time?"

"Yes," replied the Grand Master. "The UEO has attempted to send a Master to address their Superior Convocation, but they will not grant access. A representative of the Syndicate of Thaumaturgic Sciences has also attempted to gain access and been denied. We know they received the interplanetary transmission of data I sent. We are still working to convince them that the danger is greater than the short-term gains they seek."

The blue genasi female said, "Your efforts as the shepherds of temporal and dimensional matters in realspace are appreciated, Grand Master. As stated when we last met, we have consulted with our wisest sages and scholars."

The Grand Master, as Master Alisay, had addressed the genasi when they had accompanied their predecessor to meet them before. They wondered if the genasi were recognizing that. However, it was a passing curiosity of no import.

The slate-colored female genasi spoke. "We have made some important discoveries. First, although the threat of creating a greater rift in space/time that could bleed the various dimensions together is possible, it's highly unlikely. There are many, many dimensions beyond even our understanding, in addition to those we know to a greater or lesser degree. What's more, the galaxy, and in fact the whole of the Universe you know as realspace, your reality, is larger than even our minds could fully comprehend."

"We're not in danger of destroying the fabric of our reality because of folding space/time, then?" questioned the Grand Master.

"Unless hundreds and hundreds, if not thousands, of space/time folds are opened, each creating a dimensional rift, the probability of a greater, reality-destroying rift is far less than feared. Consider this: there are nearly two trillion galaxies in the reality of this universe. A few rifts within space/time in one galaxy in trillions cannot impact the sum total of the reality of the larger universe."

"That is a relief," said The Grand Master. "However, this information will not leave the UEO, for the threat the mindflayers represent is sufficiently problematic."

The red male genasi said, "We appreciate that, Grand Master."

The slate-colored female genasi said, "Secondly, once a rift is closed, that is permanent. It cannot be reopened. That's due to the inherent nature of savagespace being so alien to realspace that the denizens of savagespace cannot open a way from their dimension or to any other."

The Grand Master recalled from the prior meeting between their predecessor and the genasi that the only reason the creatures of savagespace were aware of any other dimension was the wormholes. The tunnels of wormholes crossed savagespace. When wormholes were employed for faster-than-light transit by any of the races of realspace, those who called savagespace home became aware of life in other dimensions.

The slate-colored female genasi continued. "A rift in space/time is a form of creation. The mindflayers and their pets live off destruction. Hence, cataclysms, collapses, and anything that is a negative and a dark energy force fuels them."

"That's incredible," breathed the Grand Master. "You referred to this when last we met as anti-life."

"Yes," replied the slate-colored female genasi. "The mechanics of this, of anti-life, in opposition to life as we know it, is incomprehensible to the genasi, let alone the people of realspace. Likewise, however, time as we are capable of perceiving it is not something the mindflayers can understand."

"Are the mindflayers the most advanced form of life in savagespace?" asked the Grand Master.

"That's highly probable," said the red male genasi.

The blue female genasi said, "There may be others. But the destructive power of anti-life that drives the illithids has likely made them dominant."

The Grand Master couldn't help but shudder.

REVELATIONS AND RECONCILIATIONS

Scholar Khort asked, "If I may, honored friends, how is it that creating portals between realspace and unrealspace does not create rifts in reality and similar space/time problems such as the situation with savagespace?"

The blue genasi female said, "What is causing the rifts is the artificial wormhole event horizons. In short, unlike their natural counterparts, the rift they tear in space/time doesn't self-heal. The portals between realspace and unrealspace pose no threat to space/time because of shared properties between the dimensions. Points that exist in realspace, like planets and stars, exist differently in unrealspace. Despite the difference in that existence, they are still mirrored. Space is effectively the same in both, but the flow of time in unrealspace is vastly different.

Scholar Khort asked, "And what about the dimension the genasi and tieflings call home? How does that relate to realspace?"

The three genasi said nothing. After several moments of silence, the Grand Master asked, "Can you or the tieflings provide us with aid to close the rifts in space/time? Can you help us repair the damage that's been done?"

The red male genasi replied, "We cannot."

The blue female genasi said, "As we have evolved, one consequence of this has been that we can spend only limited time in realspace or any other dimension that is not our home. When we first encountered the spacefaring peoples of realspace, we were at a point in our evolution that allowed us greater time in this dimension. As the years go by, we and the tieflings have evolutionarily advanced in ways your minds cannot comprehend. This has lessened our ability to be present for long in your dimension. But we can and will continue to observe and provide you with further assistance."

The Grand Master bowed their head and said, "We have always appreciated our connection to you and your ongoing desire to help us and those who call this dimension home."

The blue and red genasi similarly bowed their heads to the Grand Master. The slate-colored genasi said, "One final warning we must leave you with. As you are aware, mindflayers destroy. They gain power by destruction, and this is both tangible and intangible. They will likely gather to be a greater and more thoroughly destructive force, and thus pose tremendous danger to any who face them."

The red male genasi said, "The attacks you have experienced by the illithids thus far have been testing you. They learn from each engagement how life in this dimension works. For though the races of realspace are different in many ways, the essence of life is not. As forces of anti-life, they will kill and destroy to get stronger and more powerful without remorse."

The blue female genasi concluded with, "Once the illithids have worked out how life in realspace works, and they understand how its destruction further powers them, they will begin to more actively move to destroy it. Be forewarned that the stronger they become, the harder they will be to stop."

Chapter 38 – Negotiations

The flowing color of unrealspace terrified some. Ilizeva found it calming. She stood at the forward observation port aboard the *Nuummite Raptor* with the crew of the bridge behind her carrying out their duties.

Ulozov stood silently at her side. She should have technically left Ulozov behind in drow space, given that he was her second. Despite that protocol, Ilizeva preferred her Second to be present. Even though it was not anticipated that they would face combat, he was both her most trusted advisor and a good friend. Fortunately, with the drow having withdrawn from the Federation, Orizevi was back in drow space and could be in command with Ilizeva and Ulozov absent.

Ilizeva checked the display before her and shifted to video of the ships immediately to port and starboard of the *Nuummite Raptor*. Elf starships. There were three drow and three elf starships working together as a taskforce, en route to hold a conversation and negotiate with a major dwarf community.

Noticing what she was looking at on the display, Ulozov said, "It's a most surreal experience, isn't it?"

"That's one way of putting it," Ilizeva replied. "Drow and elves working together. I could never have imagined this."

"Working *with* the elves rather than against them?"

"Indeed," agreed Ilizeva. "All previous encounters with the elves tended to be from above those ships as we folded space/time to arrive atop them and attack. Look at them. Their starships have clean lines and are beautiful to behold just as ours are. Would you have thought our tech to be so similar after all this time?"

"No."

"Nor I. It's strange."

Ulozov chuckled. "It's unnatural."

Ilizeva grinned. "It is. But given what we're all up against, it's necessary."

"For the greater good," agreed Ulozov.

Despite the elf Synod giving the go-ahead for the elves and drow to work together to close the rifts in space/time, it was clear they would have preferred not to. Granted, neither did the drow relish working with the elves. Millenia of racial hatred took its toll on both sides.

It seemed that the sun, moon, and star elves had stopped considering the drow at all over the many millennia since they'd left the cradle. While the drow had held onto resentment and fomented the racial hatred across the generations, the rest of elvenkind had forgotten the actions of their progenitors.

When the drow had attacked via space/time fold, the elves had been caught off guard. Though they still held some enmity towards drow, it had been beneath the surface before the drow attacks.

Millennia of racial hatred was not an easy thing to let go of. But the greater good demanded it. To that end, the data that the Grand Master had included in their transmission for closing the portals would require something only one race in the galaxy had access to. The dwarves.

Ilizeva was not a scientist per se, but she had a basic understanding of what had gone into creating the fold in space/time. Elements of that would go into the process of closing the rifts. However, to close the rifts and the portals that would sometimes open between realspace and savagespace, they would need a mineral mined almost exclusively by the dwarves.

To power the technology for creating the artificial wormholes, the Federation had needed the drow. The degenerate matter power source that they used for that purpose was necessary for closing the rifts. One of the biggest problems they would encounter in closing the rifts was seeing them. They were not visible and needed to be made visible so their unique signature could be analyzed and matched.

This was part of why the drow needed the help of the elves. To make the rifts visible required them to focus a beam of the dark matter power source all elvenkind had easy access to and then pass it through a measure of the dwarf-mined mineral. When the rift was made visible, its energetic frequency could be ascertained.

Then the drow would utilize the space/time folding technology to engage the rift energy, now made visible by the blended elf and dwarf tech, to close the rift. Once it was closed, the tear in space/time would cease to exist and the threat of further savagespace incursions would end.

REVELATIONS AND RECONCILIATIONS

Ilizeva considered why the Federation had chosen the drow rather than the elves when they had sought the power source to make their technology viable. Reputation, she decided. The elves would have been disinclined to help the Federation, knowing they'd use the technology to attack other human territories.

"The damned Federation," Ilizeva said aloud. She turned to her Second. "It distresses me deeply that the arrogant Triad, or more probably the 'Superior' Convocation, since I believe the Triad is a myth, are ignoring the Grand Master's warnings. How can they be so contemptuous when it comes to anyone other than themselves and their power?"

"It's not everyone in the Federation," said Ulovoz. "Song was unique, though the rest of his staff were competent, save that Second the family leaders forced on him. It's the three families and their unquenchable thirst for power where the problem lies."

Ilizeva considered that. "Yes. The damnable Koh, Mallick, and Anwar families. The new Anwar general who murdered Song is considerably out of her depth leading their forces."

"But she's a member of one of the families," said Ulozov. "And given that she was the highest ranked member of a family in the military when they forced her on Song, she probably feels secure in her new role."

An idea was beginning to take shape in Ilizeva's head. "I think I might know how to destabilize the Federation leadership and end their quest for power. Special forces could be sent in to assassinate high-placed members of the three families."

"The Superior Convocation, though they are never seen, are known to be made up of the elders of the families," said Ulozov.

"Yes," agreed Ilizeva. "Though the families appear balanced and united, I suspect that's more a front than the truth. To take advantage of that, these special forces would not target the leaders of the Anwar family."

Ulozov raised an eyebrow. "It's an intriguing idea. The problem, however, is that if any drow are found to be involved in such a ploy, it could generate sympathy in other human governments, who in turn might aid the Federation."

"A fair point," Ilizeva conceded. "But that is why I suggest special forces. If they're human, there are options."

Ulozov nodded and turned back to look out the viewport at unrealspace. Ilizeva would consider her idea further, but not until the more pressing matter before them was taken care of.

Fifteen galactic standard minutes later, they emerged from unrealspace into dwarf space. Alarms began to go off. They were silenced, however, before Ilizeva needed to give the order.

There was a massive space station floating above one of the largest asteroids Ilizeva had ever seen. The asteroid was pocked and marked with numerous entry points to its core. Scaffolding and various other frames were scattered across parts of its surface and into its center. The station above it was made of two large counter-rotating cylinders. Ilizeva could not recall its name but knew that it was one of the oldest bases of its kind still in use by any race.

While numerous starships were visible around the asteroid and space station, the alarms had been triggered by the dozen heavily armed warships in the system, all of which were converging on the six starships of the joint drow and elf task force.

Dwarf starships were among the best armored in space. They appeared utterly solid, like dwarves themselves, and were as tough as they looked. Yet Ilizeva found they had a certain symmetrical beauty she appreciated.

"I knew they would have an impressive force on display," said Ulozov. "I expected that. But that is a very well-armed welcome party."

"General," a controlled called out, "Sadiro Paon-sun'kiri and a representative of the dwarves are transmitting holograms."

Even though Alizev Kaen'baer was with them, because of the dwarf patronymic culture, it was important to establish the female drow leader as an authority figure at the outset. Though the dwarves did not allow their females much autonomy, they didn't tend to apply that to other races, though they still treated females with caution and skepticism towards their authority. However, given the importance of their mission, they had chosen Ilizeva as the initial drow representative of this task force.

Ilizeva stood before the necessary station to attend the parlay. "Engage."

A moment later, holographic figures appeared before her from the chest up. One was the sun elf Sadiro Paon-sun'kiri, the other an unfamiliar dwarf.

REVELATIONS AND RECONCILIATIONS

Sadiro Paon'sun'kiri introduced himself and Ilizeva did so as well. The dwarf replied, "I am Xoc'hi-pepe ubn Cua'la-li, tribal elder. I was informed during an elder council you would be coming here."

"We have a matter of dire importance," said Sadiro Paon-sun'kiri. "Our delegation requests an audience to discuss this."

"We have a chamber prepared on Eta'palli," Xoc'hi-pepe ubn Cua'la-li said. "I will send you coordinates. You may each bring no more than three delegates and three guards."

"Agreed," said Ilizeva. Sadiro Paon-sun'kiri echoed her reply.

Ilizeva joined Alizev Kaen'baer in the shuttle bay of the *Nuummite Raptor*. They were joined by three guards and Elezevi Taen'caer. The shuttle departed from the bay, and as they flew towards the space station, another came up alongside them from the elves.

"As you have made first contact with the dwarf elder," Alizev Kaen'baer said to Ilizeva, "and as the handling of what we are requesting will be by the military, you will take the lead on these discussions."

She glanced at the ambassador but couldn't read his face. "If you wish. Is there more to it?"

"I have heard how the dwarves treat their females," said Alizev coldly. "If having to speak to one such as you in any way makes them uncomfortable, that suits me fine."

This surprised Ilizeva. But she nodded and made a mental note to be that much more respectful towards the drow ambassador.

The shuttles landed. Ilizeva and her companions exited from their ship. They met with Sadiro Paon-sun'kiri and his companions. They included his page, Nitori Loun-sun'kiro, an elf military colonel, and three guards.

Awaiting the half dozen drow and half dozen elves were twenty armed and armored dwarves. It always struck Ilizeva how, though also humanoid, the dwarves were so much shorter and stockier. However, part of it was that until she saw them in person, Ilizeva had considered dwarves to be larger, since their personalities tended to be. Maybe they seldom stood more than one-and-a-half meters tall, but they were as formidable as far larger creatures.

"Xoc'hi-pepe ubn Cua'la-li instructed us to escort you to the conference chamber," one of the dwarves called.

Ilizeva paused to see if Sadiro Paon-sun'kiri would speak, but she caught his eye and he nodded almost imperceptibly to her.

"Thank you," Ilizeva said. "Please show us the way."

The drow and elf delegations merged as half the dwarves took the lead, the rest falling in behind them.

"It never ceases to amaze me the dwarf attitude towards females," said Sadiro Paon-sun'kiri softly, leaning toward Ilizeva.

"Indeed."

The guards led them past a broad window that looked into the cylinder. Within, Ilizeva saw a large, thriving space with artificial sunlight, tree-lined avenues, and other flora and fauna beyond the countless dwarves.

"It's an impressive station," said Nitori Loun-sun'kiro.

Elezevi Taen'caer said, "Before we left the ship, I learned this station is home to half a million dwarves, most of whom work on the asteroid."

They were in another corridor, then the guards split to either side of a broad portal. The drow and elf delegation entered. Seated at a circular table, a finely dressed dwarf spread his arms expressively.

Xoc'hi-pepe ubn Cua'la-li said, "Welcome, welcome all. This is quite the sight to see. Elves and dark elves – sorry, drow – working together. There are stories," he continued, arising from his seat. "Nothing very specific, but stories about how the dark elves who, upon claiming drow as their racial identity, vowed to avenge the wrongs done to them by the rest of elvenkind when they all lived on the same world. Then, we heard of sudden, unexpected drow attacks against elves that just as suddenly ceased. Now I see before me drow and elves side-by-side."

Sadiro Paon-sun'kiri said, "We have a common goal that we agree overrides our historic disputes."

Ilizeva added, "The greater good of the broader galaxy is at stake. In light of that, our dispute is, and I never thought I would ever say these words, petty."

The dwarf chuckled. "A drow admitting to being wrong?"

"No," said Ilizeva. "Just prioritizing matters differently in light of new information."

"Compromising," said Xoc'hi-pepe ubn Cua'la-li.

"Just so," said Sadiro Paon-sun'kiri.

REVELATIONS AND RECONCILIATIONS

"Please, have a seat," said Xoc'hi-pepe ubn Cua'la-li.

Four of the guards that had escorted the drow and elf team to the hall took seats to either side of the elder. Introductions were made around the table as the elder sat back down.

"How do we address you, Xoc'hi-pepe ubn Cua'la-li?" questioned Alizev.

"You may call me Elder, or Xoc will do just fine."

"Elder Xoc'hi-pepe would be most appropriate," said Ilhi'cam-ina ubn Ne'cal-li, head of Eta'palli station security.

"That's not necessary, Ilhi," said Xoc. He turned his attention to the drow and elves. "Now that the pleasantries are out of the way, what is it that has brought you here?"

"Have you seen the Grand Master's message?" asked Sadiro.

"Of course," replied Xoc. "The technology they used for that transmission is quite impressive and a little distressing. Our elders were not pleased to learn that the Syndicate has that ability."

Ilizeva began, saying, "We drow and humans from the Federation worked together to achieve faster-than-light travel via folding space/time. As you know, there was an unintended consequence the came of this. The drow take responsibility for our part and are seeking to undo the damage we have helped inflict."

For the next ten minutes, Ilizeva, Alizev, and Elezevi detailed the initial outreach to the elves. Sadiro joined the discussion at that point. They concluded by explaining that the Grand Master's transmission had included the means to close the rifts, and to do so, they needed dwarf help.

"That is why we have come together," Ilizeva concluded. "And why we're here to address you now."

Xoc steepled his fingers and leaned back in his seat. For a time, he said nothing. But then, just as Ilizeva was finding the silence uncomfortable, the dwarf elder said, "When I was told you would be presenting yourselves here, I was skeptical. Elves and drow have been separated for millennia. Yet here you are, and you have made a cogent argument for what you need from my people."

Sadiro said, "We know that dwarf elders are largely separate and independent. You have mentioned that there was a council held."

"Yes," Xoc said. "For matters such as this, we agree dwarf greater interests come first. To that end, we will provide you the ore you seek. But for a price."

"Excuse me?" asked Sadiro, not hiding his disgust. "This is about the greater good of all the races in the galaxy, and you would exact a price?"

"Nothing of value is ever free," replied Xoc.

Sadiro looked as if he would explode in outrage, but Ilizeva held up a hand to forestall him and said, "Elder Xoc, the drow expected this would come with a price."

"And you didn't think to tell us?" demanded Sadiro.

"With apologies, Ambassador," said Ilizeva. "But all dealings with the dwarf people come with a price. We expected nothing less here."

"She is correct about that, Ambassador," said the elf military colonel. "Dwarves place value on everything."

"That is why I expect the price will not be COIN," Ilizeva said, her eyes never leaving Xoc.

The dwarf elder grinned. "Very perceptive, General."

"Name your price," said Alizev.

"The dwarf elders agree that our price is this: An open dialogue between dwarves, elves, and drow, the oldest space-faring races in the galaxy. It is long past time we discuss a great many matters, and this new threat is the perfect impetus for that."

Chapter 39 - Bridging

As they passed through the portal, the swirling colors of unrealspace gave way to stars. However, they were utterly unfamiliar stars. This was a system far from any Darius had ever visited before.

"We're here," said Sara.

"Where are we, exactly?" asked Aya.

"Charts say Vhilk Kylig Ahk," said Kaz. "Our destination is the fifth planet, Vhilk Kylag."

Darius was looking through his displays, going over what Ms. Stern had sent. He found what he needed and sent a message via the chatter. It was only a moment later that they received a signal back, and Darius tapped a screen to open the chatter.

"*Moon Raven*, this is Fhalt hur Pholm Ahk. Welcome to Ahk tribe space. Please state your business."

"I'm Darius Noble, Captain of the *Moon Raven*. We seek an audience with Chieftain Ghalt hur Kholm Ahk. He should be expecting us."

"One moment," Fhalt said. The chatter went silent.

"Lots of ships moving around this system," remarked Aya.

"No surprise, really," commented Galit. "The Ahk tribe is one of the five largest orc tribes. They number in the billions."

"More than a billion related orcs?" asked Sara.

Galit chuckled. "Orcs do not form the same familial bonds humans, elves, or dwarves do. The males and females of a given tribe breed with one another but don't form monogamous bonds. Orc females tend to birth between five and ten children in their lifetimes. The tribe raises the young in age groups called sects. So, each successive generation might be five to ten times larger than the prior generation."

Before anyone could say more, the chatter was online again. "*Moon Raven*, the Chieftain will see you. Transmitting coordinates now to Jha-Dyt Ahk Madeena."

Darius saw the coordinates and vector information populate on his display. "Confirmed. Transmission received. *Moon Raven*, out."

"Got it," remarked Kaz. Darius felt the *Moon Raven* shift course.

As they neared the fifth planet, Darius noted multiple orbital platforms, docks, stations, scaffolds, and numerous starships of various sizes, as well as a broad artificial half-ring orbiting the planet.

"That's some impressive tech," said Zya as the half-ring took up more of the ship's canopy.

"How so?" asked Sara.

"The ring always follows the dusk terminus. It won't blot the sun from the surface."

They continued towards the planet. Lights showed cities on the dark side of the world. Tol said, "I just checked, and local time is midday where we're going."

They entered the atmosphere. Darius realized something else he'd not considered as they started their decent.

"I don't know much about orcs or their culture."

"Nor I," said Sara.

Aya laughed. "My interactions with orcs have seldom been good. But then, stowing away on an orc ship might have been cause for that."

"Only saw one or two during my time at *Territory's Edge*," commented Tol. "I worried they would trample me, last I encountered orcs. They tend to be more than a meter taller than dwarves and proportionally as broad as my people."

Galit said, "Orcs can be as brutal and tough as they appear. But the truth is that they have a deep, rich culture with many diverse arts. Much of this is known only between the various orc tribes, since billions of orcs across the galaxy keep to their own kind and trade only between one another. But there are some orc communities from various tribes that actively cooperate with other races. Between this and various conquests, half-orcs are among the most common hybrids with humans, next to half-elves."

"Rape," said Sara with distaste.

"No," said Galit. "That's anti-alien propaganda. Close interaction between orcs and humans tends to produce a physical attraction, which some scientists attribute to shared primal instincts in the DNA of both races."

"I find that really hard to believe," said Sara.

"Coming from a human-only sector, such as you do, that's not surprising," said Aya. "As you travel the unaffiliated and independent sectors

REVELATIONS AND RECONCILIATIONS

further, you will see how such interactions between humans and nonhumans are far more common and unremarkable."

Darius again found that, though his service to and for the Alliance had been worthwhile to him, it had still been unsettlingly myopic. The galaxy beyond one democratic human sector of space was far bigger than he'd previously recognized and acknowledged.

As the *Moon Raven* started its landing cycle, Darius looked out the viewport at an impressive, enormous city. It looked like most of the other cities he had seen as the *Moon Raven* had traveled across space. However, there was something brutal about the architecture, though it reminded him of dwarf structures, save that it was taller, with lots of spikes and sharp points. He realized that had been true of the orc starships and other structures of theirs he'd seen in space as well.

"It's midday?" questioned Sara.

Darius noted now that it appeared unusually dim out there. As the ship slowed, making its final approach, he could see that it was a sunny day, yet the light still appeared relatively dim.

"Remember," Galit said, "orcs are especially photosensitive. They also breathe the nitrogen in the air, rather than the oxygen. Since their eyes are smaller than a lot of other races, they prefer less light. That's why most orcs wear goggles when meeting in places belonging to other races."

"That explains the message that came with the coordinates," said Kaz. "They restrict the intensity of lights on starships landing here."

"Dwarves used to be more photosensitive, too," said Tol. "But our optic nerves are more adaptable than the orcs."

A moment later, the *Moon Raven* had settled onto the landing pad. Darius noted they were at ground level. He checked his display for local information. This was one of the larger, more centrally located spaceports in the city. The information sent by Fhalt hur Pholm Ahk showed that the tribal leader was in the largest tower, about ten kilometers from the spaceport. Darius saw that a transport would be awaiting them outside their landing bay.

"Anybody care to remain with the ship?" asked Darius.

"Captain," Galit addressed him, standing, "I think it would be best to bring the whole crew of the *Moon Raven* along. First, it will show the chieftain that you feel secure in his city. Second, it will show him you are a united group. Though not a singular mind, you work as one. And lastly, *Phantom* will protect both ships."

"You think it will matter to them if someone remains aboard the ship?" asked Aya, also standing.

"Trust me, they will scan the ships to see if we left anyone behind," said Galit. "This is the tribal leader's world and his capital city. If you want to put us on the best footing to have him hear you out and help, this is the ideal way to start that process."

Darius climbed out of the captain's nest. "I trust you, Galit. Okay, crew. Get what you need, and let's go meet the chieftain."

"It will be acceptable if you're armed," added Galit.

Each member of the crew went to their cabin. Darius went to his and put on a coat and grabbed his synchronized pulse pistol. Soon they were gathered together outside the hatch on the tarmac. Darius paused, looking at the *Moon Raven* and *Phantom* atop it. He couldn't help but admire both starships.

The promised transport arrived nearby. The craft landed, and a tall, broad orc stepped out. It had been a long time since Darius had seen an orc. Despite the orc being well-dressed, it took Darius a moment to adjust to looking at his grey-green skin, small, beady eyes, pointed ears, and tusks from the lower jaw, ending just above the upper lip.

The orc looked them over. "Captain Noble?"

Darius recognized his voice as he stepped forward, and the orc offered his hand.

"A pleasure to meet you. I'm Fhalt hur Pholm Ahk."

"Thank you. How do you prefer to be addressed?"

"Tsgahn Fhalt," the orc replied. Then, gesturing, he said, "Climb aboard. The Chieftain is awaiting you."

Darius and the rest of the crew boarded the transport. He noted there wasn't a pilot as the craft began to ascend away from the tarmac.

Aya leaned in towards Darius and said for his ears alone, "Tsgahn is a title that falls somewhere between deputy, underling, and assistant."

"Thanks," Darius replied softly.

REVELATIONS AND RECONCILIATIONS

The transport joined the traffic along a route with other, similar vehicles on a pre-prescribed flight path. Darius noted that all the other transports, like the one they were on, were an odd combination of blocky spiky, and, to his human eyes, overly large. Given that short orcs were the height of the tallest human beings, that should not have surprised him.

The transport departed from the flight path towards an impressive, spiky, enormous tower. Despite its somewhat rough appearance, there was a beauty in its structure that impressed Darius. They were soon landing on a deck about halfway up.

As they departed the transport, Darius was immediately impressed by the tall portal leading into the tower before them. Six well-armed and armored orcs stood to either side of the entrance. The guards initially appeared to take notice of the mixed group following Fhalt, but then paid them no mind as he led them through.

On the other side of the portal, Darius found himself in a huge foyer. There were many orcs, a mix of armed and armored, well-dressed and casually appointed, all going about whatever midday business they had. Many paused as they noticed the humans, dwarves, half-elf, and kitsune following Fhalt. Darius wondered how common non-orcs were to Jha-Dyt Ahk Madeena.

Their guide moved purposefully through it all, pausing at the doors Darius was certain led to a lift. When they opened, Fhalt led them in. He swept his hand over a panel within, and the doors closed as the lift ascended.

"The Chieftain will be meeting you in his private suites," said Fhalt.

"Is this normal?" asked Sara.

Fhalt chuckled. "As much as it can be for non-orcish petitioners to present themselves to the chieftain."

Darius looked towards Galit and Aya, both of whom nodded slightly to indicate it was not unusual.

The lift stopped, and the doors opened to a high-ceilinged hallway. As they stepped out, Darius noted that the space opened to a reception area ahead and to the left and seating to the right.

The orc at the desk stated, "Tsgahn Fhalt, you and your guests may go right in."

"Thank you," Fhalt said as he led Darius and the crew onwards. The doors opened automatically.

The space beyond was a well-appointed office, not much different from others Darius had seen, save two major features. First, the ceiling was considerably higher than he was used to, and secondly, the eleven people within were all orcs.

Like Fhalt, they were all well-dressed, six males and five females. They had been holding a conversation, which stopped when Darius and the crew were led into the suite.

There was no mistaking who was in charge. The tribal leader, Chieftain Ghalt hur Kholm Ahk, wasn't especially taller nor broader than the other orcs in the room. The cut of his outfit wasn't particularly better tailored or of richer-looking material. How he stood, his overall bearing, and air of authority, however, was clear. It struck Darius the same as being in the presence of any admiral, high-level politician, or business leader.

"Chieftain," Fhalt said with a slight bow of his head. "The crew of the *Moon Raven*."

Darius stepped forward, offering his hand. "Captain Darius Noble."

The orc took his hand in a firm, but not too tight grip. "Chieftain Ghalt hur Kholm Ahk."

Darius introduced the rest of the crew, Galit last. The orc tribal leader showed no sign of recognizing the Blue Cybewizard, but Darius suspected that was his poker face. Ghalt did not introduce the rest of his associates but gestured and everyone took seats.

Ghalt said, "Tell me, Captain Noble, why have you come here?"

Darius proceeded to relay the quest with the late Grand Master, how they had worked to find the ancient texts to close the rifts in space/time opened by the Federation and drow. He concluded by stating, "We have it on good authority that the drow have taken the unusual step of setting aside their long-held issues with the elves and are working with them to close the portals now."

Ghalt looked to one of his associates. "We had heard that from other sources, yes, Pynol?"

"Yes, Chieftain," the orc female replied. "I still find it difficult to believe."

"As do we," added Galit.

"It is good to have additional confirmation," said Ghalt. "Please, Captain, continue."

REVELATIONS AND RECONCILIATIONS

Darius said, "Unfortunately, as I mentioned before, these rifts in space/time have opened a way to an alternate dimension called savagespace. That's given access to a race that calls themselves illithids, which translates in Common as mindflayers. They are unrelenting and here for one reason: to destroy. They are a threat to everyone."

"The Grand Master made mention of that in their address," another of Ghalt's associates stated.

"What about it?" asked Ghalt.

Before Darius could speak again, Sara said, "It is wanton destruction and the ensuing chaos from that which feeds them and allows the mindflayers to grow and evolve. They can travel faster than light by a means other than wormhole or unrealspace, which has been presumed to somehow utilize faster-than-dark travel to cross vast interplanetary distances."

"Faster-than-dark?" growled one of the orc males. "That's ludicrous."

"Not necessarily," stated another orc female. "Just unimaginable to races dependent on light to live. Even low light, such as ourselves and dwarves."

Darius saw Tol and Zya both nod appreciatively towards the orc. Then he said, continuing his prior line of thought, "Closing the existing rifts will keep more of the mindflayers and their monsters from entering realspace. Apart from where they come from, and that they can manipulate extreme gravity to orbit a superdense dark star, nobody knows anything about them. How they live, grow, reproduce, it's all unknown. Even if more cannot cross from savagespace to realspace, can those already here increase their forces?"

"Extreme gravity manipulation?" Fhalt asked.

Aya said, "After we went on the quest with the Grand Master, we sought several of the suspected rifts and tracked the mindflayers and their monster companions to learn if they were gathering their forces in one place. They are. And as Captain Noble said, it's a superdense dark star that no race can approach too closely. Darius, Sara, and Galit, with their strategic and tactical knowledge, think it's most logical that they are gathering to strike from there, in force."

"They've been testing us, thus far," said Sara.

Aya continued, saying, "The mindflayers have been indiscriminate in attacking anyone and everyone who crosses their path or whose path they cross. Thus, everyone is equally likely to be their target."

Galit said, "And they have another weapon most of us have limited resistance to. They have the power of psionic attack and can use that to inflict pain, confusion, and other means to fog the mind. They are, quite probably, the most dangerous beings to threaten the lives of the peoples of this galaxy."

The end of the narrative was met with silence. The orcs seemed to be looking towards one another, then the crew, before turning to their tribal leader.

Darius waited. Ghalt appeared to be studying him, as well as the rest of the *Moon Raven*'s crew. After a long, increasingly uncomfortable silence, Ghalt said, "You've woven quite the intricate pattern before us, Captain Noble. But you have not explained why, or what it is you have come to me for."

"As you know," Galit began, before Darius could respond, "we came to you on the recommendation of Danielle Amelia Stern."

"Yes," Gahlt agreed. "And she told me you were coming. But the why has not been explained."

"No, it hasn't," Darius conceded. "So here it is, Chieftain Ghalt. The mindflayers must be stopped at all costs. They threaten every life in realspace. The human sectors are too self-absorbed or too preoccupied to lead, as are the elves, the drow, and even the dwarves. The orcs, however, could assemble an impressive force to meet the mindflayers and destroy them before they grow in power by causing more destruction and devastation. You are one of the most powerful and influential orc tribal leaders. You could lead that force."

The orcs all looked to Ghalt. Darius saw him leaning back in his seat, reaching a hand to rub at his chin, a gesture Darius should have known was not strictly human.

"This is not something I expected. I recognize that these mindflayers are dangerous and will need to be dealt with by orckind in time. What's in it for me, if I assemble a strike force to take the fight to them?"

Darius considered how to answer that. To his surprise, though, Zya said, "Reputation. Your people, not your tribe specifically, Chieftain, but the whole of orckind, are notoriously reputed to be gruff and difficult. But that, you know and I know, is largely unjust. It's akin to the judgment of a refurbished starship by its ancient hull. An orc tribal leader organizing the

REVELATIONS AND RECONCILIATIONS

forces of all the orcs to fight a threat to all sentient life in the galaxy could build you one hell of a legendary reputation."

Darius had not expected that sort of statement from Zya. Judging by a glance towards the rest of the *Moon Raven* crew, he could tell he was not the only one surprised.

"My mate speaks the truth," added Tol. "If the orcs take the lead in combatting this threat, the unfounded notions of who you are will be forever changed. What would that do to your people and their place in the galaxy? And what would such an opportunity, to lead that charge, do for the reputation of Ghalt hur Kholm Ahk?"

Ghalt was nodding his head. "You intrigue me. This is your whole crew, Captain Noble?"

"It is, Chieftain."

Ghalt turned to one of his associates, who gestured in a way Darius took as confirmation. Galit had been correct that the ship would be scanned for any remaining behind.

One of Ghalt's associates, a male, said, "I've never seen a mixed crew such as this, particularly with human leaders, showing such understanding."

Ghalt chuckled. "Yes. The crew of this *Moon Raven* seems to understand how things work in orc society. Very curious." The orc chieftain's eyes seemed to bore into Darius. "Still, I could use further convincing."

Before Darius could respond, Kaz said, "Captain Noble has chosen, and we have agreed, to help gather allies to join together, to take the fight to the mindflayers. As destruction makes them stronger, we must destroy them, first, before it's too late. While the UEO monks and clerics are working on gathering resistance, they have only limited access to orcs and are not likely inclined to directly approach orckind in this matter. Hence, if an orc tribal leader, such as yourself, took initiative to gather forces, that would make quite the impression."

"Then," Darius added, taking the cue from Kaz, "your initiative could well encourage the kitsune, halflings, gnomes, goblins, and maybe even the beholders to present themselves for this fight. It impacts every single sentient race in realspace. Think of it, Chieftain Ghalt. What would added good relations with those races, borne of your actions in gathering all orckind together and leading this fight, do for your standing among all of orckind and beyond?"

Darius saw the other orcs looking at their leader with what he almost thought was adoration. He had them, even if he didn't have Ghalt.

"Chieftain Ghalt," said Galit, arising from her seat, "I am, as I'm sure you are aware, the Blue Cyberwizard. I've joined this crew because they continue to amaze and surprise me. Coming to you as they have - as we have – should tell you just how serious this situation is."

She had taken up a docupad and approached the orc tribal chief. At his desk, she presented it to him. "This is everything the Grand Master shared, everything we found in those ancient documents, what we learned at the dark star that the mindflayers and their monsters are orbiting, and more. You are the orc tribal leader we have brought this to. Now is your chance to make a difference in a way none before you in all of orckind has before. The choice for what to do with this, and the good or bad that may come of it, is before you. Will you answer the call?"

Chapter 40 - Disparaging

Aneesa had always known that being born into one of the three families that led the Federation came with a huge amount of privilege. Even with this truth, not all members of the Koh, Mallick, or Anwar families were created equally.

She was one of four children. Her father had married into the Anwar family, and her mother served as a secretary to one of the more senior members. That senior member of the Anwar family had seen fit to find positions for Aneesa's two elder siblings. But that meant she and her younger sibling had to find their own ways.

The military, she had always been told, was of vast importance to the Federation and its goals. She had chosen, thus, to attend the academy and work on gaining respect as a military officer. Although she knew it was her being the highest ranked member of one of the three families that had gotten her the position of second-in-command of the Federation's forces, she believed she had also earned that place with her service. Aneesa had always worked hard, given her all, and fared decently at everything she'd done.

Even as a member of the Anwar family, Aneesa's knowledge and understanding of the hierarchy, and who specifically stood atop it, was limited. While her mother served an Anwar family elder, Aneesa knew he was at least a step or three from the top of the overall hierarchy.

The Anwar family had established protocols to let the junior members know when a senior member needed to counsel them. Aneesa had received such a message. She had been told to leave her command ship and take a shuttle to meet the elder. Aneesa had gotten a pilot and was on her way.

She was both nervous and excited about this meeting. The last time a senior member of the Anwar family had used the protocols to contact her, she'd been informed she would be named second-in-command of all Federation military forces.

That, she thought, must have made her a senior member of the Anwar family. Now that she had command of all the Federation military forces, that had to be a foregone conclusion.

Aneesa paid no attention to where the shuttle was going. She didn't recognize the stars or planet they'd approached, although a glance at the instruments from her place in the cabin behind the pilot and copilot showed it was the planet Third Moonrise. Aneesa knew that name. It was one of the core worlds the Anwar family called home. That must have meant whomever Aneesa was meeting would be one of the most senior members of the family.

When her shuttle landed, Aneesa made sure her uniform was straight. She found herself outside an impressive mansion, which featured a blend of classical and modern architecture. A servant was waiting to take her to the elder. He led Aneesa into an opulent study. It was appointed with art, carpets, and furniture that only the wealthiest, most powerful people could have and show off.

A man Aneesa had spoken with via video chatter only once before awaited her. "Galen Anwar," she addressed him, bowing formally to the elder.

He waved off his servant, who left the room. "Aneesa Anwar," Galen said, his voice rich and smooth. However, Aneesa also thought that she detected a note of condescension in it. "General of all Federation armed forces now," he continued. "Quite the impressive rise in such a short time."

"Yes, sir," she said.

Galen smiled. But it didn't touch his eyes, chilling Aneesa. He said, "And the senior members of the family have been informed that you have led your first battle into Confederation space. I have also heard that it went rather poorly."

Aneesa hadn't expected that. Caught off guard, she spluttered, "That, well, you see. That was not my fault. That was the result of General Song and his overly cautious, non-confrontational command. It made our forces too soft, and it left them ill-prepared to take the fight to the Confederation. My plan was bold, unlike anything that Song gave our forces. The only reason the battle went poorly was due to his past incompetence."

Galen nodded. He said nothing, going to a sidebar and pouring a drink from a decanter. He took up the tumbler and swirled the liquor within it. Aneesa wasn't sure what to do.

"Song's failings-" she began.

REVELATIONS AND RECONCILIATIONS

Galen moved far faster than Aneesa would have anticipated. He backhanded her across the cheek, catching her utterly off guard. She stumbled, but caught herself on a nearby chair before she could fall.

"You were made second-in-command of the Federation military to keep Song in line with our goals, not to eliminate him," Galen said, his tone so cold it nearly froze Aneesa. "Your job was to keep abreast of what he was doing and to make certain that he kept sight of the greater goal."

"But...but..." Aneesa stuttered, still shaky from the blow. "Sir, was it not meant for me to assume command of Federation forces? Song was not a member of one of the families, and I thought my place was to lead in the Anwar name. And if I did not eliminate Song when I did, how long would it have been before some Kho or Mallick officer was breathing down my neck and eyeing to replace me?"

"Prior to Thomas Song, Alistair Mallick – yes, a member of the Mallick family – was the General in command of Federation forces. And he failed miserably. He was arrogant, brash, and gave no thought to the future, only what he saw before him. If he had not started out the occupation of the Alliance with all the missteps he took, it would not be going as poorly as it is. All my intel informs me that it is only getting worse, Aneesa."

Galen took a drink from the tumbler as Aneesa released the chair and righted herself.

The Anwar elder continued, saying, "Song might have taken an approach that other elders of our family, as well as some Mallick and Koh elders, found to be too cautious. But he was not wrong. Thomas Song rose through the ranks on merit, Aneesa. He had a sharp mind, and he saw the big picture for what it is, not what we wish it to be. He recognized winnable from unwinnable situations."

Aneesa shook her head. "No, sir, you don't understand. No offense, you're not a soldier. Song was overly cautious because he didn't truly have a taste for war. He was a coward and a fool."

Galen backhanded Aneesa's other cheek, this time throwing her to floor. His tone was even icier than before, if that was possible. "No, Aneesa. You are the fool. Thomas Song was probably the finest general the Federation has produced in decades. He was both a cunning tactician and skilled strategist. He knew who you were, Annesa... A communications specialist."

Galen reached into a pocket and withdrew a small device. He activated it, and Aneesa heard the late Thomas Song's voice. "She's based at a planetary station in one of the innermost Federation systems. She has no combat or strategic experience."

Galen returned the device to his pocket and said, "Song did his homework. He knew he had been assigned a member of the family to keep an eye on him. And still, he served to both expand our interests and keep the Federation whole. You have deprived us of his skill and insight."

Galen returned to the sidebar, refilling his tumbler. He took a sip from it, then turned towards Aneesa, still on the floor beside the chair.

"Because of your youth and inexperience, Aneesa, you know only that you are a member of one of the three families that lead the Federation," Galen continued. "Three families working as one, controlling and expanding their sectors of space called the Federation. But despite all outward appearances, matters are getting more and more complicated between the Mallick, Kho, and Anwar clans. The invasion and occupation of the Alliance has proven anything but simple. Couple that with the attacks on the Confederation, and there are divisions among the families over how to proceed. Still, to the galaxy at large, the Federation is a united government. But internally the cracks are starting to show."

Galen paced, and Aneesa pulled herself off the floor. Both of her cheeks stung. However, she could not be sure if that was from the blows she'd received, or the continued dressing down.

"The cautious approach Thomas Song was taking was a lesson in wisdom and smart strategy," Galen said. "Yes, our victory over the Alliance was sure and swift. But the occupation has been increasingly met with resistance. Resistance that likely would not have existed had Song been in command rather than Alastair Mallick. You received high marks in military history in the academy, is that not so, Aneesa?"

"Yes, sir," she replied. Her voice quivered ever so slightly, which she despised.

"Then you know that fighting a war on two fronts is mostly a losing proposition unless you have impressive numbers at your disposal," Galen said. "Realize, Aneesa, that the Federation is currently fighting a war on two

REVELATIONS AND RECONCILIATIONS

fronts, and we do not have the benefit of impressive numbers of soldiers or equipment at our disposal."

Aneesa searched for a response. The berating of her elder was both scaring and angering her.

Galen continued, saying, "Now that you are the General and commanding officer of Federation forces, you need to act decisively and choose a new Lieutenant General. I advise you to do so with all haste. And it would be in both yours and the Federation's best interest if you choose a wise soldier not unlike Thomas Song, and not a member of either the Mallick, Kho, or Anwar families, either."

"I'm to choose someone who can next replace me as Song replaced Mallick?" spat Aneesa, her anger rising to the surface and overcoming her fear.

Galen sighed dramatically. "You're a fool, Aneesa Anwar. You know that Song only replaced Alastair Mallick because there were no members of any of the families who'd achieved a high enough rank to safely, reasonably, or logically assume command. There were no other members of the family who understood the amazing new technology we had at our disposal and how to employ it."

Galen took another drink from his tumbler, then said, "You were not that officer, Aneesa Anwar. You were to learn from Song, gain understanding to make up for your lack of experience, not eliminate him in the middle of a two-front war. No, no member of the three families had the rank, the experience, nor the support of the drow."

"The drow?" Aneesa questioned.

Galen grunted. "Yes. That factored into the Superior Convocation's decision to give Song command. But now they have withdrawn, further lessening both our soldiers and equipment."

Galen turned away from Aneesa, returning to the sidebar. He set down the empty tumbler and, without turning back to her, said, "The drow Synod, their leaders, have lodged a formal complaint with the Convocation about the continued use by our forces of space/time folding technology. They emphasized that the consequences of its continued use are grave for all the peoples across known space, Aneesa. And the Superior Convocation takes that very seriously."

"What?" Aneesa exclaimed. "Why? The drow are ludicrous. They use this phantom of unexpected consequences to cover their own cowardice. Frankly, the Federation is much better off without them."

Galen turned on her. He wore a look on his face that made Aneesa want to melt away. She had never seen that much disappointment from anyone before.

He sighed. "Aneesa, you truly do not understand the big picture at all. This new technology for folding space/time has been sought after for millennia. That Federation scientists unlocked it is an incredible feat of science. But we did not have the power to use that technology on our own. Without the drow and their power sources, we would have naught but unusable theory. Without the drow, our invasion and overrun of the Alliance would not have come to pass. Ludicrous? Maybe. Cowards? No."

Galen went silent. He continued to eye Aneesa in a most discomfiting manner.

"As to the Grand Master and their transmission," Galen continued. "Publicly, in a show of Federation might and strength, we ignore their warning. Privately, among ourselves, the Superior Convocation takes it very seriously. It is concerning that invaders from another dimension have taken advantage of unintended consequences of folding space/time. It is equally concerning that they, when met in combat, proved formidable. That the drow have immediately ceased use of this technology is not something you should so eagerly and readily discount. The drow are ancient, wise, and neither fools nor cowards."

Aneesa considered Galen's words. She also considered that he might be testing her. Thus, she needed to tell him what he wanted to hear. And she had to do so convincingly. "Sir," she began, putting a look of contriteness on her face, "I am sorry if I have disappointed. I have always had the best interests of the Federation at heart. And I wish to do my family proud. If I have acted rashly, it is only in my fervor to show the Superior Convocation that I can lead us to greater glory."

Galen continued to give her the same silent, uncomfortable stare. He did not reply for some time. After too long in that tableau, Galen finally said, "Very well, General. I shall continue to support you in the Superior Convocation. However, it is imperative that you choose and name a strong second-in-command, preferably with lengthy experience. I recommend General Gerhardt, General Healy, or General Hara. All of them can offer you insight, experience, and strategic guidance for ongoing operations."

"Yes, sir."

"What's more," Galen continued, "be especially mindful of further rebel attacks and ongoing problems with the Alliance occupation."

Aneesa felt like Galen, with no military experience at all, was telling her how to do her job. Still, she knew what he wanted to hear and said, "I will make certain that any attacks I launch against the Confederation use only current, fresh intel."

"Focus less on the conquest of the Confederation, Aneesa, and more on the nearer issues with the Alliance occupation."

She wanted to scream at the elder, to tell him he had no idea what he was talking about. Galen was not a soldier. Maintaining her face, Aneesa said, "Yes, sir."

Galen sighed and shook his head. "Aneesa, be mindful of what I have been telling you here. You are new to this level of politics, but as the commanding officer of Federation armed forces, you cannot be ignorant of them. I told you that things are not as copacetic between the Kho, Mallick, and Anwar families as we project to the galaxy at large. You are part of that now. And you must understand that the slightest spark will burn away the fabric of the Federation. Learn from the example of Thomas Song and don't be incautious."

"I understand," she replied. She hoped she still looked appropriately contrite.

Galen continued to stare. Then, the servant who had escorted her into the study appeared, and she realized she was being dismissed. The walk back through the mansion was silent. It took all that she had not to openly seethe. Aneesa knew she was not just being escorted by the servant, but was also being closely watched.

Once back aboard her shuttle and in the air, Aneesa felt as though she'd been holding her breath. The meeting had not gone as she had hoped. Yet, it hadn't gone as badly as it might have, either.

Galen Anwar might have been a member of the Superior Convocation, but he was no soldier, and she believed that he was thinking too small. She was not Alastair Mallick. She would bring honor, not dishonor, to her family. Aneesa was beginning to formulate a plan.

Chapter 41 - Strategizing

A signal had been received at the Grand Master's temple. The halfling leadership had something they wanted to share with the Grand Master. With all the memories imparted to the Grand Master by the mysterious stone, they were fairly certain that no Grand Master before them had ever visited the halfling homeworld.

The halfling homeworld, Poluroslyyk, was situated in a particularly large solar system featuring binary stars, two asteroid belts, and more than twenty planets and dwarf planets. It was relatively not far from dwarf, elf, and beholder space.

The halflings had been part of the second wave, discovering unrealspace and faster-than-light travel around five thousand years before. They had ventured to many of the other worlds in their solar system and sent an expedition beyond. Unfortunately, the first race they would encounter was another second-wave race. The beholders.

The Grand Master had never seen a beholder in person. Unlike most of the other sentient races, beholders had neither arms nor legs. They were, instead, two point four meter-large levitating spheres, with a giant central eye, large, fanged mouth, and ten smaller eye stalks atop their bodies.

Beholder starships were as spherical as their creators and tended to be larger than almost any other race's ships. The beholder ship that the halflings had made first contact with had led to more beholders arriving at Poluroslyyk. Before the halflings could spread their wings and travel the wider galaxy, the beholders had subjugated them and occupied Poluroslyyk for two-hundred and fifty years.

The motivation for the beholder occupation of the halfling homeworld had never been clear. Dwarves, drow, and elves all reported encountering the beholders soon after they joined the second wave. Perhaps because the halflings of the time had been relatively unarmed, the beholders found them easy targets.

Some speculated that the large spherical beholders, so vastly different from the other bipedal space-faring races, felt a need to dominate the far smaller one-meter large halflings.

Over the two and a half centuries of the beholder occupation, the halflings had largely just existed. The beholders had made them use the resources of Poluroslyyk, the other worlds, and the asteroids in their solar system to build beholder starships, cities, and various other items.

Several dwarf explorers investigated after noting the back-and-forth travels of the beholders from the large, binary-starred solar system to their home system. Upon discovering the halflings and their beholder occupiers, the dwarves had chased out the beholders and freed the halflings.

Though none had ever determined what the truth might be, many speculated that one reason the beholders had largely kept to themselves, apart from travelers, trading, and their colonies, was because of their failed occupation of the halfling homeworld. Many of the Grand Master's predecessors had often pondered if the UEO should approach the beholders to learn more about them.

The halflings had formed an almost immediate kinship with the dwarves. It was not just because the dwarves had freed the halflings from the beholders but also because they were quite close in stature. The dwarves, however, were both broader and about a quarter of a meter taller. Although dwarves and halflings had become generally friendly toward one another, the nature of the dwarf elders, the incredible discrimination of their patronymic society, and their lack of central leadership, kept the two races from a closer bonding.

Using technologies liberated from their former beholder overlords, combined with their prior attempts at exploration, the better-armed and armored halflings had resumed exploring their galaxy and beyond. The next race they had encountered on their travels was the elves.

The elves had immediately felt a kinship with halflings. Despite being twice their height, the two races had similar features, such as pointed ears. The biggest difference was greater variances of skin and hair color among the halflings.

While the halflings had developed a friendship with the dwarves, they especially bonded with the elves. It was with the guidance of the elves that the halflings developed better starships, though they still remained something of a hodgepodge of elf, dwarf, and beholder technologies. The elves also helped the halflings redevelop their culture to take part in the galaxy at large.

REVELATIONS AND RECONCILIATIONS

Unlike the other races of a given wave expanding their territory, colonizing worlds and star systems, the halflings had colonized no worlds outside of their own solar system. It was halflings that worked out the finer points of terraforming, creating a process that they had refined on two of the worlds nearest Poluroslyyk in the system's goldilocks zone. Sharing the technology that they had developed for that process made them a largely wealthy race.

The halflings, despite having only three worlds they called home in a single solar system, was a large race. They were frequent spacefarers, part of mixed crews, and even monks and clerics of the UEO. Still, the vast majority of halfling society kept to themselves. That was part of why the Grand Master had been surprised to be contacted by the halfling leaders.

Starships of the halfling home fleet met the Grand Master's ship and escorted them to Poluroslyyk. As they neared the halfling homeworld, the Grand Master refreshed their knowledge of halfling leadership.

Each halfling world had a group of elected officials in charge of regions, sectors, and other various divisions of the cities and wider lands of Poluroslyyk and the other two terraformed worlds. Beneath those various leaders, committees of rotating volunteers and appointed members handled infrastructure, law enforcement, public works, the courts, and other matters of governance.

There was a larger structure atop that. The halfling cabinet consisted of more elected officials and committees that oversaw everything across their entire solar system. The cabinet officials rotated jobs and titles, which lessened the danger of megalomaniacs or demagogues arising. Among the titles and jobs that the cabinet officials rotated between, there was a president, first and second vice-president, and a dozen ministers, covering finance, defense, internal affairs, external affairs, and more.

The Grand Master hoped they wouldn't be meeting with all fifteen cabinet members. Still, they were intrigued that this form of governance, created before the halflings had made their way to the stars, had worked, and worked well, for millennia.

As their starship entered Poluroslyyk's atmosphere, the Grand Master found the light of the binary suns nearly as bright as most single-starred worlds. The twin suns of the halfling homeworld were less than a thousand kilometers apart, constantly trading elements between them. They had a tight orbit around one another and were always seen together in the skies of the worlds of their solar system.

The current captain of the Grand Master's ship, a half-elf, pulled them from their reverie as she said, "We've received clearance to land at the main government center, which is not the capital of Poluroslyyk."

"No," the Grand Master said. "It wouldn't be, Guardian Kolora. The whole-system government rotates between the three halfling worlds and several stations across their system. If you look closely, in fact, you'll see there is no capital city. Even the planetary government rotates its location around the planet."

"The seems horridly inefficient," Kolora said.

The Grand Master chuckled. "I thought so, too. But it's worked for them for thousands of years. The politics of halflings are quite a bit less important than other races seem to make them."

Guardian Kolora said nothing further on the subject, confirming their coordinates with their pilot. As they approached the city, which the Grand Master learned was called Gorod Tiijooj, they noted how many structures seemed oddly small, even when they were towers. Of course, to a one-meter-tall halfling, even a two-meter-tall ceiling would be high.

Fortunately, it was clear as the ship neared the government center that the halflings had built to receive other races. It was offset from the main portion of the city, a group of four buildings arranged around a fifth, with fountains, landing pads, and gardens between them.

There were several other starships on the landing pads, most of them halfling. One, however, looked to the Grand Master, with it's clean lines and overall beauty, to be an elf starship.

Accompanied by a pair each of cleric and monk masters, the Grand Master departed the ship. They were met by a small group of officials, representing a presidential committee. They escorted the Grand Master and their party to the main meeting salon.

Four of the halfling cabinet members awaited the Grand Master and their party. A female halfling stood, offering her hand. "Grand Master? I am President Laahooh Tarirat."

"It's an honor to meet you, Madame President."

REVELATIONS AND RECONCILIATIONS

The halfling president introduced her first and second vice presidents and the minister of trade. "We appreciate you coming here, Grand Master," President Laahooh said. "While there are a good number of halflings among the monks and clerics of the UEO, there are no temples or monasteries here, or anywhere in our solar system, for that matter."

"I had it in mind that I am the first Grand Master to visit Poluroslyyk."

"Indeed," said the first vice-president, Tiinuun Polalop. "We appreciate you coming so swiftly."

"Given my recent transmission across all chatters and the medianet, I figured what you desired to share with me was related."

"This is so," stated President Laahooh. "Please understand, the halfling people are not cowards. But we do not know how secure any transmissions might be against these mindflayers. We did not wish to invite them to target us, should they learn what we desire to share."

That piqued the Grand Master's interest. "I understand. So, unless you'd like to continue with further pleasantries, tell me what it is."

The four halfling leaders exchanged a look between them. Then, the minister of trade, Dootaat Nukikun, cleared his throat. "As you may or may not be aware," he began, "we've sent a convoy on a trade mission to Pherusah. I'm sure the specifics would not interest you. But what would interest you is their encounter with the mindflayers and a dragon during their mission."

"Go on," encouraged the Grand Master.

"An attempt to contact the mindflayers was made but to no avail," said Minister Dootaat. "Combat ensued. Though the mindflayers appeared to have superior technology, and the dragon was incredibly fierce, our convoy overcame them and won the battle."

"Were they evenly or unevenly matched in numbers?" asked the Grand Master.

"The numbers were relatively even," replied Minister Dootaat. "We did, however, make an interesting discovery. In your message to everyone, Grand Master, you discussed the psionic abilities of the mindflayers. Power that can disrupt thought, sow confusion, and in some instances cause pain. Knowing this, the leaders of the convoy reported that not a one of our people suffered any such affects."

The Grand Master leaned forward. "None? We've had reports of variable impact of the psionic attacks, and it's presumed that's due to the mindflayers still learning about the peoples of this galaxy. But everyone thus-far has reported feeling the affects of their psionic attacks."

"We found this curious as well," said Minister Dootaat. "We double-checked, and not a single halfling in the convoy felt any adverse effect on their concentration, thoughts, or anything else. That got us to thinking, and we checked into some of our most ancient texts to see if there was anything about resistance to psionics."

"I've no recollection of any such thing on the part of any race," said the Grand Master.

"There are, of course, not many races with psionic abilities," said Minister Dootaat. "But there is one we're familiar with. One that halflings are especially familiar with."

"Beholders," breathed the Grand Master.

"Yes," agreed Minister Dootaat. "Which our people were not aware of during their occupation. It went unnoted because the beholders were the first aliens halflings ever encountered. It was not until far later, long after the occupation, that we learned they were capable of psionic attacks."

"They couldn't use psionics against halflings during the occupation?" asked the Grand Master.

"No. That was what we turned to the ancient texts to confirm. In fact, a few of our scholars, following the beholder occupation, think one reason they occupied Poluroslyyk was because they wanted to figure out why we were immune to their psionic attacks."

The Grand Master shook their head. "This would not be common knowledge, of course. Halflings, though known across the galaxy, are not well known. And the specifics of your history with the beholders is not common knowledge. If you are resistant to the psionic attacks of beholders, and to the psionic attacks of mindflayers, as a race, you may well be resistant to all psionic attacks."

"That is the consensus among our leaderships, educators, and scientists," said Second Vice-President Faapiip Alitila. "What's more, our academics and scientists believe this is related to the halfling ability to shapeshift."

REVELATIONS AND RECONCILIATIONS

The Grand Master considered that. "I know that shapeshifting is an inherent trait in some halflings. Can all of you shapeshift?"

"Yes," said President Laahooh.

"However," added Vice President Faapiip. "To do so regularly, and for an extended period, requires mental discipline. All halfling children are taught this, and some are better than others. The most skilled can imitate the appearance of nearly any race, though none can maintain a given shape for more than about twelve galactic standard hours. But our academics and scientists agree that the training for this, even when they are not among the strongest shapeshifters, makes us all resistant to psionic attack."

The Grand Master considered this. "Do you believe this is a skill you can train in others, or have you some other purpose for sharing this with me?"

"It's not a skill another race could learn," said Vice President Faapiip. "Even an untrained halfling can shapeshift at will; they just cannot hold it for long. The mental discipline is specific to shapeshifting and not something to be taught."

"Our military is not known for the kind of strength humans, elves, or orcs possess," said President Lahooh. "So, for us to join any of the parties that it's rumored are being assembled to seek out the mindflayers, that would unacceptably harm our forces."

"But we feel this is too important for the halfling people to not get involved," added Vice President Tiinuun.

"We called you here to discuss this," said Minister Dootaat. "We would be willing to dispatch halflings to be embedded on the ships of any fleet from the forces of the other races."

"To what end?" asked the Grand Master. "It's only halflings who are not impacted by psionic attack."

"True," said Vice President Faapiip. "But we believe that, through shapeshifting actively, it's possible halfling presence would be disruptive to the psionic attack for all who are near that halfling individual."

"How would that work?" asked the Grand Master

Vice President Tiinuun replied, "Though we change ourselves through shapeshifting in some ways, more than anything we project those changes outwards. That's what requires such discipline. To take and hold the form of an orc, for example, who is so much larger than our people, we must project the presence, aura, sounds, and smells of an orc in addition to our physical changes."

The Grand Master leaned back in their seat. "So, you think the act of shapeshifting during an attack by the mindflayers would nullify their psionic attack for anyone in the presence of a halfling?"

"Yes," agreed Minister Dootaat. "What's more, the people we would send to perform this aid would be skilled in things that might be negatively affected by a psionic attack to the detriment of all. Hence, we'd offer pilots, navigators, and weapons specialists."

"Having a gunner able to fire in the face of a psionic attack, even as it affects others on the ship, could turn the tide of battle against the mindflayers," said President Laahooh.

The Grand Master was intrigued. "How can I help?"

"Simple," said President Laahooh. "As the Grand Master of the UEO, you have connections to those rumored to be gathering forces to take on the mindflayers. Help us connect with them and get our people embedded in their fleets so we can do our part to help."

The Grand Master nodded. "That could provide tremendous assistance to the effort to stop the mindflayers and their monsters. I understand why you did not wish to broadcast this."

The Grand Master paused, considering their next words, then said, "I am not wholly certain of the specifics going into putting together the rumored force to attack the mindflayers. But I suspect I have a contact or two I can reach out to for this."

Chapter 42 - Closing

The science behind the process made sense to Ilizeva. The logic was clear. Yet the precise calculations and how the forces came together to do all that they needed to was less understandable.

Together, drow, elf, and dwarf scientists had made their calculations, run their simulations, and came to a consensus. Hence, Ilizeva and the *Nuummite Raptor* were in the company of three elf and one dwarf starships, in a sector of elf space where the drow had previously used folding space/time to attack.

This time, the trip had been made by more conventional means, a trek across unrealspace. Once they had arrived, they compared data logs from the *Nuummite Raptor* and sensor input to pinpoint where a tear in space/time had been left from creating the fold. With that worked out, they needed to confirm that the mindflayers had used the rift in space/time to cross to realspace from savagespace.

There was also a danger that more mindflayers might arrive through the rift while they worked to close it. That was why there were two elf and two additional drow warships with them.

This would be the first attempt to close and seal a tear in the fabric of space/time. The complicated process involved multiple, precisely timed steps.

It began by pinpointing the precise location of the rift or tear in the fabric of their dimension. Once its existence was confirmed, the dwarves would move in and place their mineral in the center of the exact location of the tear in space/time. Once that was complete, they would move a safe distance away. Then, the *Nuummite Raptor* would use its space/time fold tech to focus the creation of a portal on the mineral.

They couldn't open a fold in space/time. Like the static tests, they needed to open the event horizon of the artificial wormhole but not a space/time fold portal.

Once the artificial wormhole event horizon was created, the elves would send a beam of negative energy into the center of the artificial wormhole event horizon. By interacting with the dwarf mineral, utilizing the energy for the creation of the portal with the negative energy beam would seal the tear in space/time like a tailor sewing a torn garment back together.

All the calculations made by drow, elf, and dwarf scientists, plus the work from the Federation scientists the drow still had, confirmed that this plan should permanently seal the tear and stop the dimensional bleed allowing the denizens of savagespace access to realspace. Or there was another possible outcome. The result of the combination of the dwarf mineral, drow artificial wormhole, and elf negative energy beam might lead to an explosion. A really, really big explosion.

The information provided in the broadcast by the Grand Master was ancient. Thousands of years old. Maybe even older. While it had led to the calculations for the combined technologies to work to close the rifts in space/time, it didn't account for the passage of time. The technology they had at their disposal, thus, had a considerably higher power output.

This was one point the scientists of the elf, drow, and dwarves disagreed upon amongst themselves. Some argued that the amount of total power they had available now, versus when the information had been created, didn't matter. Greater power output made no difference in the calculations. Some, however, argued that the exponentially greater amount of energy output by each race's contribution wasn't negligible and needed to be better accounted for.

There were always nonbelievers. One or two of each race's scientists argued that closing a rift in space/time wouldn't work, no matter what data they had. Time being both linear and quantum, depending on the observer and the observed, would render the tear either permanent or self-sealing. What's more, the factors of the potential difference in fundamental physics from one dimension to another made it unworkable. The majority, though agreed by a wide margin that it would work.

Ilizeva had insisted on being present for the first attempt to seal a tear. She believed in showing her faith in the science and tech by being there, rather than shying away from a potentially lethal situation. In her experience, that had led to receiving respect.

If they succeeded, they'd employ the other drow starships that had the space/time folding technology with teams of elves and dwarves to seek out and close all the rifts. The information about where the drow had opened

REVELATIONS AND RECONCILIATIONS

rifts in space/time for their attacks and return transit had been saved, so deploying more than one joint task force was possible. It was still up for debate if more than one group should be tasked with sealing the rifts. Also, the instantaneous transit of folding space/time could not be used, lest new rifts be opened. Thus, they had to cross the distances via unrealspace.

One of the drow scientists had questioned if there might be some way to automate the closing of a rift, akin to the natural process of wormholes. That had been a private conversation between Ilizeva, Alizev, Ulozov, and the other Synod ambassadors. Ilizeva had considered the idea, once they knew a rift might be able to be closed. However, before further in-depth discussion could take place, she'd said no. The potential for abuse of the technology - she recognized the irony of her concern about that – took the idea completely off the table.

That led to another concern. While the drow had taken the Grand Master's warnings to heart and changed their mission, abandoning the space/time folding technology, the Federation had not. They were, to her knowledge, still using the technology to attack the Confederation, adding to the total number of tears for the mindflayers to use.

Ilizeva's dislike of humans had found more affirmation with the Federation than not. The one human she'd respected, Thomas Song, had been murdered to advance an underqualified political appointee to leadership. However, it was not, by all reports, going well. That was but a small comfort.

As if he read her mind, Colonel Ulozov approached Ilizeva. "General," he addressed her.

"Colonel."

"I bring word from Colonel Orizevi," he said. "Special forces have their assets on the ground in Federation space. Operations have begun."

Ilizeva nodded. "Do we have results thus-far?"

"All is going as planned," Ulozov reported. "Orizevi was instrumental in creating the strategy for this operation, and it shouldn't trace back to the drow at all."

"It will take time," said Ilizeva.

"It will," agreed Ulozov. "But the impact of this operation should end Federation space/time folding."

"Well done, Colonel," Ilizeva said. "Both you and Orizevi will be receiving commendations for this quite clever plan."

"Thank you, General."

"General Ilizeva," a controller called out, "the dwarves report the mineral is positioned correctly, and is stable. The elves also report they're ready."

"Our systems?" questioned Ilizeva.

"All systems are go, at your command," another controller called out.

"Stand by the space/time fold," Ilizeva ordered. "Get confirmation that the dwarves and elves are in sync for this operation."

"Yes, General."

After a moment, the *Nuummite Raptor's* captain reported, "Confirmed. All task force ships report ready, synced, and standing by."

Ilizeva looked at Ulozov a moment, then back to the viewport and displays before her. "Very good. All ships, make ready. *Nuummite Raptor* is opening the artificial wormhole event horizon now. Engage."

The *Nuummite Raptor* fired the beam, targeting the precisely-placed dwarf mineral to open the artificial wormhole event horizon. Within moments, there was a flash at that same location. Space appeared to fold in on itself at a small point she could see, and then it erupted like a volcano into a ring of distortion that appeared cloud-like, with an inky, blurry portal at its center.

A moment later, a green and gold beam emitted from an elf starship, targeting the dwarf mineral hidden by the inky portal at the center of the distortion. Ilizeva looked at the readings on the energy output and other matters, braced for the possible explosion. But none came.

At the center of the portal, akin to looking through a window, she caught a glimpse of the darkest darkness Ilizeva had ever seen. It flashed, once or twice, like it had lightning within. Just visible in those flashes were mindflayer starships. Ilizeva realized they were waiting to cross to realspace from savagespace. But before anything could happen, the '"window" vanished, replaced by familiar stars.

The wormhole seemed to fold in on itself. Then, there was a flash of light, and it was gone. "Report," Ilizeva ordered.

"Process complete," a controlled called. "Checking instruments now."

"Glad it didn't go boom," remarked Ulozov under his breath.

REVELATIONS AND RECONCILIATIONS

"Dwarf and elf starships report no issues," another controller called out. "They're running tests now."

Ilizeva looked at the displays and the calculations on them of temporal distortions, dimensional bleed, particulates in the vacuum, and other data. Yet she had to admit to herself, she had no idea how to fully comprehend what she was seeing.

"General," a controller called out, "all readings indicate that the rift has been sealed."

"Confirmed," another called. "Showing expected norms for temporal and dimensional factors."

"The elves agree," another controller called.

"The dwarves confirm," still another controller sang out.

"One down," Ilizeva said aloud.

"Many to go," remarked Ulozov.

Chapter 43 – Networking

It felt strange to be alone in her ship. Yet that was where Galit found herself. She was aboard *Phantom*, rather than *Moon Raven*. Of course, it was the middle of the "night cycle" of the starship, and they were in unrealspace, en route to kitsune space.

While she had full access to all of *Phantom*'s systems on the *Moon Raven* and spent most of her waking hours there with the crew, she still slept in her quarters on her ship. When she'd awoken in the "middle of the night", she had decided to remain aboard her ship rather than go to the *Moon Raven*'s flight deck below her.

The kitsune crewmember of the *Moon Raven*, Aya, had made arrangements for them to meet with a representative of the kitsune people. Galit knew that Aya had been a thief prior to joining the crew of the *Moon Raven* and wondered how legitimate her contact might be. However, given the gravity of the situation, Galit knew Aya would seek as legitimate a contact as possible.

Galit rarely slept more than a few hours at a time. It was because she'd gone to her bunk earlier than usual that she was awake presently, she suspected. She was going over various messages she'd received from associates. Though many had been read from her station below on the *Moon Raven*, she felt an odd sense of detachment. As if not doing what she was doing now, on *Phantom*, somehow represented a dereliction of duty. She'd not neglected anyone or anything. Even the *Phantom*'s AI was present in the station on the larger ship that she'd taken as her own. It was just a drastic change from her usual sense of normalcy.

Galit chided herself for being a creature of habit. What's more, the months with the crew of the *Moon Raven* were almost an insignificant blip of time when it came to the life of the Blue Cyberwizard.

She leaned back in her seat, looking at her starship's flight deck. Large enough for a crew of three, it was a very different arrangement from the *Moon Raven*. Yet it was still obviously of similar design.

Galit recognized that her mind was wandering. Given the time and lack of any current urgency, she let it. Galit pondered the recent happenings of

REVELATIONS AND RECONCILIATIONS

her life that led to the meeting with the orc tribal leader, Ghalt hur Kholm Ahk. She had stepped up to the orc leader, challenging him to decide. He had chosen to support their request and offer aid in leading the hunt to destroy the mindflayers and their monsters.

Ghalt had immediately begun to reach out to other orc tribal leaders. It had been an even bigger success than Galit and the *Moon Raven* crew had thought might be possible and had led the crew into a discussion about what to do next.

↔↔↔↔

Galit and the *Moon Raven* crew were escorted to a conference room, where they were assured of their privacy. Ghalt had invited them to join him for a meal, and they'd accepted.

This gave them some time. Though it had been presented to them as an option, sightseeing around the city of Jha-Dyt Ahk Madeena didn't hold appeal for the crew. Galit suspected that being surrounded by orcs, such as they would be, might not feel like a comfortable place to be for any of them.

As they settled into the conference room, they were brought drinks and were admiring the spectacular view of the city.

"Orcs have impressively good taste," remarked Aya.

Zya chuckled. "Maybe. Seems rather ostentatious to me."

Aya gestured. "Maybe it's just huge because they're so huge."

"I've had so few interactions with orcs," remarked Sara.

Tol said, "I once got into an utterly unexpected philosophical debate with an orc back at *Territory's Edge*. It's too easy to see them as brutes. But past the appearance, they're no less developed than any other first through third-wave races."

"So it seems," agreed Sara.

"Your time serving the Alliance, even in special operations, seriously seems to have sheltered you," said Galit.

Sara shook her head. "More than I ever thought."

"You're learning," said Aya.

"We all are," added Darius.

Galit noted that he had his back to the crew, looking out the window into the city. Without turning, he said, "We keep learning there's a lot beyond what any of us have known before. Maybe we all came together by random chance, but together, we've done some extraordinary things."

Galit had learned most of their short history. The *Moon Raven* crew was singular in many ways. Darius continued, saying, "I have a thought about what comes next."

Aya sat at the table. "I know that tone. This is going to be brilliant or terrible."

Following her lead, the rest of the crew took seats. Darius turned from the window to face them. "With Galit and Ms. Stern's help, this crew has managed to meet an obviously influential orc tribal leader. And he has made it clear that he will draw in more of his contemporaries and others of orckind to assist. Now we have the start of a force to deal with the threat from the mindflayers already in realspace."

"The start?" questioned Sara. "You see more?"

"I do," Darius said. "There are many races in this galaxy, all of whom are under threat by these extradimensional invaders. The orcs are tough, and they're impressive fighters. But the mindflayers and their monsters will fight to inflict chaos and destruction with ferocity and tenacity. It will take everyone and everything that can be mustered to stop them."

"What leads you to that conclusion?" asked Galit.

Darius shrugged. "Can't say. A feeling, I guess."

"It makes sense," Kaz said. "The Grand Master would not send a galaxy-wide message via both medianet and chatter if the threat wasn't dire. The UEO doesn't take such actions lightly. You might not have a connection to chi or the energies as I do, but that doesn't mean you can't sense it, too."

There was a moment's silence. Galit, for her part, agreed with Kaz's assessment.

"So," Darius took up again, "I've been thinking. We have the Blue Cyberwizard with us, direct contact with the Grand Master, and together we represent multiple races. We have a lot of resources at our disposal. Resources we could use to broker arrangements with connections to involve more races to join the orcs to stand against the mindflayers."

Sara whistled low. "Seriously? You think we should stay in the thick of this?"

Darius chuckled. "I do. Do you have another idea?"

REVELATIONS AND RECONCILIATIONS

Sara shook her head. "No. I'm not against this at all. Just clarifying the thought."

"We are limited," said Zya.

Tol added, "Given our status among the dwarf elders as renegades for violating the tradition regarding the place of females, we can't be a bridge to our people."

Aya sighed dramatically. "I have someone among my people who could help. It's just going to be wicked awkward for me."

That was why the *Moon Raven* was en route to kitsune space. Galit had been impressed that the crew had been so willing to make that decision. She wouldn't have blamed them for moving on and perhaps genuinely taking up transportation of cargo. Yet at the same time, given their natures, that wouldn't have worked for them. They needed to serve the greater good as part of their own good.

The crew of the *Moon Raven* may not have realized it, but they'd become key players in what might lead to a rather major interstellar power shift. One that Galit saw as wholly beneficial for all the residents of the galaxy.

Her thoughts were interrupted by a chatter signal. Galit accepted it. Above the station she sat at, a holographic image of the head and shoulders of the Grand Master appeared.

"Galit Azurite," they addressed her.

"Grand Master."

"Apologies," the Grand Master said. "I know it's the middle of galactic standard night, but I wanted to make you aware of some developments regarding handling the mindflayers."

"You didn't wake me," Galit said. "Please, go on."

The Grand Master proceeded to explain to Galit the situation with the halflings and their ability to resist the mindflayer psionic attacks. "That could be of great use to those who will seek to stop them," the Grand Master concluded.

"Indeed," Galit agreed.

"As you know," the Grand Master continued, "the elves and dwarves have joined the drow to close the rifts in space/time and stop any further incursions. That will take time and much of their attention."

"And the Federation?" Galit asked.

"Still focusing on their conquests," said the Grand Master with obvious distaste. "However, there have been developments in Federation space that I suspect might lead to the end of their conquests."

Galit waited, but the Grand Master didn't elaborate.

"The first wave races, the elves and dwarves, tend to lead discussions about cooperation between disparate races," continued the Grand Master. "As they're otherwise occupied, I would like to ask this of you."

Galit nodded to the Grand Master's hologram. "You wish me to help connect the halflings to the other races, such as the orcs, that will be hunting the mindflayers?"

"Precisely," said the Grand Master.

It was, Galit knew, an honor to be trusted in that way, and it was in line with her life's mission.

"I can do that," Galit said.

"Thank you," said the Grand Master. "I'm transmitting additional information and contacts among the halflings to you."

"Very good," said Galit. "I'm sending you some information as well. The orcs are organizing a hunting party."

"Your doing?" asked the Grand Master.

"Not entirely. I'm still with the crew of the *Moon Raven*."

"An unexpected but appreciated resource," said the Grand Master.

Galit didn't need to tell the Grand Master that their involvement had begun because of their predecessor. They knew well how all the energies of the Universe tended to intertwine.

"Keep me apprised of your progress, Galit Azurite," said the Grand Master.

"I will."

The Grand Master's hologram bowed and the transmission ended. Galit leaned back in her seat. To coordinate getting the halflings connected with the various races that would be involved in hunting the mindflayers and their monsters, she'd likely need to leave the *Moon Raven*.

Despite having spent the majority of her life on her own, she'd gotten surprisingly comfortable and accustomed to having companions. It had been unexpected, but not unwelcome. However, she was the Blue Cyberwizard.

REVELATIONS AND RECONCILIATIONS

By their nature, cyberwizards lived long and independent lives. She knew that every encounter was a learning opportunity. Thus, it was not a coincidence that she'd come to join forces with the *Moon Raven* crew.

Although cyberwizards didn't believe in or use the Universal Energies in the ways of either the UEO or sorcerers, Galit knew there was something to it all. She believed in the energies of the universe in her own way. Time and again, she saw for herself how the Universe and its energies moved in mysterious yet necessary ways.

Chapter 44 - Reunion

The world they were approaching had orange clouds, green oceans, and landmasses of various shades of grey.

Darius realized he knew next to nothing about the kitsune. Prior to meeting Aya, he'd only ever seen kitsune in images and medianet programs. He knew they were part of the fourth wave of interstellar travelers. Unlike humans and their three millennia traveling the stars and settling across the galaxy, kitsune had only been doing so for about a thousand years.

Darius knew that their home system had three worlds and that they had terraformed the nearest to their original homeworld more than a century before unlocking the secret of unrealspace.

It wasn't long before the kitsune had encountered humans. Fortunately, it had been Terra Prime that they encountered. Darius found it odd that most humans had no idea where Terra Prime – formerly Earth – could be found. The world kept to itself for the most part, trading with neighbors quietly. Apart from the rest of the humans still in the Sol system, they didn't interact with the other human territories.

This world, l'Orni'Ri, was one of the first kitsune colonies, and a hub of trade and government. Darius saw that there were a variety of starships and several platforms and docks around the planet. The many kitsune starships were distinct, sleek, but slightly less organic in appearance than elf vessels.

Darius heard Aya speaking to someone via the chatter. But she had an earpiece in and was speaking in low tones he could barely hear. It was curious and quite unlike her. He wasn't concerned. Yet.

"Captain," Galit addressed Darius as she arrived on the *Moon Raven*'s flight deck. He had gotten so used to the Blue Cyberwizard being part of the crew, and being present that he was only now registering that she'd been aboard *Phantom*.

"Everything alright?" he asked.

"Yes," she said. "But you should know that I had a conversation with the Grand Master late last night."

"Oh?" exclaimed Darius. "What was that about?"

REVELATIONS AND RECONCILIATIONS

Galit proceeded to explain that the Grand Master wanted her to arrange getting the halflings, who were apparently immune to mindflayer psionic attack, connected to the orcs and any other members of the hunting party being put together.

"They could be a major asset to anyone having to deal with mindflayers," Darius concluded.

"They could be," agreed Galit.

"You might need to do this on your own, right?" Darius asked.

Galit nodded. "Yes."

"The outcome of this meeting will likely make that clear," said Darius.

"Quite possibly," said Galit.

"If the time has come for us to part ways, you will be missed," Darius said.

"Thank you," replied Galit. She moved away, seating herself at her customary station. Darius had come to admire the enigma that was Galit Azurite. Before he'd met her, all he'd known of cyberwizards were wild stories of using tech in ways nobody else could.

"We got landing clearance," said Kaz, interrupting Darius' thoughts. "City called Na'een'teru."

"Not the city itself," said Aya. "There's only the one spaceport. It's quite large and a fair distance outside Na'een'teru. We should have no trouble getting transport to meet my contact, however."

Darius found something about Aya's tone off. He was clearly not alone, as Sara said, "What's wrong, Aya? You're acting strange, even for you."

"Nothing," Aya replied too quickly.

"Does this have anything to do with your past?" asked Darius.

"No, nothing like that," said Aya. Then, she added, "Well, then again, sort of. Not in that way, though. I'm not stepping into trouble. I think."

"Aya?" Darius questioned, his tone commanding.

She sighed. "It's bound to be awkward, for lots of reasons I'd rather not get into just now. It's a lot of uncertainty that's making me nervous, and I'm sorry about that."

"Is this going to be a problem?" asked Sara.

"No," Aya replied. "My contact is someone that I know and trust. But that doesn't mean some serious awkwardness isn't going to happen."

Darius nodded. Sara said nothing more, either.

As the *Moon Raven* descended, Darius saw they were approaching over the green waters. He found it surprisingly inviting, despite the unusual-to-him color. Ahead, on the continent, a city of many impressive spires arose before them. They appeared to be largely glass and probably some metal or composite. Many were connected via arching bridges at various heights, equally looking especially delicate.

Kaz adjusted their course a few degrees to starboard, and Darius could make out the obvious and impressive looking spaceport well outside the city.

"Interesting choice," commented Tol.

"What?" asked Aya.

"The spaceport being kept so far from the city," Tol said. "Almost like nobody wants visitors to go to the city itself."

"Oh, that," said Aya. "As I recall, when our ancestors colonized l'Orni'Ri, they made very particular zoning decisions. It'll be more obvious as we approach, but there's a whole industrial zone between the spaceport and Na'een'teru. Much of it's underground. There are multiple options for transport between them all."

As the *Moon Raven* descended, Darius now saw domes between the spaceport and the city, just as Aya said.

It wasn't long before Kaz was landing them on a pad towards the center of the spaceport but nearer to the city side of it. The *Moon Raven* was set to standby power.

"Aya, is your contact expecting us all or only a few of us?" Darius asked.

"I never said, but implied I'm not coming alone," Aya replied.

"Captain," Zya said, "there is something that Tol and I would like to look for that would benefit the ship."

"Likely it will be found here in the spaceport," added Tol.

"As much as I should like to join you," started Galit, "there's another matter that I must see to."

"Kaz? Sara?" Darius asked.

"Yes, I'm going with you and Aya," said Sara.

"Me, too," added Kaz.

"Anything we need to be aware of, Aya?" asked Darius. "Can we be armed or is that an issue here?"

Aya was quiet a moment, but said, "No, armed should be fine."

REVELATIONS AND RECONCILIATIONS

"Everyone, get what you need, and let's go meet Aya's contact," Darius said.

Less than ten galactic standard minutes later, Darius, Aya, Sara, and Kaz were on a silent tram car, gliding swiftly toward the city. There were two additional kitsune with them.

"We're not going to the city," said Aya as the tram began to slow. "My contact's here, in the industrial zone." Darius saw Sara raise an eyebrow, but nobody said anything else.

They left the tram and made their way through the surprisingly not busy area between the industrial domes.

"Is it some sort of holiday or something?" asked Kaz, voicing Darius' thoughts.

Darius expected Aya to laugh, but the tension in her body was clear. Still, she said, "No. Apart from visitors and businesspeople who don't get dirty doing the work, everything moves below ground. There are at least three sublevels, maybe four or five in some cases, below. One or two are transport networks that run to the spaceport and the city."

Darius noted that what few people he did see were all kitsune and carried themselves in a manner that screamed businessperson. The crew reached a dome, marked by a glyph or kanji Darius barely noticed and couldn't identify. Aya led them inside. They found themselves in an unremarkable room with undecorated walls and a male kitsune seated at a desk, flanked by two more kitsune in light armor with synchronized pulse rifles.

Aya stepped up to the desk. "I'm expected. Aya Mah-soo-may fo Misa."

Both guards immediately trained their weapons on Aya and the crew. "Drop your weapons," one said. "Disarm, or you go no further."

Darius saw both Sara and Kaz tense. Aya, however, removed the SPP from the holster at her hip and set it on the desk. Darius drew his sidearm and laid it down on the floor. Sara did the same. Kaz removed several weapons from his person, including two pistols, his sword, and a long dagger.

Two more guards had entered from a door between the first pair. They also pointed their SPRs at Darius and the crew. "Let's go," one ordered, gesturing with his rifle.

They were led through the doorway, three of the guards following. They weren't abusive or rough, but it was clear they'd not tolerate anyone doing anything untoward. Darius suspected Sara and Kaz were both still armed. Aya, however, looked unconcerned. Still, the tension in her gait was unmistakable.

After going down a descending corridor, they were led past several doorways, and the sounds of an industrial complex Darius had expected to hear never reached them. Either those were far from the corridor they were being led down, or this space produced something that didn't make much noise.

The guard in the lead stepped up to a door, which slid open. Aya and the crew, plus their guards, followed him in. The office on the other side was not at all what Darius had expected. It was plush but also featured a number of display screens along the walls and a desk with several more atop it. Passageways led out in three directions, and though they were well lit, Darius couldn't tell what was beyond them.

Before the desk stood a kitsune woman whose fox-headed face was lined in a way that gave the impression she was older than Aya. However, it was not in any way obvious, just an impression. Her arms were crossed, and she somehow looked angry, annoyed, and indifferent, all at once.

The older kitsune approached Aya. She said nothing, but her eyes looked to Darius as though they were boring into his quartermaster. "Aya Mah-soo-may fo Misa," the kitsune woman said, her tone instantly concerning Darius. She was too calm. But that didn't last. "After all this time, after all the things you have done, you reach out to me from nowhere. I had no idea if you were still alive, and here you are, demanding an audience, acting as if no time has passed and you've been accounted for all along. Who in the inky void do you think you are, girl?"

The kitsune continued, but it was not in a language Darius had heard before or could remotely understand. He presumed she was dressing Aya down in the Kitsune tongue. Aya would respond from time to time, but never more than a word or two, as if merely upholding basic conversational contracts.

"What do you have to say for yourself?" the older kitsune concluded, returning to common.

Aya sighed. "Hello, auntie."

REVELATIONS AND RECONCILIATIONS

"Don't think you can sweet-talk your way out of this," the kitsune woman said. "You and that idiot go off into space, half-cocked, committing petty thievery across who-knows-how-many systems. Did you care at all that you might have worried those you left behind? No, of course not. And you dragged your brother along because he did anything his sister wanted him to do."

"Wait just one moment, auntie," said Aya. Darius noted that the tension she'd been carrying seemed to have evaporated. "The three of us started out doing legit business. Your dear sweet Ryn was not the innocent you care to paint him as. He could be incredibly devious, and you might want to deny it, but you know full well that it was his fault I got into thieving. He figured out it made for far better profits. And what's more, had you been so concerned about our welfare, auntie, you could have intervened after mother's death and taken Ryn and me away from our father. Talk about the true bad influence."

The other kitsune woman said, "You and your brother could have gotten away from Garm at any time."

"Not so," said Aya. "Father was suspected of being part of any number of scams and the like. Yet he was never convicted of any crime. But you knew him. He kept Ryn and me just close enough to pass all the legalities after mother's passing. But we couldn't have gotten away from him, and we didn't know better until he was gone."

"Still, Aya Mah-soo-may… No word from you for years," pressed the other kitsune woman. Then, she sighed and seemed to soften somewhat. "Ryn's body was returned here, you know. We only knew that he was publicly executed on Exopol. But there were no further details."

Aya sighed. "Ryn and Chav made a really bad deal. We didn't know it at the time, but we were set up. They got caught, and before I could do anything to get them out, they were executed. I only got away because nobody got a good look at me, so they never identified me, and I stowed away on an orc transport to *Territory's Edge*."

The other kitsune woman was shaking her head. Darius thought the look on her face was one of sadness. She turned her attention to him, Sara, and Kaz. "Which of you humans is the captain?"

"I am," Darius said.

"You a criminal?"

"No," Darius replied with a chuckle. "Far from it." He reached out a hand. "Darius Noble."

She took his hand. "Ryka Key-koo-noh fo Hava."

Kaz introduced himself and shook Ryka's hand, followed by Sara. As she completed her introduction, Sara said, "Definitely not criminals. Darius and I, in fact, are former Alliance officers. While escaping the Federation, separate from their invasion, we literally ran into Aya."

Ryka grunted. "The Alliance was fair to deal with. We don't even bother with the Federation."

"No surprise there," Sara said. "Darius and I interceded on Aya's behalf at *Territory's Edge*, and she helped Darius and I avoid bounty hunters and to get a ship. She's been a companion and a crew mate since."

"Aya serves as *Moon Raven*'s quartermaster," Kaz said. "And is quite impressive in that role."

That seemed to catch Ryka up short. She turned to face Aya. "Is this true? You've given up thievery and gone legit?"

"While it wasn't something I'd aimed to do," Aya replied, "that's the way of it. I've been on the up and up the whole time we've served together. For the first time, really, since my mother's passing, I found a new family."

Ryka nodded. She gestured, and all the heavily armed kitsune guards departed. Ryka approached Aya tentatively, then pulled her into a hug.

"Welcome back, Aya," she said.

Darius could have sworn that Aya's eyes were wet with unshed tears. That was, of course, if kitsune were capable of shedding tears, which he realized he wasn't sure of.

Releasing Aya, Ryka turned to Darius again. "I'm sure my niece didn't explain who I am. I don't hold a specific office, nor have any formal title. I know human government officials have titles like ministers, secretaries, officers, and the like. But I am a kitsune government official."

Darius nodded. "Are all the government offices in the industrial zone hereabouts?"

Ryka smiled. "Those that aren't in space, yes. Is not government also industry?"

"We aren't here for a debate in semantics, auntie," said Aya.

REVELATIONS AND RECONCILIATIONS

"You said it was an urgent matter, but I wasn't sure if you were exaggerating or not," Ryka said. "If it wasn't, I figured you were in trouble and would need my help all the same."

"Darius can best explain," Aya said.

Ryka gestured, and they all took seats. Darius explained the situation with the mindflayers. He told her about the observations he and Sara had made on the *Moonshadow*, their quest with the Grand Master, the texts they had found, and their outreach to the orcs to get them involved in fighting the extradimensional invaders.

"You have most certainly fallen in with an interesting crowd, Aya," Ryka said. "Legitimate, yes, but no less dangerous, clearly."

"It does keep my life from getting boring," Aya said.

Ryka turned her attention to Darius. "We have heard rumors of these mindflayers and their vacuum-breathing monsters that accompany them. And of course, we received the Grand Master's transmission. Though they're clearly a threat to all life in the galaxy, which seems absurd, I don't follow why you would come to us and suggest that the kitsune get involved."

"That was my idea," said Aya. "We've been highly fortunate to have avoided warfare with other races since we reached interstellar space. But we are not without capable starships and weapons. The kitsune could play a leading role in hunting the mindflayers down before everyone finds themselves reacting to them."

Ryka leaned back in her seat. "Perhaps. But I still don't see why you'd think the kitsune should get involved."

Aya grinned ruefully. "Because it would give our people legitimacy."

Ryka leaned forward. "Legitimacy?"

"Auntie, relatively speaking, we kitsune are new to the space race. The first wave of interstellar travelers started faster-than-light travel over six-thousand galactic standard years ago." Aya arose, began to pace, and continued, saying, "The second, five-thousand. The third, which included the humans and orcs, was three-thousand years ago. For a little over a millennia, the kitsune have made our way across interstellar space. We might have a half a dozen star systems under our governance, yet we're still just beginning to make an impression on the galaxy at large."

"And you think risking our ships and their crews to attack these extradimensional invaders lends us 'legitimacy' how, exactly?"

Aya stopped pacing, turned to face her aunt, and blew out a breath. "Because by stepping up and offering to ally ourselves with the orcs, the kitsune show we're not just a race of wannabe neophytes. We show our understanding and concern for a cross-species threat and join the cause, taking a stand right at the start."

Ryka nodded. "That's one possibility. But there is another. It could horribly backfire. We know our arms and armor are capable, but unlike orcs or humans, we're not battle-tested. We could be overwhelmed and prove ourselves horridly outclassed and outmatched, obliterating our standing and possibly opening the way to invasion and overrun."

"That's true," Aya conceded. "You're absolutely correct, auntie. It could backfire. But consider this: the mindflayers are the single greatest threat any race in the galaxy has faced. Even the neutral Universal Energies Ontology has stated, through the Grand Master, their opposition to the invaders from savagespace. They must be stopped."

"What of the first-wave races?" questioned Ryka. "Why aren't the elves, dwarves, and drow joining the orcs?"

"They have another, equally important mission," Darius said. "The drow helped the Federation create the technology that folded space/time. When the drow learned of the unintended consequences of their actions, they ended their campaign against the elves and sought their help to close the rifts they opened. Through the data we helped the Grand Master to uncover, I know that the dwarves have a role to play because of a mineral they mine that's essential to closing the rifts."

Kaz stated, "And if the rifts aren't sealed, more mindflayers and monsters from savagespace can come to realspace."

Sara added, "As the Grand Master has pointed out, they gain strength through destruction. They cannot be bargained with, nor negotiated with. They will not relent. The only recourse they leave us is to destroy them."

Darius finished with, "The human governments are currently too caught up in their own messes and the Federation's actions to do more than defend themselves at present. And everyone knows that the hobgoblins and trolls will only work with the drow."

REVELATIONS AND RECONCILIATIONS

Ryka nodded. She was silent for a time, and nobody else offered anything further. "What about the goblins?" Ryka finally questioned.

"Truth be told," Darius began, "I would love to reach out to the goblins to get them involved, if I knew how that could be done. I'm the captain of an independent starship with a mixed crew and am part of no government, guild, or other organization that might do such."

"Interesting," said Ryka. "What if I told you I might be able to help with that?"

"A contact with the goblin leadership?" asked Darius.

"Yes."

"I would be interested," replied Darius.

Ryka was silent for a time. She stood, turning away a moment. Then, she turned back and said, "Well, then, it's clear what the kitsune must do. I shall present your request to those who make such decisions. You make a poignant argument, and you are not wrong that the danger presented by these invaders is considerable. Separately, I will reach out to my contacts in the goblins and see about arranging a meeting with them for you."

"That's much appreciated," Darius said. While he'd not known what to expect, this was more than he could have hoped for.

Ryka looked towards Aya. "It has been too long, Aya Mah-soo-may. It does my heart good to see you and know you have changed your ways for the better. Now that you are here, do you wish to come home?"

Aya shook her head. "No, auntie. I've found a new purpose and a new family. I'm home. I'll be remaining with them."

A sly grin crossed Ryka's face. "Well, my errant niece, it is good to know you're still out there, alive and better than you were before. But I do hope you remain on the straight and narrow."

Chapter 45 – Navigators

They emerged into realspace from unrealspace without incident. The Grand Master was seated behind the current captain of their starship, Guardian Kolora. They were looking between the display before them, holographic images, and the viewport into space above them.

They were on the outskirts of gnome space. The gnomes tended to get touchy when it came to outsiders. Hence, unless you were expected or invited, it was wise to pause on the outskirts of their territory and await them.

The Grand Master had gained some useful insight both from the halflings and the Blue Cyberwizard. With that information, they'd taken it upon themselves to seek an audience with the gnomes. The gnomes were often a curiosity. They were a part of the second wave of interplanetary travelers. There were very few gnomes in the UEO and none were masters that the Grand Master was aware of.

As a race, they placed a great deal of value on culture, art, and a mindful existence. Their government structure, while known to be singular like that of elves and drow, was a mystery. Even the deepest UEO archives had no detailed information about the gnomish government, what it was called, how it was structured, and how involved in the lives of its people it was or wasn't.

"No contacts yet, Grand Master," the monk at communications called out.

"Signal our intent to meet with gnome leadership," the Grand Master requested. "We're here to discuss delicate, important matters for every race."

The Grand Master looked at the display in front of them. Nothing showed, no ships, no bases. They had arrived on the far outskirts of gnome territory, allowing their potential hosts plenty of time to see them approaching the nearest gnome world to the border.

The Grand Master instinctively pulled up another star chart. From where they had entered gnome space, they were several hours' flight, at sixty percent the speed of light, from the nearest inhabited gnome world, Gkiruna. Gkiruna was a world with a population in the billions and may or may not have been a gnomish capital.

REVELATIONS AND RECONCILIATIONS

A portal opened ahead and to starboard of the Grand Master's starship. A trio of delicate-looking ships that reminded the Grand Master of leaves emerged from unrealspace. A moment later, the monk at communications called out, "Incoming transmission, Grand Master."

"Let's hear it."

There was a hiss as the speaker for the chatter became active. Then, a voice said, "You are trespassing in gnomish space. Leave immediately, or we will open fire."

"I am the Grand Master of the Universal Energies Ontology," they responded. "I seek a dialogue with local authorities to discuss a matter of grave concern, one that impacts all gnomish kind."

There was a pause, but then the voice in the chatter returned with, "While we recognize the neutrality of the Universal Energies Ontology, you still have no business in this sector. Please depart immediately."

"But we do have business here," the Grand Master insisted. "Check with your leaders. I know that a gnome mining colony was lost some months ago to an unexpected and unknown assailant. This is directly connected to that, and it's important I speak to an appropriate gnomish official."

There was silence for a time, and then the voice on the chatter said, "Very well. We'll escort you to the local spacer's guild station, where the High Officer will meet with you."

"Thank you," the Grand Master replied.

The trio of leaf-like gnome starships took up a triangular formation ahead, leading them to a space station that was unmarked on their star charts.

Unbidden, two memories surfaced in the Grand Master's mind. The first was that eternal affairs related to the gnomes were exclusively handled by the spacer's guild. The officer in question was likely the local authority figure, at least when it came to all things interstellar. The High Officer was then directly connected to any other gnome authorities, who were in turn connected to one another across gnome space.

The second memory was about gnome space stations and the spacer's guild. Rather than a fixed station or platform in planetary orbit or stabilized at a Lagrange point, these space stations were a type of starship. They traveled all about a given gnome solar system and served as a customs/trade/

administrative hub, particularly connected to unexpected or external affairs. That was why the station was not on any charts. Because it was mobile.

The Grand Master found other snippets of memory coming to mind, none of which were their own. Previous encounters by their predecessors with gnomes and their leadership, presumptions, assumptions, and observations. There were also some loose thoughts of writing things down that never materialized.

The Grand Master leaned back in their seat a moment. How much they had learned in the time since becoming the Grand Master was sometimes dizzying and disconcerting. Much of it was directly tied to the amazing, unique crystal that was passed from Grand Master to Grand Master.

Additionally, the crystal held a vast store of the memories and elements of the personalities of all who had borne it before them. This device held knowledge beyond memory, beyond space and time. Some could be dug up at will, some came to them unbidden. Overall, they experienced a constant sensation of never being truly alone and the potential to learn things new and old beyond their wildest imagination.

Once, they had foreseen a brief glimpse of their own passing. They suspected this was to inform them that they need not be immediately concerned with seeking another to pass the crystal to, as their predecessor had with them.

As they, the current Grand Master, spent more time on studies in old archives and datacores of the UEO and elsewhere, they perceived another benefit of their crystal. Though they couldn't prove if it were so, they believed the stone increased their focus, concentration, and memory.

It could be quite daunting. In a relatively short time, they'd gone from a new master of the UEO to the Grand Master. Why were they given no choice in accepting the price they paid? The answers were in the histories of their predecessors in the crystal, and they knew this instinctually via connection to Universal Energies. Still, in brief moments, the Grand Master lamented no longer being Alisay Naun-moon'kari. Yet just as swiftly as the sorrow struck, it passed and was released. Their choice or no, they would have gladly accepted.

REVELATIONS AND RECONCILIATIONS

They shook their head and leaned forward, returning to the present. They were certain that the High Officer of the spacer's guild was the contact they needed.

It wasn't long before the space station, a remarkably large starship, really, loomed ahead. It had multiple tall spires at its top and curved to a peak below its base. As they got nearer, protrusions all along the base, including landing bays and pads, were evident.

"Grand Master of the Universal Energies Ontology," a new voice came across the chatter speaker. "You are clear to land in Bay Nine."

"Very good," the Grand Master said. Then, remembering something, they reengaged the chatter and said, "Controller, this is the Grand Master. Even though the UEO is not representative of gnome mythology, we prefer a bay not associated with the nine hells."

A pause, and then the voice, sounding more pleasant, said, "Apologies, Grand Master. Clear to land in Bay Seven."

"Thank you."

"The nine hells?" asked Guardian Kolora.

"Gnome mythology," the Grand Master said. "Long before they became an industrial society tens of millennia ago, they believed in one heaven and nine hells. Each was ruled by a monster related to natural disasters and the elements, striking at the people to inflict misery and suffering. Long ago, this was given over to stories told to every child. Even now, many reference these old myths superstitiously, with no genuine belief. But an outsider accepting docking in Bay Nine will be held suspect."

"Obscure history," a cleric at one of the flight deck consoles commented. The Grand Master didn't respond.

When they landed, the Grand Master, accompanied by a monk and a cleric, met with a gnome escort. They were led to a conference room much like others they had seen and visited. Save one notable exception. Half the seats at the table would only be an appropriate size for gnomes or perhaps smaller halflings or dwarves.

A purple-skinned gnome, male with bright red hair, entered the conference room flanked by a fluorescent-pink-skinned male with bright green hair and a brown-skinned female with similar bright green hair.

The less-than-a-meter tall, purple-skinned gnome stopped before the Grand Master and offered a hand. "I am High Officer Arvid Gmorner. I'm the local head of the spacer's guild."

"A pleasure to meet you," the Grand Master said.

"Please." Arvid gestured to the conference table. "Have a seat."

The Grand Master sat, the cleric and monk also sitting to either side of them. Across the table, the High Officer sat, but his associates remained standing.

"What has brought you to gnome space?" asked the High Officer without preamble.

The Grand Master explained the situation with the mindflayer invasion from savagespace, and the growing coalition of hunters gathering around the orc tribal leader Ghalt hur Kholm Ahk. The Grand Master concluded by sharing how the halflings were offering to place volunteers on hunting party starships. They explained that this was because of their ability to offer protection from the mindflayer's psionic attacks. The Grand Master also shared that the kitsune were joining the orcs.

Another memory came to the Grand Master about goblins and gnomes and how the former felt the latter were cowardly. Though they knew it was a bit manipulative to include, they concluded by sharing that a delegation was contacting the goblins.

Arvid was nodding as the Grand Master finished. Then, he asked, "What about the humans, elves, and dwarves?"

"The dwarves and elves are working with the drow to close the rifts," said the Grand Master. "The humans are too busy fighting amongst themselves to help in this matter, presently."

"And it goes without saying the hobgoblins and trolls only do as commanded by the drow," Arvid said with obvious disgust.

"But all races, even those not taking part in the hunt, will need to fight the mindflayers and their monsters if they come," said the Grand Master.

"And this hunting party quest is led by orcs?" asked Arvid.

"A necessity," said The Grand Master. "The mindflayers do not negotiate, will not parlay, nor accept terms. They will only attack. That's because when they destroy wantonly, they get stronger. Taking the fight to them allows us, the denizens of the galaxy and this dimension, to destroy them before they get too much stronger, and thus harder to remove."

"I assure you, Grand Master, that the gnomes will defend ourselves if need be," said Arvid. "But if you are here to recruit our forces to join the hunting party, I'm afraid you've wasted your time. No offense, but we will not seek a fight. That's not our way."

"I and the UEO are well aware of this truth," replied the Grand Master. "I know that your people are by no means cowards and that you will defend yourselves in the face of attack. But there are other ways that the gnomish people can help us."

"Is that so?" asked Arvid. "How?"

"Aren't gnomes the finest celestial navigators in the galaxy?" asked the Grand Master. "Aren't gnome navigators capable of finding anything they seek, as well as approaches no others have taken?"

"What of it?" asked Arvid. Yet the Grand Master saw the look of pride he was trying and failing to hide.

"If the hunting party had some of those incredible navigators among them, akin to the halflings offering protection from psionic attack, don't you think they'd more readily find the mindflayers?"

High Officer Arvid leaned back in his seat a moment, crossing his arms and eyeing the Grand Master. Then, he said, "You have come here to request only gnomish navigators to help the hunters seek and find the mindflayers and their monsters?"

"Yes."

"This is not a matter that I alone can decide upon," said Arvid. "I shall have to take this to my superiors."

"Understood," said the Grand Master.

Arvid cocked his head to one side and asked, "Begging your pardon, Grand Master, but this? This seems like a terrible risk. Tell me, because I should like to know, why? Why should we take part in this?"

"Simple," replied the Grand Master. "The mindflayers are a threat to everyone. Your people have already experienced this, and all peoples in this dimension are under the same threat. Perhaps it's a risk. But everyone, everywhere, across all the galaxy, is under the same threat."

"So you say," said Arvid, sounding skeptical.

"Additionally, there is the potential, if the mindflayer threat is ended, for the gnomish people to benefit from being part of this," teased the Grand Master.

"Potential? And what would that be?"

"It never hurts to be proactive," remarked the Grand Master. "And gnomes volunteering to work alongside orcs will further the cause of gnomish exploration of space while remaining largely separate from the other races. Furthermore, by volunteering your assistance in this way, it shows your courage. How could any think you cowards in the face of that?"

Chapter 46 – Complications

Ilizeva grabbed the rail before her as the ship banked sharply to port. Her mind reeled. But she knew it wasn't just the unexpected combat causing that. It was also the combatants. Psionic attacks were deeply unpleasant. Though she knew they could be far more debilitating, they were bad enough.

"Tell the dwarves to turn hard a-port," Ilizeva called out. "Target that wyvern! All drow ships, focus on the mindflayers."

They had been getting into position to close another rift. Then, before the drow, elves, and dwarves could act, it had opened to disgorge more than a dozen mindflayers, a dragon, and a wyvern. The elves were targeting the dragon.

The taskforce was outnumbered. Even though they'd caught the mindflayers by surprise as they emerged from savagespace, they had quickly been at a disadvantage. Ilizeva had assumed command. She had no time to consider how easily both the elves and dwarves accepted that and followed her lead.

The battle was ugly. One dwarf ship was lost, and one was nearly dead in the vacuum. Two of the elf starships were severely damaged, and a drow ship was soon to be lost, all the others taking damage. Ilizeva couldn't deny that they were on the verge of being overwhelmed.

The psionic attacks were slowing everyone down. They seemed more intense than she recalled previously. Everyone's reaction times were less than optimal. The dwarves were suffering the most.

Ilizeva looked to the display before her, examining where all the forces were. An idea came to her. "All elf and dwarf starships," she called, "I have an idea. Break off your pursuit of the dragon and wyvern. Take a wide sweep, elves to port and dwarves to starboard, then accelerate towards the *Nuummite Raptor*. We and the other drow will do an axial flip to attack the mindflayers from two angles at once."

Both the elves and drow signaled their agreement. Faced with their destruction at the hands of the mindflayers and their monsters, it only fleetingly crossed her mind that they'd not fought together before but were doing so seamlessly now.

"Major, come to point oh-six mark two-two," Ilizeva ordered the *Nuummite Raptor*'s captain.

"Yes ma'am," he replied.

Ilizeva checked the display. "On my mark," she called over the chatter. Then she saw the optimum position. "Now!" Ilizeva ordered.

The elf and dwarf starships broke away from the monsters and swung out wide, accelerating and changing course towards the drow ships.

"Major Onuzov, standby for axial flip," Ilizeva ordered. Then, she transmitted via chatter, "All drow ships, standby for axial flip."

"Ready," Major Onuzov replied. The other drow captains signaled their readiness as well. Ilizeva felt the ship lurch as it took more hits from the mindflayers.

"Shields at thirty percent but holding," said Ulozov calmly.

The dwarves and elves were nearly in position.

"Now!" Ilizeva ordered. She braced, knowing that the compensators were likely damaged. The *Nuummite Raptor* shuddered as it took more hits. Yet out the viewport she saw the changing perspective as they flipped around, facing their pursuers.

"Fire," Colonel Ulozov ordered. Plasma cannons from the drow, elves, and dwarves threw bolts of light into the mindflayer ships. Torpedoes and missiles were fired.

Just when it had looked potentially hopeless, the tables had turned.

The drow and elves, as if practiced, advanced on the mindflayers, tearing their ships apart with plasma cannon fire. The dwarves, slightly delayed, probably due to psionic attacks, joined with only slightly less grace.

The pressure on her mind evaporated. Either they'd destroyed the mindflayers attacking psionically, or the enemy had chosen to stop.

"General," a controller called, "two mindflayer starships, the dragon, and the wyvern have broken contact and are fleeing."

"The other drow, elves, and dwarves want to know if you want to pursue," Colonel Ulozov reported.

Ilizeva looked at the tactical display before her. The picture it showed may have been one of victory but not without too high a price. "Negative," she replied. "Keep an eye on them but let them go. Let's work together to assess our damages and make repairs."

REVELATIONS AND RECONCILIATIONS

"Yes, General," Ulozov said.

As Ulozov relayed her orders, Ilizeva thought about the battle. It had been intense, and much too destructive. As a result, she planned to request more ships to join her taskforce and recommend the same to the dwarves and elves.

She considered the elves and their combat prowess. When the drow had attacked the elves by folding space/time they'd been caught unaware and had offered little resistance. Ilizeva had maintained no illusion of any lack of skill this revealed. Responding to a surprise attack was different from direct combat.

Begrudgingly, she found that she admired the skill of the elves in combat. They fought the mindflayers and their monsters brilliantly and valiantly. The dwarves had done their part, too, but they had clearly suffered more ill-effects from the psionic attacks.

Ilizeva realized that for the first time in history, the elves had fought side-by-side with the drow. Apart from sealing the tears in space/time, it was the first they'd ever worked together in combat, let alone so effectively.

The thought of the rifts brought Ilizeva back to the present. "Colonel, what's the status of everything we need to close that rift? Did we lose anyone or anything essential to the mission?"

"No," Ulozov replied. "Recovery is underway. The dwarves are working to use the ship they've declared dead to salvage the most severely damaged. But they report they can place the ore as needed. The elves are working to repair their damaged ships, and we're recovering the crew and are salvaging what we can from our lost ship. Nobody came away from that one undamaged or unhurt."

"Understood," said Ilizeva. "Inform the rest we need to close the rift, lest it open again. We can't handle another battle like that one in our current condition. We'll work together on salvage and repair, dwarf, drow, and elf, once the rift is closed."

"Yes, General," Ulozov responded.

"Major Onuzov, damage report."

Her flagship's captain called out, "General, the *Nuummite Raptor* suffered no breeches, but shields will need major repairs if we want to restore them beyond seventy percent. Three casualties to report, shock damage across a few systems, but hull integrity is eighty-eight percent."

"Thank you, Major."

"The elves and dwarves will be prepared to close the rift within five galactic standard minutes," Ulozov reported.

"Very good, Colonel," Ilizeva said. She looked at the holographic display before her and saw the remaining mindflayers and their monsters were already nearing the edge of their detection range.

"Though they appear to be fleeing, let's not lose sight of them," Ilizeva said, gesturing to the display. "Maybe we should have pursued them."

"You made the right call, General," said Ulozov. "The mission to close the rifts in space/time is most important, so that more don't arrive from savagespace. Besides, thanks to the Blue Cyberwizard, we know where the mindflayers are gathering all their assets."

"We do," agreed Ilizeva. "But nobody can attack them there because no one of this dimension can get that close to a dark star and its intense gravity."

"Given their need to cause destruction, they won't stay there forever," said Ulozov. "Everyone believes they can receive our chatter transmissions. But apart from multiple attacks, none seem specifically targeting like that. They still appear to be testing the capabilities of the races in this dimension."

"That likely won't be the case for much longer," said Ilizeva.

"Agreed," replied Ulozov. "Have you read the reports we've received from our intelligence forces about the effort to take the mindflayers on?"

"I saw them but haven't looked closely," said Ilizeva. She grinned ruefully. "Other present matters have been more pressing."

"Of course," said Ulozov. "It would seem that the Blue Cyberwizard is working with the UEO Grand Master to build a force, a hunting party, to take on the mindflayers."

Ilizeva raised an eyebrow. "Is that so?"

"It seems thus far, they have orcs and kitsune committed."

"I hope that they understand what they're up against," said Ilizeva. "These mindflayers are hell-bent on destruction, and they're tough and ruthless fighters. What's more, the psionic attacks that disturb the minds of elves and drow can be worse on other races." She didn't care to admit

REVELATIONS AND RECONCILIATIONS

aloud just how close their taskforce had come to defeat. Though maybe less susceptible to psionic attack, they were still affected by it.

"You should read the reports," suggested Ulozov. "The Grand Master is on to something that might neutralize the psionic attacks."

"Colonel, General," Major Onuzov interrupted. "Apologies, but the elves and dwarves report ready to close the rift."

"Let's see to it," Ilizeva said. "Major, get the *Nuummite Raptor* into position. Let's not let any more of these destructive invaders come into our dimension."

Chapter 47 – Machinations

"General," a controller called out, "five more ships have arrived, and General Waheed is requesting permission to come aboard."

"I didn't expect him here," said Aneesa. In all probability, he was likely present to protest the forces she'd taken from the occupation of the former Alliance territories. "Permission granted. Have him escorted to the observation lounge and I'll see him at my convenience."

"Yes, General."

Aneesa looked out the viewport. What she saw made her smile. It was a massive force of Federation warships. The largest assembled, she knew, since the invasion of the Alliance. True to her word, Aneesa had set out to gather more intelligence about patrols, ship movements, and the happenings in Confederation space. This had led to a surprising discovery.

Advanced reconnaissance had shown a weakness in a most unexpected location, the central-most sector of the Confederation, Wolfgang-Alpha. They had withdrawn much of their force, likely in response to prior Federation attacks on more outlying sectors.

The central-most sector was a prime, ripe target. Aneesa felt that she could deliver a decisive blow with properly overwhelming forces. So, she had gathered additional starships from the Alliance occupation to guarantee that overwhelming force. The goal was to wipe out every military vessel in Wolfgang-Alpha, as well as anything else that got in her way.

Nearly all the ships she'd intended to take to the Confederation were present. All she awaited was a few more, a briefing with the captains, and final word from the spy ship doing reconnaissance to choose the optimum point of insertion. Then she'd fold space/time to decisively defeat the Confederation, striking straight at their heart. This would disprove Song's ludicrous caution, prove Aneesa was right about everything, and make her a legend, all at the same time.

"General," another controller called, "you're receiving an urgent communique. Code zero-zero-one Priority."

Aneesa took up a docupad and used her secure code to access the communique. A zero-zero-one Priority request could be made by only a

REVELATIONS AND RECONCILIATIONS

handful of authorities. A short message appeared, and Aneesa sighed. Galen Anwar demanded she make immediate, secure contact. Additionally, he'd sent a message that read, *"There is a major issue that requires your immediate attention. Do not delay."*

Tempted as she was to ignore the family elder, she knew that wouldn't be without consequences. What's more, much as she had personal distaste for Galen Anwar, he would not use that priority code unless it were truly urgent.

"Major," Aneesa called out to the *Hammer of Harmony's* commanding officer, "I'll be in my office on a secure line. See to it I'm not disturbed."

"What about General Waheed?" he asked.

"He can wait," Aneesa said.

She left the bridge and entered her office. She activated the secure systems and went to her desk to reach out to the Anwar elder. Aneesa reminded herself that she was the commanding officer of the Federation's entire military. While Galen Anwar was a leader of the Anwar family, her position technically was greater than any one family or it's members. Even her own. Still, she knew that caution was warranted and steadied herself as she signaled him.

It took a moment longer than normal, because of the level of security involved. Then, the head and shoulders of the family elder appeared via hologram at the edge of Aneesa's desk.

"General Anwar," he said.

"Galen."

"We have a grave situation on our hands," Galen said without further ado. "Several of the leading members of the Koh and Mallick families have recently been assassinated."

Aneesa balked. "I hardly see how that's my concern, Galen. The Federation military has nothing to do with household security, and I am sufficiently well protected among our forces that I should not need to worry. Unless you know of a threat to me that I do not?"

Much to her annoyance, Galen sighed. As though explaining to a child, he said, "Aneesa, the situation is problematic because it is members of the Koh and Mallick families that have been assassinated. None of our family, no Anwars, have been killed. Because of this fact, and the fact that you, an Anwar, are in command of the Federation military forces, the surviving Koh and Mallick family members of the Superior Convocation suspect that this is part of a power-grab by the Anwar family."

"But that's ludicrous," said Aneesa. "Isn't it?"

"It is," agreed Galen. "But when you look at it from a perspective outside of our family, it takes on a very different color. These deaths were not just murders but obvious assassinations. They were targeted, intentional, and decisive. And when the assassinated include only members of the Koh and Mallick clans, and elders at that, the Anwars look highly suspect."

Aneesa considered that. Galen had previously mentioned that the seemingly solid-appearing power-share of the three Federation families was more fragile than most knew. Had he told her this as a warning because the Anwar clan *did* intend to grab more power? Or was it a genuine concern for the present, as well as the future, of the Federation?

"I appreciate you letting me know this," said Aneesa. "Is there something you want me to do?"

"Yes," Galen said. "I'm well aware that you're gathering a very large force together at present. A force that includes ships and personnel taken away from the occupation of Alliance space."

"How do you know this?" asked Aneesa. It wasn't like she was hiding what she was doing, per se, but Galen was not tied to the military in any way she was aware of.

"Aneesa," Galen said with a hint of condescension she didn't miss, "the senior leadership of the Federation, be it from the Koh, Mallick, or Anwar clan, keeps tabs on everything. You might have command of our forces, but they cannot move in secret in any way we are not aware of."

"I should have realized that," Aneesa conceded.

Galen nodded. "Be that as it may, I presume that you are preparing to attack the Confederation with your force."

"I am."

Galen shook his head and said, "I respect your authority as the general of our forces, Aneesa, to command them. But you have yet to establish the necessary succession that I requested you put in place, and with the uncertain politics among the leadership in the face of these assassinations, that must be done immediately. What's more, the added tension of the Grand Master's warning about the consequences of folding space/time are too concerning

REVELATIONS AND RECONCILIATIONS

to ignore as you are. I recommend that you stand down from this operation you're planning. And with that, redeploy all forces to join the occupation of the former Alliance territories."

Aneesa found herself taken aback by Galen's suggestion. She couldn't hide the annoyance from her tone as she said, "All forces? End our operation against the Confederation and go all-in on occupying the Alliance, a territory we've already conquered?"

"Conquered and overran, maybe," said Galen. "But the ongoing resistance is becoming increasingly troublesome. Further, your prior defeat at the hands of the Confederation did not paint you or our forces in the best light. The Federation military needs to step back while we sort the political fallout from the assassinations. Redeploying to the occupation sends a message that we can use to diffuse the prevailing concerns."

"But Galen," Aneesa started to plead. She took a breath, changing her tone to one cooler and more formal. "We're on the verge of a decisive strike against the Confederation."

"Even so," Galen began, "I fear that a bold move such as you intend, led by the military leader who happens to be part of the currently-suspect Anwar family, will add to the already disturbing and messy political situation at hand. It sends the wrong message to the Kho and Mallick families at this time."

"I disagree," said Aneesa. "I think rather than stick our proverbial tail between our legs and sit in already occupied space, just to keep the locals in line, sends the wrong message. Not just to the other families, but the whole galaxy. A massive, successful strike on the Confederation, at the heart of the Confederation, no less, will show that the Federation as a whole is poised for expansion."

"Aneesa," Galen replied. "In principle, I agree. But when the Koh and Mallick families are investigating the assassination of multiple members of their clans - while the Anwar family remains untouched - an Anwar-led expansionist strike might be easily misconstrued."

"How is that possible?" demanded Aneesa. "The Federation, the whole Federation, controls the former Alliance territories. We have the capability to fold space/time and surprise attack any sector of our choosing, and we've made considerable headway into the Confederation. Ending that abruptly now would send exactly the wrong message."

"General," Galen said, catching Aneesa off guard by using her rank, "you do not understand the fragility of inter-family politics. The Koh and Mallick families have lost top members to assassins, while the Anwar family has one of their own as the military leader. You are, as such, a suspect, given that you have soldiers available who could be assassins."

"The Federation military doesn't strike against its own."

"That's good to know, Aneesa," said Galen. "But please, understand, we must use extreme caution here. Do not launch your strike against the Confederation. We need to pull back while this mess is sorted out. I need you to trust me on this and do what's right for the family, which is ultimately what's right for the Federation."

Aneesa was silent for a moment. She understood what Galen was getting at. Swallowing all other arguments, she said, "Very well, Galen. I'll alter my plans and make ready to redeploy the fleets to the occupation."

"How soon?" asked Galen.

"A few hours," Aneesa said. "At the latest, tomorrow. There are logistics to work out."

"And choosing your successor?" Galen questioned.

"A day or so after that is complete."

Galen's holographic bust appeared as if he were trying to see through Aneesa. After a few moments of silence, he nodded and said, "Very good. The longer you serve, the more you will see and understand how Federation politics work. I appreciate you doing what's best in this challenging situation. Thank you, General."

The chatter transmission ended. Aneesa leaned back in her seat. She calmed herself, considering her next move. The victory she could taste would not be ripped away.

She arose from her desk. She decided she hadn't lied to Galen. She would alter her plans, but by attacking as soon as possible. Then she'd redeploy the fleet to the occupation. Aneesa left her office and soon arrived on the bridge. "Major, have all forces arrived?"

"Yes, General."

REVELATIONS AND RECONCILIATIONS

"Excellent," Aneesa said. "Gather all captains for the final briefing in thirty galactic standard minutes. Have the space/time fold tech prepped and communicate with our recon ship to get the optimum point for our attack to begin within the hour."

Chapter 48 - Parting

"It's not the entirety of *Phantom*'s datacore," Galit was saying, "but it gives you access to a partial version of the AI, which could be highly useful to you."

"That's much appreciated, Galit," Darius said.

The Blue Cyberwizard turned her attention to Sara. "If you use the secure chatter frequency I've shared, *Phantom* will be able to interact with the partial AI variant I'm leaving you."

"That could be super helpful going forward," Sara replied. "We can never have too many resources."

Galit had disconnected *Phantom* from the *Moon Raven*, and it was on the landing pad a short way from the larger ship. It still struck Darius that Galit's ship seemed larger than it had while it was mounted atop the *Moon Raven*. He wondered if that was a trick of the eye, the genasi tech, the cyberwizard's stealth tech, or some combination of it all.

While the *Moon Raven* was set to leave l'Orni'Ri for goblin space, Galit would be going her own way to coordinate matters with the halflings. The halflings trusted the Blue Cyberwizard to make sure they got where they needed to be, whether that was with the orcs, kitsune, or goblins, if the *Moon Raven* crew succeeded in getting them to join the hunting party. Aya was convinced that her aunt's contact with the goblins would be instrumental to that end.

The crew was standing on the landing pad between *Moon Raven* and *Phantom*. They had all come to bid farewell to Galit. Darius had to admit he'd miss their unexpected but quite capable and helpful seventh member of the already diverse crew.

"I hope that I shall have the opportunity, in time, to return to the *Moon Raven* and rejoin you," Galit said. "I have never met a crew quite like you before, and I have a truly tremendous amount of respect for you all."

Kaz extended a hand to her. "You are all your legend claims you to be and more."

"Thank you."

Tol also shook her hand, Zya doing the same.

"Good luck, Galit," said Aya as she shook Galit's hand.

REVELATIONS AND RECONCILIATIONS

The Blue Cyberwizard was face-to-face with Sara. "You will consider all that we have spoken about?"

"I will," Sara said.

Galit nodded to her, then stood before Darius.

"Captain," Galit said. "Thank you for letting me be part of your crew."

"Galit, thank you for joining us while you could. Though I know you don't need anyone, you will always have a place with us. Even when you're not aboard the *Moon Raven* any longer, you are still part of this crew, as far as I'm concerned."

"Thank you," Galit said. She placed a hand on Darius' shoulder, gave a squeeze, then stepped back. "Until we meet again."

Galit turned and walked the short distance to *Phantom*. A few moments passed, and the starship engines powered up as the hatch closed. Soon, the ship lifted smoothly off the landing pad, turned to face the crew of the *Moon Raven*, then arose higher and began forward flight.

"She is not at all what I expected," said Aya.

"Cyberwizards are unique creatures," said Kaz.

"That's saying something, coming from this crew," remarked Aya.

"Kaz," Darius addressed, interrupting the banter. "Are we set to depart, too?"

"Aye, Captain," said Kaz. "I have the coordinates to goblin space Ryka gave us input into navigation."

"There's nothing more for us to do here," said Tol.

"Maybe," said Zya. "But Aya's aunt might have more to say."

Darius noted Zya looking away from the crew. When he looked in that direction, he saw Ryka Key-koo-noh fo Hava approaching with a bundle in her arms.

"Let's prep to go," Darius said.

The crew boarded the *Moon Raven*, save Aya, who awaited her aunt. Darius remained at the hatch. While the kitsune official and his quartermaster seemed to have patched up whatever dispute they had, he wanted to stay near, in case Aya needed him.

"Glad I caught you before you left," Ryka was saying.

"You could have used the chatter to check," Aya replied.

Ryka laughed lightly. "I could have. But I wanted to leave it to fate that I might or might not get here before you departed."

"Oh?"

Ryka offered Aya the bundle. Aya took it, and Darius saw it was a coat.

"Your brother probably would have wanted you to have this," Ryka said. "I thought, if it was meant to be, you'd be here to take it. And here you are."

Aya was nodding absently, all eyes for the coat she held out. "Thank you, auntie."

Ryka closed in on her niece and enfolded her into a hug. "I'm proud of you and what you're becoming, Aya. You were always special, you know." Aya said nothing. Ryka released her. She held her at arm's length, her hands on Aya's shoulders, for a moment longer.

Ryka turned her head to Darius and gave him a nod. He returned it. "Good luck to you and your crew," said Ryka to Aya.

"Thank you, auntie."

The kitsune official departed. Aya approached Darius.

"You set?" he asked.

"Let's go talk to some goblins, if they'll hear us out," replied Aya.

A few moments later, Darius was climbing into his seat behind Kaz as Aya took her usual station.

"All systems are looking good," Tol said.

"*Moon Raven* is good to go," added Zya.

"We've got clearance for uplift," said Sara.

"Take us out, Kaz," called Darius.

The *Moon Raven* shuddered ever so slightly, then rose off the landing pad. Kaz yawed to port, then pointed the ship's nose to the sky and began forward, ascending flight. The *Moon Raven* crew said nothing as the ship accelerated through the sky, which darkened as they left the bounds of l'Orni'Ri's atmosphere.

"Clear of the planet," said Kaz. "Five minutes to gravity well clearance and portal to unrealspace."

"I guess I can cross kitsune space off my list of places to visit someday," commented Sara.

Darius looked to his first mate. "You had a list of parts of space you wanted to see?"

REVELATIONS AND RECONCILIATIONS

Sara chuckled. "No. This is not where I saw my life going at all. I had planned to serve in the Alliance Interplanetary Navy until I made Captain, then resign my commission and work in the private sector as a security consultant. Do you have any idea how much COIN big corporations pay for former security and intelligence officers who make Captain or the equivalent from the Alliance, Confederation, and Union?"

"Impressive?" asked Aya.

"Bordering on obscene," confirmed Sara. "You can make good pay as a retired officer at any level, but what they pay a former captain? Crazy. But things change."

"That they do," said Tol.

"The other thing I never expected was this," said Sara.

"What?" asked Darius.

"Serving the Alliance as I did meant a lot to me. But this? Being an ambassador between disparate races to form an alliance to face the threat we're fighting together is another matter entirely."

Darius chuckled. "Yeah, I can relate. This was not somewhere I ever expected to find myself, either." But he felt there was more to it. So, he added, "I can't say how, but... But I know we are doing the right thing."

Zya said, "Tol and I stood against the status quo of the expectations of our people. We just wanted to be equal partners, despite the 'status quo'. That was good, until we were separated. But we are together again, stronger than before."

Tol added, "And this is where we ultimately belong."

"Nobody signed on for this," Aya said. "But then, the way we came together, everything that brought us here and that we've been a part of since? Like Darius, I can't say how I know, but it feels totally right to me, too."

Darius was grinning. "I could not have asked for a better crew. But you're all crazy."

"I don't know about crazy," muttered Sara.

"Eccentric might be a better description," remarked Aya.

"We're clear of the gravity well," said Kaz.

"Right," Darius replied. "Open a portal to unrealspace and let's go visit the goblins."

Chapter 49 - Transit

It wasn't long before things felt mostly normal again. Galit hadn't realized just how little time she'd spent aboard *Phantom* over the past several months. Apart from sleeping in her bunk on the starship, most of her time had been spent aboard *Moon Raven*.

For the first day, she had to remember that *Phantom*'s belly hatch no longer led to *Moon Raven*. She was on her own, and conversing with Sara, Darius, or any other member of the *Moon Raven* crew wasn't a short jaunt from one vehicle to another but a chatter call.

Soon, however, she was back to her old patterns. She'd read, study, play chess and converse with *Phantom*'s AI, check systems, and take care of duties and correspondence as necessary. Still, being alone again would take some getting used to.

Galit was in unrealspace, letting *Phantom*'s AI do the flying. The trip from kitsune space to halfling space was no short hop, so she pushed her ship not to its limits, but to an impressively fast velocity relative to unrealspace travel. *Phantom* had multiple automated systems in addition to its almost illegal AI. The drones and bots maintained much of the ship in the same way a sentient being might but with the single-mindedness of robotics. Relatively simple as much of the tech was, at least for a cyberwizard, it was impressive in its capabilities.

Galit had not neglected what needed to be overseen while mostly aboard the *Moon Raven*. However, she had allowed herself to take more time with some responses and searches than she might have otherwise. Fortunately, cyberwizards tended to have constant and steady employment, as they had many specialties that attracted adventures, businesses, political and business leaders, and others.

Galit had made a lot of contacts and connections along the way. Some were closer and more personal than others. Some an enigma. The new Grand Master, while an enigma, was proving more of the former than the latter.

Galit was alerted that they were requesting a live communication via chatter. She sat at the console she preferred for communications and

REVELATIONS AND RECONCILIATIONS

accepted the chatter request. A holographic image of the Grand Master, mid-chest up, appeared.

"Greetings, Grand Master," Galit addressed them.

The Grand Master nodded. "Galit Azurite, the Blue Cyberwizard. It is a pleasure to speak with you again."

"How many I assist you?" asked Galit.

"You are en route to coordinate with the halflings?"

"I am," Galit replied. "I'm about five galactic standard days away, maybe four and a half if I push *Phantom*'s engines harder."

"Do not harm your ship, please," said the Grand Master. "But I do appreciate your haste."

Galit was starting to recognize when the new Grand Master was concerned. "Has something new happened?"

"No," the Grand Master said. "Nothing bad, at least. I have successfully negotiated with the gnomes and made an arrangement to get some of their navigators to join the hunting party."

"That's impressive," complimented Galit. "They are not big on being in combat, but they are the best celestial navigators in the known galaxy."

"Agreed. That's why I took it upon myself to see if I could get their help. I sense that the mindflayers will need to start actively destroying sooner rather than later. They will not remain at the dark star much longer. Especially as they gain fewer numbers from home."

"The rifts are being closed," remarked Galit.

"By a combined task force of drow, elves, and dwarves," said the Grand Master. "My warning spurred the drow to not only cease folding space/time, but to actively close the tears they helped create."

"Impressive," said Galit. "The drow have hated the elves a long, long time. That they made the first move to enlist their aide was not something I'd have foreseen."

"Nor I, nor any of my predecessors," agreed the Grand Master. "And with these new alliances to combat the mindflayers being forged, the fabric of interspecies politics and cooperation will be forever changed."

"Time will tell," said Galit. "Everyone came together to combat the AI during the awakening, after all, then largely went back to separation and independent politics after."

"True," said the Grand Master. "But humans had barely come into their own, and the fourth wave wouldn't occur for almost another two thousand years. Things have changed, and the threat of the mindflayers does not carry the same types of blame the AI did, created by multiple races before threatening the lives of all."

Galit considered that. She knew the Grand Master had a more thorough history and knowledge on the topic of the AI Awakening and all that had occurred around it than she did. "You don't think the blame towards the drow or Federation will have a similar effect?"

"Only time will tell," said the Grand Master.

Galit agreed with that sentiment. "This is all rather momentous when you consider it."

"It is indeed," agreed the Grand Master. "And right at the center of it, the crew of the *Moon Raven*."

"Yes," said Galit. "I do not think they expected to be so intricately involved in these interspecies and interplanetary matters. Given they were all running from something when they met, it defies logic. To that end, they are making their way now to speak with the goblin leadership."

"How did that come about?" asked the Grand Master.

"The kitsune government representative. Who happens to be the kitsune quartermaster Aya Mah-soo-may fo Misa's aunt."

"I know your beliefs as a cyberwizard are not the same as mine, but doesn't the interconnection of all things amaze you?"

Galit chuckled. "Yes, and no. When the crew of the *Moon Raven* and I answered your predecessor's call, none of us knew what that would amount to."

"Nor I," said the Grand Master. "I knew, from the moment we started our quest beneath the ancient temple together, that the crew of the *Moon Raven* came together as they did because they are special."

"In many ways," agreed Galit. "That's probably how they wound up aboard a genasi starship."

"Quite a fascinating topic in and of itself, that," began the Grand Master. "There has been much speculation among UEO scholars over the genasi and how they - and the tieflings, for that matter – have interacted over time with races, as well as groups and individuals."

REVELATIONS AND RECONCILIATIONS

"There's much speculation among cyberwizards of the same," said Galit. "Like how every cyberwizard, almost like a rite of passage, acquires a genasi starship."

"My predecessors and I have wondered about that," said the Grand Master. "All cyberwizards?"

"Yes," replied Galit. "There is sufficient empirical evidence, though much of it appears more circumstantial, that it's as if old genasi vessels are left to be found in specific locations and at distinct times."

"Indeed," said the Grand Master. "The UEO has speculated a long time about that. We know the genasi exist outside of realspace or unrealspace in an alternate dimension that runs parallel yet separate from those we know, and they live outside of our time, too."

"Really?" asked Galit. "You think the genasi exist in a parallel dimension where time functions differently?"

"Not exactly," said the Grand Master. "And it's not the whole of the UEO, but some scholars who've believed this. The genasi, they suggest, don't exist in time in a way we are capable of understanding. Thus, it may be that they can see how we perceive time and work in our framework from their own, unique perspective."

"Similar to the inexplicable physics we see from the mindflayers and their savagespace monsters?" asked Galit. "Their ability to ignore the extreme gravity completely and travel faster than dark, rather than light?"

"Something like that," said the Grand Master. "Though, to be honest, my own understanding is limited, as that's never been my area of study."

"Most can only barely manage understanding realspace and unrealspace as unique but connected dimensions," said Galit. "That there are more, and that they can defy laws of our universe, is a lot to swallow."

The Grand Master chuckled. "It is. Which is why such matters tend to stay with the UEO, sorcerers, cyberwizards, and a few other random mystics."

"That's why even the tech-bound like cyberwizards recognize the invisible-energy-bound monks, clerics, and their abilities. Connectivity is the key to all, organic, inorganic, or blended."

"Yes," agreed the Grand Master. "Even when those, like most of the crew of the *Moon Raven,* are non-believers. I agree it is no coincidence they travel space in a genasi starship. They have been an unexpected key to assembling the hunting party. To that end, there are monks and clerics of the UEO, as well as Syndicate sorcerers joining in. The signs and portents in the Universal Energies speak of a potentially disturbing conflict, and soon."

Galit lacked the Grand Master's connection to such energies. Yet somehow she knew, in the depths of her soul, that the Grand Master was correct.

The Grand Master continued, saying, "Let's hope between the drow and their efforts to close the rifts and the hunting party gathering to face the mindflayers and their monsters that are already here, that we can stop them. Before they begin to truly destroy and grow too powerful."

Chapter 50 – Surprise

They emerged from the artificial wormhole into Confederation space. Just as expected from the reconnaissance reports, there were only ten Confederation warships. As orders were being called out across the *Hammer of Harmony's* bridge, they were raising shields.

"All ships, assume attack formation Bravo One," commanded Aneesa, proud of herself for having memorized several of the basic fleet formations. "Prepare to wipe them out."

Knowing that the Wolfgang-Alpha sector was a central sector of the Confederation, Aneesa found it hard to believe they had left so few forces on patrol. There were five inhabited planets in the sector, plus multiple bases, platforms, and space stations. Billions, maybe tens of billions of Confederation citizens called Wolfgang-Alpha home.

Consistent intelligence reports and reconnaissance observations confirmed it. The far greater number of ships that should have been in this sector either had been rerouted to the less-central sectors the Federation had previously focused their attacks on, or they were redeployed to sectors considered more vital than Wolfgang-Alpha.

It hardly mattered. The Federation would show them they could not stand against a fleet that could fold space/time and go anywhere they desired in Confederation space, or anywhere else in the galaxy.

Just as she was about to order the attack, Aneesa saw something unexpected happen. All ten Confederation starships dropped their shields. Seconds later, they opened unrealspace portals and departed.

"How can this be?" Aneesa asked. "We've been here less than thirty galactic standard seconds. How could they possibly have portaled away?"

Much to her annoyance, General Waheed was at her side. He had insisted that if she was taking so many of his ships from the Alliance territories occupation on this attack, he would join and attend her on the *Hammer of Harmony*. Rather than risk him contacting Galen or some other member of the Superior Convocation, she'd agreed.

"This is not good," he said. "The only way they could depart to unrealspace so quickly would be if they had their drives spooled because they were anticipating the attack."

"Impossible," said Aneesa.

A number of different alarms sounded across the *Hammer of Harmony's* combat information center. Aneesa looked at the holographic display before her in utter disbelief. Her impressively large fleet paled in number compared to how many starships were surrounding them.

It appeared as if all the ships that should have been in the Wolfgang-Alpha sector had arrived via unrealspace portals. Along with those, there appeared to be another sector's worth of warships.

General Waheed pulled up the schematics of the unexpected warships on the display before them. "It's worse than not good, General."

Even with her limited experience, Aneesa knew the difference between the ships of the various human sectors. The schematics Waheed had brought up on the display was not Confederation, but Union.

Aneesa's overwhelming force was extremely outnumbered and outgunned. "How could this be?" Aneesa called out. She was utterly caught off guard and totally unprepared.

Aneesa considered that it had to be some sort of bait and switch. They were set up. There was no other explanation. "Who betrayed us?" she questioned aloud. "For this to be so incredibly wrong, they must have been told we were coming. We have been betrayed."

"No, General, probably not," said General Ishii, standing across from Aneesa at the holographic display. "This was not the result of a betrayal. We were fed a target of opportunity that you could not resist, and you led us right into their trap."

Before Aneesa could reprimand the security chief, the deck beneath her feet shifted and she had to grab the edge of the display before her to keep her balance. "Open the fold and take us back to Federation space," she ordered.

"General," the major in command of the *Hammer of Harmony* called out, "to open the artificial wormhole to fold space/time, we'd have to drop our shields. Doing so, surrounded and under fire as we are, is ill-advised at this time."

REVELATIONS AND RECONCILIATIONS

"Damn," Aneesa spat out. "Have the first group cut to port, the second group to starboard. We need to move the *Hammer of Harmony* out of this fire zone to a more open position. All ships need to fire all weapons and clear paths so we can regroup."

"Say again, General?" someone called out.

Aneesa was staring at the holographic display before her. She could see no openings, no obvious path to move any ship in her fleet out of harm's way. They were all being attacked, the impossibly numerous forces they faced were mercilessly firing synchronized plasma cannons, missiles, and torpedoes at her fleet.

It had always looked so easy on screen and in plans. But this? The chaos, the confusion, the noise... It was utterly overwhelming. For the first time since assuming command of the Federation military, Aneesa found herself feeling out of her element.

A rough hand at her shoulder, turning her away from the display, interrupted her thought process. "General," General Waheed got her attention. "You need to let me take command and salvage what I can to get us out of here."

Aneesa became angry. Staring daggers at Waheed, she spat, "I will order the retreat when we have no other options."

"We are outgunned and outmatched, General. We *have* no other options," Waheed said.

"Mind your place, General," Aneesa almost shouted.

"I need to assume command now, General Anwar, before we lose everything."

Aneesa's temper flared. How dare Waheed be so presumptuous? As her anger flared she drew her sidearm, pointed it at his chest, and fired. A moment of stunned surprise crossed General Waheed's face before he collapsed onto the deck.

Aneesa was about to bark orders, though to do what, she was just not certain, until she glanced towards the holographic display. The large force of superior Federation combat ships she had brought to the Confederation's Wolfgang-Alpha sector were being obliterated.

Without direction from their central command, the Federation ships were scattering as best they could but had nowhere to go. The forces of the

Confederation and the Union had the upper hand, in addition to the greater numbers.

The horror of her failure washed over Aneesa. The cries and shouts of the crew aboard the *Hammer of Harmony* grew to a distant roar in her head as she felt everything she had expected and championed fall apart, with zero hope of recovery or reconciliation. Aneesa saw no way out, just destruction. But not destruction wrought by her forces, but by their inferior enemies.

She barely noticed how the *Hammer of Harmony* kept being rocked by enemy weapons fire, her mind adrift as her eyes saw the representations of her fleet on the holographic display disappear one after another after another. A rushing, whooshing noise dominated her mind, and she heard none of the shouts or requests for orders from her flagship's scrambling crew.

A bright blinding flash was the last thing to get Aneesa Anwar's attention. Her final thought was that Song had been right after all.

Chapter 51 – Domino

Only three starships were being worked on. Two were undergoing minor repairs. One was a relatively expansive overhaul but was still utilizing very few of her mechanics and engineers. Nomira Luon-star'koam was at her station, glancing up through the scaffolds and framework of *Territory's Edge* above her. Having so little work to do was beginning to become extremely frustrating.

The blame was being placed by the platform administration on the Federation's overrun of their neighbor, the Alliance. Nobody had ever truly accounted for how much of the station's business was a result of its proximity to those two human sectors. Most, like Nomira's partners in the repair yard, thought traffic was largely from the many independent territories that the station skirted.

While there had been some truth in that, it turned out that movement between the two large human territories and the independent systems had been more dependent on the Alliance than anyone cared to believe. Though free and willing to trade with the unaffiliated worlds and nonhumans, the Federation tended to venture less to the independent territories than their now-occupied neighbor.

Nomira wondered if the leaders of the Federation realized that their invasion had cut off their primary trade partner. What's more, post-invasion, travelers from the Federation were increasingly infrequent. She suspected that the rumors of Federation forces using surreal tech to invade far-away sectors might have something to do with that. Still, Nomira was an elven businesswoman, first and foremost, a supervisor of workers second, and only involved herself in matters beyond that if her partners required it.

A trio of dwarf mechanics were crawling over the body of one of the starships. Nomira had never trusted the dwarves fully and was even more distrustful after the departure of Tol'te-catl ubn Chi'mal-li.

The little sneak had somehow quietly purchased engines and an unrealspace drive without her noticing. Then, he'd managed to get them into a restricted, abandoned section of the platform where Nomira and her partners had long deposited wrecks and junk that, while not immediately useful, might be salvageable in time. How a whole starship had been hidden and restored right under their noses angered Nomira. And what about station security? They had done nothing.

One way she kept her less-needed - and as far as she was concerned, less-skilled - workers busy was combing through that disused sector. If Tol'te-catl ubn Chi'mal-li had found and restored a previously missed spaceframe, there might be others. But so far, everything else was just junk.

Now that he was gone, the other thing Nomira had been forced to accept was that Tol'te-catl ubn Chi'mal-li had been among her best. More than a mechanic, he'd been a talented engineer. She'd not realized what all he'd done until he was gone and the jobs that were once taken for granted were no longer being handled effectively.

As she seethed over that, a human and halfling mechanic passed her station. Why was it always dwarves, halflings, and humans? Nomira was increasingly missing the faces of her fellow elves. She'd been away from elven space for too long and was realizing she should make one of her partners take her place so she could go visit for a time and get away from this platform in the middle of nowhere.

Nomira shook it off. These ruminations were a waste of time and energy. She looked at progress reports on the work her mechanics and engineers were doing and debated who needed to be yelled at.

A piercing, distressing wail reached Nomira's ears. Glancing around, confused, she was caught off guard by whatever it was. Then she remembered. Proximately alarms to warn everyone within *Territory's Edge* of ships or unexpected debris potentially impacting and damaging the platform. Or, worst-case scenario, an attack of some sort.

Who would be brazen enough to attack a platform such as *Territory's Edge*? Nomira looked up through the platform framework again. What she saw froze her heart and chilled her blood.

Massive creatures with broad, flapping wings, impossibly flying in the vacuum. Alongside them, disturbing starships, sporting a hammerhead fore, with strange protrusions at the very front that almost stuck out like tentacles. It wasn't long before the disturbing starships were firing energy weapons of some kind at the platform. These, Nomira realized, must have been the

REVELATIONS AND RECONCILIATIONS

mindflayers that the UEO Grand Master had transmitted a warning about across the chatter and medianet.

"Attention," an authoritative voice called on the local chatter network, coming across the public address system and joining the alarm sounding across the platform. "*Territory's Edge* is under siege. All departures are authorized. Station personnel to defense positions. Prepare to repel boarders. Repeat, all departures are authorized. Station personnel to defense positions. Prepare to repel boarders."

Nomira shook herself once again and called out, "Drop what you're doing and take up arms, now! Report to your assigned support stations and defend the platform! Move, people, move!"

Nomira watched as, for once, everyone followed her orders without question or hesitation. Then she checked the board before her and patched herself into the platform's feed.

Externally, sections of the platform were being destroyed by weapons fire from without. Station defenses were firing but were doing little to stop the attack.

Internally, video showed disturbing humanoid monsters. She presumed they were the mysterious mindflayers. They were marching on station personnel, many of whom were clutching at their heads as though deeply pained. They were being killed without mercy or remorse. How had matters become so bad so quickly?

Suddenly, Nomira felt as though someone had applied a vice to her brain. She felt disoriented, nauseated, and distracted. She took several deep breaths and was able to shunt that feeling to a less-dominant place. Nomira realized that what she was feeling must have been a psionic attack.

A loud, unexpected crashing sound reached her sensitive ears and got her attention. Looking up again, Nomira saw an enormous, impossible beast crashing through the dome and framework above.

New alarms sounded as the repair bays were depressurized. Nomira saw that the monster had landed on a scaffold nearby, where it started blasting some sort of beam out of its mouth, vaporizing anyone it touched.

There was no time to run, nowhere to hide, Nomira's last sight was the dragon turning to face her, the beam from its mouth engulfing her. The unbearable brightness, an instant later, turned to black.

Acknowledgments

There are several people I need to thank for all their continued assistance, encouragement, and more. In no particular order:

Rose Butcher, my cover artist. I cannot say enough about how amazing she has been with what I have tossed her way, and what an incredible job she's done for this series! I'm really looking forward to partnering with her for more.

Vickey Skinner, my new editor. I appreciate your keen eye and insights. Thank you.

My wife Chrissie. She is my rock, my sounding board, and she's amazing. I couldn't do this work without her! She's my best friend and my biggest cheerleader (even if I keep failing at being her emergency contact).

My dad, for supporting me by paying attention to all I do and buying everything I write.

My friends and their continued support. Thanks for following along on social media as I keep oversharing my work.

Last, and certainly not least, YOU. I love and appreciate my readers. I hope you've enjoyed reading this first entry in this series as much as I enjoyed writing it.

Before you go – please leave a review on whatever platform you purchased this from, and/or Goodreads. Also, please tell a friend or two!

REVELATIONS AND RECONCILIATIONS

Links

Author website (where you can join my newsletter and learn more about me and my ongoing process):

mjblehart.com

YA Fantasy series *The Source Chronicles*: **sourcechronicles.com**

Instagram **@mjblehart**

TikTok **@mjblehart72**

Facebook **@blehartmj**

Also by MJ Blehart

Forgotten Fodder
Unexpected Witness
The Clone Conundrum
Unraveling Conspiracy
Bold Moves

Savagespace
Alliances and Consequences
Revelations and Reconciliations

Void Incursion
Opening Gambit
Critical Position
Strategic Crush
Antipositional Moves
Check and Mate

Standalone
Infamy Ascending

Watch for more at https://mjblehart.com.

About the Author

MJ BLEHART has been writing fantasy and sci-fi/space opera all his life, the first when he was nine years old. *Star Wars* and *Star Trek* were some of the biggest influences in his youth.

He is a history aficionado. MJ has been a member of the Society for Creative Anachronism (SCA - a medieval re-enactment society) for over thirty years. As part of the SCA he studies and teaches 16th century rapier combat (fencing) and court heraldry, enjoys archery, and spending time with friends.

When not writing sci-fi and fantasy, MJ blogs regularly, exploring mindfulness and creating an amazing life. He strives to live a kickass life and consciously create his reality (and sharing that process to help others do the same).

MJ lives in New Jersey just outside of Philadelphia with his wife and their two feline overlords.

Read more at https://mjblehart.com.

Milton Keynes UK
Ingram Content Group UK Ltd.
UKHW051004081024
449371UK00020B/1122